CODE OF HONOR

COL. JOHN A. DRAMESI, USAF

WARNER BOOKS

A Time Warner Company

W
01.NOV90
MCLL

WARNER BOOKS EDITION

This Warner Books Edition is published by arrangement with the author.

Cover design by Don Puckey
Cover photo by Le Clerc Du Sablon/Gamma

Warner Books, Inc.
666 Fifth Avenue
New York, N.Y. 10103

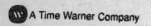 A Time Warner Company

Printed in the United States of America

First Warner Books Printing: October, 1990

10 9 8 7 6 5 4 3 2 1

TO BE FREE

"Quick," I whispered to Ed, "cover yourself with the net and lie still."

The guards surrounded the pond below us and after a few moments departed.

We waited, according to plan, for the patrolling guard to pass, but he did not appear. The rain was doing its part well.

"We're wasting time," I said. "Let's go."

On my stomach and head first, I crawled down to the edge of the roof overlooking our small wash area. I removed an overhanging tile, then signaled Ed to join me. "What are you going to do with that?" he asked.

"Nothing," I said, "but the rope over the edge against the wood support is better than crumbling another tile. Here, take my rope, tie it to yours, and anchor it to the lightning-rod brace. We're going down." The rope proved to be an essential item as we had thought it would be.

As I moved from Station One, next to our building, toward Station Two, Ed started his descent. The cement walk that ran through the middle of the garden was the longest open stretch we had to cross. I crawled up to the path and stopped. This was our second station. I was lying on my right side in the mud beneath the camouflage net, my chin tucked between my knees. I raised my head slightly and was about to scurry across the path when I froze.

A pair of boots was less than three feet away from my head . . .

To Edwin Lee Atterberry

To give or assist without credit, benefit, or return is man's most highly praised virtue, kindness.

J. A. D.

For their unselfish assistance I thank
Ann Robertson
Mrs. Marge Sands
Robbin Broyles
Mrs. Pauline A. Shacklette
William K. Orr
Mrs. Betty Orr
Jane Walker
James L. Monroe
Starling Lawrence
John D. Warwick
and especially Leonard W. Lilley
for his encouragement and friendship

Contents

Author's Note

The object of this book is not to disgrace anyone or to dwell on the past but to present the clear and convincing truth so that we may prepare our young men and women for the future. If there is anyone who thinks that the image of the American fighting man is marred by the events and personalities presented herein, I suggest that he read this book carefully, for there is ample evidence to prove the courage, honor, discipline, and determination of our military.

CODE OF HONOR

I

Lover Lead

War is not big or little, hot or cold, limited or total.
War is death; it is life. Ask the man on the battlefield,
war is absolute.

On April 1, 1967, right after dinner, I went down to the briefing
room in Korat Air Base, Thailand. I had originally been scheduled
to strike a North Vietnamese barracks the next day. However, an
RF-4C on reconnaissance had spotted a truck park in Package
One at the south end of North Vietnam. This new mission would
be my fifty-ninth since I started flying the F-105 fighter-bomber
in the air war over North Vietnam.

My code name was to be Lover Lead. It sounded like an April
Fool's Day joke. Love what?

The next day, an hour and a half before scheduled takeoff that
afternoon, I was back in the briefing room along with the other
assigned pilots. Intelligence briefed on what targets were off
limits for the day, what antiaircraft and surface-to-air missile
(SAM) sites in the target area were active, and the best escape
routes. The Vinh SAM site was reported active again. It had shot
down Durat a week earlier. Also, Cadillac, who had gone down in
the area ten days ago, was still there and reported evading. "Listen for his call sign," the intelligence officer said, "and keep your
eyes open."

Next the weather. "Clear with puffy white clouds at ten thousand feet," the weather officer reported. He described the winds
at all levels and gave a ground temperature of 78 degrees. "There
is a light haze," he continued. "The seas due east of target are
running four-foot crests with wind from the north at ten knots."

Finally, the operational briefing. The strike commander repeated target coordinates and as much detail as he had on the truck concentration found the day before by the RF-4. "The same RF-4 will be back in the area today, spotting the target and acting as our forward air controller," he said. "The area is a plateau with a fall-off to the east toward the sea. There is a 500-foot ridge in a half moon around the target to the north, west, and south. When we leave here, I will be in the first flight. We will be in two flights of four with Dramesi leading one flight of two. The first flight of four will come in from the west, the second flight from the south. Dramesi will cap us and drop last."

I briefed my wing man, Ken Gurry, on bomb settings, bomb angles, refueling procedures, and what to do in an emergency if one of us went down. I had no worry about the mission. Gurry, I knew, was a good pilot, enthusiastic, dedicated, a good man to have around.

We took off after the briefing and linked up with the RF-4 on the radio. We had no sooner made contact, it seemed, than we could hear over the radio the other 105s already on the target dropping their bombs. Ken and I went in, made one strike, then a couple of re-strikes.

Rejoining over the target, we still had fully loaded guns. I called for and received a secondary mission, to run armed reconnaisance along a road northwest of Dong Hoi just ten minutes north of the truck park. The valley the road ran through was a likely enemy staging area for strikes into Steel Tiger, the border area between North and South Vietnam.

As we went up the valley at five hundred knots, Ken was in the right position—behind, to the right, and high. He was in the midst of reporting what small arms and 37-millimeter antiaircraft fire we were attracting, when suddenly I was hit. I felt "whump, whump, whump" three times, and the plane shuddered.

"Lover Lead," Gurry called, "your wing tanks are gone, and you have fire in the tail."

Smoke suddenly filled the cockpit. I was at 2500 feet, moving fast, and unable to see the instruments. It was time to get out. I pulled the handles and squeezed the trigger; as the canopy flew off, I followed. The air blast knocked me out.

When I was conscious again, I was already on the ground, on

the side of a hill, and by instinct halfway through unbuckling my harness. Quickly I shed my gear, clawed my parachute into a loose bundle, shoved it under some bushes, gathered up my survival equipment, and started up the hill. Except for a tall tree here and there, it was covered with small brush about chest high. I could hear faint voices down in the valley, and rifle shots where I had landed.

At the crest of the hill I turned north. I thought a helicopter would have an easier time finding me up there. Being on a small trail was bad. Still, I had a commanding view of the area. To the west was a small cliff. Nobody was likely to come at me from that direction. It ran around to the south, so the North Vietnamese were not likely to come from that direction, either.

A path ran along the ridge, going north. Down below, people were coming up from the east. And to the northeast, at the bottom of the valley, near a small hill across a road, more North Vietnamese were running onto a path that looked as if it swung around in a semicircle to join up with the one on the ridge. I had to hide.

I ran down the path to a thick clump of bushes. Using a rolling dive, I leaped over the bushes so I would leave no sign of where I had left the path. I stood up and called Ken on my radio.

Ken responded. He had notified the helicopters. They were on their way, including at least three A-1s. As I held the radio to my ear, I heard Ken say "I'm running low on fuel, be right back." "Rog," I answered. "See you later."

Just seconds passed. I could hear the Sandies, the fighter escort that would protect the rescue helicopters, but couldn't tell where they were. Covering one ear, I cupped the other and began slowly turning my head like a human radar receiver. By isolating the engine noise, I could tell they were south of me. I shouted into the radio, "turn north, turn north." The engine noise grew louder, and when I finally spotted the aircraft, they were east of me.

"Sandy One, this is Lover Lead," I said. "Turn west, stand by, and I will direct you over my position. Turn left, roll out, a little more, that's it . . . Straighten out . . . You are over my position *now*, Sandy One . . . *Now*, Sandy Two . . . *Now*, Sandy Three. Swing left and come around, heading north."

As they did, I asked, "What's your load?"

Sandy One had four White Phosphorous rockets, machine guns,

and 2.75 rockets. The others had machine guns and rockets.

"They're coming up the hill," I said excitedly. "Fire on your first pass."

"We can't see a thing," the leader shouted over the radio. "Keep coming around," I directed. "I've got you. Roll in there to the left; more, more, roll out, fire, fire. Fifty feet to the left and higher up the hill, Two." "That's where you are, isn't it?" the number two man questioned. "I'll be all right," I insisted. "That's good, fire. That's good, Three." I could hear the screams of the North Vietnamese soldiers as the rockets crashed into the east side of my hill, exploding about two hundred yards down from my position. "The same place, Number Three," I commanded. "Great great, Three. Keep it up, right in that area." The whole valley seemed to erupt with rifle fire each time an aircraft dove to fire.

No more than five minutes had passed since the Sandies had arrived. I felt I was back in my own element, doing what I had trained, taught, and demonstrated for more than two years. Directing airplane fire-power in support of ground operations, my area of expertise. I turned the Sandies around, brought them in again, this time on the North Vietnamese coming up the northeast side of the hill.

"That's great, Lead, I've got a new target for you."

"Start your roll-in, *now,* Sandy One . . . Fire *now* . . . Lead, you're off . . . Two, hit to his twelve o'clock . . . Good show . . . Three, closer to the base of that hill."

The Sandies were doing their job. I could see soldiers fleeing back down off the brush-covered northeast slope, hunting for cover, and diving into the ditch on the other side of the dirt road.

"Good show, good show, we stopped them. Pull off and get some altitude, the whole valley's opened up on you."

I was planning to bring them in on the trail to discourage anyone from coming after me from that direction, when suddenly I was hit. "They got me," I transmitted. "They got me."

The idea raced through my mind that they couldn't be more than fifty yards away. Only my head was visible. That must have been the target, but the Sandies going over had rattled somebody's aim. As I thrashed in the brush, they were on me, two North Vietnamese with rifles and behind them a young boy in short pants with a machete.

I was stripped immediately and left with only my flight suit. Two soldiers started shoving me rapidly to the north up the path. We had just started when the Sandies came screaming overhead, very low. My captors yelled and jumped into the brush. The Sandies suddenly disappeared. The silence was as threatening as the roars just seconds before.

The soldiers were in a hurry now, but I limped and dragged along as slowly as their poking weapons would allow.

The bullet wound in my right leg didn't bother me much, but I had twisted my left knee, and it was swelling and starting to hurt. Evidently, it had twisted during ejection or upon landing. My hands were tied behind my back, my right leg was covered in blood, but I was alive.

We made our way to a stream, following that downhill, first to the east, then south. As we approached a village, I slipped and fell face down into the knee-deep water of a rice paddy.

Each time I tried to get up, the guard pulled on the rope, turning me face down into the water again. It happened three times before I realized that, because of either the guard's stupidity or his anger, I was going to drown if I did not do something. I grabbed the rope and jerked the guard into the rice paddy with me.

The boy laughed. I managed to scramble to my feet and struggled out of the paddy. The guard crawled out, even madder now. Suddenly the valley floor trembled and the thunder of jets and exploding bombs created a scene of fear and confusion. I was shoved into the entrance of a shelter under one of the houses. The entrance was a tunnel, actually, with two right-angle bends in it. Inside, the shelter was small with a very low ceiling and dimly lit.

As I settled into a corner, a woman with a baby sucking at her breast crawled into the place from another entrance. Soon the little hole was crowded elbow to elbow. The bombing stopped. The thunder was gone. My pant legs were slit up the sides, and the North Vietnamese examined the swollen left knee and the bullet wound in my right leg. They gave me a dirty rag to tie around the wound.

Some time later, after the bombing had stopped, an officer pressed his way into the hole. He motioned for me to get out and walk. I pointed to my wound and swollen leg and shook my head.

I knew if the officer checked with the soldiers who had brought me in, they could verify that I had stumbled and fallen several times on the short trip to the village.

He threatened me in a loud, angry voice. Stubbornly, I shook my head. The officer seemed almost beside himself with anger. He held up first ten fingers and then ten again, indicating that the capture had cost him twenty of his men. He unholstered an automatic pistol, cocked it, and swung it up at me.

The other people in the little basement put up their hands and started to yell. Any shot in there would probably hurt more than just the new captive. They gestured and shouted at the officer to put the gun away. He kept it pointed at me and shouted, "Get—up, Get—up."

I shook my head again and said I could not walk. The swollen knee bothered me more than the wound, but because of the blood splattered all over the lower portion of it, the right leg looked worse. I kept pointing to that. Finally, the officer holstered his gun and left. The other people in the hole relaxed.

In a short time, the officer came back and motioned for me to get out of the hole, crawling if necessary. I did. Outside, two soldiers tried to pick me up, but each time they did, I pretended to collapse. Sooner or later, I thought, my seeming inability to walk or even stand up ought to give me a chance to escape. Finally, they sat me on some boards that formed the roof of the shelter. The officer pulled his pistol out again and threatened once more to shoot if I did not try to walk. I shook my head again, and pointed again to my bloody leg.

After we had repeated this exchange a few times, the officer departed and then returned with some more soldiers. They had a net and a long bamboo pole. Stringing the net like a hammock, fastened at each end of the pole, two of them picked me up and placed me inside. Two others picked up the pole and started carrying me. A third soldier carried the guns for all three of them. The trail showed up light gray in the starlit night. As they walked along, one of the bearers stumbled. I grunted. My left knee was bothering me. When the bearers realized that the bumps must hurt, they began jiggling the pole now and then, trying to make the ride even more uncomfortable. I now grunted on cue, even letting out a yell every so often, not because it hurt but because it was what they expected. But, eventually they stopped, realizing they had a long way to go. They settled down just to getting me to the next village.

Late that night we arrived at a small house. The people in it acted nervous. They had one candle lit in the main room, and each time they heard, or thought they heard, an aircraft in the area, they put the candle out. A soldier pulled off the dirty rag and looked at the wound. It had stopped bleeding. He put a standard-issue army bandage on it. An old man who had been hanging on the edge of the group, glaring at me, became annoyed at all the attention I was receiving. Suddenly he rushed at me and began beating me around the head and shoulders. The guards took their time pulling him off and lectured him mildly.

It seemed almost a signal for an elderly man to come into the house. He clearly was in charge. He asked, "Parlez-vous français?" and I said "No." He handed me a piece of paper and indicated I should write something down. I knew the old man was after my name and a description of the aircraft I had been flying, but I tried to demonstrate that I did not understand what I was being asked. The old man went into the next room and I could hear him cranking the handle of an old "coffee grinder" telephone. He spoke into it for some time, then came back into the room. He had the paper he had given me in his hand, and, while the old guy who had attacked me hovered close by, he handed it to me along with a pencil and pointed to it.

The directions were in clear English. He had left a small space for me to fill in my name, rank, serial number, and the type of aircraft I was flying. I looked at the paper. I wrote, "John Dramesi. Captain. FR 60532." I refused to write more.

The old man went back to the telephone, rang someone up, and read them the information. Then he came back and issued some orders. I was placed on a flat pallet of bamboo stalks with ropes looped at each end. They draped the loops over a large bamboo pole and picked me up. Once more we were on the move. As we left the house, one of the first bearers was heading back toward the other village, carrying the hammock-net.

I lay back and looked up at the stars overhead. I found myself wondering if the Hanoi prison food was going to be as good as the North Vietnamese propaganda claimed. I thought, Hanoi or Hell?

The First Escape

A good soldier is a man aware of the cause and willing to make the necessary sacrifices.

The sun was just coming up the next day as we arrived at another
village. They placed me in the middle of an S-shaped trench. As I
lay there with the sun rising at my back, I began to think about
escape. We had been taught in survival school that an early try
was best. But I decided to gain some strength first. I was tired
from the trip and had no trouble going to sleep in the muddy
bottom of that trench.

When I woke up, I had to go to the bathroom. No one appeared to be around. I walked, crouching. A few paces away in
the trench I relieved myself. I continued to think about escape.
I seemed free to move from one end of the trench to the other.
I recalled something else I had learned in survival school. Patrolling the compound, the escape committee had discovered an obvious and untended hole in the barbed wire prison walls. I had
told them not to use it, that it was too obvious and they had to be
more ingenious than that. I was overruled and they plotted their
escape. Sure enough, even with a diversion, their "captors" were
waiting that night on the other side of the hole when they broke
through. They were "mowed down" with machine-gun fire. Now,
in real life, escape again looked too easy. This was not the time.

Just before the sun went down, my escort came back and loaded
me on the pallet. We all started off again. It was an easier trip
this time, but slower. We reached the next little village well before
sunrise. Inside a wooden building I was stripped down to jockey
shorts and put into a square hole with only one entrance. Thick,

heavy planks were laid over the top, forming a roof. In the same large shed, along three walls, were stacks on stacks of ammunition and grenade boxes reaching clear to the beamed ceiling. I sat on a board in the hole and waited.

As the sun rose, guards removed most of the planks, leaving the hole open. In the early morning, village kids circled the hole, threw rocks and other debris, and poked me with sticks. The shouting and jeering helped their game. Finally I threw some rocks and grabbed and pulled their sticks. It took all the fun out of their game. They tired of it and left for school or work.

I had been alone just a short while when one boy crept into sight, stood up, and threw a knife. I ducked to the side. It hit the clay wall and fell to the ground. I let it lie there.

Later in the morning I could hear people moving back into the village, coming in from school and from the fields. Several gathered around the entrance to my pit. Then a young man wearing boots arrived, gesturing for me to come up out of the shelter and sit on a plank. While I sat there in my shorts, the young political organizer began to harangue and excite the gathering crowd. Only after the weeping women became hysterical and the men brandished their tools was I returned to the hole.

Shortly after that, I was taken out of the hole again and set on a stool, once more on exhibition. I was given a tiny bowl with greens over rice. On top of it all was a globule of something that looked very unappetizing. A dog sat off to my left and a swirl of flies hovered between us. A red-headed fly landed on the strange piece of matter that crowned my meal. As I picked up the morsel with my chopsticks it changed shape. I "accidentally" dropped it. I looked up at the crowd and shrugged my shoulders. They smiled. The dog ate it.

I ate all of the rice and dried greens, knowing that sooner or later I would need the nourishment. As I did, I looked over the crowd. The old women were thin; most had missing and rotting teeth. Everyone except the uniformed soldiers wore black clothes. It was possible to rank the people in the village according to what they wore on their feet. Besides the political lecturer, I saw one army officer in a pair of boots. That was the highest rank of village authority. Next to the "booties," as I labeled them, there were the "sneakies"—the military men and a few others who wore sneakers.

The middle class, the "sandies," wore sandals; and the rest were the "baries," those who were barefooted all the time.

That night I heard vehicles moving. I was given a red T-shirt and red pants. My hands were tied behind me. I was carried to the outskirts of the village and dumped in the back of a small truck. For camouflage, foliage was fastened to the tailgate, the sides, and across the top of the cab.

We were part of a small truck caravan, traveling at what I thought was a dangerously fast pace on a narrow road without lights. Heading east, I thought, that is good, for I regarded the sea as friendly territory. We stopped only once, when flares suddenly illuminated the sky overhead. Other than that, we spent the night at breakneck speeds, barely missing trucks and walking troops. Two guards in back of the truck with me slept soundly.

I had managed to untie my hands and eventually was able to move sticks and leaves apart to make a hole in the camouflage on one side of the truck. It was big enough for me to dive through if necessary. A few times, when the truck slowed, I thought of jumping, but I finally dropped the idea simply because I believed we were traveling east in the direction I wanted to go.

Just before dawn on April 5, we arrived at another village. We took quite a while getting settled this time, because the whole area was packed with trucks, bumper to bumper, all trying to squeeze as close as they could to the village huts and still stay hidden under the broad leafy canopies. Trucks had been crammed together like that in nearly every village we had passed. Ammunition was stored everywhere—in the trucks, on the roads, and in the homes. It was all obviously done for just one reason: the North Vietnamese knew the villages were off limits to American air attack. That civilian shield was better than antiaircraft guns for keeping U.S. fighter-bombers away from the North Vietnamese army, as it moved south to fight.

When the truck finally parked, my companions carried me through the village to a small house. That night my bed was a twelve-inch-wide plank.

The next morning I examined the room as I ate a small bowl of rice. In the middle of the room was a solid-wood double-bed frame with no mattress. Opposite that, in the center of the wall were double doors leading outside. Off to the left was a single

door which led into an open but roofed-over kitchen area. In front
and to the right of where I lay was an arrangement of chairs and a
table. In the right front corner of the room was a table, and above
it, where the outside wall and the roof joined, was a hole large
enough to crawl through. The walls were made of long bamboo
stalks bound together with bamboo ropes. Escape began to fill my
mind. When I finished eating, I told the guards in sign language
that I had to go to the bathroom. The guard pointed to the open
door. I crawled out of the house and up a path on hands and
knees. This gave me a chance to look around.

When I was crawling back to the house, several old-looking
women with babies approached. One sat her baby on my back.
They all laughed and giggled except the baby, who started to cry,
probably more because of the dust than out of fear. As the others
giggled, the mother danced around me in a cloud of dust insisting
that her son ride the American horse. Later that day, the villagers
crowded around the house. The children showed up to poke bamboo poles at me through openings in the house walls. Finally, the
owner of the house began helping me ward them off, obviously
worried that they were going to tear the place apart.

Before sunset, I had a meal of rice and dry chopped peanuts.
For most of the peasants in North Vietnam, sleep is not far behind
sunset. Two soldiers in their uniforms slept, one on each side of a
uniformed girl in the big bed. Each cuddled a weapon.

They left me untied. I assumed my performance that day had
convinced them I could not walk. But as they locked the front
doors for the night, they moved the table away from below the
hole in the wall. The kitchen door was the next alternative. Late
that night, I crawled along the floor, past the bed. I stood up beside
the kitchen door and tried unsuccessively several times to open it.
I got back down on my hands and knees and crawled to the front
doors.

Thinking I might be able to get away before they woke up, I
stood up directly in front of the three sleeping figures and tried the
door. The door was locked and bolted. Anything I tried would be
too noisy. I got back down on my stomach, slipped back to my
corner, and went to sleep.

The next morning a pretty but very businesslike and expressionless girl, carrying a tiny baby, fed me a meal of crushed peanuts

sprinkled over a small bowl of rice. Throughout the day, she also gave me water when I asked for it. She did not seem to mind my being in her house.

That evening I was taken out of the house and put on a stretcher. A corridor of villagers was lined up from the house to a small truck. As the guards picked me up, the villagers closed in and began beating on me with small sticks and their fists. The old woman and the kids were the biggest menace. To get away from the pounding, I rolled off the stretcher and hit the ground. Two guards rushed forward, pulled my arms up around their necks and dragged me. Now, because they, too, were being hit by sticks and flying rocks, they yelled and threatened the crowd with their guns. As the angry mob ceased, the soldiers piled me into the truck. We rumbled on, still going east.

Much later, still at night, we drove into an intermediate prison. I guessed it was the last stop before Hanoi. If I was going to escape, it had better be soon, I thought. This probably was as far east as we were going.

The guards half pulled, half carried me into a cell that seemed about five feet wide by seven feet. In one corner of the dirt floor lay a board—my bed, no doubt. They took my shoes with them when they left. The wooden front wall of the room had four iron bars set into a small window some three feet up from the ground. There was a wooden shutter over the window.

What interested me most was the inside wall. It was made entirely of bamboo and tied down in a number of places with wire and bamboo twine. Making a pillow out of an old burlap bag I found in the cell, I went to sleep, thinking about that wall.

When I woke up that morning and looked out through slits in the bamboo wall, I could see a cooking area with pots and pans and a large double bed, again without a mattress. At the end of the house, to the right, was a livestock pen, thick with muck and straw. Tethered inside the pen was a large black bull, far more handsome than any other water buffalo I had seen. In the front yard, an ugly yellow dog yelped as he chased some chickens.

The bamboo wall, I decided, was the escape route. If I could loosen its bindings and slide it to the left toward the door frame, I would be able to go out through the gap at the front end of the cell. I yelled for a guard and gestured that I had to go to the bathroom. When the door opened, I crawled out and to the right at the corner of the building.

I relieved myself. Behind my cell I saw barbed wire and a cluster of houses. Discouraged, I crawled back inside the cell. After the guard had latched the door and left, I got up and started unwinding wire and untying bamboo twine, loosely refastening it each time to cover the activity.

By hanging onto some rafters, I pulled myself up to peer over the wall I was working on. An old farmer was on the other side shelling peanuts. I hung there watching for a long time before the old man saw me. Silently, the North Vietnamese came over and passed me a handful of peanuts. They tasted good. I asked for more, and he gave me another handful. I went back to untying bamboo twine while watching the old man.

That afternoon, with a new guard in the area, I indicated that I had to go to the bathroom again. This time, I crawled out and to the left where the bull was penned. It swung its massive head to watch as I rose up on my knees and peed into his stall. There was a brass ring in his nose, and his sleek coat looked well brushed. He looked so powerful, it seemed as though nothing could hold him if he decided to move. How many people, I wondered, are willing, like this bull, to give up their freedom.

That afternoon I was given a small bottle of wintergreen, apparently to clean my bullet wound. I hid the wintergreen for later and went back to dismantling the wall.

The next morning two guards came in, picked me up, and carried me out of the cell, off the one-step porch, past the bull pen, through a small gate in the building's courtyard, into the courtyard next door and up into the open side of a three-walled building. They placed me on a stool in front of a bare table and tied my hands behind me. On the other side of the table sat four men, two young men flanked two older men. One of the old ones wore what looked like an officer's uniform. The other had a scar on his face. At the end of the table on a high-backed chair sat another, older man who turned out to be the interpreter. The old man with the scar was in charge. Through the interpreter, I was asked, "How do you feel?"

"All right," I said, "except one leg is swollen and no one has cared for my bullet wound."

Scarface said it would be attended to. I was asked my name. "Captain John Dramesi," I replied.

"Your name is John Dramesi," the interpreter said sternly. "You have no rank here."

I was asked, "What type of aircraft did you fly?" I refused to answer.

"Where are you from?" I refused to answer.

"What is your wing commander's name?" I was asked. The questions were repeated, and again I refused. With each question, my interrogators became more and more agitated—except for the interpreter who sat, placid and expressionless, working like a machine.

Suddenly, Scarface grabbed a three-foot-long bamboo pole, rushed around the table and began beating me about the head and shoulders. Fortunately, each time Scarface raised the pole over his head, it hit the low ceiling. That took some of the force out of each blow. Still, they were hard enough so that I slowly slumped off the stool and dropped to the ground. Scarface started kicking me. His boots dug into my ribs and back. I was sure it would not last long and I would be able to remain silent.

My interrogator went back behind the table. I was hoisted back up on the stool, and the questioning started again. I refused to answer. This time, when Scarface rushed at me, he swung the bamboo weapon like a baseball bat, hitting me mostly on the back. For some stupid reason I forced myself to stay on the stool this time. Once more, I refused to answer and once more the whole process was repeated.

When I refused to answer a fourth time, the interrogator shouted to the guards while waving a finger in my face. Two guards sprang into action. One guard turned my hands until the backs were against each other, then tightened the wrist ropes until I could feel the circulation stop.

The other strung another rope around my arms three or four inches above the elbows. With a knee in my side for leverage, he forced my arms together, tighter and tighter. I grunted with each jerk of the rope, but because I thought I was expected to show no emotion, I grimaced, tightened my jaw and remained mute. I could feel my arms swell as the blood tried to pass the rope barrier. My heart pounded in my chest. I wanted to cry out, but I kept telling myself I must not show weakness. How much longer could I restrain that expanding balloon of emotion and pain? When my elbows were touching, and my bones felt ready to pop from their sockets, the guard cinched up the rope. Then, in a solemn and orderly manner, they all rose and left me there.

In fifteen or twenty minutes, I no longer had any feeling in my arms. I thought gangrene would set in soon.

Finally, the interpreter came back. Shaking his head back and forth, he said unemotionally, "You are a diehard." He took his seat, gestured by showing me the palm of his hand, and said, "This will get you nowhere. It is stupid." He paused and then said, "Now tell me the name of your wing commander."

"No!"

"Then you must just lie there. Perhaps you will lose your arms."

"No! I don't want to lose my arms. Take me out and I will tell you the name of my wing commander."

"No! No! No!" he corrected. "You will tell me the name of your wing commander now, and then we will remove the rope."

With all my strength, I screamed, "I'll rot first."

He sat there studying me then said softly, "I will take you out, if you will answer the question."

"Yes, Yes, I will."

Involuntarily a piercing cry forced itself from my throat as a guard released the ropes. The stabbing pain was overpowering as my blood rushed to return life to my arms. Was I obligated now to tell the truth? My thoughts were interrupted.

"What is your wing commander's name?" I told him and immediately realized I had committed a terrible error. It was not honor that had caused me to tell the truth, it was stupidity and fear. I think he realized I was not going to answer more questions. The conversation drifted to more personal matters. Even I asked some questions.

The interpreter told me that he had a wife, who was a doctor, and a son in Dong Hoi. "My son was killed there," he said, "in an American bombing raid." He told me, proudly, that he had been to Moscow and that he was a teacher of mathematics. "What will you do after the war?" I asked. "I will be a professor in Hanoi," he replied. He seemed friendly and relaxed, but underneath, no doubt, cold-hearted enough to do whatever was necessary to get the information he needed.

"I have interviewed many of your friends," he told me, "and it is no use resisting. It is of no use being a diehard. If you will answer the questions, many of the uncomfortable things will not happen to you. It will be much easier for you."

I explained to the Professor, "I am a military man. I am expected not to answer those kinds of questions."

"You are a diehard and a fool," the Professor said, and left the room. Shortly afterward, he came back with the interrogators. They asked about dive angles, aircraft speeds, altitudes, what kind of munitions I used, and how I got away from antiaircraft fire. With each question, I said either that I did not know or that I was not permitted to answer. With each refusal, Scarface's anger increased. Finally, as if by signal, two guards jumped up, grabbed me, tightened the ropes, and again marched out of the room. And again I felt my arms go dead.

I decided this time to scream and cry. I was on the verge of it anyway, so it wouldn't be very difficult to put all my heart into it. I wailed, "My arms, my arms, my arms are dying. My poor arms. My arms will leave me. My arms." After what seemed like an hour, but surely was no more than twenty or thirty minutes, I was released from the ropes.

I began to lie, hopefully, in a convincing babble. I told them I was just a pilot and could not answer technical questions.

The old man next to Scarface, an antiaircraft officer, took over the questioning. The Professor asked, "How do you get away from the gunners?" I told him, "It is very simple. We just fly straight ahead to get out of range as fast as possible."

"No, you do not. It is not so," said the Professor after talking to the old man.

"Oh, yes, we do," I said. "Because it is very logical." I was speaking very deliberately now, attempting to be convincing. "If you want to get from one point to the next outside the range of the guns, you obviously do not go in a curve because your time exposed to fire is increased. Going straight ahead is the quickest way to get from one point to another. Turning left or right is not."

He thought that over for a moment, then asked what I would do if the bullets were coming up straight ahead of me. "I would fly straight ahead," I responded, "because if I saw the bullets, they would already be past me and the air ahead would be clear."

The old man told me I was lying. The old man suggested I was possibly a very dumb pilot because no other Americans flew straight ahead. I insisted that is what I would do. We argued about avoiding antiaircraft fire until, late in the afternoon, the interrogators left. I was returned to my cell.

Alone again, I realized I had failed my first test. I had given them my wing commander's name. To say I had done it because I had made a promise or they probably knew the name anyway was a rationalization. I didn't know they knew, I told myself, and I was expected not to give that information. They could use it any number of ways, to intimidate, to show someone else how much they knew, or to expose someone else's attempt to lie. From now on, I promised myself, I would have to do better. I would have to think more clearly. The tortures were going to get worse, and I would have to endure. There will be other men stronger than I, I thought. How will I explain my behavior to them?

I resolved that I would say nothing even if I lost my arms. I knew now it was easier said than done. I knew also there would be another time. Finally, I went to sleep with my problems.

The next morning, I again worked on the bamboo wall. The old man was there again and gave me some more peanuts. That afternoon, one of the young men from yesterday's interrogation showed up and placed a small table outside my cell. He told me to crawl out to a chair set up beside the table. A political indoctrinator, he spread several propanganda pamphlets across the table and began to talk. He claimed America was losing the war and the North Vietnamese were going to win eventually. He stated that Americans did not want to fight and that the American people were against the war. He spoke like a man who had memorized a prepared thirty-minute speech and had recited the words many times.

He asked me if I was afraid of the surface-to-air missiles and the North Vietnamese MIG fighter aircraft. I said I was not afraid.

"Why? Many pilots are afraid. They wear good luck charms

and tiger's teeth. They are afraid of the North Vietnamese pilots and the missiles that protect all of North Vietnam. Many American pilots are afraid."

"No, I am not afraid of them," I responded, "simply because they do not exist all over North Vietnam." The young man braced himself in the chair and was astonished when I accused him of lying. "There are no SAMS in the south of North Vietnam, and the MIGs cannot go that far," I emphasized.

In an attempt to regain the offensive, he said, "Johnson is very unpopular because he takes heavy taxes from the people to pay for the war. Do you realize that all the people of the United States are very tired? They are tired! They do not want to give all of their rice and buffalo to Johnson to fight his war."

"Rice and buffalo?" I asked, relaxing a little.

"Yes. They don't want to give their rice and buffalo to Johnson. Soon they will rise up." He launched into another of his prepared speeches. At the end of the lecture, he gave me some of the communist and North Vietnamese booklets on the war and ordered me to read them.

I realized I had made another mistake, more subtle than giving my commander's name, but still a mistake. I had talked too much.

By the start of the third day, I had the bamboo wall bindings completely loosened, though from the outside the wall still looked sturdy. Nevertheless, it was held in place only with the few strands that I had retied. I feared it would all fall down if someone came along and leaned against it.

On the tenth of April, they left me alone, except for one time when I had to relieve myself. I didn't, but I wanted a look at more than I had been able to see from the bull pen three days earlier. I was led, crawling, to the right again, farther down the path, across a small courtyard, and past a small pond. Beyond the pond, in the opposite direction, the path went right and then left. It appeared to angle between two houses, connecting to a road which went off through the village and across the fields. That looked like the way out.

Down the path a short way, the guard pointed to a red brick pedestal with a lid on it. I pulled myself up onto it, lifted the cover and sat over the hole. While I feigned the commotion of relieving myself, I surveyed the whole area more closely. Yes, I decided, down the path and out across the fields was the way to go. I climbed down off the pedestal and made the long crawl back to the cell. As I went up the porch step, I picked up a bamboo pole and used it as a support as I stood upright on my knees. Negligently, the guard allowed me to keep it.

Initially, the dog had been a worry because of his constant barking. But for the last day and a half I had neither seen nor heard him. I wondered what dog meat and peanut soup tasted like.

That evening, just before the sun went down, the rain I needed to cover the sound of the escape began to fall. Shortly after dark, it seemed, everyone went to sleep. No lights were on, no community games, no social activities. My guards were sound asleep in the big bed no more than six feet away on the other side of the door.

I put the bottle of wintergreen into my shirt pocket, put on the burlap "jacket" I had made, and began to loosen the wall's bindings. As I untied the bindings near the floor, I sat down. My thoughts were to push the wall out about four inches and slide it to the left in front of the door.

As I gently pushed on the wall, the bottom moved slightly. Suddenly, the unbalanced wall started to topple in over me. Quickly, I reached up and stopped it with my left hand. I sat there for five minutes with the wall canted in over me. Finally, fighting to keep even from breathing hard, I managed to grab the bamboo pole and used it to prop up the wall.

On my hands and knees I made my way through the Delta-shaped opening, picked up my shoes at the foot of the bed, crawled across the porch and out into the front yard. On my way out on the opposite side of the bed I saw three machine guns. I hesitated, then left them. In survival school, during one of my two "escapes," I had "shot" three guards and two commanders. In the debriefing that followed, I was told it was best to use brains, not brawn, and to avoid the enemy, if possible and that opportunities for escape can be created.

I crawled through the courtyard out to a small tree by the path. I put on my shoes and stood up. The rain was still coming down hard, noisy and heavy enough to obscure any movement. The air was cool. Nobody was around. If the ugly yellow dog was alive, he was probably keeping dry with the bull. I walked through the little village and out into the rice paddies. The first thing that startled me was the racket I set off from frogs and crickets each time I took a step. To the North Vietnamese, it was natural noise. No one came out to investigate.

I had traveled some distance when I heard the beating of metal in the distance. The rain was light by now, and far back in the dark I could see lights going on and torches being lit. My absence had been discovered. But around me the night was dark and the rice fields were filled with water. I felt my chances were still good. I kept moving in what I was sure was a straight line east. In a little while I could see the headlights of trucks and cars racing down a road which paralleled my course. They were trying to get out ahead of me.

III

The Bug

Given the opportunity, I will attempt to be a hero, for I most certainly prefer to be a hero, dead or alive, than to live the life of a coward.

After traveling for some time, I saw in the distance flashlights bobbing in the night, searching. They came very close. I sank down in the water between two rows of rice, took a deep breath, and submerged. When I came up for air, they were past me, moving away. I stood up and walked until I came to the hard ground of a dike. I climbed it and, looking back over my shoulder, saw the searchers returning, their lights sweeping back and forth across the field.

I slipped down the other side of the dike and struggled into a dense thicket, standing still while the flickering lights probed the brush around me. When they turned and started away again, I moved down to the edge of a pond and started across. The bottom was mushy. About halfway across, I was nearly up to my nose. A few sniffs revealed what I had suspected: I was in an open cesspool. Once out of it, I climbed to the top of another dike and started heading—I hoped—east. Behind me I could see the lights of the search party combing back and forth across the section of field I had just left. Finally, they were out of sight. I was alone, my stumbling and splashing triggering the clicks and croaks of a thousand crickets and frogs.

It was very near morning. I had just crossed a footbridge when I almost stumbled into patrolling guards. I slid down into the rice paddy until they passed, and then I hurried off, looking for a hiding place.

Other than walking right through two villages, most of my trip had been over the paddies. The sun would be coming up soon, and I needed cover, a chance to rest. I hunted in vain. I was in open country. Finally, I just lay down beside one of the paths running through the rice fields.

I was tired, cold, wet, hungry, and shaking. In the dim dawn light, I knew I was still going in the right direction. I looked down and groaned. My lower calves were covered with black, slimy leeches. Instinctively, I grabbed one of the disgusting creatures, but then I stopped. Fortunately, the small bottle was still in my pocket. I dabbed some wintergreen on my thumb and forefinger. Calmly I touched the head of each leech. Instantly the repulsive parasites fell to the mud, slithered down the small embankment into the water and wriggled to safety. After clearing them from my legs, I examined my body carefully to ensure that I was clean of the black bloodsuckers.

When I was finished, I realized I was very thirsty. Picking leaves off nearby bushes, I wiped them across my lips to get the early morning dew. I went through a good many leaves before I realized I was getting nowhere.

People were beginning to move into the fields. To my left, three water buffalo were slowly making their way in my direction. On my right, twenty-five or thirty people were working in a rice field already.

I could see no good place to hide. Three children came by. I was positive they saw me, but they failed to recognize me as not one of their own kind.

I started across the fields heading east, trying to stay as far away from people as possible. I remembered the intelligence officer at Korat saying one time, "People catch people." When I came to a stream, I stopped to fix myself up a little. The bandage on my right leg was ripped and hanging loose. I took it off, cleaned the wound as best I could and packed it with mud. I ripped the legs off the red pants and made short pants out of them. I then spread mud over my legs, arms, face, every exposed bit of skin to darken my complexion. I took off my boots, tied the laces together, and hung the shoes around my neck and down my back underneath the burlap jacket. It made me look like a hunchback. I uprooted a big bundle of rice straw, and held it in front of my face as I walked. This made me feel a little more secure.

To the North in the distance I could recognize a soldier on a narrow bridge. I started along the stream to the south, looking for a place to cross in order to head east again. I approached a group of old women washing clothes in the shallow stream. In order not to get too close to them, I crossed the stream heading east. They each looked at me and went back to what they were doing. On the other side I passed some children riding a water buffalo around in circles, apparently threshing rice. They also paid little attention to me.

It seemed my props were working well. I was a poor old peasant with an ugly deformity. Past them, I was into open fields again. I felt safe because I couldn't see anyone around any longer, and my disguise seemed to be working.

About noon, I came up to a canal running north and south. To my right was another canal, cutting east to west. Over the latter ran a bridge connecting a path from the fields in front of me to a small village. I waited until the bridge had cleared of traffic, then slowly walked across toward the town. Suddenly, coming down that road I spotted some people on bicycles. I hurried across the bridge, moved off the road down into a gully, and bent over, pretending to work with the rice bundle. No more than thirty yards away a boy sat on a water buffalo allowing it to feed. Fortunately, he ignored me, and the bicycles rattled the loose boards on the bridge as they disappeared. I climbed out of the gully. As I got closer to the town, I saw there were many people milling about doing their chores. It would be too risky, I decided, trying to go through or circle around that sprawling place. So I retraced my steps back across the bridge and headed north toward a smaller bridge I had seen earlier, which crossed the larger north-south canal. I would have to trespass the grounds of a small, stately house to reach the bridge. Then I spotted what might be my first break, a small banana grove near the house. There was no one in sight.

The bananas were small, green, and hard, but I thought if I carried them for a day or two, they might be edible. I tucked a small bunch inside my shirt, and started out into the rice paddy on the other side. Off to my right at the far end of the field, a road gang was working on one of the canal levees. Many hours of target study paid off. Ahead of me, on the far side of rice fields, I saw a familiar landmark, a solitary hill on the coast, no more than four miles away. That is great, I thought after walking with the sun in my face all morning. I was dry and no longer hungry or thirsty. New strength surged through my body. I was elated.

Suddenly, an old man popped up in front of me, no more than twenty-five feet away. I wondered if he had been hidden among the rice stalks, or if I had been careless. I tried to walk away but the old man persisted in moving after me, shaking a finger, and scolding me in Vietnamese. When he was almost on top of me, the shouting stopped. He realized I was not merely a trespasser. He snapped his head right and left, then took off running hard toward the road gang, screaming and waving his arms.

I suddenly felt the energy and drive drain out of me. Even the clouds were rolling in to witness my recapture. The field in front was wide open; but running would be slow through knee-deep water, and then there was my bullet wound and swollen left leg. I buried the bananas in the mud so I couldn't be accused of stealing anything. I started to walk the field but, as the road gang rushed up, I stopped, took one last look at that sign of freedom in the distance, and turned to face them. They slowed down when I did that, stepping toward me very carefully, as though I were a dangerous animal about to attack. I stood perfectly still. When they saw I possessed no weapons, their courage was boosted. Four of the boys jumped me, pulled me down, and tied my hands behind me. The yapping mob started off toward the village. Soldiers arrived in a few minutes, tied a lead rope around my neck, and took over the march.

As we neared the town, I heard the swelling sound of shouting people. The kids were running around spreading the word. No one acted as if he knew who I was, but they were all obviously very excited about having a prisoner of some kind. At the edge of the village, the civilian gang and the military stopped, evidently to talk about what to do with me. After a short session, we started through the village walking on the bank of a canal.

By now a corridor was formed by a solid line of people on one side and the canal about half a mile long on the other. One guard was leading me, pulling the rope, while two more walked behind. Because of my earlier experience, I was not surprised that it was old women and children doing most of the shouting and cursing, closing in to throw rocks and sticks, and even trying to take a swing at me.

While I ducked and dodged, I kept an eye on one man who, instead of falling in behind the parade, ran along behind the crowd, looking for a gap in the line. About halfway to a bridge, at the end of the line, he found one. He dashed through it, leaped in the air and took a karate chop at my neck. I pulled in my neck, lifted my shoulders to soften the blow. I had to fend off three more chops before the guards finally shoved the man away. Just before we turned right to cross the bridge, he charged through the crowd once more. He managed to punch my back and ribs a few more times before the guards shoved him out of the way. On the other side of the canal, they led me to the right again, going back toward the village. The crowd was thinned out now, with only the kids following, still throwing whatever they could pick up.

We stopped eventually at a rustic little cottage. It was well furnished, by far the most attractive little home I had seen in North Vietnam. The handsome, healthy-looking family in it seemed pleasant. They gave me a large bowl of rice over which were the usual greens and crushed peanuts; but one of the younger girls also offered me a new delicacy, a small portion of sweet rice. As I ate, I could hear more and more people flocking near the house.

Later, the young political interrogator and a soldier showed up. The soldier, tall and handsome, was the same one who had ridden with me to prison after my initial capture. They were very angry. The young political officer commanded the attention of all. His quick glances in my direction during his discussion with others told me that he was contemplating his next move. Finally, the interrogator moved me outside into the front yard. As we left the house, there was an immediate and noticeable hush.

They formed a circle around me while four guards stood by. The political interrogator started his speech, slow and almost inaudible. Deliberately, the words came faster and there was no need for the crowd to move closer or lean forward to hear. In his own language he was an excellent speaker. With the sun gone and a light drizzle beginning, I began to tremble seated there on the ground. Some began to sob. The young political officer's high-pitched, staccato words and vigorous gestures caused one woman to scream. That was the signal. The crowd surged forward. No doubt the political officer was satisfied with his finale. I was being hit with fists and bamboo sticks. The crowd was crammed so close that many couldn't reach me. While they wildly flailed away, I tried to protect myself by putting my head between my knees. The interrogator apparently realized he had gone too far, for he began to shout at the crowd while the guards pushed with their rifles, driving the people back. With the young officer leading the way, the guards picked me up and dragged me to an opened wooden door of a silo, threw me inside on top of a pile of rice, and closed and locked the door. Rain was falling. It had turned into a dismal day. But, inside I was dry and comfortable, and able to go to sleep.

Light streaming through cracks in the silo wall woke me the next morning. I lay there, thinking. I had been caught, I decided, because my early success had made me overconfident. At the same time, I had proved an American could move over the North Vietnamese countryside undetected if he had an adequate disguise. Now, I wondered, where was I going? I would probably meet the Ropes again, the Professor, the man with the scar and some other very unhappy people. Was I headed back or to unknown Hanoi?

A truck arrived. I was pulled out of the silo with my hands still tied, and walked to the truck through a chanting crowd brandishing their fists and clubs at me. Inside the back of the truck, two guards tied my ankles as well. Besides me and the guards, the truck carried some gasoline cans and hundred-pound bags of rice. It surprised me that we were going to travel in broad daylight. The truck had very little camouflage on it, but most disconcerting of all was the speed with which we rumbled past the cratered countryside. The driver seemed in an almost frantic hurry. We were headed in a northerly direction. I asked a guard, "Hanoi?" and he nodded. Other than that, they paid me little attention. I stretched the tight ropes on my wrists as much as I could to make myself comfortable on the rice bags, and decided to rest, certain I would need it.

We stopped only once, after nightfall when aircraft roared over and started dropping flares. We were in the middle of a truck convoy by now. It stopped immediately, and people started bailing out over the sides. The flares were popping a good distance from us. It did not seem that the pilots would be able to see us.

It was time to do some serious thinking. I knew I was heading into trouble, and I knew I had to do better. One thing I had to do always: stall for time. You never know when the rules of engagement are going to change in your favor, I thought. I also realized it was necessary to absorb as much punishment as possible before talking.

They seemed to judge your answer by attempting to determine if you had succumbed to their pressure. They thought that if you had given up, your answers were probably true; if you were still able to resist, they thought that most likely your answers were false.

If I became afraid, intimidated or confused, I must remember to resist. If they wanted me to sit down, I would stand. If they wanted me to sleep, I would try to stay awake. If they wanted me awake, I would try to sleep. And I must lie. I must lie about almost everything. I would not worry about whether I used the same lie when answering the same question at different times. Let them sort out what was a lie and what was the truth. They would believe what they wanted to believe. I knew I could not lie immediately. It was definitely clear in my mind that I had to say no first and absorb the inevitable tortures to make my lies convincing to the enemy. Unfortunately, many people back home would read my lies and believe them. Even the lies had to be unacceptable for the enemy's use. Above all, I must remember to say as little as possible.

I would not be able to sidestep cruel reality, I thought. At all costs I would attempt to avoid cameras, the press, the pen, and the tape recorder. Failure was my greatest fear.

Very early that morning, before sunrise, we entered the city. Once out of the truck, guards in green uniforms stripped me of all my clothes and gave me a black, short-sleeved shirt and a pair of black short pants. Again they tied my hands, blindfolded me, and walked me through the gate of what I was sure was the Hanoi prison. They led me first to what I felt was a small office, a checkpoint, then into a hall or tunnel that echoed with the footsteps of the soldiers. When the echoes stopped, we immediately turned left, went up a few steps, and turned sharply left into a room. I stood there in the middle of the room, bound, blindfolded, barefoot, and waiting.

It was still very early in the morning, I thought. I waited a long time, then heard shuffling feet. It sounded as if some "booties" were there and maybe some "sneakies." No "baries" here, I thought. After some shuffling of feet and scraping of chairs, the room went silent. I was moved more precisely to center of the room, and the blindfold was removed. I blinked and attempted to focus on the area between the two lamps located at either end of a table. Finally, through the glare of the lights pointed in my direction, I could see the outlines of five uniformed men seated behind a table covered by a large blue cloth. Each had a pad of paper in front of him. The one on my right looked the oldest, but the one in the middle seemed to be in charge. The two to the left seemed to be in slightly different uniforms. I tried to sort out which of the group were North Vietnamese and which were Chinese. The man in the middle motioned to the guard to untie my hands. I considered saluting but none of the uniforms showed any rank, so I abandoned the idea and waited.

I heard one of them say, "You are very ignorant. You have no manners. You must show your respect. You must bow to those who sit here."

I looked straight, said nothing, did nothing.

"Do you understand? You must stand at attention and bow. Do you understand?"

"Yes, I understand," I said, but I did not move. The man in the middle then indicated I should be seated. A small stool was put behind me. As I sat down, I saw to the left, in the corner of the room, my boots, my torn flight suit, and my ragged clothes and burlap bag from the escape. I sat straight up, looked straight ahead, and sat on my hands so that I would not show any signs of nervousness.

The one in the middle, who identified himself as the camp commander, spoke poor English. Quietly, he said, "You are a criminal. You are the blackest of criminals. You must answer truthfully all my questions. You must do whatever I order. If you repent, you will be treated in a humane manner." He stopped, waiting for a response. I had not been asked anything, so I wasn't going to volunteer anything. I wanted to make it as uncomfortable for them as it was for me. The object was to end this interrogation as soon as possible.

Irritated, he stood up, glared at me, and snapped, "You are a diehard criminal. A diehard. You must pay for your criminal acts. You are the blackest of pirates. You must pay! Do you know you are a criminal?"

"I understand what you have said," I answered. The interrogator sat down. He seemed to relax, apparently knowing what was to come.

"Many will go home," he told me, "and you too can go home; to go home even before the war ends," he added. "Do you want to go home?"

"Yes, of course," I said. "Of course, I want to go home."

"Well, it is possible," he said. "And while you are here, you can have good food, you can have exercise. You can have some—" he hesitated, trying to think of the word, then almost shouted, "liquor! You can have some liquor!" He smiled. Puffy lips parted showing a mouth full of large teeth. He probably thought I smiled because of what he said, but the fact is I did not drink. I was positive that his price for going home before the war ended was far more than I was willing to pay.

That approach having failed, the center three started their questioning. They wanted to know what I had been flying. I refused to answer. It did not take long for tension in the room to increase. The old man on the far right asked, "Why did you escape?"

"I am a military man," I said. With this, the middle interrogator stood up.

"I will think of your bad attitude," he said. "You have not done well. I will give you time to think."

A guard came to me, tied my hands behind my back again, and pushed me. I was to sit on the floor. One by one, the interrogators filed out. As the doors were closed, I could see it was now daylight. I was alone, thinking. It was April 13, 1967.

Later in the day, a skinny North Vietnamese with a thin, expressionless face came into the room. As I looked up at him, he seemed tall. He wore a long-sleeved shirt and a belt that was much too long for his thin waist. The heels and toes of his big feet extended beyond the sandals he wore. He had a long, thin neck— a goose neck.

The Goose indicated that I should sit down on the stool. He then dragged to the middle of the room a monstrous iron bar and a pair of ankle irons. The anklets were fitted to my ankles. Through eyelets on the front of each anklet, Goose threaded the oversized bar. It was about two inches in diameter and about ten to twelve feet long. He adjusted the bar. The full weight of that frightful contraption pressed on my ankle bones and arches. I could feel that relentless force immediately. Goose promptly left the room, leaving me alone again, sitting on the stool, hands tied behind, and the irons hung on my legs.

I looked carefully around the room for the first time. On a small table in the back corner to the left was a clutter of what looked like nylon or rope cords and some handcuffs. I also saw some other irons, similar to those I wore, but much smaller. To the right were the double doors which locked at the center. Iron-barred windows were covered by frosted paneled glass shutters which opened inward. The floor was a rough red tile. Five feet up from the floor the white plaster walls were filthy and in some places streaked with a dull green. In the corner in the rear and to my right, the place was especially dirty, as though it had been used as a toilet area. A large hook was anchored in the ceiling over my head. I sat facing the table with the blue cloth. Five high-backed chairs were still behind the table, but only one lamp was left on it. A picture of Ho Chi Minh had hung on the wall behind the table when I first entered, but it too was gone now. To my right front was a large drainhole. I had already seen a rat come in, look around, and leave through the hole.

Later in the day, I heard keys jingle again. The Goose returned. I noticed a slight shuffle in his walk as he approached. He opened the doors wide so the room would air out. I was able to see the archway entrance to the hall that led past the room. Beyond the arch was a garden.

In a short time, the camp commander returned with the two interrogators who had sat on either side of him. I stood up and waited. The pain in my ankles was intense. The camp commander stopped beside me and indicated that I should sit down. As I began to do so, he took a full swing, hitting me flush in the face. I toppled backwards over the stool.

"Get up! Get up!" he screamed. I looked up at him; he reminded me of an insect. He yelled again, "Get up." Although it was awkward with my hands tied and my feet anchored, I managed to regain my balance. The Bug said pleadingly, "You must be respectful! You must greet me! You must bow!" Then he demanded, "Bow, Bow!"

I nodded my head and leaned forward slightly. The Bug rushed at me and hit me again. This time I did not fall.

"Bow! Bow!" he repeated. I did, but not to ninety degrees. This seemed to satisfy the Bug for the moment, although when he took his place behind the table he was still irritated. He gestured for me to sit down. The irons were beginning to eat into my skin. The tension and the pain in my feet were becoming unbearable.

The questioning started. This time they wanted to know about my personal life, my family, my parents. Was I married, did I have children? To all these questions, I gave wrong answers. They asked if my father was alive. I said no. Was my mother alive? Yes.

"Where does she live?" I said I didn't know; she had moved away after my father died.

"What work does your father do?"

"My father does not work, he is dead."

"Before his death?"

"He was retired for a long time."

"Before, before," Bug demanded impatiently.

"I don't know, I was a little boy."

Another asked what my wife's address was. I said, "I do not know, because she moved after I left to come here."

The Bug switched to military questions, lowered his head, gave me a stern look and asked, "What is the name of your wing commander?" Without hesitating, I answered, "I do not remember." Bug jumped up: "You must tell! You are the blackest of criminals. You must tell me!"

"I do not remember."

Bug waved his hand. The Goose came over and knocked me

off the stool onto the tile floor. Goose went to the little table in the corner and came back with two long strands of nylon webbing. While I lay on the floor, he put one strand of rope around my arms above the elbows, cinching it tight. Putting a foot on one of my arms to brace himself, he pulled on the rope until my elbows were as close together as was possible without breaking my arms. The circulation stopped.

Goose went back to the table and picked up a pair of strange-looking handcuffs. He returned, untied my hands, and then turned the backs of my hands toward each other. As Goose grunted, I cried "Not again, oh, no, no, not again." He put the wrist cuffs on, screwing them down tightly until I thought my bones would snap. I expected them to leave. The numbness would follow, and if they did not return, I knew I would lose my arms.

I was surprised. Goose took the other length of nylon, tied one end to the wrist cuffs and ran the rope up and over my shoulder. From there, he looped it underneath the leg iron and back up over my shoulder. Then he put one knee between my shoulder blades and pulled. My horrible scream excited Goose to pull harder. I fought against him, preventing him from getting the full leverage he wanted. We fought against each other. Finally, he threw the rope aside, pushed me over on my side, and began to kick at my head. His hysterical whinnying grew louder and louder as he kicked and kicked and kicked. The Goose was going mad. Realizing he was completely out of control, Bug jumped out of his chair to grab Goose's shoulder. When Goose moved away, Bug turned to me and, at the top of his lungs, shrieked, "Get up! Get up!"

When I started up, Bug ordered Goose on me again. This time Goose used his foot between my shoulder blades. Jerking the rope, he raised my arms until I felt as if my bones would pop out of their sockets. My screams echoed throughout the camp. The Bug shouted, "Will you tell me the name of your wing commander?"

"Yes, Yes, I will," I wailed. The Goose continued to pull. "Yes, Yes." Finally he stopped pulling. When the Bug asked again, I answered his question. Before my tormentors stopped, more questions were asked and the cycle was repeated.

That night the ropes and wrist cuffs were removed, but the

handcuffs were clamped on and I remained on the stool with the burdensome weight on my feet.

The next day, Bug brought a tape recorder with him. He plugged it in and played two tapes while he and his friends stood watching me. The first tape started out, "This is Col. Robinson Risner." Immediately, I stopped listening. Colonel Risner was a Korean War ace and a well-known tactical fighter pilot. No doubt they were playing the tapes to convince me it was easier to cooperate, easier than suffering. If Colonel Risner could do it, then why not Captain Dramesi? I wanted to believe it was not Colonel Risner; it must be somebody else. It made no difference. Regardless who it was, I knew what I should do.

IV

The Golden Key
and Nancy

A realized word relationship is a thought provoking
word equation which when solved reveals but a bit
of your total mental outlook.

Those first two days in Room 18 set the Bug's relentless routine.
The pain was a constant reminder that the jumbo irons were always there and that my hands were handcuffed behind my back
continuously. I was fed twice a day—a dark-green liquid, some
rice, and a cup of water. I was forced to remain on my stool at
all times. When alone, although I managed to sleep in the very
early morning hours when the guards were away, the effort was
to keep me awake.

During the daily interrogations, after I had listened to two
tapes, they wanted me to make similar tapes, denouncing the
war. They insisted I write letters to the other members of my
squadron. They wanted me to write a letter to Senator Fulbright.
They wanted a signed confession, admitting I was a war criminal.
They wanted to know how many and what kind of missions I
had flown. They wanted the names of my squadron's pilots. Regularly, my answers were unsatisfactory. Just as regularly, I was
put through the Ropes. After the twelfth time it was stupid to
count the number of times Goose triggered an agonizing cry of
pain. At the end of a week of murderous torture they wanted me
to write out a statement, telling the world the North Vietnamese

were lenient and humane in their treatment of American prisoners. I refused.

I was growing weak from the tortures, the starvation diet, and the endless pressure of the irons. What had I accomplished? Other than some names I recalled from an old squadron, I had given up little else. I had given Bug the name of my wing commander. I revealed that I had been flying an F-105D. In an effort to stop their trying to beat military information out of me, I had told them I was only a captain from Korat, Thailand.

"The generals and colonels assign targets," I insisted.

"I do not know what targets will be next," I shrieked.

But the Bug persisted. Finally, I told him of an attack planned on a barracks north of Thud Ridge, a mountainous area used by F-105 pilots as a check point, and wondered how long it would take him to find out that I had fabricated the story.

Except for having revealed my wing commander's name, I felt proud. I had not written a single word in the biographical questionnaire the Bug constantly thrust before me.

After dark, I attempted to relieve the weight of the bar that was eating into my flesh. When I was confident the guard was not outside the cell, I would rise up off the stool and crouch down so I could grab and lift the bar. Then I would inch the ankle irons along the bar until I reached the corner. Reaching backwards to pick up the screwcuffs, I was able to shuffle the five or six feet back to the stool and position the cuff rings between the bar and the tile floor. A good portion of the bar's weight now rested on the metal wrist rings. At dawn, when I heard footsteps along the hallway, I learned I had about thirty seconds to lift myself off the stool, force my arms over and below my buttocks, extract the support, and throw the cuffs back to the table. The rattle of the guard's keys in the padlock, the clang of the door bolt being slammed open, plus my loud cough, all covered the clattering cuffs as they hit the table or landed in the corner. I was never caught, but the shock of sudden pain as my ankles again bore the full weight of the irons was staggering.

Another thing I did at night was pee on the floor several times. One late afternoon after a grueling session with Bug, I managed to convince a guard I needed a latrine. I pointed to my rear and grunted; he nodded and returned my grunt. The guard took off the heavy irons, untied me, and escorted me out of the cell, down the hall to the left and left again into another cell. This seven by four and one-half foot dungeon was some prisoner's little world.

It was windowless, unventilated, close, and dirty. The stench was choking. There were two bunks, one above the other. Could it be that two lived here? A banana rested on the lower bunk. The guard pointed to a bucket with a lid in the back of the cell. There was no toilet paper in the room, but from a string near the bucket a small brown rag hung. The stifling odor drove me back when I removed the lid, but the pain in my bowels forced me to squat over the bucket. I delayed as long as I dared. I thought, here at least there is a bucket, a rag, and a banana. In my room there is nothing but agony.

I had not shaved or been allowed to bathe since my capture. Several times, the Bug pointed to my bullet wound and asked, "Do you want the doctor?" "Yes," I would say. "It is infected and needs stitches."

Invariably, he would disregard my answer and ask another question. Because I either gave false information that did not satisfy him or refused to give any, the bullet wound went untended.

At the end of a week of interrogation the question was now "Why did you try to escape?" I told him I was a military man. I wanted to be free. If tortured, any man would try to escape. "Any North Vietnamese soldier," I said, "would do the same thing if he were captured in South Vietnam. Would you not do the same?" This always provoked the Bug into raving about my poor attitude.

The Bug was more interested in military mission intelligence. "What missions did you fly? How many missions? In North Vietnam? In Laos?" When he tired of getting no answers to those questions, Bug would go back to why I had tried to escape. The whole tedious circle, combined with the Ropes and beatings, was repeated again and again.

Finally, on the eighth day of torture, Bug and Goose came into the room, took off the heavy irons, and untied me. I could hardly hold myself under control. I wanted to cheer. I have made it, I thought, I did it.

I walked very slowly and stiffly out of the cell. I had a large growth of beard and my hair was very long. They led me through the archway, down three steps into the garden area. We turned left and walked to the other end of the garden. A large double steel door opened. Immediately after we entered the large corridor, which was similar to the one at the main entrance of the prison, we turned right. They opened another smaller door, and I stepped into a dark hall. I counted eight ominous-looking doors, four on each side of the hall. A lock snapped, and the sound of metal against metal echoed in the dingy and dank passageway. Above the squeaking door was stenciled a black number two.

I was pushed to a dirty, five-and-a-half-by-seven-foot cell. Twelve inches separated two bunks side by side. Each had mounted on the end closer to the door a set of old-style stocks, the bottom made of wood, the top a heavy flat iron bar. They sat me on one of the wooden bunks. The Goose placed my ankles into the stocks, slammed down the hinged iron bar, and locked it in place. Then he grabbed my left wrist, put a handcuff on it, and pulled and fastened the other half of the cuff to the iron bar where it crossed my right ankle.

A great cloud of doom descended over me. I could not believe what was happening. Could it be that the tortures were not over but just beginning? Is death the only means of retaining honor?

Twenty-four hours a day, I sat in this doubled-over position. I was not released to eat my inadequate ration of food or to use the bucket in the far corner.

When my bowels moved or I peed over my left leg, the Goose would rush in and pound my head against the wall.

My feet began to itch, but the stocks were so tight I could not reach the irritation. Eventually, I noticed, they were starting to swell. I could feel the rough wood on the bottom of the stocks cutting into my skin. My ankles felt hot, and I knew they were infected.

Mosquitoes were everywhere, landing on my feet they gorged themselves on my blood until they simply fell, too full to fly. I imagined a black streak inching up my leg. Should I call for Bug? I looked at the raw flesh hanging from my right leg. The bullet wound looked worse. It was amazing, I thought, how I can sit here knowing my pathetic condition and say that I will accept my badge, the loss of a foot or a leg.

There must be some way I can escape. Physically I could not escape reality, perhaps mentally I could. I indulged in a mental exercise I decided to call "Realized Word Relationships."

It wasn't enough to wander in the caverns of thought. To survive I had to return to reality. I had to do something. I had to do something to help myself. I rubbed my feet and legs hour after hour. I examined specks of dust. I found a small, V-shaped nail.

The nail was thin enough to enter the keyhole. Maybe I could pick the lock on the handcuffs. Indiscriminately I poked and probed, twisted and turned. At times I became frustrated and fatigued very easily.

After two days of failures I almost tossed the nail aside in disgust. But it was all I had to do, so I kept at it. On the third day, I twisted the nail in a new combination of moves. To my amazement the metal cuff around my wrist fell open. I was overwhelmed with joy. I did it, I did it! I wanted to cry out, "Free, free."

Very carefully, I straightened up, stretched, and leaned back. It was a wonderful feeling. It seemed as though new-found energy cleansed my body of its stiffness, cramps, and aches. I had to move slowly. For over a week now, I had been bent over in one unchanging position. I was prepared to revel in ecstasy as I rested on my back. Suddenly, instinctively, I sat up, leaned forward, and grabbed the handcuff with my left hand. The cover over the peephole was opened. From the peephole, the guard couldn't see the handcuff, but he would be able to tell if I was in the right position. When the peephole cover slid closed again, I thought the guard would leave. Instead, keys rattled.

I coughed to cover the sound of the handcuff clicking closed. The guard suspiciously looked me over, then left the cell. With practice, I was able to open the lock in just a few seconds. The ideal time to release myself and lie back was at four in the morning. A gong off in the distance would sound, starting people off on their early-morning chores. Within the compound music would accompany group exercises. When the night guard departed, my morning attendant would not peep in at me until seven A.M. I had three hours to pass into oblivion, forgetting the sight and feel of my infected swollen feet.

It was only a short escape; but for a little while each day, the Golden Key freed me.

I stole sleep when I could. I developed a subconscious trigger, an alarm which told me who was approaching and whether I needed to sit up. It became automatic: I was not consciously aware I was jerking into a sitting position until I had done it. Goose's shuffle and the opening sound of the outer door initiated this reflex action.

After ten days my condition was getting worse by the hour. The days were hot, the nights hotter. I lived in my own filth. I sensed the ache of infection in my bullet wound. I knew I had lost a great deal of weight. My feet looked horrible.

Undoubtedly, if I didn't get out of the stocks soon, I would lose my feet. My toes stuck out like elephant's feet. Someone forgot to blow up the ears of my Mickey Mouse balloons.

Horrified, I thought: If I cry for help I lose; if I do not, I lose.

Nightly entertainment for the North Vietnamese was listening to the radio. The loudspeakers in the courtyard brought to them music, speeches, and melodramas. Normally the modern North Vietnamese music and the fight songs were played until eleven. Between eleven and eleven-thirty the old traditional wailing melodies were played. When the radio was turned off someone in the compound began to play Western music. It was Nancy Sinatra singing. Training, discipline, and physical strength were on the verge of failing. It was the woman, Nancy Sinatra, at that critical moment who kept me loyal to my purpose.

But I did have some help in this Heartbreak Hotel. A rat used my cell as an access way to the hall. It always looked under the door before scampering out into the hallway. One time as I was ready to lie back and rest, the rat abruptly pulled back from the door and raced off in the opposite direction. I quickly grabbed the handcuff. In seconds the peephole cover opened. The rat, I decided, was an excellent sentinel.

On the third of May, the Bug and the Goose came into my cell. The Goose unlocked the iron bar and lifted it off my ankles.

"Turn and sit on the bed," snapped the Bug. "Sit!"

I tried to move, but my legs were fused to the stocks. I was too weak to lift them. The Goose leaned down and yanked on both legs. Flesh was ripped from my legs. My ankles started to bleed. Numb, with my mouth slightly open and my eyes unblinking, I sat there staring at the Bug.

"Now," demanded the Bug, "you will write about your missions." Irritated with my silence, he asked loudly, "Will you write about your missions?"

I still said nothing, glaring. Angrily, the Bug shouted, "Do you want to go back? Do you want to go back? My guard will put you back," as he pointed to the medieval torture device.

"No, no," I pleaded. "I do not want to go back."

"Then write!" he yelled.

"Yes," I said, "Yes, I will write." The Bug shoved paper, an ink bottle, and a pen into my hands. "Write about your missions," he said. The Goose followed the Bug out of Cell 2 of Heartbreak. At last I was out of the stocks for the moment at least. What next?

The following morning, a guard came in wearing a pith helmet with bits of cloth on it which were supposed to look like flowers and leaves. Such a simple attempt at camouflage seemed silly. I promptly nicknamed him after Ferdinand the Bull. Ferdinand told me to clean the room and the unused bucket. I put my feet on the floor. The pain was too intense. I could barely move, let alone walk. I was too weak to hold a broom or lift the bucket. I just left a trail of blood as I tried.

Ferdinand watched for a few minutes, then left. Later that day, evidently on a report from him, a "doctor" arrived. He examined my swollen feet and my infected ankles, shot penicillin into me, bandaged my ankles, and left. Once more that day I was pumped full of penicillin. They ignored the bullet wound. Have they forgotten about it? I wondered.

Between doctor's visits, Ferdinand returned. It was back to business. He was the Goose's partner, but his behavior was altogether different. Goose was vicious and emotional if I did not do as I was told. To Ferdinand, what he did was simply a job he had to do. Pointing to the paper Bug had given to me the day before, he indicated with a series of short grunts that I should start writing. Bug still wanted details of my missions over North Vietnam.

Both Ferdinand and the Goose peeked in several times during the day. Each time, they grunted and mumbled something in their own language. After the second warning, when I heard them approaching the door, I would pick up my pen and pretend I was beginning to write.

That night, for the first time, I wondered how many prisoners were in this rat-infested "hotel." It was possible, if all eight rooms were alike, that there could be sixteen prisoners, but I could not recall ever having heard a whisper.

Once more I tried. I said aloud, "Is there anyone here?" thinking if they were American they would answer.

There was silence. Ten minutes later from Cell one came "dah . . . dah, da, dah . . . dah." I "bump . . . bumped" an answer with my fist. There was no reply.

All I could do was yell again, "If there is anyone here, say your names." No one ever answered. In the time I was in Heartbreak Hotel, I talked only to myself.

On the fifth of May, the guards evidently were under instructions to see that I wrote on the paper. Each time one passed my cell, they would look in the window, pound on the door, and point at me to write. For the brief seconds until they left, I pretended to scribble.

That same day, Ferdinand gave me a pair of crutches. They were too long but I managed to follow him. Slowly, I was led through the arches out of Heartbreak and into the Hanoi Hilton's main courtyard. We entered one of the interrogating rooms on the right side.

In it were two men. One was the old interrogator who had been sitting on the right when I was first interrogated in Room 18. Speaking English, he was concerned solely with my escape. He seemed very familiar with Air Force survival-school manuals. He mentioned and seemed to know all about Stead Air Force Base in the United States where Air Force pilots were trained in survival, escape, and evasion. He kept asking me over and over again why I had escaped.

No guards or ropes or wrist cuffs were in sight. I assumed the old soldier was not going to use torture to extract from me what he wanted to know. I listened to him do most of the talking. It soon was clear that he had three objectives: to find out why I had escaped, to learn how strongly I felt about escape, and to convince me that escape from North Vietnam was impossible. He repeatedly insisted that escape would result only in pain for myself and others. Just once, he tried to tell me I was a criminal, but I could tell from the way he said it that he was not convinced himself that it was true.

At the end of the session, he signaled. Ferdinand entered, and we started back—into the courtyard, under a canopy of grape vines, through the archway and back into Cell 2 of Heartbreak Hotel.

That evening, Ferdinand woke me up to take my black shirt and shorts. He gave me in return a long-sleeved shirt and long pants, both of them dyed in wide pale-red and grey stripes. When he left, I took off the jockey shorts I had been wearing since I had been shot down. They were caked with my own excrement, but they were dry. I wrapped my brown shorts with some old bandages I found on the other bunk. I now had a pillow but no blankets or mosquito net. I placed my only possession on the top of the iron bar of the stocks, rested my head on it and immediately fell asleep.

On the afternoon of May 6, Ferdinand came in. Without looking at my papers he crumpled them, picked up the bottle of ink, snatched the pen from my hand, and walked from the room. That afternoon I was led to a shower in Cell 8. I was clean for the first time since I had been captured on April 2. Ferdinand used a pair of clippers to "shave" me and cut my hair.

During those three days after my release from the stocks I tried to sleep as much as I could, rising only for my two meals a day or when a guard would bang on the door. While I slept, I dreamed. They were some of the most vivid dreams I had ever experienced. I seemed able to take myself completely out of the cell and out of Hanoi. The dreams were so real at times that I had trouble coming back to the realization that I was in a prison in Hanoi. One dream occurred over and over. No matter where I was, or with whom I was talking, I was always explaining that because I was not free I had to go back to Room 2 of Heartbreak Hotel. Each time I did return, knowing it would have been easy never to return. In one dream, I was in a swamp. I slipped and fell into a quagmire. As I struggled to get out, I sank deeper and deeper until my head was submerged. It was dark. I thrust my hand above my head, thinking I had done everything I could. Maybe someone would come along and grab it. With a final effort to get out, I woke up.

V

The Mold
and the Casting

Realizing the objective is to win, and having experienced the cruelties of defeat, the good loser is the stout man who will try again.

Seemingly endless hours provided the opportunity to look back over my life again and again. Where were my strengths and weaknesses? What had I learned in living that would help me stay alive in my private war with the North Vietnamese? Or, if it came to death, would I be able to die with honor?

I was born in South Philadelphia on February 12, 1933, proud of having the same birthday as Abraham Lincoln, the greatest man the nation ever produced. There, I used to say when my friends would listen, was a man who had the courage to make the right decision at what appeared to be the wrong time.

My father, known as K. O. Leonard, had boxed for the world Bantamweight title once. My mother taught music and played piano well enough for Mario Lanza to come once to sing and hear her play.

Like nearly all the other kids, I belonged to a "club," the Jessup Street Gang. We scraped close to the edge of trouble many times. Building a snow fort across the street to stop traffic was nothing compared to wrapping one of the gang in a bundle of rags and trying to sell him to the junk man who bought rags by weight.

That same junk man bought the scrap metal we swiped from the World War II street-corner collection points.

My father helped me to be a man in many ways. There was not another boy in the neighborhood who ate raw clams and oysters with his Dad. When the oyster cart, shaped like a fish boat, would come by, Dad and I used to race the short, fat oyster man to see if we could eat oysters faster than he could open them. We always lost, but it was fun for me just being close to Dad. Doing something together, that was the important thing.

There were many lessons to be learned in South Philadelphia. Once, another kid had beaten me up and I went home crying. Dad ordered me back out to fight the kid again. "But he's bigger than me," I cried.

"I taught you to box," Dad answered. "All you have to do is use what you learned. I know you'll win. Now, go back, and don't come back crying."

I won. Is it possible that the will to succeed can be transferred from one man to another by the example of an everyday experience?

Because it was a tough neighborhood, I was forced into a lot of fights. It happened when another kid named Bruggy tried to swipe some of my marbles. I grabbed the thief to stop him. The kid picked up a milk bottle and swung it at my face. The bottle shattered against my front teeth. As I looked at a portion of my broken tooth in the palm of my hand, chubby Bruggy ran off. Some older boys, seeing what had happened, caught him and dragged the struggling Bruggy back where I stood sobbing and talking to the piece of tooth. In the battle that followed, I punched Bruggy hard enough to drive his head through a hole in the brown cement railing of one of the fancier corner row houses. The spectators spent the next few moments pulling poor Bruggy from the railing that seemed determined to have his head.

In South Philadelphia many types of baseball were played in the cement schoolyards surrounded by wrought-iron fences. Playing with a broomstick for a bat and a hollow rubber ball cut in half was one favorite, but there was one form of baseball which required only a sponge-rubber ball instead of the rubber half ball and broomstick. In this game, the batter used his fist to hit the ball. One day during recess period some blacks attempted to disrupt the game by stepping in front of the batter and swinging at the pitched ball. As one stepped in front of me, I grabbed the black's arm. The fight started, blacks against whites. The bell rang ending the lunch hour and immediately stopping the fight. There were rivalries in Philadelphia. There was discipline also.

Shortly after World War II started, the summer place called Farm Camp near Willow Grove, where Dad had always taken the family for summer vacation, was turned into a training camp. Dad went hunting for a new vacation spot and ended up moving the family permanently to a town in New Jersey called Blackwood. My younger brother, Leonard, said, "We're moving to the country. We'll never see a trolley again." The street through town was the main road to Atlantic City. The last thing Leonard and I did in South Philadelphia was to pitch my model airplanes from the roof of 1943 South Jessup Street. The whole block turned out for the mock air battle. Many streaked flames as they crashed into the black street below. The models were too fragile, too bulky, and too numerous to be taken to our new home.

In Blackwood, I continued learning the discipline that goes with growing up. And the problems of a boy were not left behind in Philadelphia. Mother insisted through the eighth grade that I wear knickers all the time. I was teased about my pants constantly and regularly had to defend my pride and Mother's judgment. One young antagonist was unfortunate enough to end up with his head between my legs. He struggled and kicked to get away, but I squeezed so tight that the corduroy knickers imprinted lines down both sides of his face.

At Haddonfield High School I always had to wear a tie and either a sports jacket or sweater. I made the swimming team as a freshman and was disappointed when the school dropped swimming the next year. Leonard talked me into trying for the wrestling team. Richard Buckalou was the school track and gymnastics coach, and the new wrestling coach. I didn't know any more about wrestling than the rest of the team did, so we learned together.

We ran into trouble early. Our first practices were held in a room where band instruments were stored. During these first tryouts, which turned into free-for-alls, I flipped a guy. The flying body crashed through a base drum. The boom of the drum and falling cymbals sounded Haddonfield's and my entrance to South Jersey wrestling.

In the first wrestling year, I lost all my matches. The second year, I lost half. By my senior year, as captain of the team, I lost only to the South Jersey champion. It was Mr. Buckalou's way—keep trying, and even in defeat, don't be disgraced. I was never pinned even during that first year of wrestling.

I excelled at gymnastics. In my senior year there was a class trip to Washington, D.C., and a classmate offered to pay me a nickel for every step of the Washington Monument I walked down on my hands. When I walked on my hands down all the steps of the high-school stadium for practice, my friend withdrew the offer. But the challenge was still there. The small group of classmates who followed and my coal-black hands told of the victory.

Wrestling in high school helped me in later life. I had been conditioned to an individual sport where I had to rely on my own skill and determination to win. Nobody was going to come out onto the mat to help. I relearned that lesson in Hanoi, North Vietnam.

In 1951, I went to Rutgers University. I went because all my friends from Haddonfield were going to college. That need to compete pushed me. Mom also urged me. I had a wrestling scholarship, but it wasn't enough. The money for my first year I earned working all summer in the Grenloch, New Jersey, iron foundry. It was, I thought, the most primitive iron foundry in the United States. I wore a piece of gauze over my mouth and nose when I was pouring molten metal. Because of it, the rest of the crew called me "The Kotex Kid." The white gauze would turn black with soot before the day was over. The old-timers would say, "You'll get used to it, John." My reply was, "No, thank you."

Trained and pushed to test myself constantly, I found a challenge even here. It faced me when the foreman asked me at the end of the day shift if I wanted to make some extra money working that night. A big black, built like Atlas, told the foreman, "I don't think he can do it, Charlie."

So I went home, ate, cleaned up, and came back. Just the black man was still there and it was then I learned that only the two of us constituted the night shift. All night, I shoveled sand into a machine to recycle it for the molds. I had proved to myself I could do it; but one night on the second shift was enough.

In the first year at Rutgers I won all my wrestling bouts and did well in the classroom as well. Then as a sophomore, I thought I knew it all, and I almost flunked out. The third year was better, and my grades were top notch in last year. In my senior year the 150-pound football team had gone undefeated until its final game. We were playing Princeton, which had been beaten by Navy. Rutgers had already beaten Navy, seven to nothing. Rutgers lost to Princeton, seven to six. We had come close to perfection but missed. Alone I walked across the field, head lowered, crying. A teammate ran by, slapped me on the shoulder pad, and said, "Forget it, John, it's just a game." But I would not forget it, and to me it is more than a game. It's a way of life.

But there were victories too, being voted Rutgers's outstanding wrestler one year; joining Lambda Chi Alpha, the Scarlet Rifles ROTC precision-drill team; being named drill-team commander, and being awarded the Outstanding Military Bearing trophy. I decided when I was a junior to make the Air Force a career, mainly because I adapted well to the regimen, routine, and the discipline of the military.

My biggest fault is a constant mistake—expecting too much from others. Most of that frustration in my college days was in what I saw at the Jamesburg State Home for Boys. I took a job there during the summers, primarily to run the swimming pool.

There were no fences at the Home, but boys eight to eighteen were in there for every imaginable reason. My waiter was a kid who had shot a school principal between the eyes with a .22 pistol.

The boys at Jamesburg had an unwritten but very real chain of command. Cottage 6 was the top of the caste or "duke" system. (This term was derived from the expression "put up your dukes," an invitation to a fist-fight.) All the black seventeen and eighteen-year-olds lived there. A duke's number indicated how important he was. Duke Three did not mess with Duke One. Duke Upstate was the top leader among the dukes in all other cottages.

My introduction to the boys was one of the toughest challenges of my life. Mr. Fitch, the superintendent, introduced me to Cottage 6 as a wrestler from Rutgers. The demands for a match came thick and fast. Stunned, I watched the superintendent walk off smiling. After I beat two of the upper-echelon dukes from Cottage 6, none of the lesser dukes issued a challenge.

Because of the slight difference in age, I had to earn the boy's respect before my authority as an instructor was accepted. Once they found they could respect me, friendship followed. But Duke Upstate was not friendly—not yet, anyway. Everyone knew sooner or later he would have to challenge me. The system required it.

Duke Upstate was about six-two and weighed 200 pounds. At first, after seeing me wrestle, he suggested a boxing match. But he canceled that when he saw me box an Italian boy and beat him with one hand. Finally, Duke Upstate decided we would wrestle under water. That made what had been a big worry for me very easy. When I dived in, I simply took a deep breath and remained just out of reach, like a mongoose toying with a cobra. Duke Upstate started up for air, but when he realized there was a vise-like grip about his ankle that prevented him from reaching air, he panicked and thrashed about trying to reach the surface. From then on, though other counselors had trouble with escapes from the fenceless home, because of respect and friendship nobody ever "pulled out" while I was on duty.

One result of incidents like that of beating Duke Upstate—incidents of inspiring respect—was that the younger boys magnified everything I did. I could do anything better than anybody. I was Tarzan and Superman and the Lone Ranger all in one.

After graduation, and as a favor for a friend, I accepted a job as a lifeguard at the Fontainebleau Hotel pool in Miami Beach. Although it was for a short time, life in Miami Beach soon became boring. There was nothing to do except rub ladies' backs with suntan lotion, perform handstands on the high diving platform, date a Peruvian airline stewardess, and lie on the beach.

Finally, in January of 1956, my Air Force career began with preflight training at Lackland Air Force Base, Texas.

In 1957, I received my first operational assignment, flying F-100s out of Myrtle Beach, South Carolina. All I could read into the orders was adventure. I drove my Thunderbird across the country as fast as I could to get there.

With the 355th Tactical Fighter Squadron, I met two men who became part of me. One was Lt. Col. "Rock" Brett, 355th Tactical Fighter Squadron Commander. Colonel Brett gave me a chance to show if I had any potential.

Besides flying nonstop aerial refueled flights to Norway, Turkey, Panama, Alaska, Italy, and Germany, I became involved in preparing the manuals on how to ready and then deploy the logistical support for an entire F-100 squadron to anywhere in the world.

I had some fear of failure, but acceptance and success were more important to me. Colonel Brett gave me a chance at more. He taught me the importance of learning to play the game and of accomplishing the objectives within the laws, regulations, and rules of the engagement established by society for the military.

"If you play the game and excel, you'll be noticed and appreciated," Colonel Brett said. "If you do not play by the rules, you'll be a detriment to the group even if you personally succeed." He taught me how to be what I was claiming to be, a military man. The exposure to Colonel Brett triggered a change from the carefree to the serious, from the fighter pilot to the dedicated soldier.

In September, 1959 I stopped racing my T-bird at 135 miles an hour to "clear out the carbon." At a water-skiing party in Myrtle Beach, South Carolina, I met Dorothy, a tall, slim blonde. Later that year we were married. Call it a transition or growing up, it's all the same.

Lt. Col. Clyde McClain took over the 355th when Colonel Brett moved to a new assignment. Like Colonel Brett, he challenged me to perform to the best of my ability.

The Cuban missile crisis erupted while I was at Myrtle Beach Air Force Base. My assignment was to lead a flight of eight F-100's fully loaded with bombs, guns, and napalm. Our target: the San Cristóbal missile site. My flight was standing in their cockpits, expecting any minute to see the pickup truck come racing down the runway with its red light flashing, our signal to take off. While we waited, we watched eight B-52s leave, one after another, a fantastic and exhilarating sight. But the tactical fighters were not called to action that day.

From Myrtle Beach, I moved in 1963 to Seymour Johnson Air Force Base, North Carolina, and was assigned to the 336th Tactical Fighter Squadron, Fourth Tactical Fighter Wing. I flew the F-105, an airplane ridiculed by many and loved by all who flew it. The commander of the Fourth Wing was Colonel John Murphy, a man who probably looked like a general when he was a major. From Colonel Murphy I learned of the all-important human factor in command, a need to relate to the people in any organization. Colonel Murphy made it a practice to listen, to attempt to understand others. I began to realize that there is more to being a good officer than simply being a good pilot.

After I had spent one year at Johnson Air Force Base, Colonel McClain called from Myrtle Beach. Colonel McClain was reassigned as the tactical air liaison officer with the Fourth Infantry Division at Fort Lewis, Washington. "You've just volunteered to go to Fort Lewis," McClain told me. I was smiling as I hung up the phone. Well, I thought, if the commander wants you to go to parachute-jump school, you go; if he wants you to go to Fort Lewis, Washington, you go to Fort Lewis, Washington. It's all part of what is expected of you.

In the early sixties there was a need for tactical air command to learn more about the Army and how best to provide additional firepower to the Army field commanders. Colonel McClain was dispatched to Fort Sill, Oklahoma, to demonstrate Tactical Air Command's ability to support the ground commander with tactical air power. I approached the Fort Sill air liaison officer, an Air Force major, to discuss the planning of the combined firepower demonstration. The major said, "We're really going to put on a show this year. We'll have the aircraft come by every five minutes instead of the normal fifteen-minute separation."

"What I have in mind," I countered, "is to have flights of four aircraft each strike the targets at ten-to-fifteen second intervals.

The major was apprehensive. "Too close," he said. "Impossible."

But Colonel McClain backed me up, and the plan was executed in spectacular fashion; more important, the potential of the tactical fighter bomber was demonstrated. Because of that kind of coordinated effort in South Vietnam, combat forces, forward air controllers, and close air-support pilots were able to work very effectively together.

My assignment at Fort Lewis was rewarding professionally, but more important was the opportunity to know the people that live in the Great Northwestern part of our land. I realized more clearly that my duty was to safeguard their freedom.

One evening my wife and I traveled across American Lake in Tacoma to a dinner party in our outboard motor boat. Late that evening, we returned the same way. The boat moved slowly over the dark mirror created by the placid lake and moonlit sky. Except for the motor, the night was quiet. About halfway across, Dorothy moved to my side, put her arm around my neck and asked, "Do you really have to go to Vietnam?"

I just looked at her.

"Oh, yes, I know you do," she answered her own question. "But promise when you get there, you'll fly low and slow."

I laughed. "From what I hear," I said, "I think the safest thing to do over there is fly high and fast." Dorothy made room for herself on the same seat with me.

"At least," Dorothy said, "I have Andrea now."

"That was nice," I said.

Looking slightly confused, Dorothy asked, "What was nice?"

"When it happened," I replied.

Dorothy threw both arms around my neck and squeezed. "I remember," she said.

It happened during a boating and camping vacation.

Our tent was glowing orange-bright in the morning summer sun. At the campsight, hot water for tea was boiling but Dorothy was not around. I found her nearby in a small cove hidden by the rocks but open to the sun. The water in the small cove was crystal clear. I could see the many colored pebbles on the bottom. I walked into the cool, ankle-deep water and picked her up, interrupting her bath. With both arms raised she prevented her only garment, a large yellow terry-cloth towel curled high on her head, from toppling to the ground. The tent was not far away. Nine months later Andrea was born.

Dorothy drove me to Fort Lewis the next morning after the dinner party. The Air Force contingent of the Fourth Infantry Division was assembling behind Building 600, a large administration building, to say goodbye to their families, load up on trucks, and drive to nearby McChord Air Force Base for the long air transport flight to Pleiku, South Vietnam.

I was the last one in my group to arrive. Two of the sergeants came to my Thunderbird to help me with my bags. The car was nine years old now, sporting new red paint and new red upholstery. Dorothy had said of the '57 Thunderbird, "If you could sleep with it, you'd divorce me." As the luggage was carried to a truck about twenty-five feet away, Dorothy, with Andrea in her arms, climbed out of the car to chat with Colonel McClain. An enlisted man who, I knew, was partial to gorgeous women and sleek sports cars, said, "Damn, Captain Dramesi, with you leaving, who's going to take care of all that?"

"Oh, there's someone to take care of it all while I'm gone," I said. I whistled. My white French miniature poodle leaped from the car and raced across the pavement, jumping into my arms. "This is Louie Johndee," I said, "the guardian of all I possess." The enlisted man looked at me as though I were crazy while everyone else who had heard laughed.

During the next several days, by ship and C-141 transport aircraft, the 4th Infantry Division and all its equipment moved from the security of Yakima and the mountains surrounding Fort Lewis to Pleiku. Now the games we had practiced in The Great Northwest would be played with real bullets.

The Fourth Division's battlefield was the Paul Revere area, a stretch of plateaus, mountains, and jungle from Pleiku to the Cambodian border, bounded by Kontum in the north and Ban Me Thuot to the south. Only a few days after we arrived, the Fourth Division suffered its first fatality in action, an Air Force captain. He had been, like me, a forward air controller. I now realized that death or capture were realities.

"The idea is to survive," said another of the forward air controllers, "and that means flying as high as possible." I said, "We're here to do a job. We're supposed to help the Infantry, and you can't do that from 2500 or 3000 feet in an 0-1. Find the enemy; if necessary try to draw his fire. The more we fight, the faster we'll win."

By December, we were working as a team, trained in the state of Washington and welded together under fire in South Vietnam. Thirty-two Air Force officers were assigned to the Fourth Infantry and each FAC in the air knew his counterpart on the ground by his first name. It was a well-coordinated operation between the Army and the Air Force. After approximately six months in South Vietnam I went to Colonel McClain and said, "I would like to start flying the F-105 again to help fight the air war in North Vietnam." Colonel McClain replied, "John, in the time we have been together you have performed outstandingly well. I hate to see you go; but I'll do whatever I can."

I was assigned a squadron but was sent first for a month to

Kadena Air Base to get checked out again in the F-105D tactical fighter-bomber. I had not flown one in more than two years, but when I shattered the dart with the 20 mm Vulcan cannon on my first pass, I knew I was ready. It was a great feeling. I had not lost anything.

I was back in Korat by January 1, 1967 and quickly realized I had a lot more to learn. My first mission was in southern Laos, flying formation with one of my flight members. The airborne forward air controller over southern Laos had sighted a troop concentration. My leader dived his aircraft and dropped his bombs. I did the same. The forward air controller came on the air, yelling excitedly, "Hot shit! Hot shit! Right on the button. You must be an old Tactical Air Command pilot!"

"Ah, Rog," I said. "I'm TAC. Glad we could help."

With our bombs gone, I thought we would return to base. But my mission leader contacted airborne control and received an OK to go into North Vietnam on an armed reconnaissance mission. When we arrived over North Vietnam, the ground was covered with a heavy undercast. Surely we would return now. But suddenly Walt said, "Look. Down there. A truck convoy." He said he could see them through a hole in the clouds. I felt a surge of anticipation, set up my Vulcan gun sights and waited to follow as he turned, dived, and disappeared into the clouds. He came back up shortly; we rejoined and went back to Korat.

In the debriefing, I said I was sorry, after the first part of the mission had gone so well, that I had not fired my cannon. "But, honestly, I just could not see any trucks."

I was taken aside in the briefing room and told I had a lot to learn. "Of course, there weren't any trucks to shoot at; but you should have fired some rounds anyway."

"When you get clearance from the controller," he said, "you don't get credit for a combat mission unless you shoot at something."

"Are you serious?"

"Oh, yes. That's the way we get credit for a mission sometimes. That's called a counter."

After a series of trips into Package Six, the heavily defended area around Hanoi, Walt requested to be relieved of combat flying and accepted a desk job for the remainder of his tour.

I began to hear another expression, besides "counter." It was "no way." There was "no way" we could win a war in Vietnam. There was "no way" we could get to the moon. There was "no way" a mission could succeed. My roommate and flight commander, Lash Lagrou, and I discussed that totally negative philosophy a few times. I could not understand the attitude and told him so. "How can men who talk like that be leaders?"

"First of all," Lash explained, "all officers are not leaders, and secondly, it's a way they justify their own weakness. If they can't do it, they will explain very quickly it can't be done."

Under Lash the attitude in the flight changed from "no way" to "no sweat," from "let's go Cricket" (a less dangerous mission in the southern area controlled by an airborne command center code named Cricket) to "get me a Package Six mission" (a Hanoi-area strike).

There is always the battle to eliminate an ever-present small percentage of weak and undisciplined men.

One day a major was briefing his flight and complaining about having to go on a "real white knuckler," another term for a mission in the Hanoi area. The name comes from one who, out of fear, grips the flight stick so hard that his knuckles turn white. The briefing was the poorest I had witnessed. The major was saying, "We're going to ziggy here and ziggy there—then when we're over the target we'll play it by ear." Finally, a gutsy captain stood up and said "Major, if you're so afraid and haven't the faintest idea what you're going to do, how about giving someone else the lead?"

The day after I was told I would be wing tactics officer, I asked my squadron commander if he wanted to play squash when we returned from the morning Hanoi strike. The squadron commander looked at me and said, "Don't you know we're going into Package Six? If we get back that calls for a beer. Everyone will be at the bar."

"That may be, but I want to play squash. How about it?"

The squadron commander got the message. No Package Six mission was going to interfere with my squash game.

"OK," said the commander. "Reserve the court." The attitudes were changing.

VI

Octoberfest in the Zoo

> To prepare your son for the man you would like
> him to be—prepare first the example.

On the evening of May 6, the Goose led me, not blindfolded this time, out of Heartbreak. We went down the left side of the Heartbreak courtyard this time instead of the right. At the end of the courtyard, through a small hallway, and up onto a porch. There, in a room beyond the porch door, behind a small table, sat the camp commander. In front of the table, on a stretcher, lay a tall, slim, crewcut American. He was thin-faced and pale and had a cast from his waist all the way down his right leg. He looked sick and in pain.

I walked into the room, stopped, and stood at attention. The Bug and I looked at each other a long time, saying nothing. Obviously he wanted me to bow, but I ignored him and looked down at the man on the stretcher.

"Do you want to live with this man?" the Bug asked.

I hesitated. I did not know yet how imaginative the North Vietnamese were in attempting to extract information from their prisoners. I had always assumed that sooner or later they would put me in a cell with someone whose mission it was to pump me. And above all else, I did not want them to learn I had been with the Fourth Infantry around Pleiku and was considered an expert in tactical close air support.

Reluctantly, I said, "Yes."

The camp commander asked, in his poor English, the same question of the man on the stretcher. He seemed at first not to understand. "No," he said.

The camp commander repeated the question to him a couple of times before he said, "Yes." Either we are thinking the same thing, I thought, or he's playing his part very well.

Goose promptly steered me out of the room and through an archway in the opposite direction from Room 18. He blindfolded me and led me out of the Heartbreak courtyard into another section of the camp. It was Room Three of the Golden Nugget in Little Las Vegas, another part of the Hanoi Hilton complex. Room Three was a little bigger than the rooms in Heartbreak, with about a foot more distance between the two bunks. The door to the cell was solid wood, and there were one-by-two-foot windows in the wall on each side. The windows were barred and shuttered. When the shutters were closed, which was most of the time except for quiet hour, all light and ventilation was blocked out.

A short time after I arrived, two guards carried in the man on the stretcher and laid him down on the other bunk. He was Al Meyer, a very independent-minded navigator from Texas. His father was a farmer. In my very first conversations with Al, I was reminded of a warning my Dad had given me many years earlier to discourage me from acting selfish.

"Hooray for me and to hell with you!" That, it seemed to me, was Al's attitude. He would say, "Hey, get the pot," or "Hey, get some water." One day I said, "Listen, Al, I don't mind wiping your ass, and I'll do anything to make it easier for you, but please—it's John, not Hey."

For the next three days, I helped Al as best I could, but we were in a pitiful place. Mosquitoes were everywhere. The food was bad. Except during quiet hour, there was a continuous, clanging thunder, like the pounding of cold steel, coming from behind the back wall of our cell. People were working there, but by putting my ear to the wall I could tell nothing except that they were Vietnamese. One day, from back there, we heard a worker whistling an American tune, "Cherry Pink and Apple-Blossom White." It hardly started before it was stopped by a scream. For the next three days, we could hear the man being beaten and screaming, just for whistling a Western song.

Because of his broken leg, Al received, for a while, what the North Vietnamese called "special food," a thicker broth with some potatoes and slices of pork in it. I was still given my usual

rice and bowl of thin green soup. But for the first time, we each
received a banana. And two or three times while we were there,
we were given some bread, the first I had seen since being shot
down. It lifted our spirits, and from time to time after that we
would wager when the next loaf of bread would come through the
door. Eventually, the odds on receiving bread were fixed at nine
to one.

While Al still wore his cast, I had to help him to the pan to
go to the bathroom. When he needed it, Al would signal; I would
help him over, try to get the pan in position, then wipe him as
best I could. To pass the time, we played quiz games. And at
times I tested my strength against the wall, pushing away from it
until I was strong enough to do pushups off the floor.

During the quiet hour, signals were arranged and lookouts
posted so the guards could be spotted when they entered the
alleyway which ran between the Golden Nugget complex, on our
side, and the Thunderbird layout of cells across from us. The first
man I talked to was Dave Gray. We were even able to see each
other by looking through the open cell windows. In our first conversation we traded names and dates we had been shot down and
types of aircraft we had been flying. Gray then disappeared, but
returned again to ask when I thought we'd be going home.

"No chance," I said, "At least not within the next year."

Gray's head sank slowly from sight. I could tell he was de-
pressed. Eventually, Gray came back to ask why I thought that.
"Because U.S. forces have just moved into South Vietnam in
strength. Progress seems good but I think it will take a year to
reach our military objectives." I learned later Gray was passing
all this on to Commander Stockdale, who was senior ranking officer (SRO) in the camp.

The next day, I learned that Charlie Greene, a friend from my
days flying 105s at Seymour Johnson Air Force Base in North
Carolina, was in a cell two windows away. Knowing there was a
friend close by helped lift my spirits in that dismal place.

While I had been in Heartbreak, I had heard bombing raids
only faintly. In Golden Nugget, it was like being out in the open,
almost at ringside. The roar of engines could be heard easily, and
at night we could see the curtain of tracers being thrown up at the
fighter-bombers as they attacked. One particular night, the raid

seemed like a huge, roaring Fourth of July. Guards ordered us under our bunks whenever the air-raid sirens sounded, but several times I watched, trying to spot where the Vietnamese positioned themselves, and how many carried machine guns.

Once a day, often for only ten minutes, I was allowed out of the cell to wash myself and my clothes. Once a week I was given a razor so old it took a lot of scraping and several cuts to get any sort of shave. But even with the cuts, the shave always left me feeling a little bit closer to being civilized.

Pigs were kept in an old shower stall across from our cell. Their stench, wafting across the narrow, muddy walkway, was revolting. The smells, the noise from the back wall, the filth, all of it was unnerving and oppressive. They treat us like animals, I thought, to tear away our human dignity.

One day, after some time in that rancid place, I was given two sets of striped red-and-gray long pants and long-sleeved shirts, another set of short-sleeved shirts and pants, and my first pair of rubber sandals. I was also given a toothbrush and was told it would have to last six months, and a tiny tube of toothpaste that was to last for the next three months. Also I received a blue sweater, an odd thing to have, I thought, in that stifling room.

One day I was taken to a small room the Americans called The Riviera. There, one of the five interrogators I had met when I first arrived at the Hanoi Hilton told me, "You are going to move to a better place, someplace where they can care better for your roommate." They were doing this, the interrogator said, because my attitude had improved. He told me he hoped I would continue improving, and he reminded me to do as the guards and interrogators ordered. I said only that I understood. The interrogator spoke of how badly the war was going for America, that my country was losing, and the war would soon be over. When the lecture ended, Goose came into the room and led me to a medic's shack at the other end of the alley.

The medic's face sneered in disgust when he looked at my still-untreated leg wound, suggesting he was appalled at the way I had been taking care of it. I thought back quickly, trying to count the number of times the Bug and others had told me the bullet wound would be treated if I did what they wanted. The medic attacked the wound with a pair of tweezers, pulling out large slivers of

dead flesh, and the pain flared up and down my thigh. Finally, the
medic bathed the open sore in hot water, patted it somewhat dry
and packed it with sulphur. He put a compress over it and bandaged that in place with gauze.

That night guards came to the cell. They had Al and me gather
up our small store of belongings and put us on a truck. We were
driven about three and a half miles from the Hanoi Hilton to another prison called the Zoo. It once had been a French movie
studio. The now-unused swimming pool was full of discarded,
strung-out reels of "decadent" Western film. We were put in the
last room of what the prisoners called the Stable. We were there
together for only two days when I was taken out to meet Colt 45,
an arrogant little man with an elongated face and very dark skin
who always wore a .45 strapped to his side. The Zoo, he explained, was a very disciplined place, and I was to follow his
orders and those of the guards. When I refused to sign a statement
shoved in front of me, Cold 45 pulled out his automatic, cocked
it, put it up to my temple, and threatened he would pull the trigger. I said I would not sign.

Suddenly, as Colt 45 began to snarl, an air alert sounded.
Guards started scurrying. One of them pushed me in the direction
of an old garage near the main gate. Inside, he forced me down
under a crude bed. He left, locking the door behind him. Looking
at me were two other Americans in the room, each under other
beds. Bill Baugh, I promptly learned, was an F-4 pilot; and the
other man was Don Spoon, the backseater in the two-place aircraft. Baugh, it turned out, knew many of my friends from Myrtle
Beach Air Force Base.

An Ohioan, Baugh was a big man, six feet four, with a large
head and heavy jaw. One of his eyes was glazed. It looked as if
the pupil had slipped off the center of the eyeball. He had had an
accident, he said, during bailout in a mountain area. Whether the
eye was damaged on bailout or landing, he could not remember.
He could see only shadowy movement out of it.

When the raid ended, the guard came back and marched all of
us at gunpoint back to Colt 45. We stood there in front of his
table. He pushed a paper in front of us and told us to write down
that we would obey everything we were told. He looked at Spoon.
Don refused, setting the pace for the rest of the group. When Colt

45 looked at Baugh, he also refused. But when he finally shoved the paper at me, I picked up the pen, scrawled some illegible lines and signed my name. I asked Bill and Don to do the same, which they did.

At first, just watching us, Colt 45 had a slight smile on his face—until he picked up the paper. He looked at it, reddened, crumbled it into a wad, and yelled for the guard who prodded us at bayonet point to a cell in a building called the Barn. We were ordered to stand in the room side by side with our hands raised high. The guards left the door open so that they could come by periodically to make sure our arms were still up. Colt 45 also checked on us. We soon determined we could position ourselves to see the guards before they arrived. When we spotted one, we would move back to the middle of the room and put our arms back up. As the day wore on, I told the others to start holding their arms down a little as though the struggle to keep them up was becoming more difficult. We knew the show was working when passing, guards screamed, "Hands up! Hands up!" That evening, when our meal arrived, we were allowed to lower our arms.

We were together for three days. We talked a lot during that time. Don, a bright electrical engineering graduate from the Air Force Academy, was most worried over one question for which he did not have an answer: "Why hadn't we declared war?" He had been victimized by interrogators occasionally, he said, because he did not know the answer. The reason, I told Don, was that because of the complex treaty arrangements on both sides, if the United States declared war on North Vietnam, China and Russia would both be forced to declare war on the United States. Or at least there was very high likelihood of that kind of escalation. The United States wanted to avoid a direct confrontation with those two nations, an escalation that would risk nuclear world war.

Another thing Don wanted to know was why, if the United States had not declared war, "aren't we all criminals?" The North Vietnamese berrated all the pilots on that score, accusing us regularly of acting on our own, killing women and children, bombing hospitals and schools.

"That's nonsense!" I said, "We are briefed time and again on where the hospitals, pagodas, and schools are located. We are restricted, and in many cases, we have had to take otherwise unnecessary risks, exposing ourselves and even losing men in order to avoid hitting off-limits civilian areas. The North Vietnamese know this. That's why they use these sanctuaries to hide troops and store ammunition."

"Remember this," I told them, "the North Vietnamese are constantly attempting to prove the pilots are intending to bomb civilian targets. If you sign a confession or a statement acknowledging the bombing of civilian targets, you are admitting and indicting yourself. You are now a criminal."

After the three days, we were blindfolded and taken out of the cell. When the blindfolds were removed, Baugh and I found ourselves in an end room of the building called the Office. Spoon was not there. In his place was Don Heiliger.

Don Heiliger had been an accountant and had played the trombone in school. He had originally flunked the pilot training exam because, he said, when asked, "Would you prefer fast cars or listening to a symphony?" he had answered, "Listening to a symphony." After having been briefed on what the right answers should have been, he took the test again, passed, and went through pilot training, not because he was really suited to be a pilot but because he felt he had to do it to be "one of the boys."

By the end of May, the Office had fallen into a routine. It was an oppressively hot summer. No matter what we did, we could not cool off. When it rained, we frantically wanted to be out in it. Even at night the cell was hot, a dreadful discomfort made worse by the sound of breezes whispering through the trees outside. We were covered with blisters and heat rash. Once I counted fifteen large boils on Don's back.

We were given two meals a day, usually including that green soup which I still was unable to identify. We were expected to eat quickly and Don did so. I tried to convince him to eat slowly because, if he did, then we all could take more time, and the guards would have to wait. But Heiliger feared the guards, who banged on the door shouting for the dishes. He continued to finish his meal as fast as possible; then he would sit on his bed, ready to jump up and hand over his plate as soon as the guard opened the latch.

In addition to the two weak meals, we were allowed a washing period early in the morning and a "quiet hour" that lasted about three hours. Once a week we were subjected to an inspection by sometimes as many as seven guards. We had to stand facing and leaning against the wall with our hands up and feet spread. The guards would search carefully all of our clothing and every crack and corner of the cell, including the three small ventilation holes high up on the wall next to the ceiling. We were searched also, but they never did find the "Golden Key" hooked into my shorts between my legs.

Baugh was the joke teller in the group, the expert on mixing drinks, on movies and TV. Don talked about music and religion. I told them what I knew of boating, mountain climbing, skin diving, and sky diving.

Always, our long evening talks ended up back on the same subject, our predicament. Heiliger said he was happy that he was with Baugh and me now.

"I was with three Navy types. They had a different attitude about this whole thing," he said. They had told Don that the trend was to do and say anything the North Vietnamese wanted "because it wouldn't hurt the United States anyway."

I said they had no right to speak that way, and Heiliger agreed they were probably just rationalizing to avoid torture. However, he added, "It was very difficult to follow the Code of Conduct. I had the heavy irons on only once, for about thirty seconds, and could not stand the pain." Some American prisoners in Hanoi justified the information they gave the North Vietnamese during interrogation by insisting if something wasn't classified "Confidential" or "Secret" or "Top Secret" it could be told. Our aircraft manuals were not classified, so some pilots claimed it was all right to tell them about the radar, the armament, and some other F-105 systems.

I told Don that he was wrong.

"Name, rank, serial number and date of birth are all you're required to give."

The North Vietnamese demanded that all prisoners bow ninety degrees from the waist. I insisted that we resist. But Don persisted in bowing ninety degrees, even while Baugh and I were being beaten for merely nodding. Don never accepted the idea that he could gain more if he resisted. Even in the shower outside, he would rush to go back to the cell when the guard yelled that time was up. Baugh and I always lagged, finished our washing chores, and strolled back to the room.

In little ways, we tried to jar self-respect back into Heiliger. Don always bowed to the water girls as all prisoners were expected to do. Once, marching back from the shower, we came upon one of the girls. Don stopped, assumed his customary heels-together, arms-at-his-sides stance; but before he could bend down, I gave him a kick in the rear with my knee. Heiliger stumbled, almost fell, and resumed his trot back to the cell.

The water girls came around twice a day to fill our small teapots with water. I named them after the water boy in the Kipling poem "Gunga Din." The first one I saw, a rather pretty girl but with the largest feet I had ever seen on a woman, I called Gunga Dinnie. I gave others names like "Gunga Baby Doll" or "Gunga Bitch." Finally all but one had names. It was agreed that Don Spoon's cellmate, Irv Williams, would label her. She was easily the ugliest in the bunch, but Williams did not know that at first. He waited for her by his peephole. As she opened the small square door and put her ladle through the hole to pour water into his tiny teapot, he looked and groaned, "Gunga . . . Damn!"

When the Gungas brought water, the prisoners were supposed to bow as they opened the peephole door. Don, of course, did. Baugh and I played games. Our favorite was sitting in the corner on the latrine bucket, pretending, to the accompaniment of loud disgusting noises, to be relieving ourselves. It always made Gunga Dinnie angry and she would slam the door closed.

Three different times she actually did arrive when Don was sitting on the bucket, its sharp rusty edges digging into his buttocks so much that he had trouble getting up each time he heard her bang her ladle on the window announcing her arrival. He would leap up so abruptly he nearly spilled the bucket. I finally told him if he did it again, I would belt him.

Don had been totally intimidated by the North Vietnamese. He ran out to pick up his food in front of the cell door because the guards became angry if the prisoners took their time. When we were sweeping in the yard, Baugh and I took our time, soaking up the sun; but Don, in a tornado of dust and leaves, would be finished sweeping in minutes. Ironically, once when Don saw another prisoner from the cell across the hall rush out, grab his food, and rush back, he cursed him for his weakness.

During that hot summer, and because of the poor ventilation, men began to faint regularly from heat prostration. Apparently afraid of losing some of their victims, the prison authorities ordered small windows to be built into the walls of some cells. Two old men came to our room one day, banged out a one-foot-by-two-foot hole in the wall, and fit bars into it. Two plasterers followed to finish the job. Bill and I were delighted, because the way the bars were installed, we were certain they could be yanked out at any time.

We had good communications with every room in the cell block except the one immediately to our right. Three people lived in it. Only once did they give us their names. All the rest of the time they refused to respond to our calls, except once to explain that a guard was stationed outside their window waiting to jump them if they tried to speak. So for the next year, twenty-four hours a day, they remained silent to avoid being caught by that imaginary guard.

One day I was talking from our cell to Spoon, Mike Christian, and Irv Williams, who were at the other end of the building. I learned that Major Everson had been taken out of his room. He had been the building senior officer, which meant until he came back, I was in command. I was asked if I had any message for the three men who "were being groomed" to go home early. "Being groomed" meant that they were doing something that made the North Vietnamese very happy, something that would give them a propaganda gain.

My message to them was "Back U.S." It was a code originated by Commander Stockdale back at Little Vegas. The "B" stood for "Never bow in public"; the "a" for "Stay off the air"; the "c" for "You are not a criminal"; the "k" for "No kiss goodbye, do not sign a statement claiming humane treatment when you are about to be released." And the "U.S." meant "Unity before Self." I added to Stockdale's order "R.S.R." and explained it meant "Through Resistance, you can come out of here with your Self-

Respect as a soldier and a man." The message was passed, but the very next day the men were taken from the room, which meant they were still being groomed. My attempt had failed.

Baugh, Heiliger, and I were forever trying to pick up messages by looking out the small air holes high on our cell wall, or by peering through what we called "the star," a small hole we had discovered on the cell wall by the door. We had named it because in daylight, with the sun's rays streaming through, it looked like a star in our dimly lit world. I had the best view of the whole area when Baugh stood on my bunk and I stood on his shoulders, looking out the high air holes.

One day, over the compound radio, we heard recorded tapes made by a pilot to his family back in the States. He told us why the war was all wrong and how he hoped his brother would not participate in this "dirty war." I wondered what he had gone through, what pressures had made him make such statements.

Shortly afterwards, we saw a new face seated on a stool in the courtyard. A guard called "Samson" because he considered himself a strong man was giving a man a haircut with a comb and scissors. It was an unusual sight, because on all of us this same guard regularly used clippers, moving as fast as he could until we had almost no hair at all. However, with this man he was doing a careful job, even trimming the hair in his nose and ears. When Samson finished, he handed the prisoner a mirror. As soon as the stranger was led into one of the cells in our building, the tapping started. Who are you? It turned out to be the same pilot whose voice we had heard over Radio Hanoi.

They put him in a cell only two doors away. I asked why he had given in to the North Vietnamese. Talking under the door, he said he was afraid his grandmother was going to die and he had wanted her to know he was still alive before she passed away. I said that didn't seem like much of an excuse. My neighbor promised to stop helping the North Vietnamese. Little by little he began to fight back. Eventually, his special food and haircuts were no longer available. The North Vietnamese dropped him from their list of those they constantly badgered for military information and propaganda. He became a good soldier. But it was a harder road for him than it would have been if he had expended that same effort from the beginning.

We worked constantly, day after day, trying to bolster each other's morale, knowing sooner or later each of us would be challenged. Some prisoners went out to "quizzes" and interrogations more than others.

I was never called out except once with my cellmates to go to what was called the Library, a room filled with piles of communist propaganda.

That day, on the way, we passed a group of prisoners digging foxholes in the yard. The diggers were ordered to crouch down and cover their heads so the three of us could not see who they were. "What the hell are you guys doing?" I demanded. I received no answer except the guard's grunts to hurry past the area.

The guard who took us to the Library was the one we called Shrimp. He was constantly coming up to the cells to talk, trying to learn English. Each newly learned word or phrase seemed to please him immensely. He seemed genuinely disappointed when none of his three prisoners showed any interest in reading what the Library had to offer or in listening to him rattle on about the benefits of communism. We did not stay long in the Library.

We were constantly looking through the windows or the "star," listening to the pounding, the tapping, the cadence of the brooms sweeping in the hall, always trying to pick up messages, to find out what was happening.

Very seldom, except in the morning ritual, did our room door open. Just as with the interrogators, guards would avoid those prisoners who made them uncomfortable and their work difficult. Even Samson, who was a tough guard, preferred directing others to work in the yard because it was easier.

We made Samson uncomfortable. We worked at it. One time he wanted us to move some dirt from our courtyard to the Pig Sty courtyard a short walk away. The prisoners always seemed to be doing something like that, moving a dirt pile or a stack of bricks from one spot to another, moving it back again a few months later, digging holes in the ground, filling them up again.

At this particular time, with Don shoveling, Bill and I were to haul the dirt in a crude wooden trough. We had to pass another guard each time we made the trip, and each time we did, Samson would rush over and pound on our backs and shoulders, yelling, "Bow! Bow!" As planned, the next time we reached the guard, we dropped the full trough of dirt. After all, we reasoned, the bow is considered a salute, and we can't be expected to salute while carrying such a burden. It would be awkward and impolite. The trough burst, splashing dirt all over the narrow concrete path. In a rage, Samson charged at us, kicking and hitting as we bowed "politely." He ordered us back to our room, and it was months before we had to work out in the yard again. In the cell, we laughed until we ached. Samson and his broken trough—things like this kept us going. It was like winning a battle.

Toward the end of summer, we realized something was happening. We could hear screams around the prison, and we were unable to communicate with the other end of our own building. We decided someone in Don Spoon's room had been caught talking or looking out the window. I proposed to stop communicating for a while, but Baugh said we had an obligation to stay in touch. So we continued talking to Jack Davies, our neighbor.

After a few days of fruitless effort. Don Heiliger, who had been at the "star" watching for guards, suddenly jumped up and, without a word to us, walked over to his bunk, sat on the edge of it, and crossed his legs. One elbow in his lap supported his chin cupped in his hand. It was his own "security" pose. Immediately, we knew trouble was coming. I jumped down off Baugh's shoulders onto the bed, and Baugh had barely reached the floor when keys rattled in the door and Samson charged into the room. Quickly, Baugh told Samson, in sign language, that I had simply been doing push-ups on the bed because the floor was dirty; and had stood up on my bed when the door opened. Samson was suspicious, but Baugh appeased him, indicating that I would stay off the bed and do my push-ups elsewhere.

To pass the time we concocted imaginary escapes. Baugh was best at this, most often turning himself into Lamont Cranston, The Shadow. Invisibly he could kick the hell out of Samson, Colt 45, and a few guards. The North Vietnamese would be so shaken that they would run away, leaving all the prisoners to escape. Don's only idea was to sleep until the war was over. My one contribution was that if I hollered, "Shazam!" I could turn into Captain Marvel and fly away, taking everyone in prison with me.

One day, in the shower, I shouted, "Shazam!" It brought a rush of guards, grunting for quiet and waving their rifles around while I answered, "Huh? Huh?" Later, laughing in the cell, Baugh suggested it hadn't worked because Shazam was old and hard of hearing, but perhaps we could try it another day.

"Damn it, no! No!" Don snapped. "You'll just get us in trouble and we won't be able to wash any more."

The laughs stopped toward the end of summer. We came to realize that we were probably at least partly to blame for the start of what came to be called Octoberfest. An airplane had gone overhead without the air-raid siren blaring first. I was looking out the window to see if I could spot it—just as Samson opened the peep hole. The guard said nothing, but the next day we heard the clanging of keys and the movement of guards at a cell called the Gatehouse. Then came the painful cries. The same small caravan moved to the Barn; and again we heard the same tragic sounds. After five or ten minutes there was silence, and we knew it was our turn.

A key clattered in our lock. Don was up immediately and into the middle of the room, ready to bow. The bolt rattled free, the doors opened, and with a stream of sunlight, Colt 45 came in with Samson and a number of guards. They ordered Don off to one side of the room. He went to sit cross-legged on the far end of his bunk, trying to isolate himself from what was about to happen. "You are to be punished," Colt told us, "because you have been caught looking out the window."

I could think of only three principal reasons why the North Vietnamese tortured: initially to extract military information; to achieve a propaganda gain, a "confession," or a tape recording; and to strip us of our individuality, our self-respect, our American identity, to break the American spirit.

They sometimes did it for two other reasons as well: to counter the incessant bombings by showing they could do as they pleased in spite of the air raids; or to insure discipline, discourage what they called "those dark schemes," the planning of escapes.

Once charged, Baugh and I were ordered to kneel down on the hard tile floor. A husky, relatively tall guard we called Big Moon then started to slap Baugh as sharply as he could, first with his left hand, then his right, lashing back and forth across Baugh's head. He had absolutely no concern for Bill's bad eye. After ten such blows each way, Big Moon moved to me.

He stopped to rest and the Colt asked, "Do you know what you did wrong?"

"No," we both answered.

"Do you know you are not supposed to communicate?" Now we knew the real reason for the beating; the guards were trying to disrupt, if not stop, communications between the rooms.

The beatings started in again and went on like that every morning for two weeks, with Don all the time sitting on his bunk staring into space. When the beatings ended, we were expected to stay kneeling in the middle of the room the rest of the day, our arms raised high over our heads. But, as before, when the guards left, we would get up and take turns watching at the "star." When a guard returned, we would get back into position, and sound agonized, crying that our knees were burning and we could not keep our hands above our heads.

Our only real problem was Don. At his turn to watch, if someone was coming, he never said anything, but just left his post to rush back to his favorite sitting position on his bunk. That would normally be clue enough, except that several times, after we assumed our painful poses, no guard appeared. Don was more frightened than we were, but we were the ones paying for his fear.

At the end of two weeks, Colt came in with his entourage. He said, "You will not look through the window." Big Moon gave us each two slaps before they left us. Oktoberfest was over.

VII

Planning "The Party"

> Without purpose man is like an egg without its filling. Like that shell, he will crumble under the slightest pressure.

November turned cold, and two pairs of thin black pajamas plus the blue sweater were not enough to keep us warm. To compensate, we did a lot of walking around the room, and we exercised.

On Christmas Eve, 1967, we were marched, one behind the other, out of our cell, around the bamboo wall that was our barrier from the rest of the world, and up to the Office. Waiting were Colt 45 and Big Moon. In one corner of the room was a long-needled fir, its branches decorated with 50-watt bulbs painted different colors to make it look like a Christmas tree. In another corner were a makeshift altar with a nativity scene, a small snowman beside it, and four or five packs of cigarettes and matches in front.

"It is Christmas!" Colt said. "It is your holiday." We nodded.

"You are permitted to have some tea," he said. "Enjoy yourselves."

He poured hot tea into demitasse cups in front of him, and offered us some candy as well. He giggled. He sounded drunk. He was not his usual arrogant self. "Look at the tree. Enjoy the tree," he demanded.

We looked at the tree. "Look at the altar." He began to sense from our manner that we did not give a damn about his tree or his silly, makeshift decorations. He got angry. "Pray! Kneel and pray!" he bellowed. On the "altar" were five packs of cigarettes and a little paper snowman. Disgusted, Baugh and I turned our backs and stared at the tree.

"Go to your rooms! Go to your rooms!" Colt howled. Our Christmas was over. But we felt better for it, especially after we heard over Radio Hanoi of the things others had done during Christmas ceremonies elsewhere. They gave the impression that everything was peaches and cream in Hanoi.

The cold of winter was replaced in spring with a new menace: mosquitoes. In one day, in a rampage of killing, we squashed 846 mosquitoes. If the blood that covered our hands and spotted the walls was not our own, no doubt it had once belonged to other prisoners.

Samson was relieved of his duties. We named the new guard the Kid because, like most North Vietnamese guards when they first began their jobs, he tended to be meek. Like the others, he was inclined to let the prisoners carry out orders in their own way—until he had the routine down. Then he would demand we do it his way.

Samson had liked to punch prisoners like Don Heiliger in the stomach every once in a while just to keep us obedient. The Kid's favorite trick was to twist an ear. He grabbed my ear only once. I reacted by reaching up, clamping on the Kid's wrist and squeezing until he let go. I was never bothered by having my ears twisted after that. But those who accepted the harassment without resistance continued to be subjected to the Kid's indignities. There was a kind of tacit understanding between the guards and the prisoners about the acceptable limits of such harassment and resistance. Had I reacted more violently to the Kid's ear-twisting the incident would have been reported, and I would have been severely beaten to maintain discipline in the camp.

A short time after the ear incident, I was summoned by the Kid. Next to the shower area was an open cesspool with two pipes, one running into it and one out, each about two feet below the level of the filth. A prisoner I knew was crouched on his hands and knees leaning over the edge, his face only an inch or two from the stench.

"Hey, what the hell are you doing down there?"

"The Kid wants me to unclog the pipe. I've got to get the pipe unclogged."

"I can see that but what are you doing now?"

"I'm resting."

"Well, for Christ's sake, stand up. You keep your nose that close, you'll asphyxiate yourself."

"No, no, the Kid wants the pipe unclogged."

"We'll get it unplugged. Just get out of there for a while."

But he would not budge. And when the Kid came back with a long, flexible, metal pole, the prisoner stretched out flat on the ground, stuck his arm back in the muck, and started shoving the pole around. After fifteen or twenty minutes, he was exhausted.

"Will you try it for a while?"

"Hell, no. I don't want to get down in that damn stuff. And you don't have to, either. If they want that damned thing unclogged, let them do it themselves."

"Oh, no, we've got to do it." A few more minutes went by, and he was close to tears. Taking pity on him, I said disgustedly, "get the hell up out of there. I'll do it." Before slipping my arm into the liquid brown mass, I looked up at him, smiled, and said, "Marlon Brando isn't going to like this scene."

In three or four minutes, with strong thrusts of the metal rod, I shoved loose whatever had been blocking the pipe.

Samson had allowed us out of the room maybe three times in six months. But the Kid apparently had taken a liking to us. Not only were we out fairly often, but the Kid, unlike Samson did not badger or shove us around when we worked in the yard.

It was a break because pulling weeds permitted me to scout the area. Once I even worked my way to the top of a bunker. From it, I could see over the prison wall, locating roads and houses, searching for the most promising escape routes.

The other pressures from the North Vietnamese had not eased up much, though. Colt 45 was still demanding that I, Baugh, and Heiliger fill out "The Book," a biographical sketch. At one session, Baugh and I both scribbled down haphazard sentences full of meaningless lies. Don needed more paper to complete all the questions as fully as he thought he must. Afterwards, I was angry with myself. I had made another mistake, not in giving pointless answers, but in writing at all. Resistance was the only successful way to deal with this enemy. Because I had agreed to do anything at all the first time, I knew, Colt probably would call me back expecting more the second time. And the punishment would be harder and more prolonged when I refused. The energy expended in the beginning to develop the proper relationship with the enemy is far less in the long run than the mental and physical effort required to resist later.

At the same time I was making my mistake, Don Spoon was being put through the rope torture out in the courtyard. He confessed he had been communicating through the walls of his room with other prisoners. Retelling it through the wall, Spoon said, "John, you said I could do it. And I did. But John, on the fifth time I shit my pants and gave up." His wavering voice continued. "Then they put me through a sixth time to show me the determination of the North Vietnamese people. They wanted me to denounce the president but I remembered one other thing that you told me." There was a pause before Don Spoon said, "I wrote very patriotically." I made no attempt to hide the tears that were falling to the floor from my cheeks as I heard his story. I cursed the wall that prevented me from embracing that man. Who could ask for greater loyalty? There was strength, that is discipline.

A short time later, it was Peaches, an easy, almost feminine interrogator, who started me thinking of escape again. I saw Peaches in the summer of '68 during the "big move," when many of the prisoners were shifted around. I was the last to be moved from the Zoo into the Zoo Annex next door. The Kid had come for me, acting a little sad that he was no longer going to be my keeper. He did not bother tying my hands behind my back. He just put a blindfold over my eyes and led me from the room. I left the Office in the Zoo for the last time.

I could sense where we were headed. I had studied the wall between the Zoo and the Zoo Annex many times, weighing the chances of escape in that direction. I had memorized the terrain. From the amount of time we walked and the sound of a gate opening, I knew I was in the Zoo Annex.

In the interrogation room, I did not bow, but Peaches, smiling anyway, invited me to sit down. Peaches asked, "Would you like to live with one or two or three, maybe nine or even twenty people? What is your choice?"

"Naturally," I said, "I would prefer to live with a number of people, but, of course, the decision is up to you."

Peaches said he had been told my attitude had improved. "But," he asked, trying to look stern, "have you been thinking of escape?"

"Oh, no," I answered. "Look around you. The walls are high. It would be very difficult to escape from here."

Peaches laughed. "Ah, yes, it is difficult. You cannot escape from this place."

A large door, similar to the one at the main entrance to the building, had been left open behind Peaches. A guard was standing outside. Behind him rose a high wall with twisted barbed wire along the top. As I agreed with Peaches, I tried to examine the area closely. Could this be a way out?

We bantered back and forth a bit more about the high wall and barbed wire and my attitude and Peaches said again that escape would be difficult. Then he said, I'm going to allow you to live with eight people. What do you think of that?"

"That's fine," I answered, "but, of course, that's up to you. It is good to hear, but I can't say more because I cannot do anything about it either way."

"Ah, yes," Peaches said, "but here you will be in a good place because you will be living with eight other people." His tone suggested that, therefore, out of gratitude, I should not stir up trouble.

I said, "Fine," and was guided out of the room and along a walkway to another. As my new cell's big iron double doors were pulled open, I saw Heiliger, Baugh, and six other people in the room. They bowed down to the guard 90 degrees from the waist. My anticipation turned to dismay. Why do they do it so obediently and so correctly? I thought.

I walked into the room. Immediately, Don rushed over to shake my hand. The rest crowded around. I saw Al Meyer, still with his leg heavily bandaged. I met Red Wilson, Wally Newcombe, Lorry Lengyel, Mike McCuistion, and Ed Atterberry.

Heiliger took the floor. Exercising his excellent memory for everyone's date-of-rank, he announced that I was the cell's senior officer. From previous discussions Don knew I had made the list for promotion to Major. Baugh had also made the Major's list, but I outranked him because I had made Captain earlier. The only other contender was Red Wilson, who had been promoted to Captain two days before me but had been passed over for promotion to major.

A couple days after Don made that announcement, we were all moved to another cell within the Zoo Annex. As we were being herded in, I looked at the rooms' big iron double doors very closely. The two doors, which locked together in the center, were actually made up of two vertical sections. The inner section of each looked as if it could be lifted off its hinges if the door could be shoved just a short way out from its frame. One day, when we were out washing dishes, I experimented while the guards were busy elsewhere. The iron doors were standing open. I lifted one of the vertical center panels, carefully, I thought. But it not only came off, it came off too easily. A little tug and I suddenly was standing there holding a loose door panel in my hands. I looked around for the guard. The rest of my roommates were wide eyed. They closed in quickly to help put the panel on its brackets. A guard came around the corner just as we finished and ordered us back to work. The guard was puzzled by the commotion but unable to determine what had happened.

Later that same day, back in the cell, we were given pen and paper. The guard said he wanted the names of everyone in the room, our ranks, serial numbers, and home addresses. He would be back the next day, he said, to pick them up. I decided to use the paper for notes to the next room. The question I intended to ask was "How many want to try to escape?"

Notes would not be passed until the work period the next day. In the meantime, I organized our cell. All expressed the desire to make the attempt, but we would have to leave Al Meyer behind because of his leg. I divided the remaining eight men into teams of two: myself and Newcombe, Ed Atterberry and McCuistion, Wilson and Baugh, Lengyel and Heiliger. The reason for the pairing was that each man on a team was about the same height as his partner. Thus, from a distance, it would be difficult for anyone to tell whether the pairs were five feet five or six feet four. A small thing, at a distance, but it could be just enough edge for us to move undetected.

They all seemed eager. They agreed excitedly that escape from the cell was a simple matter of clearing the door from its frame and lifting the panels off their hinges. It was easy. The planning for escape began.

In the note Red Wilson passed through the wall the next day to our neighbors, I had explained we had a way of getting out of the cell. I said I was not interested in names but only in the number of people who were interested in making the attempt. I added that whoever was interested should, as we had done, divide up into teams of two or three, depending on how many were ready to try to escape.

The note I received the next morning in our "mail drop," a hole in our common wall with our neighbors, said simply, "Are you kidding?"

The answer I passed back to them said, "No, I am not kidding. Who is interested in escape?"

The answer this time was that all the men next door were physically fit, all were interested, and they had divided themselves up into three teams of three men apiece. The word started to pass to the other eight rooms in the prison compound.

As we plotted the escape in our own room, enthusiasm climbed. A new kind of emotional strength lifted our spirits while we analyzed where to go, what we needed to do, and what could happen. I handed out assignments, some with seemingly silly titles but all having a purpose. Lengyel was health and sanitation officer and Baugh communications officer because his code tapping was the best in the room. Heiliger was religious activities and entertainment officer, which translated, "Keep our morale high."

Red Wilson was to be security officer and second-ranking officer on the escape committee. Ed Atterberry was to be "historian," keeping track of when things were happening and what we agreed to do in the escape plan. Mike McCuistion, who rapidly lost his enthusiasm to participate in any group project, was to do nothing at his request. As Senior Ranking Officer, I was chairman of the escape committee, and everybody would be on the escape committee. We would all discuss and develop this plan together.

At the start, coordinating a plan was almost impossible because the North Vietnamese kept moving people around all the time. As part of their program to keep us off balance and insecure, they moved the group, for instance, first to Room 4, then to Room 10, then to Room 6, all in less than three weeks. By the time we were all settled in Room 6, we had our first major disappointment. We realized that Room 6, according to the numbering system we had created for the Zoo Annex buildings, was in the center of the compound, farthest away from the outside prison wall.

The room itself was also a problem. It had inner doors of iron like the other rooms, but it also had a pair of wooden outer doors. Between the two sets of doors was a small foyer. And to increase security, the guards locked both the inner iron doors and the outer wooden ones every night.

Using pieces of wire we picked up in the cluttered courtyard during work periods, I attacked the wooden door panels. I nicked my wires with my Golden Key to give them a sawtooth edge, and I used these saws on the door at every possible unwatched moment. As I worked, I realized that the outer door would actually be an asset. Through cracks in it, we would be able to watch for guards and be sure we were not seen leaving the cell. Little by little, mostly when everyone else was washing clothes, shaving, or getting some exercise, I worked on the door. I used the wire saw on it sometimes, and sometimes I cut at it with a razor blade or piece of nail. Many of the wires I found were rusted and broke too easily. But my constant search finally produced one strong enough to make a decent cutting tool. Progress on the wooden door panel speeded up.

My work was easy to camouflage with dirt and mud. But when I had cut down one side of the door panel and was halfway across the top, I began to feel a more insidious setback developing. Dedication to the escape scheme was beginning to weaken.

Our first planned escape date was sometime in the fall. That was when the monsoon rains came, the rivers were swollen, and most of the fields were flooded. It was also a time when the North Vietnamese had regular flood warnings. They would be staying indoors. From my earlier experience, I knew the best time was at night and in the rain. Now, I started to hear grumbling that the rainy season was the wrong time, the plan was poor, and the escape should be delayed. In short, "We can't make it."

The noise from breaking out of the cell, I insisted, would be covered by the rain. "Besides," I said, "with most North Vietnamese naturally staying inside out of the rain, our chances of being seen will be much less, both moving through the camp and through the city." But I could tell we were no longer as enthusiastic about escape planning and preparation.

In the face of waning interest, Lorry Lengyel announced one day, as a contribution to escape preparations, that he was going to start exercising, cut down on the amount of bread he scavenged, shape up, and lose his pot belly.

Until his announcement, Lengyel had seemed obsessed with a need at every possible moment to lie on his pallet sleeping or, with his head propped up, to stare off into space and endlessly twirl a lock of his hair around a forefinger. So his promise amounted to a drastic personal change. Red Wilson immediately jumped up and announced, "Project Greek God is now in effect."

Duties were assigned. Wally Newcombe was named "dietary consultant." I was to prescribe exercises to make Lengyel the "Adonis of Hanoi." Part of the spartan discipline was that Lengyel would no longer be allowed to sleep except at night and during "quiet hour," from 10 A.M. to about 2 P.M. each day. Wilson bet Lengyel would not be able to stay with Project Greek God for as long as a week.

Wilson was right. Three days later Lengyel was back on his pallet, sleeping or propped up on one arm with a finger ceaselessly twirling his hair. It was Lengyel's search for a way of escaping the present, but his obsession made his cellmates nervous, especially Red Wilson. Stomping around the room, Wilson would call Lengyel a baby or sissy.

"God damn it, Lengyel, quit messing with your hair!"

Lorry's answer was usually that he was sick or very tired.

Other than little flurries like "Project Greek God," and outbursts from Wilson, the routine droned on. But with my insistence and prodding, escape preparations continued.

None of the plans were written down, because of the guards' weekly inspections. They were always thorough, inspecting every inch of our clothes and pallets, peering into every crack and crevice in the cell. The guards required the men to lean forward against and facing the wall, while they searched each individual from neck to ankle. The North Vietnamese officers and guards banged wooden pallets about and created a cloud of dust by shaking clothes and blankets.

Here in the Zoo Annex I detected that we were building up to a clash in Room 6. Getting people to carry out information- or material-gathering assignments was becoming more and more difficult. The best time to do these jobs was when we were out hoeing or picking weeds in a small garden in the courtyard. Ratface, our usual keeper during these work periods, gave us plenty of time. In addition to cultivating, he had us watering the plants with a precise mixture of manure and water from the cesspool pond. He seemed very proud of his delicate measuring techniques. Just the right amount of manure, which only he seemed to know, was carefully stirred with the foul water from the pond, a central collecting point for all urinals in the camp. While he stirred, we could survey the area carefully, spotting lengths of wire, pieces of glass, and iron bars that could be used for tools or weapons.

At first, full of enthusiasm, we examined piles of insignificant bits of wire, glass, string, and metal after each foray. But slowly, as the days passed, disagreements over the escape began to surface, and assignments, as they became more difficult, were neglected. A man was instructed to count the number of lights along the prison wall, and note those that were broken. Though he had plenty of time he came back into the room without the information, and invariably armed with a flimsy excuse. Another man, assigned to count the number of steps leading to the top of the northeast watchtower in the Zoo Annex wall, failed in the same way.

Once, I found a couple of iron bars in the yard. I picked them up and slipped them inside my pants, looping my waist-string around them to hold them in place. But when I straightened up and started walking toward Room 6, the string broke and the bars clanged to the ground. The guard did not notice, however, because I was near the walkway close to the room and the guard was across the yard on the other side of the group. Quickly, I bent over and began pulling weeds. As I did, I whispered to Lengyel who was nearby, "Lorry, pick up the bars, tuck them in your pants. My string broke." Then I moved away and positioned myself between Ratface and Lengyel. Later, as we assembled to go back to the room, I saw Lengyel straighten up from where he had been working. The bars were still on the ground. I moved over and bent down slowly, quickly picking up the bars, and slid them inside my pants. Holding them as though I was just trying to hold my pants up, and hoping the guard would not stop me, I smuggled them into the room myself.

When I asked Lorry later why he had not done as asked, Lorry said he couldn't because the guard was always watching him. That, I knew, was just not the case. During all our time in the yard, Lorry was on one side of the group and the guard was on the other side. Besides, I had made a point several times of drifting over to where the guard stood and, in a manner which seemed obvious, distracted or demanded Ratface's attention. Lorry, I decided, was more worried about doing something he was not supposed to do and getting caught than he was about helping to get himself or someone else over the prison wall.

Ed Davis in Room 3 had named our escape project the Party, and it was known that I was the Party Committee Chairman. In a note to the P.C. (Party Committee) I was informed that a machete had been kicked into the open shallow cesspool near Room 6. The note also explained that the guards were not aware that it was missing.

The opportunity to attempt to retrieve the machete came when the prisoners in the Zoo Annex were allowed outside for the first time to see a movie. Blankets were draped over chairs to form small cubicles so that each room would not be able to see or talk to the others. I switched places with Newcombe so that I was sitting on the cement rim of the cesspool. Lengyel was seated to my right. I leaned over and whispered. "Somehow I'm going to make a try for it, be ready." "Be ready for what?" Lorry said excitedly. "Just be ready for anything—to help," I snapped. "With the movie going, the darkness and the confusion I expect, I'll be able to pass the machete to you."

"You can't do that."

The movie started, and the guard sitting directly behind me poked me in the back with a stick and grunted, "Ugh—be silent."

Lorry persisted, "They'll catch us."

I whirled to face Lorry and now, thoroughly disgusted, grumbled, "Forget it, Lorry. Just forget it."

The guard was becoming angry also. He leaned forward on his chair and grunted, "Ugh, ugh."

If Lorry is unwilling to handle the iron bars he is certainly not going to risk being caught with a slimy cutting tool, I thought. I decided to go ahead, and if I were successful I would conceal it in the sleeve of my black, long-sleeved shirt.

Gunga Dinnie, who was a frequent visitor to this side of the camp, passed on her way to the guard room. She picked up a chair and was headed back toward us. This was going to be my chance. As she passed the guard seated behind me, he turned and said something which caused Gunga Dinnie to throw her head up and to the left. It was then that I pushed myself backward and sat in the muck. I sank up to my chin. As I sat on the soft bottom, I began snorting and blowing to keep the dark liquid from my lips. The guards were momentarily stunned with what had happened. Then the laughter began. The guards laughed till they held their sides while I groped around, hunting for the machete in that dank, filthy water. Acting as if I was struggling to regain my seat was not difficult. I pretended clumsiness until I realized that the machete was not to be found. It was the kind of act I felt I could put on only once, and I had failed. As I climbed out of the hole I was surprised by a most unnatural sight. The Goose was laughing.

The next day we received two notes. The first apologized, "Sorry we did not realize there were two holes near your room." The second simply asked, "How do you get out of a cesspool with honor?" "Honor is the frequent companion of success," I said. "When there is purpose and the willingness to make the necessary sacrifices there is no cesspool."

Disappointment followed disappointment. During one of the kohlrabi-watering periods, someone spotted a railroad spike. "We certainly can find a use for that," I said to Baugh. While watering the plants most of us removed our sandals, since they were cumbersome while we were working; but when I gathered them, attempting to hide the spike among them, several men objected to having their sandals used in such a "dangerous" trick. The spike was saved, but the disheartening thing to me was that the will to escape had been replaced by "John, you can't do that," or "John, you're going to get caught."

As fall drew closer, I realized opposition to the Party was strong. Excuses were mounting. It was time for a meeting.

That evening after the second meal, I gave a short progress report on the Party. Then, looking directly at each man in turn, I asked bluntly, "When the time comes, will you escape?"

Newcombe was the first one I asked. Wally said to me, "You're trying to cross a swift river in a rickety raft with a waterfall downstream. It is easier to wait until a bridge is built."

"That may be five years away," I answered.

"I am not going to risk my life for nothing," Wally said. "They are feeding me, and sooner or later I'll get out, and not feet first."

"What about if we could get some outside help?" I responded.

"No."

"You mean to tell me you would be willing to stay here the rest of your life?" I leaned forward.

"I'm alive," Wally answered flatly.

"Even if that door was opened you wouldn't give it a try?"

"That's right."

I felt myself sinking. All I could think of was the sleek black water buffalo I had seen right after my capture—with a ring in its nose. I turned my head. "What about you, Lorry?"

"Not right now."

"What do you mean, 'Not right now?' "

"We do not have the proper equipment."

"Just what are your minimum requirements?"

"We'll need knives," he said. "And it's necessary to have a compass and a radio."

"A radio?"

"Yes, a two-way radio."

I detected a slight smile on Lengyel's face as he emphasized "two-way".

I realized what Lorry was up to. He was trying not to say, as Wally had, "I will not go." Lorry knew we would have knives when the time came. They were to be made with the pieces of metal and bamboo stalks already gathered. Maybe he did not know we could make a compass by rubbing a nail over the magnets we could easily pull out of the small loudspeaker in our cell. It rested on the cell window sill, a simple thing to take apart. But, of course, Lorry knew a radio could not be had, especially a two-way radio. He was asking for the impossible and knew it.

Red Wilson understood also. He knew that Lorry did not have

the strength or discipline required to escape. He jumped to his feet and jabbed at Lengyel, "Who are you kidding? You were half dead for months just because you wouldn't stop guzzling some bad water; and now you talk of escape. Christ, if you had two machetes, a map, a compass, and a couple of radios, next you would want a sky hook." Lorry said nothing.

I looked at Al Meyer. I already had a pretty good idea what Al would say. While in the Golden Nugget, he had told me he despised his wing commander who was "so eager to make general he had no regard for the safety of the other pilots." Meyer did as I expected. He called me "a medal-hungry glory-hound in combat who cared for nothing except how to become a hero."

"I will not contribute to Dramesi's hunt for glory," he said.

Baugh said simply "I don't think you can make it, John."

I looked at McCuistion. "Do you have anything to say, Mike?" Staring at a spot on the floor, Mike shook his head, "No."

Wilson saw another opening. "Mike, I can now understand why you were shot down. You probably had to make a decision to turn left or right but couldn't make up your mind. So you ran into the bullets straight ahead of you." Red was well primed by now.

I walked over to the water bucket, scooped some up with the tin can we used for a ladle, filled my cup, turned, and asked, "What do you think, Don?"

Don reacted as if he'd been stuck with a needle. Speaking rapidly, his voice excited, he said, "You know what's going to happen. As soon as they find you gone, they'll find out everything."

"Oh, I think we can work out something to give us plenty of lead time."

Don smiled. "I'll tell them you are not going for the river."

I winced. Don's negative statement would give the enemy positive information. The North Vietnamese would know that a volunteered statement coming from an intimidated person would mean, in this case, "The river is the destination." Answering indirectly was a standard way to avoid torture and bad treatment. The prisoner could then tell his cellmates he had not answered the question, and the interrogator would smile because he had his answer. It was fascinating to me the mental gymnastics a man went through to convince himself and others that he had not confessed any vital information.

Don broke my silent stare with a shout. "Why should I be tortured just for you?"

"You will not be doing anything just for me, Don," I said. "You know damn well——"

"I know they'll get what they want," Don interrupted. "They'll get statements and confessions. It's not worth it!" Almost crying now, he said, "I'm not going to do what you want!"

"Do you mean you will not help?"

After a long pause, without looking up, Don said softly, "I'm sorry. I'll try."

"I know you will, Don. That is all that is necessary."

Red was up, stomping in a circle by now, his rubber sandals slapping against the red tile floor. He stopped when I finished, looked at Lorry and then Wally, and snorted, "You make me sick. All your stupid talk about stealing airplanes and trucks and killing guards to get out of here." With his eyes fixed on Lorry, he waved an arm toward me and continued, "He comes along to tell you it can be done and you all run like a bunch of frightened pussies."

At first I was amazed at the speech; but I quickly learned Red was not a new-found ally. Wilson was just doing what he liked to do most, find a weakness in someone else and throw it in his face. Now Red confirmed it. He turned, leaned forward, pointed a freckled finger at me and growled, "You! You! What the hell makes you think you're always so right. Nobody here wants anything to do with you. We all regret the day you walked through that door."

From the corner of the room, Ed Atterberry snapped, "Just speak for yourself, Red." They were the first words he had spoken all evening.

Red whirled. "You going to follow him?"

"I did not say I would or would not. I just said speak for yourself."

Red said, "Nobody's going to get out of this fucking hell hole. You people just like to hear yourself talk!"

I interrupted. "The question is, Red, will you help?"

"Sure. Sure. I'll help you to kill yourself." Red had a habit of pushing out his lower jaw when he was mad. He was mad.

"Ed?"

"I'll have to think it over. I'll let you know in a few days," Ed answered.

Progress on the wooden door slowed down now. Only Ed seemed interested in helping. The others were always busy being unavailable for some reason or other. I decided if anybody was going to go over the wall with me, it would be just Ed Atterberry. I also decided going out through the door was not such a good idea. We would have to scale two walls, the wall around our small courtyard and the higher wall surrounding the entire prison.

We'd have a better chance, I thought, if we left through the roof. There, we would be high enough to observe the two guards who patrolled within the prison at night. We could rest on the roof instead of being committed to move without a stop once we started.

The ceiling of our room had four ventilation holes in it. Each was big enough for a man to pass through, but they were covered with barriers of barbed wire, five strands running in one direction and five or six in the other. With the availability of iron bars and the spike, that barbed-wire grid seemed less formidable each time I looked up.

At another meeting of the escape committee, it became obvious that few men liked the idea of prying one of the wire grids loose. I wanted to start on it immediately so that, on the day of the escape, we would have the smallest amount of work left to do. Some of the others argued that the job should wait. When I asked each man's opinion in turn, only Ed wanted to open up the hole ahead of time. I decided we would loosen the wires right away.

At that point, we all knew Ed had made his decision. He had come up to me earlier, told me he had shocked himself by his own weakness when he was captured and he was looking for a second chance. He also said that, after thinking it over, there was no other choice for him.

"The chances are not good," he said, "but they're good enough."

The problem with the ceiling was how to get up there to work.

The ceiling seemed a little higher than twelve feet. Even by standing on someone's shoulders, it was still just a shade too high to reach and have good leverage for working. Lengyel, after agreeing with the majority that it should not be touched at all, was caught up in the challenge. "Why not have four men hold a pallet over their heads," he suggested, "so a fifth could stand on top and pry away?"

For ten minutes each day, Bill, Red, Mike, and Ed held the pallet aloft while Al, Don, Lorry and Wally kept watch for approaching guards.

It worked. After the guard had left at the end of the second meal, I was able to loosen the fasteners which held the wire in place. Finally, I was able to fold the grid back, and, after climbing through the hole, I examined our new escape route. Before I came down, I pulled the grid down and fastened it into place. From the floor, it looked undisturbed.

We had one scare the morning before the work was completed. Ratface walked in with a long pole. I could feel my heart pounding. Anxious glances darted back and forth. Ratface walked over to Don, who now had the look of a trapped animal. Ratface handed Don the pole and, with sign language, told Don to tie it to one of the small hand brooms which were used to sweep the pallets. It turned out that Ratface wanted Don to sweep away the cobwebs that had built up in the ceiling corners. While the rest of the group relaxed, Don tied the broom and pole together in seconds.

Rushing from one corner to the next, Don swept at the cobwebs so vigorously that dust flew everywhere. Coughing and satisfied with Don's enthusiasm Ratface left. The dust and tension settled. That evening the wire trap door was securely in place, and Party preparations were nearly complete. As fast as the rainy season approached, the objections to the escape mounted.

Big crisis or little, one followed the other. Ratface started the peanut crisis when he deposited in the room two bags of unshelled peanuts. It was obviously intended that the camp would eat small amounts of peanuts as a side dish until they were totally consumed. As we shelled the peanuts, someone mentioned they'd be very good for the escape because they would not spoil quickly. Ed and I already had made two neat bags about eleven inches long and four inches wide with double liners. Each looked like a sausage with a string through the top so it could be closed tightly. They were meant to carry sugar and other food, and now, I decided, our peanuts.

That first day, Atterberry and I shelled and put the best raw peanuts in the bags. We had the bags full before the room chores were completed. Occasionally, someone else tossed a peanut into one of the bags, but most of the time they grumbled that Ed and I were taking peanuts away from the rest of the camp.

Three or four times a week small amounts of roasted peanuts were served with our meals. Roasted peanuts would keep longer. I asked each man in the room if he would trade some of his roasted peanuts for the raw ones. Lorry simply said, "No."

Newcombe said, "I don't like raw peanuts."

Each man made up some excuse for not donating his roasted peanuts to the escape.

But while Ed and I lost that kind of help, the group was still willing to hoist me up to the ceiling so I could fold the wire back and pull myself up through the hole and examine the attic. While doing that, I found a hiding place for our collection of gear.

Like the other pairs of cells, Rooms 5 and 6 butted up against each other. A common wall between the two was built all the way up to support the roof. But on each side of that wall was another one which went up only to the ceiling. I put our stores in one of the big peanut bags we stole from Ratface, tied it to a rope, and lowered the bag between the two walls. I tied the rope to a ceiling brace. Even if someone climbed up to repair the roof, I was confident our supplies would not be seen.

While in this little attic, I loosened a couple of shingles so that I could look over the prison wall out into the countryside. Trees blocked most of my view in the direction in which we intended to escape, but on the other side I could pick out a small community close to the prison. During these sorties into the attic, I found it relaxing and enjoyable at times to watch the kids playing in mud puddles or riding and feeding the buffalo.

Though nothing had been said to the group, it was understood now that Ed and I were the only ones going to the Party. Knowing that, our program started to move along very well again. While the rest talked of cars and women, Ed and I sat off in a corner planning and analyzing the strategy of our escape. While the others played cards or chess with scraps of paper, Ed and I worked meticulously on a map of the prison area, marking down each bush, each garden furrow, the places where the guards walked and stationed themselves, where the foxholes were, and where the prison-light shadows fell at night. We worked out precisely how we were going to get off the roof, where we were going to crawl, and where our planned stops along the escape route were to be.

We went over everything time and again. We also talked of what might happen if we were caught developing a strategy for how best to defeat the enemy in their attempt to make psychological gains at our expense. Most important of all it was necessary to condition ourselves mentally as well as physically for the mission.

Caught up again in the excitement of preparing and planning, Lorry said one evening, "John, when you get ready to go, if Ed can't go with you, I will."

"For Christ's sake, Lengyel," Red yelled. He was up on his feet in an instant insulting Lorry and calling him a hypocrite. "Lengyel," Red sneered, "if you got sick, Dramesi would have to carry you out on his back."

They all knew Lorry was only trying to regain a little respect, but after a few minutes of Wilson's tongue-lashing, Lorry agreed that maybe he wouldn't be able to go.

Such flickers of concern for the escape became more and more rare. What became almost routine was an insistence from everyone except Ed that nothing further be done to prepare for the escape until that moment arrived. I pointed out regularly during these arguments that waiting until the last minute to accomplish all the critical preparation would mean no escape attempt. We would not have enough time. I could see that they hoped to force me into that situation. Finally, in the middle of one of these debates, Ed stood and said quietly, "You know he's right. So why don't we get on with it?"

VIII

The Party

> A hero is one who, being master of himself, masters the situation avoided by others.

While Ed and I worked on our agenda and the checklist, the rest of the group stuck to their growing resistance. The checklist was the next crisis. Since Ed and I worked on it all the time, it was kept in the room, not stored in the attic. The others were afraid it would be found. At their insistence, I agreed to hide it in the brick wall of our small courtyard until we could memorize it. Unknown to the others, Ed made a duplicate and I put it in the attic between the walls with the other equipment.

Even after the original was secure in the outside wall, the others continually worried over what would happen if it were found. Only after it was memorized and the note destroyed did tension in Room 6 ease considerably.

One day we were given a new bucket to be used as a latrine inside the cell. This was a big break. Stolen items could be hidden in it and transferred up to the attic. It was a good temporary hiding place because the guards never looked in the buckets on inspections. It was important to keep it clean so that fresh water could be carried on the escape. I gave an order not to use the new bucket.

Once more, I heard grumbling and complaining of "unfairness." "The North Vietnamese gave us the bucket for a certain purpose," Don said. "It should be used for that."

"Besides," Lorry complained, "the other buckets are filling up too fast."

"I vote we use the extra one," Wally added.

Saying each word clearly and slowly, I repeated "Do not use the bucket."

Knowing now, only Ed and I were committed to the Party, I sent a four-part message to the other cells:

1. Who was willing and physically able to escape?
2. When would they be prepared with the necessary supplies?
3. Did they each have a way out of their cells and, if not, when would one be ready?
4. Would they escape without outside help?

This, to me, was the critical question. Colonel Risner, the Korean jet ace, had passed the word earlier that there would be no escapes without outside help. Although Colonel Risner was not the Senior Ranking Officer in our camp, most prisoners looked to him for leadership because of his outstanding record. But that was in 1966. I assumed it probably related to the specific situation at the time, and that we were not obligated by that order now— especially since Colonel Risner had not been heard from in more than a year and a half.

There were seventy-two prisoners in the Zoo Annex. All the rooms said they had men physically able and willing to escape. All said they had or were gathering the supplies they needed. All but one said they had a way out of their cells. Room 7 figured it would take them a month to prepare an escape passage. But they all said they would not escape without outside help.

I learned later that this was not how all the men really felt, but that the phrase "without outside help" had been manipulated by the cell S.R.O. or by the man writing the message to discourage escape from their cell.

As it became more evident that there would be an attempt, the objections to escape grew stronger and more vocal. The time was near when men were going to have to back up promises to uphold the Code of Conduct, or admit they were afraid under pressure and did not really intend to back up their own boasts. Some already had flatly refused to cooperate.

Our escape plan was to start hoarding food on a Wednesday with the goal of making the attempt on a Saturday. The reason for Saturday was that, on Sunday, the North Vietnamese people usually came in from the fields and we would be able to move across the countryside more freely. Besides, on Saturday nights, especially rainy Saturday nights, the people remained indoors socializing. I had moved through the streets at night on my other escape and it seemed to me Saturday night would be the best time to be making our way through the outskirts of Hanoi toward the countryside.

The noise of the rain on the rooftops would mask the sound of our escape through the roof, moving across it and sliding down it into the compound, and moving across the yard and over the wall. "All people hurry to get out of the rain. They wouldn't be looking for anything except shelter," Ed said.

One day, we received a message from the Zoo. It said that the senior ranking officer in each cell would be determined only by date of rank at the time a man was shot down. That meant that, although Red had not made the Major's list, he would be, according to the new instructions, the S.R.O. As a captain, our shootdown rank, Red outranked me by two days. We also received a note from Konrad Trautman in Room 5. He was recognized as the S.R.O. for the Zoo Annex. He wanted to know if we were going to comply with the new instructions. I wrote back, "Yes." Though I continued to be escape committee chairman, the rest of the group became a little bolder in arguing against the whole escape idea. The mounting objections to the escape were motivated by fear of the consequences for anyone who assisted an escape attempt. One delaying tactic devised by Lorry was to insist that we send notes to the Zoo asking for information on other camps, the surrounding area, and any other information that they could give us which might help the escape. I pointed out that we had already asked twice and received no answers. But seven in the room insisted we ask again.

Three American prisoners, Lowe, Carpenter, and Thompson, were released. A month and a half later their parting "press conference" was broadcasted over the camp radio. One of the voices coming through the loudspeakers urged us to tell the North Vietnamese everything, that there was nothing we could not tell them, and that the North Vietnamese were good and did not want to hurt anyone. We were told why the war was wrong and how President Johnson was to blame. The POWs should be remorseful about bombing the North Vietnamese and repent what they had done.

The broadcast was the subject of conversation before going to bed that night. As he positioned his giant frame under the mosquito net, Baugh said, "People have a right to say what they believe about the war and what they think of the president of the United States."

"Bill," I said, "a military man in an enemy prison does not have the right to say any such thing, especially not the right to tell his captors things they could use psychologically against Americans in the South and in North Vietnamese prisons."

"But suppose they believe it?" Baugh insisted. "Suppose they really believe it?"

I rushed to the foot of Baugh's mosquito net, dropped to one knee, clasped my hands and pleaded, "Bill, if you never learn anything else while you're here, remember this—you are in the Air Force. Regardless of what you personally think of the president, regardless whether you think the war is right or wrong, you do not have the right to tell that to these people. Your own words will be used against us and against our soldiers in South Vietnam."

Lorry punched the palm of his left hand and said, "Those bastards. They went home."

Meyer and Wilson said that they hated Lyndon Johnson. Wilson said, "First he said we would not have to come out here and now he's playing games. The lying son of a bitch."

"I think he's trying to do the best he can to end this thing. No president wants to prolong a war."

"Your fucking blind loyalty makes me sick," Wilson said.

"And you're beginning to be a real pain in the ass," I snapped back.

Both of us were moving closer to each other. Wilson snarled, "What makes you think you know so much? Well, you know that much!" He held up his right hand with the index finger and thumb about a quarter inch apart and shook it in my face.

I held my hand up in the same manner in front of Wilson. "If I know that much, it's that much more than you know."

The shutters on the small barred window at the end of the room flew open. A guard stuck his rifle through the bars, banged his fist on the sill and shouted, "Shleep! Shleep! Shleep quickly!"

Wilson and I went back to our pallets. The room was quiet. Sleep was a long time coming that night. That Sunday morning, the lights, which were usually on all the time, were out because of a power failure. And the guard was late. It was a perfect time to sleep. It would be cool for another two hours before the sun rose.

But Heiliger and McCuistion had different ideas. "How did you sleep, Mike?" Don asked. It was pitch-black in the cell.

"Oh," said Mike in his lazy manner of speaking, "I had a great sleep. I had a wet dream."

"Really? A wet dream? Tell me about it."

McCuistion went through a long, involved story about a girl who liked sleeping on a slanted bed.

When he finished, Don started patting his own stomach rapidly. Whether that was funny or not, it was enough to wake Red Wilson. As he stumbled over to one of the buckets, he was scratching himself, snorting and coughing. When he was finished he slammed the lid down on the bucket. He was the only person in the room who seemed not to give a damn if he woke everybody up when he went to the bathroom.

Ed and I resumed our planning for the Party. Originally we favored going over the wall at the east watchtower because there was an open field behind it. But, after studying that possibility more closely, we decided it would take too long to get up into the tower, dismantle the barbed wire over its windows, and climb down the wall on the other side. We assumed also that on rainy nights like the one we expected, the guards would seek shelter in the tower.

We decided it was best to go over the northwest wall located behind the guard shack. When it rained, the guards had a tendency to go to sleep earlier than usual. The location had good tree cover, and we expected to be able to take plenty of time climbing the wall. There was an outside privy built against that wall. From the top of the privy we would make our final assault on the wall. We also noticed that the armed guards did not frequent this area during their inspection tours of the compound. Again the group objected, insisting we should stick to the tower route. It was obvious they had not really studied the problem but were only seizing on another chance to thwart the whole escape attempt. The session ended with Wilson charging, "You'll never reach the wall." I tried ignoring him this time. Wilson was ready to explode.

That evening, after Ed and I finished another planning session, I was scrubbing my teeth when Wilson came at me again.

"You think you know everything. You won't listen to what any of the rest of us have to say."

I tried quietly to explain that I did listen. "You and the others are not giving the escape the attention it requires."

I could see the teeth of his lower jaw as Red forced his chin forward. "You thick-skulled nut," he hissed. "You don't listen to anybody. God speaks and we must listen. Why, with all that junk you're collecting, you'll sound like a gypsy caravan going across the yard. You won't make three yards."

I set aside the toothbrush. It would not do to have that stick of plastic protruding from my mouth with an angry Red Wilson so close.

"All I'm saying," I told Red, "is you have to spend the time and effort to look around and examine the plan. When you do, perhaps you will come to the same conclusion. But until you do look at this thing carefully, it's my life and I do not care to risk it on some stupid idea that you've just pulled out of your ass."

Wilson rushed at me with clenched fists. I braced myself, prepared to swing first if he lifted a shoulder. But Red stopped short, turned and stomped back across the room, grumbling and repeating, "You bastard, you bastard." Red was bothered by my refusal to submit to the will of the majority. He was trying to speak for them. Yet, as the room commander, he could not bring himself to order me not to plan and prepare. His concern was not really the escape, anyway, but whether he was acting properly as a kind of elected representative of the majority. He is not trying to lead, I thought, but is trying to be everybody's "nice guy."

Shortly after that, Lorry asked if I would object to his sending a message to the camp S.R.O., telling him of the feelings of the group. I said, "Go right ahead, it's your duty. The camp S.R.O. should be totally aware of the situation." Then I added, "And your message will go out with my monthly 'Party Committee' report."

When I told Ed what happened, he said, "Damn, John, you should not have allowed that."

"Why not?"

"You know it will cause more trouble for us. It's something else Trautman can get hold of to beat this thing down."

"You're probably right, Ed, but this escape will go because it is right, not because we cheated."

Not long afterwards, word arrived from Konrad Trautman,

camp S.R.O., that we should delay the escape so that we would not destroy the chance that some men might be released to go home for Christmas.

Ed looked at me and nodded, "I knew it would happen. I guess that is as good an excuse as any."

My personal feeling was that the only release should be the release of all of us at once as part of the peace negotiations. Any early release would do nothing to reveal what was really happening in North Vietnam; and what the North Vietnamese demanded of prisoners in order for them even to be considered for early release was totally unacceptable conduct according to the Military Code of Conduct.

On the first of December, Wilson ordered, "There will be no escape attempt until after the holidays." Ed and I rescheduled for May 1. We would wait for the warm weather and spring thundershowers. One unexpected benefit of the delay was our peanut party. Realizing that the peanuts wouldn't keep for four months, we decided to make a feast of them. We agreed that May 1969 would be our OTF—over the fence—month.

After the order, the group wanted immediately to dismantle all the gear we had taken months to gather. We had made camouflage nets from three stolen blankets. The "grass" clumps stuck in the blankets were made from rice straw collected from old brooms. The other rooms in the camp did not know why the "Party Committee" had requested the brooms; however, one week after the request we were showered with brooms. One after another came flying over the walls from one enclosed brick courtyard to another. Red demanded that the blankets be returned from the attic so that they could be used on cold nights. Ed and I strongly objected.

I told Red, "You're crazy if you think I'm going to help you destroy what we sweated blood to make." Red himself climbed into the attic and retrieved the three blankets. The group proposed rotating the blankets every three days.

"Nobody," Ed told Red, "is going to get any use out of them." Ed also pointed out that, if the blankets were detected during an inspection, they would be taken away. "No extras for anybody, and our camouflage nets for the following spring will be gone." As predicted, in the next inspection they were spotted and taken out of the cell.

The argument over the bucket was even more heated. Should the clean bucket be used as a latrine? Ed and I were speechless as we listened. It was needed in winter, they said, because the cold makes men go to the bathroom more often. To defecate and urinate in the bucket would deny Ed and me the one place in the room for hiding smuggled goods until they could be transported to the attic. And the ideal water container was ruined.

Ed and I lost on all counts. In the midst of our losing the bucket, Red snarled, "What is this, some kind of symbol? Do we need a symbol? Is it that damned important?"

"Yes," I shouted. "Yes, it is that damned important!" I hesitated, then said quietly, "It is a symbol. It represents the spirit you've lost."

All through the month of April 1969, Ed and I worked out the smallest details of our plan. The iron bars and the spike were for digging and protection, if necessary. We washed the food bags, which had stored the peanuts, and we gradually accumulated some sugar, planning to supplement that food with bananas that we received once in a while. We now had three extra pairs of sandals modeled after the shoes of the North Vietnamese peasant.

We acquired enough iodine to fill two small vials. We would use it to purify water along the escape route. To combat diarrhea, some prisoners were given little brown pills we thought contained iodine. After some experimenting, I found a mixture of ground "iodine" pills and red-brick dust which matched the average skin color of the North Vietnamese.

We had knives also. The blades were made from pieces of metal used by the peasants to fix their rubber sandals when a strap slipped out of place. It was not difficult to grind the metal on brick to make a point and sharp edge. Two pieces of bamboo bound together formed the handle. We had gathered bits of cloth and string and made white "surgical masks" to disguise our facial features. Two mosquito nets replaced the blankets for camouflage.

With thread pulled from our small towels and needles made of copper wire picked up in the yard, we had fixed our black prison clothes to look like peasant dress. But I had needed help. The only long-sleeved shirt I had was a prison red-and-grey striped one. I notified Room 5 of the problem. Bill Austin owned a long-sleeved black shirt. We hung our shirts over the brick wall which separated our two small yards. "Accidentally," he picked mine up, and I pulled his long-sleeved black shirt off the wall.

Out of strips of rice-straw pulled from our sleeping mats, Ed and I wove two conical hats. One hat was the only part of our booty ever discovered during an inspection. When the officer demanded to know why I made it, I explained that I used it to protect me from the rain when I was washing dishes outside. The officer made me throw it in the murky pond.

Ed had stolen a burlap bag, one of the peanut bags, and I managed to hide two baskets and a bamboo carrying-pole during the confusion of serving the evening meal. These props were the perfect things necessary to complete our disguises. The cook was always glad to be finished delivering the food and did not bother to hunt for his missing baskets and carrying pole.

To prepare ourselves physically, we exercised and ran a mile and a half each day. It was difficult running in little circles around the room, but we could feel our bodies becoming accustomed to the strenuous work. The respect of one man for another was the basis for the friendship that followed. We found pleasure in our talks of people, philosophy, and our travels.

To prepare mentally, we talked of three possibilities: success, recapture, or death. If recaptured, we agreed, our answer to the question, "Why did you escape?" would be that one man already had been beaten to get him to write an autobiography, the dreaded "Blue Book." Therefore, we knew we would be tortured again. We were going to tell the North Vietnamese that we were only trying to escape certain torture and the miserable conditions. You cannot torture people all the time, we agreed to tell the North Vietnamese, to get what you want. But from past experience I knew that the North Vietnamese would not accept the real reason men are willing to gamble with life—to be free. I suspected that our torture, if we were recaptured, would be more brutal if we admitted that one of the objectives of the plan was to destroy the public claim of the North Vietnamese at the Paris peace talks that American prisoners were being treated humanely. We knew from the propaganda broadcasts in the compound that the question of our treatment was being debated in Paris at the peace negotiations. The North Vietnamese were claiming, with help from some Americans back home, that we were being treated well. Our side was no doubt insisting on improvement in our treatment. We hoped that if people received word of our escape, they would wonder why, if the treatment was so good, we would risk death to escape. More important, we wanted our side to know we cared less about how good or bad the treatment was; we wanted the United States to get us the hell out of there.

Ed was born in Dallas, Texas, and had worked as a telephone lineman before joining the Air Force. His telephone experience was a key part of our escape plan. The concrete prison wall was fifteen to seventeen feet high. Five strands of barbed wire supported by metal poles were strung across the top. In addition, two bare, exposed electric wires were strung on insulated posts also along the top of the wall. Ed pointed out that if he could hang a hooked wire over the top electrical wire and allow it to fall against the bottom live wire, a short circuit would result, putting out half the lights in the prison. Because power failures were common during rain, it would probably go undetected.

To reduce as much as possible the chances of being detected, I asked Room 4 to break the light in their courtyard. When we heard the explosive sound of a bulb breaking, I knew we were a fraction closer to success.

The guards would probably never get around to fixing it.

We began the countdown on April 30, hoarding food and going over the checklist to insure nothing was forgotten. There was no rain on Saturday, May 3.

But on Saturday, May 10, just before sunset, the rain came.

I asked Red, "If Trautman says we can go, can we go?"

"Sure," answered Red, confident that the answer would be no.

Once more I was hoisted up and climbed into the attic. There were two holes in the brick wall which separated the attics of Rooms 5 and 6. I was able to attract the attention of the men in Room 5 by throwing pieces of plaster through the hole in the wall and into the ventilating hole in their ceiling, which was similar to ours. After the second throw a voice from Room 5 asked, "Is that you, Dramesi?"

"Rog," I answered. "Ask Trautman if Ed and I can go tonight. It's raining, the perfect night! Tell him we have everything we need and we're ready."

There was a long pause. I could hear a discussion taking place.

Finally a voice whispered, "Dramesi, this is Konnie Trautman. Do you think you can make it?"

"I would not be asking," I answered.

"Well, I can't say yes; but I can't deny you the chance," he said.

"Does that mean we can go?"

"That's up to you," Konnie replied.

"Thanks, we'll see you later."

I started to turn away but heard Trautman ask excitedly, "You going?"

I turned back, cupped my hands once more around the hole, moved close, and whispered, "We're going."

The beam of light coming up through the ventilating hole was enough to dimly light up the attic. I looked down into the room and said, "Let's go, Ed."

It looked as if the group were dazed as they mechanically went through the motions of lifting Ed up on the pallet. Not a word was spoken. Not a single departing handshake.

Suddenly Al Meyer reached up, shook Ed's hand, and said, "Well, if you have to go, God bless you."

"Thanks, Al." Ed looked at the others.

There were no words of encouragement, no "good lucks," and no more handshakes.

We talked as we carefully completed and checked off each item of our long list.

"What happened?" Ed asked.

"What do you mean?"

"Have they lost all their spirit? I at least expected something from Lengyel."

Ed, Lengyel, and Wilson had lived together before the rest of us moved into the Zoo Annex.

"I guess we're finding out you cannot expect everyone to master fear," I replied.

But Ed was not listening; he seemed to be groping within himself to answer his own question. Finally, he said, "You know, Wilson is the first man I ever met that I did not like anything about."

I finished smearing the brown paste onto Ed's face. "You look great," I said. "Oh, oh, wait a minute. That does it," I said as I dabbed more coloring on his right ear.

The last remarks on the checklist read, "Drink water, return jugs, replace grid." We took our time and drained our jugs.

I dropped the teapots through the hole, replaced the wire grid, and said, "All set."

Ed nodded.

"We're off with a cloud of dust and a hearty—"

Ed interrupted with, "San Francisco, here we come."

I removed four roof tiles and handed them to Ed; then I lifted myself through the hole onto the roof. Ed handed me the tiles, then followed. The roof looked undisturbed after I replaced the tiles. On our backs, flat against the roof, we inched to the peak of the roof where the lightning rod was located. A tile broke, clattered down the slanted roof and burst into a hundred pieces as it hit the cement floor of our wash area. There was some commotion by the wall between the Zoo and the Zoo Annex. A group of guards carrying bamboo poles and torches approached. Had they heard?

"Quick," I whispered to Ed, "cover yourself with the net and lie still."

The guards surrounded the pond below us and after a few moments departed with five large frogs dangling from their oversized belts.

We waited, according to plan, for the patrolling guard to pass, but he did not appear. The rain was doing its part well.

"We're wasting time," I said. "Let's go."

The heavy lightning rod was our way to the ground, but when I grabbed it, I withdrew instantly. The rod was electrified. "How are we going to get down?" asked Ed.

"I don't know yet."

"Should we go back?"

"Wait a minute," I answered. On my stomach and head first, I crawled down to the edge of the roof overlooking our small wash area. I removed an overhanging tile, then signaled Ed to join me. "What are you going to do with that?" he asked.

"Nothing," I said, "but the rope over the edge against the wood support is better than crumbling another tile. Here, take my rope, tie it to yours, and anchor it to the lightning-rod brace. We're going down." The rope proved to be an essential item as we had thought it would be.

As I moved from Station One, next to our building, toward

Station Two, Ed slipped off the roof. The cement walk that ran through the middle of the garden was the longest open stretch we had to cross. I crawled up to the path and stopped. This was our second station. I was lying on my right side in the mud beneath the camouflage net, my chin tucked between my knees. I raised my head slightly and was about to scurry across the path when I froze. A pair of boots was less than three feet away from my head.

I watched the guard in a raincoat and storm hat walk toward the guard shack at the gate. Although I could not see the guards, when I felt sure they were together inside I stood up and walked behind the guards' sleeping quarters. There, I waited at Station Three for Ed. Hidden by tall weeds, two walls, and the privy, I sat huddled in the corner and relaxed. Unexpectedly, Ed plopped beside me two minutes later.

"How did you make it so fast?" I asked.

"Simple, when you got up and walked across the path, I figured you knew it was safe so I just followed you."

I hugged Ed, and we laughed, a little hysterically perhaps, but we were beginning to relax.

"I didn't think we were going to make it off the roof," Ed said.

"One way or another we were going to make it," I said.

Ed whispered, "All that crap you took about wanting to look like a bush was worth it. Those camouflage nets saved us."

"Well, so far, so good; you ready?"

Ed nodded.

"We'll both climb to the top of the outhouse and work from there," I said. "The trees should cover us."

I climbed to the top of the wall. Following Ed's instructions, I gingerly placed the hooked wire over the two live wires. They sizzled. Far down the wall there was a loud crack, and sparks flew wildly. Instantly the north side of camp was in darkness.

Guards shouted from three corners of the camp. It was then I realized the rain had stopped and the clouds were parting. Through the trees I could see them gathering around the switch box on the outside wall of Room 4. As they jabbered, first one and then another would try his hand at moving the crude lever up and down. For the next fifteen minutes they will persist in cranking that thing. Good, I thought, we'll be long gone.

Halfway over the barbed wire, I realized a wire prong snared in the crotch of my pants prevented me from going any farther. I was using both hands to maintain my balance. I was stuck on top of the wall.

"Ed, Ed," I called. "Get me loose."

Ed pulled the wire from the cloth. I was free to climb to the other side of the wire. Ed passed our bundles of gear to me, and I dropped them to the pavement. Not until I was hanging from the wall did I realize I was still very high off the ground. Here is where my parachute-jump training is going to come in handy, I thought, and I let go.

"Let go, Ed, let go," I whispered. "I'll break your fall."

As soon as he hit the ground we scrambled into some bushes between two huts in a tightly bunched collection of homes. Suddenly we realized we had plunged ourselves into a garbage bin of decaying fish heads. But it was dark, no doubt a good place to rest and hide for a moment.

Working mostly by touch, we took what we needed out of the baskets and burlap bag. We again smeared the skin dye on our faces and hands, put on our sandals and the common white surgical masks which are worn by many in the Orient to restrict the spread of the flu. I donned the conical hat and Ed wore a black cloth hat. We attached the baskets to the bamboo carrying pole, and Ed hoisted the burlap bag over one shoulder. Once more we were ready to move.

Because the houses around us were packed so close together, we decided to change our route to get away from the wall. We walked down the road past the main gate of the Zoo Annex, then north to the main road into the city. Three white-uniformed policemen on bicycles passed within a yard. Others passed, not realizing there were two American pilots in their midst.

Only once did we think trouble was coming. A man who had just finished filling his water containers from a crooked pipe which protruded from the ground stood up suddenly before us. When I nodded, the village peasant returned my greeting. After walking a short distance, I looked back at Ed. No doubt he was smiling beneath his white mask also.

On the outskirts of the town called Cu Loc, a villager approached waving his hand and speaking in Vietnamese. "What are we going to do?" Ed whispered. "Nothing," I answered. "Ignore him and keep walking." We left a perplexed man in soiled jacket and baggy pants standing in the middle of the road holding the back of his neck. When I looked back he was hurrying off toward some large buildings.

"Do you think he knows?"

"It's possible." We started into a trot. The road ran north and parallel to a canal. I took my mask off, stuffed it in my shirt and said to Ed, "Just to play it safe, let's cross." When I reached the other side I waited for Ed and helped him up the steep embankment. We walked along the bank of the canal, heading north. Suddenly Ed hit my arm and said aloud, "Get down." A truck was moving slowly on the road. Men with flashlights were walking along the opposite bank. "Shh. Someone is coming up our side. This way!" We moved beside a building and heard the familiar grunts of hogs. I lifted a heavy shutter and we stepped through the low opening. When the shutter was closed, it was absolutely black inside. The pigs could not see us. We could not see them. They grunted occasionally. We said nothing.

When we thought it was safe to continue we bade farewell to our roommates.

After traveling a short distance, Ed said, "I think we should find a place to hide."

"You're probably right. Let's get away from the canal."

Outside a broken wall which once enclosed a small church, we found our hiding place. The church was surrounded by thickets of barbed brush. We crawled into the thicket and found a suitable place next to the wall.

While we rested, Ed said, "Even if we don't make it now, we've accomplished something. I never thought we'd get this far." We leaned against the wall, sitting side by side.

"We may have made a mistake, Ed."

It was still dark. How long before daylight? We had lost track of time. We had planned the escape to give ourselves the maximum lead time before the guards would discover we were gone. We had to make it at least outside the heavily patrolled security perimeter, which meant getting somewhere between five and seven miles away from the prison. After the sun came up I was satisfied that we had found a good hiding place, but I suspected that we had not traveled more than four or maybe four and a half miles.

It was a clear, beautiful day to be free. As the sun rose, groups of fifteen to seventeen men and women, all armed with rifles and Russian AK-47 machine guns, moved past us, searching the nearby fields. If only we were just a little farther out. We were so close to Hanoi that it was easy to organize these large search parties. It seemed like hours had drifted by, but I realized I had completely lost track of time.

Finally, one group invaded the churchyard. They tore down the barricades and searched inside the church. They were gathering to leave when one of them, perhaps as a reluctant afterthought, decided to crawl into our brambled thicket. The young soldier was no more than three feet away when he cocked his .45 automatic pistol and let out a yell. It sounded like a hundred guns were cocked on command.

"Well, that's it, Ed."

"What do we do?"

"Nothing. Just crawl out slowly."

The major in command of the unit was very proud while we stood there in our mud-covered black pajamas. Back inside the walls of the Zoo, before being separated, Ed shook my hand and said quietly, "We tried."

IX

The Jaws of Hell

Dedication is the knowledge of what is right and the willingness to expend all energies to prove it. Determination is a strong mind and a stout heart.

The guards hauled me off to what the POWs in the Zoo called the Ho Chi Minh room of the auditorium. I was dressed only in my black shorts and short-sleeved shirt. By pulling on my handcuffed wrists, I was stretched out face down on a small table. The flailing began with what we called the "fan belt." It was a strip of rubber cut from an old tire. The guards and prisoners used it as a rope to draw water out of the compound's filthy wells. Once, when a piece broke off, a guard had discovered it made a very effective whip.

In the Ho Chi Minh room, I began to whimper, then cry, then with each stroke scream. As the lashing continued, my screaming turned again into crying and, as the guards exhausted themselves, the crying to whimpering. I do not know how long it was before they stopped and dragged me to one of the Office rooms where three interrogators waited. They were North Vietnamese I had never seen.

They all spoke very good English. In the beginning they concentrated on asking mainly one thing: Why had I tried to escape? These new people hinted that higher authority wanted a personal report on what happened.

The game was about to start once more. To survive meant sticking to lessons already learned. The physical punishment had to be endured. But to keep it that last margin short of unendur-

able, I had to lie, delay, beg, try not to answer, confuse, even
outwit them, if possible. But to make it all convincing I knew
I must endure, I must endure, I must endure.

One of the interrogators approached me. He stuck his face
down close to mine, pointed a dirty finger at me, and shouted,
"From now on, from now on, you will be given one small piece
of bread and a cup of water twice a day! And no cigarettes! *And
no cigarettes!*"

"No, please," I begged. "You cannot take my cigarettes away."

"*And no cigarettes!*" he yelled.

I groaned and dropped my head. What he did not know, obviously, was that I did not smoke.

Although Ed and I agreed to answer questions about the escape, in the beginning I refused to answer any questions. In the
long run this was the best approach. Two guards grabbed my leg
irons, jerked me off the stool, and dragged my butt across the
rough red tile floor to face another interrogator. This was repeated a number of times. When one interrogator finished or hesitated in his questioning, two guards yanked on my leg irons and
raced to the opposite side of the room where another interrogator
waited. Soon I could feel the seat of my black shorts turning
damp with blood.

"You have done a bad thing," the new interrogator would say.
"You have done a very bad thing, but I am going to try to help
you now. All that is past is spilt milk," he said, "and we won't cry
over spilt milk." He smiled, proud of his clichés. "That's all water
under the bridge."

If I "confessed," my friend assured me, the beatings would end
and my tormentors would leave.

Of course, as soon as an unacceptable question was asked, the
beatings would start again. The number of interrogators dropped
from three to two. The camp commander also took a personal
interest in what was happening. The brutal punishment continued
without slacking.

I could always tell when the camp commander was going to
hit me. The guards would blindfold me first. His wallop was the
hardest. I received steady attention from the Goose and "Vocal
Cords," a methodic, professional torturer who seemed pleased
with his shabby job. The Goose was as emotional and excitable

as when I had first been subjected to his talents two years earlier.

A routine developed. The Goose and Cords, who was constantly and loudly demanding something, would pull my head back by the hair so that the other could steadily slap my face with the full leverage that comes from not having one hand tied up doing something else. Taking turns, they beat me about the face, then put me through the Ropes.

When my answers infuriated them, another beating followed. Each would start out slapping me with his right, then his left, hand. When they realized they could not hit me hard enough with their left hands, they concentrated on getting full power out of their right-hand roundhouse swings. As they concentrated more and became more tired, the hand slowly became a fist. It was not long before the left side of my face was swollen and bleeding. My left eye was closed. A cloth was available to wipe the blood from their right hands.

They had developed some new variations of the rope ordeal. Initially, they had simply tied the rope to the wrist cuffs, thrown it forward over my shoulder, and threaded it down underneath the leg-iron bar and back up over the shoulder again. Then either Goose or Cords would plant a foot or knee between my shoulder blades. Goose was the more vicious. With that leverage, he would then pull on the rope with all his strength, trying to lift my arms up over my head. My scream accompanied his grunt.

Later, to that excruciating ordeal, they added a new twist. They would remove the handcuffs, position my arms in a double hammerlock, and tie my forearms and wrists together. With another rope they pulled my elbows in as tight as possible. Again they threw the rope forward over the shoulder, then looped it under the irons and up again, as before. The jerk and then the steady pull increased tremendously the pressure on the tight double hammerlock. With a crafty smile, Cords attempted to assist the interrogators and please himself by anchoring the rope to my thumbs instead of to my wrists.

The method used during my first exposure to the ropes was part of Cord's repertoire of tortures. As before, he tightened the ropes until there was no circulation in my arms. He fastened a string around each thumb, and after twenty or thirty minutes he would prick my thumbs to see if I had any feeling or circulation. If I did not, he realized, he had to allow some circulation or my arms would rot. Having the ropes loosened was almost as painful as having them tight. The stabbing and tingling sensation ran through my arms, shoulders, and hands. That searing rush of blood returned life to my arms, but they remained unresponsive to my commands.

During those first five days, I was manacled the entire time by the leg irons and the handcuffs. At night, aided by a bright spotlight, the guards attempted to keep me awake, banging on the door, shouting, and coming in to slap my face if they thought I was asleep. I became conditioned to raise my head when they banged the door.

During the day, by plan or in uncontrollable agony, I cried, screamed, and begged them to stop. Experience and training had taught me not to attempt to meet them head on and not to antagonize them needlessly. For me to win, the enemy had to think their torture was beyond my threshold of resistance.

At the end of five days of torture in the Zoo, I was blindfolded and taken to the Hanoi Hilton. Even blindfolded, I knew that once before I had walked this path.

If I had been able to look up, I was positive I would see the black number 18 painted above the barred, wooden double doors. Room 18 was about twenty feet square with solid, dull-white plastered walls. The floor was the same rough red clay tile used in the Zoo. Down the center of Room 18 the floor had a row of jagged steel stumps, most likely the foundation for a wall that no longer existed.

Room 18 was both my cell and my interrogation room. As soon as I was seated on a small wooden stool, the guards worked as fast as possible to clamp the jumbo irons to my ankles. As I felt the relentless weight of that rusted metal begin to bore into my flesh, I knew I now faced the beginning of the worst.

Dao was my North Vietnamese name. "Pain" was the English translation. The North Vietnamese referred to the heavy irons as their "iron discipline." The terms were synonymous. The jumbo irons were an oversized version of the traveling irons. The traveling irons merely held walking to a shuffle. The jumbo irons were a ceaseless, unyielding pressure bearing down on both ankle bones and the tops of the arches. Through eyelets in the ankle cuffs was threaded an iron bar two inches in diameter and ten to twelve feet long. The traveling irons were only half that diameter, and the bar was only three feet long. Twenty-four hours a day for two and a half weeks I bore the oppressive weight of the jumbo irons.

When the irons were in place and the blindfold removed, not shock but despair gripped me.

Expressionless, the Bug examined me.

"Do you remember this place?" he asked.

"Yes."

"Do you remember me?" I hesitated, then said, "Yes, I remember you."

The Bug was considered by most POWs the meanest interrogator in prison. To me, he was a professional. His assignment, among other things, was to obtain acceptable answers.

Calmly, the Bug asked the first question, "Who ordered the escape?"

"I did."

He placed his hands on the table and raised himself from the chair. His face was assuming the features of the Bug I knew. Almost unnoticed, he nodded his head a number of times and departed. Apparently the first answer was unacceptable.

In the hours that followed, Ferdinand tightened the ropes and pulled, loosened them, and repeated his gruesome task. Two guards stood by, undaunted by the screaming and the ghastly scene of the brown perspiring body repeatedly attacking the pitiful helpless creature. The three departed while I was still crying, "What do you want? What do you want?"

I knew Ed was in the Hanoi Hilton in a room close to Room 18. No doubt the whole camp heard his cries. On the night of the eighteenth of May, I could hear them beating Ed. Suddenly the hush of death seemed to fall over the whole prison. I could not hear any noise anywhere. I held my breath, afraid I would miss a sound. I leaned toward the door, and I heard them patting Ed's face and talking to him in low voices as though they were trying to revive him. They knocked him out, I thought.

The routine was well established. Early every morning, about six o'clock, I would hear the jingle of Ferdinand's keys. Locks clicked, bolts clanged, and Ferdinand entered, still wearing his pith helmet with the meager camouflage of flowers.

I would be sitting the way Ferdinand had left me the day before, wearing the heavy irons, my hands tied behind me, and a rope around my neck tied to the rope which held my elbows together. Ferdinand would leave the doors wide open and walk around the room sprinkling disinfectant. That done, he would circle the room again, spraying perfume. Then he would reposition the two lamps to insure that the beams converged on my face. Finally, he would set a fan on the table and point it toward the interrogator's chair.

When the fan was turned on, the Bug entered. The ritual ended, my day began. After over two weeks, the throbbing pain of the heavy irons was my chief concern. The irons began to eat into the flesh of my ankles and arches. My infected feet were like balloons, and the toes on each foot looked like five little nodules. I felt that I could push a button in my mind and easily release the cord which bound me to the reality of the guard's jingling keys and unrelenting pain.

"Stand up!" the Bug ordered.

I began to whimper, "I cannot stand."

"Stand up," he demanded.

He asked, "Why you cry?"

I made the mistake of telling him, "My feet are burning."

"You will stand there until you write in the Book."

"I cannot stand. My feet are burning."

"You must stand there! I order you to stand there."

As the tension rose, Bug's right eye closed slowly. The dark-skinned Cyclops said, "Come here. Walk forward."

I began to cry. "I can't walk. My feet are burning. With these heavy irons, I cannot walk forward."

"Walk forward! Walk forward!" he screamed.

I cried, "I can't walk forward!"

Again he commanded, "Come here."

I took one shuffling step, then another. It was agony.

"Now you stand there—all day."

I was now about six to seven feet away from the table where he was sitting. "I can't stand here," I told him. "My feet are burning."

"Be silent! Be silent!" he snapped.

He began to arrange his papers. He used his books as paperweights. An inkwell and pen were placed on the "Blue Book" to prevent the fan from blowing the questionnaire to the floor.

I stared at the present cause of my torment, the "Blue Book".

The pain was so great that I decided to try a desperate trick. The thump, thump of my heart beating in my ears grew louder as I planned my next step. I had learned as a gymnast to arch my back and fall forward. This time I would have to fall with my face turned to the left to avoid the kicks in the face. Secondly, I had to insure as I fell forward that I did not strike my head on the Bug's table.

It was necessary to wait until neither the Bug nor the guard was watching. Otherwise they would know I had fallen on purpose and not collapsed. With the pain mounting, I could not wait long.

The Bug was soon busy staring carefully among his papers, playing the part of waiting until I submitted and picked up the pen.

I moaned and swayed, adjusting my stance so that when I fell forward I would miss the steel studs embedded in the tile floor. My body was not going to allow me to wait much longer.

I sniveled, "My feet, my feet, my poor feet."

The Bug lowered his head, intent on being unconcerned with my suffering plight. The guard, following Bug's example, nonchalantly turned to gaze into the courtyard garden. I arched my back, let out a loud sigh, leaned forward, and fell. My head barely missed the table. The momentum of my fall lifted the heavy irons high off the floor and the clanging crash of their return echoed throughout the entire compound.

The Bug sprang from his chair, rushed around the table and yelled, "Get up! Get up! You must get up!"

To be convincing, I had to remain there for a few minutes. The renewed pressure on my ankles would be agonizing. The few moments of relief would be paid for later. The Bug was screeching, "G-g-g-get up! g-g-get up!"

The guard leaned over and looked at my open mouth and unblinking blank stare. Bug jiggled my shoulder with his foot, now hysterically screaming, "Get up! You will be punished, you will be punished."

Saliva had begun to dribble out of my half-open mouth. While lying in a pool of my own sweat, I could feel the coolness of the tile floor. My feet no longer burned. I wanted to close my eyes and sleep—sleep. When I began to stir, the guard dragged me back to the stool.

The Bug returned to his side of the table, packed up his papers and left Room 18. Twice that day Ferdinand watched as I chewed one mouthful of bread and gulped my water. Finally, alone with the great hum of invisible mosquitoes, the heat and the pain, I thought.

Day after day, the sweltering heat; throbbing pain; my nemesis, the ravenous, ever-present pests. Escape, escape to the caverns of thought.

Soon after the gong sounded announcing the beginning of another day, I heard the inevitable jingle of Ferdinand's keys. Wearing a white cap and robe, a surgical mask over his face, a stethoscope draped around his neck and thick spectacles, "Ben Casey," one of the camp's doctors, entered the torture chamber. Behind him paraded his assistant, dressed the same way and carrying a metal tray loaded with surgical instruments, knives, probes, tweezers, needles, and scissors. He also carried an assortment of gauzes, bottles, and tapes. It looked like they were prepared for a heart operation.

While the guard removed the heavy jumbo irons, "Ben Casey" jabbed me with penicillin, I hoped. Then the doctor used his tweezers to pull the decaying flesh from the holes made by the gnawing metal. When he was finished placing the slivers of white, dead flesh on a small metal pan held by his assistant, the holes were clearly visible. Of the three holes on each foot, the deepest were on the outside of each ankle and the largest spotted the top of the arch of each foot. Then he packed the holes with sulphur and bandaged them.

When he finished, I stood up and pointed to my rear. I tried to explain to him that there was something wrong with my butt, but because my arms were always bound, I could not lower my black shorts. I knew my shorts were fused to my skin. The "doctor" started tugging, then ripped my shorts down. My sudden piercing cry startled "Ben Casey's" timid assistant. Finally they cleaned my bleeding buttocks and bandaged them. After the blood was hastily wiped from the tile floor, my shorts were returned to their proper place, tools were gathered, the marching formation was resumed, and "Ben Casey," followed by his medical assistant, departed.

Ferdinand removed the heavy irons from the room and returned with the light traveling irons. These irons were considerably smaller and were used primarily to hobble the prisoner. I was astonished with what was happening. Three and a half weeks after I had been recaptured and finally, after the jumbo irons were removed, my torment had not ended. Ridiculous as it may seem, Ferdinand was carefully fitting the lighter irons over the white bandages of my ankles.

The routine did not change. The interrogations and torture continued during the day, and in the evening the harassment began. At night, the cell door was locked, and before leaving, my keeper, always with his pith helmet, turned on the spotlights. The frosted windows in the double door were closed. Periodically, on their nightly tours, guards would quietly open the window a crack and peek inside the room. If I was asleep, slumped forward, straining against the rope looped around my neck, one guard in particular would bang on the door and window bars to wake me. If I refused to react, he would rant and rave all the way down the corridor to where the cell keys were kept. He would rush back to Room 18. It sounded as if he was about to crash through the doors without unlocking them. I nicknamed him Kid Crazy, K.C. for short. He was sick.

During the time I had the jumbo irons on my ankles, I would attempt to slide the ponderous twelve-foot bar through the anklets so that one end and most of its weight rested on the floor. Every time K.C. saw what I had done, he would come in and meticulously move it back so that all the weight was pressing evenly on my ankles. After adjusting the bar, he would squat down, look up at me, and wait for the mosquitoes to settle on my ballooned feet.

They swarmed quickly, and K.C. would watch as they bloated themselves on my blood until they were too heavy to fly. When K.C. was sure they were helpless, he would slap my calf, and they fell struggling to the floor. K.C. giggled. Then, while I watched, he would squash the insects one at a time. My blood squirted out from under his thumb. When he was finished with his game, he would stand and give me a stern look. Pointing at the bar and shaking his head he would say, "No, no," as if scolding a child.

Room 18 had other visitors during that first month. Almost every quiet night, a huge rat with a crooked tail came in through the drain hole. I simply sat on my stool and watched. The rat would move from one corner to the next. He usually ended up by the bowls in which my bread and water were served. He sniffed everything first. After finishing the bread I could not eat, he unceremoniously left me to my misery.

One night, I had another visitor, a black tarantula as big as my hand. It moved slowly across three walls of the room and finally across the floor to within inches of my hideous feet. I could not move and was afraid he was going to attack the feasting mosquitoes. Finally, not knowing why, he turned to make his new home under the interrogators' table. Since this black, hairy creature had spared me, perhaps he would bite the leg of the Bug.

One day, after Ferdinand had completed his ritual preparation of the room, the Bug walked in with a blue Chinese tape recorder and microphone. This was going to be another hellish day. From the very first day when I heard Colonel Risner's voice on tape and the voices of other POWs over radio Hanoi, I knew I had to do everything humanly possible to avoid that disgrace. I feared that tape recorder more than death. Although my body was dripping wet with perspiration as I stared at the tape recorder's case and its tangled wires, I no longer felt the heat or pain.

The Bug was not long in assuming his role. He ordered the guard to push the stool close to the table. A number of newspaper clippings and a typewritten sheet were thrust before me. He said, "Today we must record your voice." My heart skipped a beat, and then the blood began thumping in my ears. I said, pleading, "You know I will not be able to perform for you." His right eye began to close. "Do you want me to call my guards?" he screamed. "No, no," I cried. "Then talk," he said as he pointed to the microphone. "I cannot," I said, "I have never done anything like that, I do not know how." In an attempt to ease my fears, he leaned forward and said softly, "It is very easy." As his face came close to mine I recoiled slightly.

"You must be a good reporter," he said. "Listen!" He produced three small reels, placed one on the machine and pushed a button. An American voice commenced to explain why the "American imperialist aggressors" were not going to win the war. Then he replaced the first reel with another and said, "This is a very good reporter. You listen." The second American voice clearly and forcefully explained why and how the North Vietnamese were defeating the United States in the air war over the North. When the second small reel was finished, he said, "Now you must be a good reporter like your officers." It seems my answer was anticipated. Before I could pronounce the second "no," I felt the agonizing pain of the merciless ropes. The Bug was yelling, "Now you read." The Goose was tugging on the rope with all his strength, and I was screaming, "Yes, yes, I'll do it." My hands were untied. I picked up the papers and said, "I cannot see." The desk lamp was swiftly moved so that the papers were flooded with light. There were four articles. They were titled: "The U.S. Failure in Laos," "The Failure of the U.S. Marines in I Corps," "The Development of the North Vietnamese Dictionary," and the "World Congratulates President Ho Chi Minh on His Birthday." While watching closely, Bug said, "It is easy. You can be a good reporter." He handed me the first article and said, "Read first." I could very easily convince myself that recording the articles was harmless, but I realized that if I recorded these articles it would be the beginning of a total defeat. It would become easier and easier to give in to the demands of the North Vietnamese, demands that would disgrace my country, the other prisoners, and me.

In the hours that followed, I was given hot sugar water so that I could do better. I angered The Bug with my inept ways, and again, feeling the pressure of the ropes, I screamed, "I will do better. I'll do better." But long after the late-afternoon gong, when the Bug finally packed his equipment and departed, I had only finished the language article and was halfway through "Ho Chi Minh's Birthday." As he departed, the Bug said, "We will finish tomorrow." I was satisfied that the tape was worthless. I never saw the tape recorder again.

On the Friday of the last weekend prior to June 17, Smoke Stack, a chain-smoking interrogator, came into Torture Room 18. He set his paraphernalia on the table and made a cigarette. Ferdinand untied my hands as Stack took what obviously were pleasureable puffs on his well-made cigarette. He handed me eight typewritten pages. The title astonished me. It read "L.B.J. America's Greatest Disaster." Stack said, "Do you know about Nixon?" I replied, "I know very little about President Nixon." Stack said, "When you finish reading, write like that about Nixon." As he spoke, he tapped the papers I held in my hands with an extended finger. I looked up at him and said, "You insult me." He stared back and said, "Think carefully about your condition." He gathered his smoke-generating equipment and, before leaving, said, "I will come for the papers Monday. Think carefully."

I examined the eight sheets of paper closely. On those pages was an attempt to damn and disgrace former President Lyndon B. Johnson. But it was not LBJ who was disgraced, but the author, for he showed himself to be totally ignorant of the word "loyalty." In that situation, the author of those pages proved to me and no doubt to himself that he was an undisciplined coward unfit to be called an American soldier. Of these eight pages, I memorized word for word six passages.

That tragic event (referring to the assassination of John F. Kennedy) was but an ominous prelude to the tragedy and suffering which Johnson himself has brought to the entire nation.

Armed with the knowledge of the political gullibility of the people he shrank from nothing to gain and keep his seat in the Senate and to advance his career and personal fortunes.

A student of both psychology and semantics might readily find in Johnson's prattle about commitments a tacit admission of guilt, of knowledge that it was actually wrong for the United States to be involved in Asia, particularly South Vietnam.

He reckoned wrongly though for his aims ran counter to those of the people, the people of South Vietnam, of North Vietnam, of the U.S., and of the world.

In only 17 days after he took the oath of office to his own elected presidential term he again committed open aggression against North Vietnam by starting aerial bombardment which is still going on after over three years.

(In reference to LBJ's decision not to run in 1968). It means that the office of the President of the United States has the chance to regain the dignity, honor, and stature which Johnson's deceitful tricks and devious ways have tarnished and diminished.

I was going to tell Stack when he returned that I would attempt not to dishonor myself as he well realized my colleague had dishonored himself.

I changed my mind. I wrote: "I am not as intimate with the political and personal life of President Nixon as my fellow prisoner is with the life of Former President Lyndon B. Johnson. I can only say that as Mr. Nixon looks to the people of the United States for guidance, they in turn will come to understand his ways. It is my opinion that in time Mr. Nixon will not only be regarded as a great president of the United States but also as a great leader of mankind."

I was apprehensive when I riffled through the many blank sheets, but I waited, satisfied with my effort.

On Monday morning Ferdinand arrived to pick up the papers. As he shuffled through the pages and noticed that they all were blank except one, he grunted, giving me a puzzled look. I nodded and smiled. He departed with the papers.

On June 16, Stack walked in with an armful of folders and papers. He had the guard untie my hands. "I have seen your friends. You have not told the truth." "There are many differences here," he said as he patted the stack of papers. He counted out twenty sheets of blank paper and dropped them on the table in front of me. "I want you to write about all the things you lied about, everything you did not tell me, and I want you to tell me the conditions which allowed you to escape." I said, "I told you before, we waited for a rainy night." "No, no," he said, irritated with my stupidity. "Tell me of the conditions in the camp." "Oh," I said. "Now write," Stack ordered. I said, "But I've told you everything." His stern face came closer and he said, "You foolish man. Baugh and Trautman will not save you." Stack turned and spoke to Goose. Obediently, Goose came forward and forced me to my knees. Hour after hour I sobbed and pleaded to be allowed up. Stack simply said softly, "Stop crying," or "Hands up, higher, higher." Stack continued his threats, and Goose enjoyed kicking and slapping me when I sat back on my heels or lowered my arms. The perspiration was dripping from the tip of my nose and elbows into a pool. I knew I should not continue this self-induced punishment, but there had to be a right time to refuse to kneel. The tension in the room increased.

Stack said, "Tell me how the other rooms helped you."

I replied, "No one helped. Ed and I were the only two who escaped."

"No, no. Here is the truth," Stack said, pointing to the pile of papers. They were two neatly bound bundles, three or four inches thick. "Hmm," he said. He paused momentarily, then said, "I will allow you to read them. For all the differences you will be punished. Do you want to read?"

"No, no, I told you everything."

"No," Stack said, shaking his head slowly, "You have made forty, fifty, sixty mistakes." He completed the sentence with a growl as he slapped the stack of papers. "I will punish you four times for every mistake you have made."

I said, "I know there are no differences. I know it's the same."

"Will you read?" he asked curiously.

"I know there are no differences," I replied. "Yes, I will read the papers."

Perhaps Stack knew I was going to refuse to kneel or collapse soon. Disregarding what I said, he replied, "You know what you must write." He moved toward the table and carefully arranged the papers, pen, and ink bottle. Then he said, "Write about the help the other rooms gave to you and the conditions that allowed you to escape." He quickly added, "Use all twenty pages, and if you need more, tell the guard." "Yes, yes," I uttered, sobbing.

I leaned forward slowly and placed my hands on the tile floor. I stood there momentarily on all fours with my chin against my chest. Suddenly, involuntarily, a hideous scream leaped from my throat. As the pressure was relieved from my knees it seemed as if two daggers were thrust into my knee caps.

I was left alone to write. Late that night Ferdinand picked up the twenty pages. In twenty pages I explained that the lighting and wiring were poor, the guards made too much noise, and the camp needed more guards. That night, with my hands and arms tied and the irons still curled around my ankles, I was allowed to sleep while sitting on the stool.

X

Isolation

Time. Time is paramount and man's worst enemy.
Time is the sky during the day, the darkness at night,
the step of a man, the thoughts in his mind.

With each passing day, with each forward stride,
with each burning idea, time and man race forward
to arrive only at the beginning. Thus, time is mea-
sured in terms of the future, the goal is man's to
create, his destiny is his to mold, man's fate is his
faith.

Time is the ultimate judge.

Time is paramount and man's worst enemy.

On June 17 I was alone in Room 18. Though the harassment continued, the daily interrogations and tortures had stopped. After
thirty-eight days of torture, I attempted to determine what I had
accomplished. I had been in heavy irons for more than three and a
half weeks. During the entire thirty-eight days my hands and
arms had been tied behind me. I had experienced the twisting ropes
more than fifteen times. I had been beaten continually with fists and
a fan belt. For thirty-eight days my only food had been two small
pieces of bread and two cups of water each day. There was no
mosquito net available. During that period my little stool was my
living room, my bedroom, and my bathroom.

The odor and discomfort of living in my own filth no longer
bothered me. I was exhausted and as close to death as I had ever
been. My weight must have been between 100 and 110 pounds.

I had told them about the escape and how it had been accomplished without revealing the involvement of others. I had not told

how the others had helped with the brooms, putting out the lights, the communications, and the attempts to acquire materials and the machete. I laid the blame for the escape on the North Vietnamese themselves, because of the torture and their callousness, for our miserable existence. Although I denied having communicated with others, I was told by what means we had communicated with the Zoo and within the Zoo Annex. I referred to the escape organization within my room only.

After seven days of torture, I had refused to write a letter to the camp commander, but a letter was written for me. After another two days of torture I signed it. In the prepared letter, I evidenced remorse for my actions and admitted what a tremendous job Stack had done in averting a great escape. It was obvious who had written the letter. I refused to write a statement praising the "lenient and humane treatment" of the American prisoners. Instead, when I finally said that I would write, I wrote, "As civilized men grow to better understand the peoples of this world, the tortures of medieval Europe, old black Africa, and the uncivilized wastelands of ancient Arabia can be found only in North Vietnam."

I did not make a single tape recording. I was badgered to sign an amnesty statement which was apparently written by an American. I refused to sign the request for amnesty. I was tortured to denounce the war and to denounce the president of the United States. I did neither. I was tortured to write a statement to the prisoners. I refused. And, finally, I was tortured to fill out the Blue Book, a complete autobiography revealing military information as well as pertinent things concerning myself and my family. After the completion of my torture, I was unable to write in the Blue Book.

In the end, having considered what had happened and the tortures I had endured, and having come closer to death than ever before, I felt that I had won. But the victory was not completely mine. In one respect it was ours—Ed Atterberry's and mine—because in our discussions and in our mental and physical preparation we had decided what we were going to do. Although I did not know what fate had befallen Ed, I felt at this point that, in view of what we had vowed to do, he had won also. I had attempted to perform not only for myself but for Ed Atterberry, for all the prisoners and for all those who would call themselves American fighting men. The people in the United States had won also, because there was no doubt in my mind that now there was greater respect for Americans in the eyes of the North Vietnamese.

On June 17, Ferdinand came into the room. But this time he did not open the doors wide, flick perfume and disinfectant about the room, and start the fan. He untied my hands and my arms and threw the ropes into a corner. Then, taking the stool, the fan, and the lamps, he left the room. For the rest of that day I lay on the cool tiles, completely exhausted and unable to move. Not a single guard bothered me that day or that night. For the next two nights, Ferdinand came into the room and put up my mosquito net. He tied it to four chairs placed in the middle of the floor. I was permitted to lie under the mosquito net and sleep with the light irons still fastened to my ankles. Each night he looked into the room. If he saw that I did not have my net up, he would come in and put it up. It took all the strength I possessed to crawl under and go to sleep. The next day came too soon, yet passed not soon enough. I was now being fed a small bowl of soup and half a loaf of bread. Ferdinand finally provided me with a small cup and a jug of water.

On the twentieth of June, Ferdinand unlocked the "traveling irons" from my ankles and motioned that I should follow. He indicated that I should pick up the bucket in the corner and carry it with me. Next he led me out into the courtyard and toward Heartbreak Hotel. Walking was a tedious task. At first I stood outside the door, and he waited for a moment before he allowed me inside Heartbreak. Apparently there was some confusion as to who was going to use the shower in Room 8. Ferdinand motioned for me to sit in front of the door of Room 1 of Heartbreak Hotel.

The outer door connecting Heartbreak with the corridor which joined the courtyard to the Vietnamese camp in the rear of the Hanoi Hilton was wide open. The door blocked me from the view of anyone passing through the archways. As I leaned against the door of Cell 1 of Heartbreak Hotel, hidden from Ferdinand's view, I realized that perhaps this was the opportunity to notify someone that I was alive after the escape. I put my hand underneath the door of Cell 1 and began to tap out my name, saying that Ed and I had escaped on May 10 and that J. D. (John Dramesi) was alive. When I stopped, waiting for some kind of a signal, there was none.

I tapped it out again then suddenly stopped, for I could feel some fingers very gently stroking the palm of my hand. It was indeed a weird feeling, and I just sat there motionless. In that cell was some-one who knew nothing of how to communicate or what to do. But he was fascinated with my white hand. My impulse was to withdraw my hand, but I kept it there underneath the door, attempting to visualize the poor soul who was kneeling on the other side of the door lightly stroking my palm.

As Ferdinand approached, I had to withdraw my hand quickly. Suddenly there was a whine and the person on the other side of the door stumbled as he tried to withdraw as fast as possible from where the hand had been. No doubt he was curled up in the far corner, frightened and staring at the peephole.

Inside the shower room Ferdinand clipped off my beard and most of my hair. When he was finished, he indicated I was allowed five minutes for a shower. In that time I could hardly take an adequate shower, so I just stood there enjoying the water running over me. I did not wash but stayed there, feeling the pleasure of the cool refreshing water. When Ferdinand returned, he was angry that I was not dry. I put my black drawers on and struggled back to Room 18. The traveling irons were again locked in place over my bandages.

I asked myself who was the person in Room 1 of Heartbreak. Whoever he was, he wasn't going to make it.

In the next week the routine for the months to follow was established. I was fed twice a day, each time being given a bowl of soup and a loaf of bread. The irons were kept on continuously, twenty-four hours a day; I slept in them. Some of my old clothes and straw mat were returned to me. I had an old, small, white towel, which was no longer white but brown with filth. Also, Ferdinand required that I put on my long pants and my long-sleeved shirt. This was to be a part of my harassment in the sweltering heat of the summer in North Vietnam. I was required to sleep at night with all my clothes. Also, I was not allowed to sleep during the nap hour, and the guards would come by, waking me each time they found me asleep. I had to wait until the guard indicated that I should put my net up and go to sleep at night. This usually happened sometime after eleven o'clock. Once a week Ferdinand would come in, unlock the irons, slide the small bar through the eyelets of the anklets, take them off, and allow me to march with him to Heartbreak Hotel, where I would empty my bucket, wash my clothes, and take my weekly shower.

All I wanted to do during those weeks which followed the torture in Room 18 was to sleep and eat as much as I could. Although the guards continually harassed me, I would sleep when I could and take my clothes off when I was able. The guards would scream and threaten me, so I would put on my clothes, but as soon as they left, off they would come again. When the guards were no longer in sight, I would sleep.

For two weeks I ate and slept, ate and slept, but I realized there was one thing that I must do. That was to attempt to contact Ed Atterberry to find out how he had fared, where he was, and what he was doing. Were they now harassing him as well? Before we attempted the escape we had devised two written codes, agreed to use the tapping code when possible, and developed a method of identifying each other. We each had a song that was to be our identification code. Ed's was "Maria," and my song was "Put Your Dreams Away for Another Day." If one of us heard the other's song, he would realize the other was in the vicinity. During the evenings and during the quiet hours when no one was around I would begin to whistle, first low and then louder and louder. If the guard did not show up, soon I whistled as loudly as I could. I was whistling "Maria" and "Put Your Dreams Away for Another Day," but there was never any response. It seemed Ed was nowhere in the area or did not hear my whistling, but at least it made time pass faster. Sometimes I began to whistle and for hours never repeated the same song. I was amazed at how many songs I could recall.

At first, when I could tell the guard was approaching, I would stop immediately. Later I continued to whistle when the guard approached. Although I was able to see his shadow under the door, he would not open the window. Knowing that he was there, I continued to whistle, and he would stay there listening for a while, then finally leave. It seemed the guards were entertained also.

There were a number of different guards who came by during that period. Ferdinand was my steady keeper, with K. C. (Kid Crazy) coming occasionally to take his place. When that happened,

I had to shuffle out into the hall to pick up my food. This was K. C.'s way of harassing me. When he was on duty at night, he would come by and tell me to sit in the middle of the room, and I would. As soon as he left, I would move back to leaning against the wall sitting on my dirty blanket and clothes. He would come by again and bellow, indicating that I was to sit in the middle of the room. I would return to the middle. When he left, I would return to my usual position. This was the game that K. C. and I played. But eventually, K. C., although always very angry, knowing that he could not come in and beat me, finally gave up.

There were a number of guards, and I had names for all of them, depending on their actions. Two of the guards would very quietly open the window a crack and peek in, never opening the window wide and always preferring to look into the room without my knowing it. One I named the Shadow and the other Lamont Cranston. I called Lamont Cranston, Lamont for short. He was the quietest one, very small and meek, hardly ever allowing me to see his face.

Another pair was Big Stupe and the Piss Ant. Big Stupe was a stupid, very large North Vietnamese. He would come into the room and insist that I bow. The tiny Piss Ant, Big Stupe's counterpart in size, would do the same. He would throw the doors or windows open, as did Big Stupe, look in and start screaming, "Aw! Aw!" That meant I was expected to come to attention and bow. I never paid any attention to either of them, and finally Big Stupe gave up. But the Piss Ant would persist, and although I would not bow, he would continue to rant and rave and threaten me because I was not bowing. One day he was overzealous. He threatened, banged, and stuck his bayonet through the bars of the window, yelling, "Bow! Bow!" It sounded as if he were going to wake the entire compound. Finally I did get up from my sitting position and gave him a nod of the head. He glared at me while I sat down. He yelled, "No! No! Bow tree times, bow tree times!" as he held up three fingers, and sticking his arm through the bars of the windows.

I was thoroughly disgusted by this and waved my hands as if to say, "Go away," and sat down. He banged the bars and slammed the window shut and walked away. I was not sure whether he was going to get the officer or the keys until I shuffled to the window to see where he was going and what he was going to do. As I looked out, I saw him as he sauntered past someone else in the courtyard. He just smiled and continued to walk. He had a rifle that was larger than he was, and the extended bayonet made the sight even more humorous. He had it over his shoulder as he swaggered down the courtyard. The rifle swung in an arc behind him, about five feet from one side to the other, as he took his steps—left, right, left, right—through the courtyard. Anyone approaching him within five feet would have his throat cut from the bayonet arching through the air.

The Piss Ant was no menace. He was a person who could hurt you only if you allowed him to do so. I never bowed to him, nor did I ever have any intention of bowing to anyone again unless forced to do so.

However, there were more important things than the Piss Ant. Occasionally I would see the big spider appear. One night, while I was intently listening to the music being played over the loud-speaker in the courtyard, I realized suddenly that to my left was a big black spot. It was the spider. I turned slightly and looked at him. It seemed he was prepared to spring, because his legs were flexed. I was no more than twelve inches away, looking at him from the corner of my left eye. I moved very slowly, getting in position so that I could strike him with the towel I held in my hand. I could see that the spider was slowly moving also, perhaps to get into a better position. Suddenly I struck. Simultaneously the black creature sprang, but my blow carried him back to the wall. Although crippled, as soon as he hit the floor he struggled to reach the sanctuary of the table. I twisted my towel and struck again. The spider went sliding to the middle of the floor, completely finished. In a very short time the ants were upon him. Within twenty-four hours there was not a single piece left.

Across the hall from the torture room there was a small office with a typist. She was a small girl with a pretty face. Most of the day she typed, sometimes even during the most severe tortures. To her it was apparently a way of life, and her only concern was that it was not happening to her. She may have felt fortunate that she was where she was, doing what she was doing and being who she was.

In the months that I observed her, I determined she owned

two pairs of slacks, six different printed blouses, and one pair of sandals. She never wore a dress or a skirt. As I watched her month after month, she grew bigger and bigger. By the time I was ready to leave in December, there was no doubt she was a pregnant woman.

I wondered what her life was like, for I witnessed some of it. Twice a month someone would come in with a small package. They would hand her one of these packages, which she would open and examine. There would be anywhere from four to six pieces of meat, very thinly sliced, looking like veal cutlets. This apparently was her ration for the month. Finally I recognized that when she received her portion, others were carrying identical paper bundles. In these small bundles was a ration of meat for the month. Seeing what was going on around her, she probably thought she was a most fortunate woman to have two black silk pajama pants, six blouses, one pair of shoes, and the opportunity to eat meat twice a month.

One evening the window of my cell flew open and three girls stood there looking at me. One was tall and slim faced, with deep, dark eyes. She was unsmiling. The one in the middle reminded me of Pia, a pretty waitress who worked in the Officers' Club at Korat, Thailand. She smiled. Next to Pia, on her left, was a small girl I called Little Moonface. All had long black hair. They stood there, the tallest on my left, smallest on the right, not saying a word, just staring at me. I smiled at them slightly, and as I did, they all turned and left, not forgetting to close the window.

Apparently it was Pia who expressed a liking for me. The next day there was a commotion and suddenly the window flew open. A number of girls and boys struggled with Pia to prop her up so that she could see me. She struggled, attempting to move away, but they persisted, and everyone laughed as they tried to get Pia to look in at her prisoner. They were all laughing and finally left.

But that was not the last time I saw Pia. At the beginning of the quiet hour someone would walk by my door and invariably bang twice very hard while passing by. Finally, after three or four days, I decided to be ready to jump up to see who was banging on my door. Sure enough, the knocks came and I was ready. There was Pia, walking into the courtyard after having knocked on my door. She went to where the bicycles were kept and rummaged among them, attempting to get hers untangled from the rest.

In the first week of July, Ferdinand came in one night and took all but one of the chairs from the room. There was quite a bit of commotion in the courtyard. From the sounds it was evident that a movie was being shown. I picked up my bar, shuffled sideways, opened the window very slowly, and looked out. Standing there right on the corner of the archway was Pia. She just stood there, looking at me for a moment. Everyone else was busy watching the movie. A stream of light coming from my room pierced the blackness of the courtyard. After a few moments she turned and left.

I closed the window, went over to the light switch, and turned off the light in Room 18. I shuffled back to the window and again opened it wide. I positioned myself so that I was sitting on a chair looking into the courtyard. I could see the screen and watch the movie. As I sat there, I wondered about Pia and whether she would be there next month when a movie would be shown again.

After a number of short films, showing how the North Vietnamese were winning the war in the South, the air war in the North, and the many great things within their own society, the feature movie began. As the credits were flashing on the screen there were many screams, and from far away, at the foot of a small hill, a boy was crying. It was apparent that the South Vietnamese, led by the Americans, had invaded a village in South Vietnam and the boy was looking for his mother.

Huts were burning. Women were screaming. At the top of a small knoll was an American officer. He wore camouflaged fatigues with a large hat and a large .45 automatic pistol strapped to his side.

The boy came closer and closer, screaming and wandering through the village. He approached the sneering American officer standing by his jeep on the top of the small knoll. The little boy threw himself to his knees, clasped his hands, and pleaded with the giant American towering above him. The passionless American drew the large .45 and fired four or five times point blank into the quivering body. That was the opening of the movie. There were more atrocities and many scenes to show how cruel the Americans were. Ultimately the North Vietnamese won.

As might be expected, near the end of the movie an old man

whose dog had been shot by the Americans managed to get his hands on the oversize .45. The last scene showed the old man, looking very much like Old Ho Chi Minh, shooting the sniveling American who had shot the Vietnamese boy earlier.

In the middle of June, before I was able to determine who was there, the windows flew open and in through the bars came a handful of litchi nuts. There were six of them. The litchi nut has a brown coarse cover and is about the size of a very large cherry. Beneath the coarse cover is a thin layer of sweet meat. If one chews this off, beneath it is a small seed about the size of a hazelnut. I took the covers off and ate all that was available. Remaining were six round seeds. I was able to shine them so that they looked very pretty. With a small nail I managed to drill a hole in each seed. From some string that I removed from my mat I braided a very small piece of twine. Next I threaded the twine through the seeds. I ruined one nut, but now I had a necklace of five very shiny litchi seeds.

I waited. As I expected, in the first week of August, Ferdinand came in one night and removed all the chairs in the room and once more the noises indicated that everyone was about to enjoy their monthly movie. In the Hanoi Hilton, all the guards, keepers, and those who lived in and about the buildings attended the movies.

Again I shuffled to the window, put the light out first, and cracked the window. Pia was there. When I opened the window, she turned and we looked at one another for a short moment. I motioned for her to come close to the bars and she did. As she came close, I lifted the necklace that I wore so that she could see it. Then I held the string wide with both hands outside the bars and coaxed her to come closer. She came closer, bowed her head slightly, and I put it around her neck. Then, without releasing the string, I moved very close to her face and through the bars our lips touched. There was a slight smile as she turned slowly and left, fingering one of the polished seeds with her left hand.

The scene was not repeated in September. There was no movie for the people that week. Although everyone continued to work around the compound, I could feel the effect of a change. Something had happened to the North Vietnamese. I had suspected Ho Chi Minh had died because suddenly and somberly everyone was wearing a black armband. I was positive when, shortly after the armbands appeared, they had a procession and jet aircraft flew in waves overhead. Following that, I listened to music and the typist across the hall crying. She could not control her whimper and tears as she stared out of her window in the direction from which the music was coming. Ho Chi Minh was dead.

Suddenly cannons boomed. Before the twenty-one-gun salute was over I opened my window and, in full view stood erect and saluted. When I had counted twenty-one, the booming stopped. An officer who was walking by jumped back out of sight when he saw me standing there at attention and saluting. He did not come again until the twenty-one-gun ceremony was over and the window was closed. He came over to the cell, pushed the window open, looked at me, said nothing, closed the window, and walked away. I thought that as a soldier I should render my salute and that, as a soldier, I should try to defeat my enemy.

The heat was less intense at the end of September, and I was surprised at how much I had improved. I was beginning to put on some weight in spite of my diet of bread and squash or pumpkin soup. Although I did start a light exercise program, there was still plenty of time to think. In one way, time was on my side. One day, sooner or later, I would be released. While my health improved, I knew that one day I would be able to help myself.

Tutter

From thoughts to dreams, reality to fantasy, voluntary to involuntary, conscious to subconscious, need or escape mechanism—sleep, sleep.

On the banks of a river which flowed into a great sea to the north, there existed a pulsating center of activity. More so on a particular day, for from the arteries which connected it to the rest of the world came streaming additional multitudes.

The marketplace swelled liked a giant amoeba, engulfing a large section of the city. Two men neared each other as they examined the wares of the vendors. It was noted that both commanded a great deal of respect, for although the market was extremely crowded, no one dared venture closer than twice the arm's length of a man. It was inevitable these two would clash.

Khan, who seemed to be as wide as he was tall, with powerful muscular arms, stepped on the tip of Mecca's flowing white toga. Mecca was a big man with a huge middle which made up the greatest portion of his massive body. Without words, long scimitars were drawn, and the hisses and grunts of a fierce battle followed. No one could determine which would prevail, the mongoose-like tactics of Khan or the heavy blows of the massive Mecca. Again without words they stopped, prepared to face a mutual threat.

A circle of one hundred inward-pointing spears was formed, and on command, step by step, the circle of death drew smaller and smaller, closer and closer. As they stood motionless, a Captain of Tutter's Peacack Guards approached and said, "To you the words of Tutter. The coming events of the day will demand all of your courage, skill, and strength, so enough, you will again meet one another." Both understood and parted to prepare themselves.

The sun was halfway down its slide, and the great glistening white stoned arena was already filled to capacity. The people waiting, munching on their favorites, roasted locus and crisp fried slices of squid. Then from the uppermost parapets surrounding the entire arena, one thousand trumpets announced, "Look to the arch! Tutter is arriving." The munching stopped and the twisting and turning began as all attempted to gain a better view.

Through the arch came Tutter and the colorful Peacock Guards. Her eyes were like precious crystal. Her crown was formed by silken strands of gold curled high on her head. She had almond skin as smooth as satin, scented lips, pink and delicate as rose petals, more intoxicating than a hot spiced wine, proud breasts yearning for attention and a lethal flair accentuated by a wide band of gold around a waist you could clutch with both hands. Some called her "Heaven." Others, not being familiar with the term, assumed "Heaven" was all a man could desire. As she took the last step to her place, long strips of white cloth parted, revealing thighs no man could resist. With an eloquent wave of an exquisite arm, she acknowledged her greeting.

Suddenly, for miles around, the animals stood still. The leaves stopped fluttering momentarily, stunned by the hysterical roar of that mysterious two-legged creature called man. The most spectacular event in the history of all mankind was about to begin.

Again, the one thousand trumpets blared and a greater number of multicolored birds darted into the air trying to top the high walls of the oval enclosures.

This was the signal. The contestants started their parade. All had fine teams and elaborately decorated chariots. Of the races I could go on for hours telling of the fantastic array of color, the victories, defeats, and misfortunes. But most important of all, who won the final race of champions?

On the last lap Khan attempted to turn abruptly inside of Mecca's massive four-horse chariot. With an ear-splitting snap the tongue of Khan's chariot broke, catapulting him into the air. It seemed as if an invisible hand picked him up and hurled him against the stone wall. The limp form fell to the track, and in

quick succession the pack of spinning wheels and thundering
hoofs delivered their crushing blows. The screams turned to
cheers. Mecca passed the finish line, and already the trampled
mass on the now scarlet stained sand was forgotten. The festivities
followed. For the next week Mecca was conspicuously absent. It
was said that after his glorious victory, no doubt, Mecca was in
"Heaven."

When did this spectacle take place? It happened on September 17, 1969, for on that day I learned to daydream.

XII

The Hawk
and the Lock

*It may very well be that you are regarded as you re-
gard yourself, but remember you may be viewed in
the same light you see others; thus seek not the
respect of others but of yourself and the former will
surely follow.*

So strong was my effort to concentrate, it seemed that I could
remove myself from reality. The arrival of Kid Crazy, K. C., as my
keeper, returned me to reality. He was taking the place of my
regular keepers—Ferdinand, Tonto, and The Hawk. The Hawk
was the sharpest, watching very closely everything that I did.

The Hawk arrived at 6 P.M. every day with an officer I called
Frankenstein. Frankenstein was taller than Hawk, and his pitted
face reminded me of the movie character. Religiously, they made
certain that I was in the irons at the finish of each work day.

Tonto was a businesslike, very quiet individual. He was thin,
long faced, and dark complexioned. Most of the time Tonto and
Ferdinand shared the chores of caring for me, but now I had to
contend with K. C. He was not as smart as the Hawk, but I'm sure
he thought he was. In the past, he was the only one who insisted
that I lock myself in the irons after my weekly trip to Heartbreak
to shower, shave, and wash my clothes. After the bar was threaded
through the eyelets of the anklets, a lock was placed through a
hole so that the bar could not be pulled through again. Kid Crazy
was the only one who would kick the lock toward me and then

face away, listening for the click, the signal which assured him that the lock was in place. Smiling and quite satisfied with himself, he would strut off. I had anticipated that K. C. would arrive again and, in his arrogant manner, insist that I lock the bar myself. However, this time I was ready for him.

Following a trip to the shower room, he kicked the irons over to me. Once more I put them on my ankles. Again he sent the lock sliding across the floor to where I sat. As he stood by the door, I put the lock in place. I knew he was listening for that familiar click. I also knew that if he heard the lock snap closed he would not look back. This was his way of saying to himself, I am the master. Knowing this would happen, I had been practicing tapping the Chinese-made lock against the iron trying to duplicate the sound he expected. There was a "click click." K. C. broke his arrogant pose, locked the door, and walked off leaving me with a wide grin on my face. I put the lock in a position that looked like it was secure and waited. Sure enough, when the radio in the courtyard made its common beeping sound, Frankenstein and the Hawk opened the window to complete their six o'clock inspection. I was in my usual position, sitting leaning against the wall. The irons looked secure. They looked around the room, closed the window, and departed. That night, I realized I would be able to sleep without the irons on my legs. On time at eleven o'clock, the guard came by to permit me to go to sleep. I crawled under my net and removed the irons from my aching legs. With my arms clasped behind my head, I stretched out on my rotting rice mat.

The pleasure was in being able to cross my legs. In every possible way, I crossed, uncrossed, and again crossed my legs. It seemed it was something I had been unable to do all my life. And now, all of a sudden, I was able to cross my legs.

I slept well that night. The next morning, I put the irons back on but without fastening the lock. No one would examine the lock for the next week. Somehow I should be able to fix the lock so they could not tell it was not fastened. With lead from a toothpaste tube, I shaped two inserts to be placed in the teeth of the padlock latch. If the idea worked I should be able to close the lock, yet because it was not seated properly, I should be able to pull it out at any time. Fixing it took a day and a half.

When the guards were not around, I kept pushing the latch further and further into the lock, testing it. Finally, I pushed it all the way, and felt a dull thud as the ratchet inside thumped against the lead I had molded inside the notches of the latch. Thinking that something could go wrong, I tested my idea with the lock in place on the iron bar. It happened. I yanked. It wouldn't budge. For the rest of the week, I tugged on it hour after hour until I was sweating and exhausted.

Shower day arrived. Tonto came in and in his businesslike manner, he moved right to work. He inserted the key in the lock and turned it. I knew it was unlocked but he could not pull the latch open. It seemed that the lead inserts had either expanded or moved out of line slightly restricting the movement of the latch. Tonto thought there was somehing wrong with the key. He became confused and decided he needed help. A short time later he returned with Frankenstein and Ferdinand. The three of them looked, tugged, and tried everything possible but they could not get it open. I was wondering what they were going to do to me once they found it was my doing. I sat looking as confused as they were. Finally, they decided they needed more brain power. They went out and returned with the Hawk, the brain. Hawk's first act was to give me a suspicious glance. One held the bar, one pulled the lock, and one worked the key while the Hawk squatted there thinking. He could not figure out how, but he knew I probably had something to do with what was wrong. I was amused by Hawk's pursed lips and wrinkled brow. When our glances met, I cocked my head and shrugged my shoulders. My concern for missing my shower simply warranted a grunt from Hawk. Tonto finally decided that a few squirts of oil might help. He came back shortly with a very small can. He squirted the oil inside the key slot and all around the lock then tried again and again nothing happened. They finally gave up. Tonto indicated before he left that he was going to saw the lock off, and then I would be able to shower.

I figured I would give it one more try. I did not want them to know that I had tampered with the lock. Again I tried and tried with no success. After resting, I figured I would give it one more try and give it all the strength I had. I took a deep breath and strained every muscle in my body. Nothing happened. One last desperate effort, I thought, and pulled harder. Suddenly the lock popped open, the two lead pellets were squirted out and oil splattered everywhere. I was so happy to see the lock open that I laughed. Once under control, I picked up the pieces of lead and wiped the oil from my face, the lock and the floor.

Now the question was—what to do? But first, I had to go to the bathroom. I took the irons off and, neatly arranging the lock, the anklets, and the bar in the middle of the floor, I went over to the bucket and sat down. I really did not know what to do, but in any case I was going to think about it while I enjoyed relieving myself on the bucket without the irons. I was almost finished when the door opened. Tonto looked in as he opened the door, and before he could look behind the opened door, he noticed the irons in the middle of the floor. He stopped dead in his tracks. He was halfway in and halfway out staring at the irons hoping I would materialize where he knew I should be.

When I made a noise he turned abruptly and looked in the corner. His sheepish smile told me he was thankful that I was still in the room. Having regained his composure, he pulled the door closed, locked it, and went again to fetch help. Ferdinand, Frankenstein, Tonto, and, sure enough the Hawk returned. I explained that when I pulled on the lock it opened. "It must have been stuck," I said.

Hawk put the irons back on, put the lock into the bar, and closed it. It clicked sharply into place. The Hawk reached down, tugged on it, then gestured that I try to pull it apart.

"I can't," I said.

But the Hawk insisted. So I banged it on the floor a couple of times, trying to suggest that is what I had done to get it open. They went through the routine again, first Hawk pulling, then me. Frankenstein gave Tonto a key. He turned it in the lock. It snapped open. Tonto repeated the process several times. Satisfied, he looked at me and said, "You strong man." It was the first time I heard Tonto speak. It was a good new Chinese lock, but that was not good enough for the Hawk. In a very short time he came back with another lock exactly the same. He opened and closed it with the key several times and ordered me to pull the lock apart. Still a little puzzled, but satisfied that I could not do it, he left. I guess Tonto was happy that I was still there, so he permitted me to shower and allowed me to wash my clothes. My freedom from the irons was short-lived.

XIII

The Cat and the Cubicle

In replacing hope and fear, purpose and knowledge are the facets of life which make it hard and precious.

On November 17, 1969, Tonto came into the room and gave me the signal to roll up, meaning that I was going to move from room 18. I gathered what few things I had: my old brown tattered rag, which was a part of me, my mosquito net, and the rotting straw mat. I had always felt that leaving room 18 would be a good omen. I looked around once more. The room was dirty, there was blood on the walls and the floor. I noticed where someone had put a calendar showing how many days he had been in this room. A number of people kept calendars. Some were there two weeks, some three, and one fellow had a record thirty-five days. There were no six-month calendars. I looked around and said goodbye to some of the names that were written on the walls, hidden in various manners and in various codes. I said goodbye to the corner, where the bucket was, looked around once more, and finally departed.

Tonto took me across the courtyard, and before going through the arch on the opposite side, he sat me down on the steps and blindfolded me. I waited. I waited for a long time. The sun was gone and it was getting dark. Finally Tonto came over and tapped me on the shoulder. It was time to go. I mounted the two or three steps through the archway, and instead of going straight toward little Las Vegas, we turned left down an alleyway behind the northernmost large administration building. This part of the camp was referred to as the Stockyards. I stumbled up four narrow steps and into a room that seemed already to be closing in on me.

I could tell that the floor was part dirt and part filth. If I could be relieved from the harassment and the irons, perhaps it would be acceptable, but right now it seemed that my situation was depreciating rather rapidly. After the blindfold was removed and the squeaking door locked, I noticed that there was only a straw mat on the grubby damp floor. The walls were so close, I could touch them as I extended my arms, and with three normal steps I could move from one end of the room to the other. There was only one small louvered window and a three-inch round peephole cut in a solid wood door. There was not even a light. Then I was aware of the most disturbing characteristic of all, the stench. A toilet was next to my new cell. I strugled with my irons and my net in the blackness. Finally I escaped my miseries by sleeping.

The next morning, when a ray of light came through the 6-inch by 10-inch window, I took my net down and saw that even in the light the room looked as bad as I had suspected. I was determined not to be despondent and said aloud to myself, "This must be better than torture. This must be better." Especially in a place such as my cubicle, it was necessary to be active mentally and physically.

A week after my arrival Tonto installed a single bare light bulb, and I was also given three blankets, one large yellow towel, a smaller white one, a toothbrush, toothpaste, new clothes, a broom to sweep the filthy floor, a clean mat, and a pallet which was raised on two sawhorses. In addition there was a strange looking basket. I thought at first there might be a snake in it; it looked like the baskets that cobras usually came out of when enticed by Indian flute players. It turned out to be a teapot warmer. It was very brightly colored and very well made, complete with a lid. The Hawk also gave me some soap, the first I had since I was recaptured, a clean white cup, and finally, the thing I appreciated more than anything else, a pair of rubber sandals for my poor feet. The scene was fantastically ironic. Green socks and colored handkerchiefs were added to my enormous wealth.

Before leaving, Hawk wanted me to sign my name next to each item listed in a booklet. I refused. He shuffled angrily through the pages and pointed out that he had signed for some of the things already. I nodded and picked up the pencil and signed with my initials JAD. Hawk grimaced, but accepted it and left.

I thought the surprises for that day were finished, but that evening my food consisted of a flat plate half of which was heaped with beans and the other half with pork and pork fat. I also had one large round loaf of bread. I could not finish the fat and kept half the bread for the next morning. Now my meals consisted of a small side plate of squash, pork fat or beans, a bowl of soup, and a loaf of bread. The side plate was a welcomed addition. I could feel my body absorbing everything I consumed. I called for more and more water and Tonto brought me all that I needed, a full teapot of water three times a day.

There are no good days in North Vietnam, but, as the North Vietnamese say, there are "improved situations." They can be spoiled. Any improvement can be spoiled by an interrogation with the Bug. I followed Ferdinand into one of the interrogating rooms, and, surprisingly enough, the Bug smiled, showing his large teeth. He motioned that I should sit down. I sat before him and waited. Finally he said, "How are you?"

I replied, "Very well, thank you."

He said, "Ah, the situation is very good." I said nothing.

"The political situation is very good for you. What would you like?"

"Nothing," I answered again. "I would like nothing."

"Would you like to go home?"

"Of course, I would like to go home."

"No! No! NOW! Would you like to go home now?"

"Of course, if that is possible."

"Do you know the North Vietnamese people have released . . ." As he said it, I felt my heart jump into my throat, thinking I was about to hear that all the P.O.W.s were sent home, but instead he said, "Three more prisoners. Did you know that?"

"No, I did not." My excitement died. Bug mentioned three names. "Do you know them?" "No," I said, "I do not."

"Hegdahl," the Bug repeated, "Do you know him?" "No," I answered.

"Well, he knows you," the Bug chuckled. "He knows you. Do you know Colonel Burdette?" Bug did not speak English very well, and sometimes he spoke so softly he was hard to understand. I thought he had said "Colonel Brett." I was on the verge of leaping at the Bug's throat. I leaned forward.

"What was the name?" I asked sharply.

"Burdette."

"How do you spell it?"

"It is here," the Bug said. He pointed to the name on a paper, spelling it out.

"No, I do not know Colonel Burdette." I sat back, relieved.

"Colonel Burdette is dead." I felt sorry for whoever he was, but I also felt a load had been lifted from my shoulders. As I tried to figure out why Bug had told me that, he pushed some pamphlets in front of me and said, "When you are ready to go, call my guard." He got up and left.

The pamphlets were propaganda. They were of no interest to me. I called Ferdinand and was taken back to the cubicle.

The next day, Tonto took me back up the alleyway and through the archway to Bug's interrogation room again. There was no need for a blindfold; I knew the area well. Again, the Bug was grinning. He pointed to the stool, then pushed a bag of candy in front of me. I must have reared backwards slightly, for he said, "Eat, yes, you can take it. You can take it." I opened the plastic bag, took one piece of candy, took off the wrapper, and put it in my mouth. At that point, the Bug pushed the blue book in front of me, the book I had earlier refused to fill out while in room 18. Still showing his teeth, he said politely, "Write in the book, write in the book." And he left the room.

After he departed, I thumbed through the pages looking at the questions. It was complete, there was no doubt about that. They wanted answers concerning my military background, squadrons, aircraft, where I was shot down, my family, their addresses, income, everything. Normally the answers were first written on ordinary paper and, when accepted by the Bug, carefully transcribed to the blue book. By giving me this pen, he was obviously willing to accept anything that I might write in the book. So I began to write. I answered some simple questions. Mostly I lied and many of the questions I did not answer. I finished very quickly and waited.

In about half an hour, the Bug came back, surprised that I was finished. He glanced through the book and did not seem pleased with my performance, but he accepted it and said sternly, "Go back to your room."

When I got back to the cubicle, I began to think and finally realized that I had made a mistake. After so much crying, after enduring so much torture, I had successfully refused to fill out that damned blue book, but now because I was told the situation was good, because of a smile coming from the master, because of a bag of candy, and because, no doubt, of the fear of going through all of it again, I had failed. I could rationalize that it would be of no use whatsoever considering the few questions I had actually answered and the lies, but again, as I sat there, I realized that it was not in accordance with my plan. The blue book was the Bug's gain and my greatest failure. The next time the Bug will probably want more.

The next day, no doubt feeling good because of his success, I was again summoned by the Bug. Small cups of hot tea replaced the bag of candy. He presented me with a magazine written by P.O.W.s entitled "The New Outlook." He insisted that I read it. I thumbed through it and recalled it was a magazine that I had heard of previously and with which I was determined not to be associated. Anyone who had written in that book had simply been intimidated into doing so. It was a professionally prepared booklet which gave a totally erroneous picture of our imprisonment. The Bug pointed at the book and said, "You will write about your situation, you will write as your fellows have written." I looked at him and said, "I will attempt not to do that."

Then, seemingly disregarding what I said, he put another pen and piece of paper in front of me and said, "You will write to the Camp Commander. You will ask him to take your irons away and he will help you."

Again I said, "I will attempt not to do that. Whatever I say or do will have no bearing on whether the irons will be removed. If the irons are to be removed, it's up to you." I repeated, "It is your decision to remove the irons."

Perhaps the Bug saw that I had regained my balance. He simply gathered up the books, paper, and pens, and on a piece of paper he wrote down, "Write in the 'New Outlook', write a letter to the Camp Commander asking to take away your irons, and write saying your injuries." He explained that I was to list all of my injuries and tell him what was wrong with me. He sent me back to the cubicle with pen and paper and a copy of "The New Outlook." All the articles and drawings gave the same impression—life in the North Vietnam prison camps was just grand.

Torture? Of course not. The magazine would show anyone in the world that there was no torture in North Vietnam, especially since it was so written by Americans. I felt that someday it would be slapped on the table in Paris, and the North Vietnamese delegation would say, "See, here. Regardless of what you hear or think you know, the prisoners in North Vietnam are being treated humanely." Whoever wrote those articles was simply helping to prolong our stay in North Vietnam.

To the Camp Commander, I wrote, "It is not up to me to ask for my irons to be removed. It is up to you. No matter what I do or what I say, the removal of my irons is up to you." On another paper I listed all my injuries and the tortures that had caused them. I wondered, when I finished, how they were going to use that. I hoped without much confidence that maybe, with Ho Chi Minh dead, some new political leader would see it and decide it was more profitable to end the tortures and be civilized.

It was a Sunday when Tonto came and picked up my very short letter to the Commander, my listing of my injuries, and the copy of "The New Outlook."

I did not see the Bug again, but one day the Staff Officer, whom I called Jeff Chandler, came in with Big Stupe and Baby Face, a very young looking interrogator. I had first met Baby Face when he was interpreting for Peaches. They opened the door to my cell, and I motioned them in, saying, "Come in, I have no hot tea, but surely you are welcome into my home." It was a surprise to Baby Face, and he grinned, and both Big Stupe and Jeff Chandler looked at him, wanting to know what I had said. He interpreted and when they understood, they both looked at me and smiled broadly. They came into the small cubicle, which was crowded with three people. Big Stupe waited in the doorway.

Since my initial comments seemed to go over well, I said to Baby Face, "Excuse the dust but my cleaning woman has not arrived today." He laughed, and again Jeff Chandler looked at him inquisitively, waiting for his interpretation. When he told them,

Big Stupe seemed to be a little puzzled. He wasn't quite sure what was going on.

Jeff Chandler started asking questions through Baby Face. He wanted to know if I had escaped before. When I answered "Yes," Big Stupe's eyes widened. Would I be able to escape from this place? was the next question.

I said "No" and smiled.

Interpreting for Jeff, Baby Face said, "It would be very dangerous for you to attempt to escape." He asked me again, "Could you escape?" I said, "No, of course not. The irons are very heavy and it is very difficult to move. I certainly could not escape with them."

He smiled and seemed to enjoy this response. He said that perhaps he could help me, so that I would be able to shed my irons. I told him truthfully that I would appreciate that very much; but, at the same time I stressed there was nothing I could do. Taking my irons away was simply up to them. I always wanted to make this point clear to insure they realized I had no intention whatsoever of doing anything which they might interpret as weakness and a willingness to comply with their wishes.

During the questioning, I watched Big Stupe leaning over Jeff Chandler's shoulder, intent on listening to everything that was said. I am not quite sure whether he knew I had escaped twice, and when it was mentioned, he was very interested in everything that was said. When the interview was finished and they were ready to depart, I looked at Baby Face and said, "Please come again, perhaps next time I will be able to have some hot tea to offer you," and I pointed to my colorful teapot warmer. They laughed and departed.

The door was clanged shut and the bolt put into place. As the door closed behind them, I looked at it again. It was obvious to me that if it were not for the irons, I would be able to get out of that room. I examined it very closely. It was on two hinges, and because of the space between the door and the top of the frame, it could actually be lifted off the hinges. It was a simple process, and I thought that one day I would try it. But, with the irons on, it was useless even to entertain that idea.

It seemed that everyone was interested in my ability, or lack of it, to escape. I was permitted to go once a week to the Heartbreak

Hotel washroom without my blindfold. On several occasions I was met by someone I later found out was called Major By or The Cat. He introduced himself as the camp commander. He was tall, thin, and dressed fairly well, compared with most of the North Vietnamese I saw. He had the piercing eyes of a cat. Considering the polite manner in which everyone greeted him, I assumed The Cat was the camp commander. Cat would stop me someplace in the courtyard or in the archway or alley, and we would talk. He said that he was trying to help me to get the irons off my feet. It seemed that everyone was trying to help me. I could not understand what was going on. But, in any case, I recognized it all to be a method, and I was hoping not to be fooled.

Like Jeff Chandler, the Cat seemed to be obsessed with my capability of escaping, and one day he asked me if I could.

"Oh no,'" I said laughingly, "I am in irons and it is very difficult even to move, let alone escape from that little room." I added, "It is getting very cold, and at night I cannot sleep. My feet become very cold because I cannot put them under the blanket."

He said, "If you were to ask, perhaps I would be able to get the irons off."

I looked at him and repeated, "No, I do not think it depends on what I say or do. If the irons are to be removed, it is up to you."

Just before we parted, he looked at me and said, "In the future, if you want to escape, you should tell me."

I stared at him, at first not really understanding what he had said, but it then became clear, and I smiled and said, "Of course, of course, I will tell you." He must have realized the humor of the situation, for he slapped me several times on the back, and we parted laughing and smiling at one another.

The Cat had a room at the end of the alley, no more than twenty-five feet from the cubicle. I could identify his walk when he passed my cell and his voice when he talked to the Bug or the staff officer outside my door. I could also recognize the Cat when he woke up in the morning and went out to brush his teeth. There were two spigots next to the urinals, which were directly adjacent to my room. Those who lived in the complex, including some of the girls, would come there, sometimes before sunup, and scrub their teeth. The Cat was usually the first. He would brush his teeth and gargle very loudly. When he was finished, he would put his toothbrush in a can, fill it with water, and then bang the toothbrush against the sides of the can as he attempted to clean it. Later, I began to mimic him. I would gargle loudly, and since I had no can, I used my cup to clean my toothbrush. The next time the Cat saw me as I came back from my weekly trip to Heartbreak, he stopped me and, to my disbelief, handed me a shiny tin can. "Save your cup," he remarked and walked off.

On one of my weekly trips to Heartbreak Hotel, I was stopped abruptly by Tonto. Before he could push me back, I saw through a large crack in one of the bamboo screens that the Cat was helping the kitchen girls roll fish in cabbage leaves. He was squatting, giggling, and having fun. When Cat heard Tonto's commotion in the hall, he jumped up and ran behind some big barrels of fish sauce. Only then did Tonto wave me forward. Helping maids do menial tasks was apparently not in keeping with the Cat's image of authority.

There were three kitchen girls. One was Zorra, the youngest and probably the prettiest. She wore a white face mask to prevent the dust from rising onto her face. She expertly handled the poker she used to stoke the furnace every morning. She was the female Zorro of North Vietnam. Another was Piggy. Needless to say, she was short, plump, and looked like Petunia Pig. Dusty was the chief in the threesome, and the oldest. She looked as if at one time she might have been a good looking woman, but she had worked too hard, too long, and now was just a little beyond her years.

On occasion I would look through a hole in the top of my door into the kitchen area. It seemed to be a well organized place. There were some tools, baskets, carrying poles, and a ladder. I had everything spotted and knew where each thing was supposed to be. Perhaps, I thought, I might find a use for that ladder.

One day during quiet hour when no one was around, I shuffled to the door and lifted. Its rusty hinges barely budged at first. I tugged harder. Suddenly, as had happened once before at the Zoo Annex, I was holding a door in my hands, free of its hinges. I frantically attempted to get the door back in position, but because of its length, I was never able to get both hinges on at the same time. Finally, with the top hinge on, I decided to take a rest. The guard came, but fortunately he did not notice anything as he peeked into the room. Later that day when Tonto came to give me my second meal, the door opened a little awkwardly, but he did not notice anything. That night I went to bed not knowing whether I should attempt again to get both hinges on or simply leave it that way. As I lay down on my mat, the rain started. A tropical storm was coming, a perfect night for sleep or escape.

I got up, picked the padlock on my irons with the Golden Key, rolled up blankets so it would look as if I were still under my mosquito net, and went to the door. I lifted it off its hinge. I crawled behind the coal pile, past the furnace and into the kitchen. I picked up the ladder, some rope, and a machete.

I moved outside and climbed up a drainpipe that went up the side of the administration building. I hooked the ladder over a battlement-like protrusion that stuck out from the roof. I released my hold on the drainpipe and swung out into midair on the ladder. Carefully, I went up the ladder, over the protrusion and onto the roof.

Quickly, softly, I headed across the building roof, jumped to the next one and moved across that to the edge overlooking the prison wall. I tied my rope to one of the steel protrusions on the roof and lowered myself down. Toward the end of the rope, I stopped. Shoving against the building with my feet, I arched out until I could slide down the rope on the other side of the wall.

When I reached the ground I left the rope hanging over the wall, the end of it barely seven feet from the ground. The rain was falling hard now. The river was rushing by almost in front of me. Almost no one was out in the streets.

I jumped into the river, cluttered with tree limbs and branches torn loose by the storm. It seemed the river and the air around me were in a rage. A little boy screamed as he was swept into the flood. I grabbed him, pulled him out, told him he was safe and to go home. I dived back into the fast moving Red River.

The roaring Red River carried me down until I was near the sea. There was a boat. As I climbed into it, an old man began beating me with a stick. I pulled him over the side of the boat and held him under the water. The boat was mine.

The flood carried me out to sea and for the next day and the next and the next, I lay in the boat waiting. It was up to the United States Navy now. My lips were parched. The reflection of the bright sun off the calm sea was dazzling.

I looked across the boat. Ed Atterberry was sitting there with his head lowered and elbows resting on his knees. "Regardless," I told Ed, "we tried." Ed said nothing. I stood up in the boat, lifted both hands toward the sky and screamed, "We tried! Tried! Tried!"

Startled I sat upright. I was still under the mosquito net. The irons were still on my feet. I had never left the cubicle.

That next morning I stood there thinking about the dream. I had saved a boy and killed a man; I was successful at removing myself from reality but a failure at escaping. As I stood there a ray of light pierced through cracks in the little louvered window of my cell and illuminated the opposite wall. Tiny particles of floating dust were caught and reflected in the beam. I imagined each of them as separate little worlds, not really part of this place. When I looked straight ahead, the shaft of light out of the corner of my eye seemed to grow until it filled the whole room. The walls seemed to shimmer as if they were alive. Not looking directly into the light but only out of the corner of my eye, I could very easily visualize anything my imagination wished to create, a God or an angel, or some other form of help. I was simply going to have to help myself. And in the end, if anyone was going to help me, it would be those I knew had this same attitude back in the United States who were working to get us out of this place. If I stood there and then knelt, perhaps I could later tell the story of how I looked to God to gain my strength, but there was no God in that cubicle. The only people who could help me were myself and those attempting to defeat the North Vietnamese.

In the far end of the alley were located the Cat's room, four bins of lye, a shower stall, and two spigots. This is where the officers usually washed in the morning. Only the kitchen help used the stinking toilet next to the cubicle.

The last week of November, the routine changed. Tonto would come into the room in the morning, unlock my irons, and put them in a corner behind the door. Every day I was allowed to shower in the same area the Cat used to wash himself. It was located next to the toilet. Instead of going through the Heartbreak courtyard and into Heartbreak Hotel once a week, I was now given an opportunity to wash my clothes every day. During the quiet hour, Tonto would take me out to the Heartbreak Courtyard to sun myself, and sometimes in the mornings I was allowed to do exercises in the alleyway. The usaul morning meal arrived around 9:30 and in the late afternoon, at about 4:30, the second meal was served. When Tonto came to pick up the dishes, he insured that the irons were on and locked in place. Noting these changes, I wondered what would follow. I now was given the opportunity to exercise and to sun myself, I had two large bowls of soup a day, I was getting as much water as I required, and I was able to shower every day. And the most appreciated change of all, I wore the irons only in the evening, at night, and in the morning prior to the first meal. Still I was permitted to shave only once a week.

Now, with as much time as I required to complete my chores, I undressed and put my soiled clothes in a bucket to soak while I prepared to shave myself. Standing there nude, I attempted to shave while peering into a broken mirror. Then I had the feeling someone was watching me. I looked up to my left and saw Dusty squatting on the rim of one of the lye bins. She was watching me. Tonto probably had something to do and instructed Dusty to watch me. That is exactly what she was doing, watching me as I stood there shaving. I did not know quite what to do. I thought it silly to attempt to hide myself. So I just stood there and continued to shave. But it was becoming more and more difficult to shave as I realized what Dusty's presence was doing to me. I saw myself smile in the mirror. If Dusty could do what she was doing, then I would have no trouble adjusting when I returned to the good old U.S.A. Finally, perhaps satisfied with her own womanhood, she climbed down off the rim of the lye bin and walked off.

During one of my periods out in the sun, I met, of all people, the Little Ox, one of the real-life actors who performed in the Heartbreak Courtyard while I peered through the barred windows of Room 18. This short, muscular North Vietnamese always seemed to be in a good mood. He saw me there with my shirt off attempting to get some sun. He stood for a moment, watching. Then he approached me, and in his sign language he asked me if I could box.

I said, "Oh yes," that I could box a little bit.

He asked me if I knew any judo. He put his hands up, taking the classical stance.

I said, "No, no, I do not know any judo."

This, no doubt, was his opportunity to show me just how

talented he was. He started into a routine that lasted for ten minutes. He twisted, turned, and poked his fingers here and there. When he was all finished he came strutting toward me, waiting for an approving comment. I shook my head indicating that it was a magnificent show. Apparently quite satisfied with himself, he turned and waddled off, whistling a North Vietnamese fight song.

Another of the Heartbreak Courtyard troupe that I used to watch from Room 18 was the gardener I called Young Ho Chi Minh. He was always there in Heartbreak Courtyard attending to his plants and watering the garden. Now every time he passed, he would nod and smile; I would do the same. We came to know each other although we never said anything. One day I could not determine what he was doing. Finally he came close. With a small eye dropper he would squirt a little bit of the fluid onto the plant. I looked at him and pointed to the bottle and to the eye dropper. "What are you doing?" He showed me some leaves; on each there was a little bit of disease. On the bottle was written in English "Disinfectant." Young Ho Chi Minh was "spraying" his plants with an eye dropper.

Having broken the ice, Young Ho Chi Minh attempted to start a conversation. He indicated by diving his hand into the ground that he wanted to know what kind of airplane I flew. I wrote in the dirt "F-105." His reaction was "Oooooh." It seemed that young Ho Chi Minh knew indeed what an F-105 was. He then asked how many missions, holding up his fingers indicating five, ten, and so forth. I smiled and shook my head, "No." I was not going to answer that question. He wasn't too interested in pursuing the question either. He was more interested in knowing if we ate greens in the United States. He picked up some of his prize greens and started chewing. I tried to tell him also in sign language that we did not eat very many greens. On the ground I drew a cow, meaning "this is what we ate most of the time." He seemed quite surprised, for, obviously, most of his diet consisted of greens and vegetables.

As I watched young Ho Chi Minh go about caring for his garden and applying his medicine to the plants, I noticed a young boy standing off to one side watching. I was picking up small pebbles and tossing them into the garden. The boy had in his hand a small cloth pouch which contained a number of coins. They jingled as he tossed them up in the air. Two small feathers tied to the tiny bundle caused it to act like a badminton bird as he paddled it with his hand. I picked up a small pebble and tossed it at the boy. He caught it. He tossed me his bag of coins and I caught it. I tossed it back to him. When it flew back to him, he hit it with his hand. I caught it again. I threw it back to him; again, he smacked it with the palm of his hand. I caught it. By now, I had the idea and the third time he smacked it to me I paddled it back toward him. Thus, our modified badminton game was on. If you missed, you lost a point; if you hit it beyond your opponent's reach, you again lost a point. On three occasions, the boy missed batting it back to me. It seemed that I was winning the game.

The boy was so absorbed in the game that he did not notice his father approach. The father was a tall, good looking man whom I had previously observed from Room 18. He was the "supervisor." When he finally noticed his father, the boy was not sure what his actions should be. He did not know how his father would react to his playing with me. But it was obvious that the father was quite proud of the young boy. He looked at me and smiled as he placed a hand on his son's shoulder. I smiled and nodded, showing approval of the boy. The father held up thirteen fingers. I nodded and smiled again. They turned and departed. The boy looked back once before they disappeared in the shadows of the Hanoi Hilton's main entrance arches. He may not have known that I was an F-105 pilot, but I was sure both realized that I was the enemy. Perhaps the torture of American captives was not approved by all North Vietnamese.

Apparently because of these incidents, I was no longer allowed into the Heartbreak Courtyard. My sunning and exercising were restricted to the alley between the administrative building and the kitchen. I had been doing more exercising. Now it was time to test my strength.

I was going to do a handstand on the rim of one of the lye bins. I knew if I could do it and hold it, I was doing well physically. There was no one in the alleyway. I placed my hands on the flat rim and pressed up into a handstand, stood there for a moment, and realized that I had regained my strength.

When I came down, I turned and looked to the other end of the alleyway. A little girl about seven years old walked toward me.

I took a few steps toward her. When we were near each other, I gave a slight bow. She returned the bow. Then I gave a curtsy and she tried to duplicate my motions, but having never done such a thing, she did not know quite what to do. Very carefully I showed her how, but not touching her. I showed her how to place her feet and how to hold her arms while making a curtsy. Finally, she did it. I was surprised that she was able to learn so fast. She was able to do it and enjoy what she was doing.

Suddenly, Dusty came trotting up to where we stood. Sneering, she grabbed the little girl by the arm and marched her back into the kitchen. In a short while I could hear the little girl crying, probably because Dusty had spoiled her fun.

As usual that night, Tonto locked the irons onto my ankles. After the guards, the "keepers," and the kitchen girls had their dinner, they started singing. I could hear a flute and a guitar. It was customary for an instructor to tour the camps attempting to teach various groups new propaganda and war songs. They would sing the same lines over and over again. The instructor, when he did sing a song all the way through, sounded very good.

I was surprised that evening. It was December 9, 1969. When it began to get dark, the door opened. It was the Bug and Ferdinand.

In a practiced manner, Bug said, "The Camp Commander has decided to forgive you." He signaled Ferdinand.

Ferdinand unlocked the lock, pulled the iron bar through the eyelets, slipped the anklets off, and stacked them in the corner.

I bundled up my new possessions, anxious to leave the cubicle.

XIV

Rendezvous in Vegas

Show me one who has failed, failed failed, and I'll
accept that man who has tried, tried, tried.

One had to pass through two large doors before entering the Mint
of Little Vegas. All the cell blocks in the section of the prison we
called Little Vegas had been named after the casinos of Las Vegas.
In the Mint, there were three cells. Looking down a small, narrow
hall, I could see three solid green doors with large locks and
latches on them. It was a most discouraging sight. It seemed that I
was going from bad to worse. From Room 18 to the cubicle and
from the cubicle to the menace of the Mint. A wooden slab, waist
high, was my "bed." Less than a foot separated the edge of the
bed and the opposite wall. Any walking or exercising would have
to be done on the bed. There was one large window, but it was
covered by a bamboo screen. It seemed to me that I would have
to dismantle that screen to get some air into the room. In the door
was a peephole with four small iron bars. Over the peephole was
a metal plate which could be opened from the outside. The
guard could look through the small metal grating into the room.
I was in Cell One of the Mint.

In one of my conversations with the Cat, prior to moving to the
Mint, he had mentioned that he was going to give me a roommate
or roommates. "Those who think in the same manner," he said.

On the night of December 10, 1969, the doors clanged again
and I waited. I knew someone was being moved in next to me.
Both cells Number 2 and Number 3 were being occupied. As soon
as I could determine that the guard was gone, I immediately banged

on the wall. Pushing out the iron cover of the peephole as much as I could, I shouted into the hall, "Who is it? Say your name." The first man called, "George Coker," and the other bellowed, "George McKnight."

"George, is that the George I know from Laredo?"

All of a sudden the tiny cells were filled with the sound. "Dramesi, you goddamn bastard, I knew you'd end up in this hell hole."

Sure enough, it was the George McKnight that I knew!

Immediately the guard came in raving, "Be silent, be silent." We were off on the wrong foot already. Nothing happened, but no matter what, it would have been worth it to know that George McKnight was in Cell 3 of the Mint. It was amazing that after twelve years we should meet each other again in Hanoi, North Vietnam. As soon as we had the opportunity, we arranged danger signals, and the routine we were going to use for communicating. While George Coker watched the hallway for shadows, George McKnight and I talked.

I asked him about his escape. He and Coker had escaped in the fall of 1968 from a small prison near the Red River.

He said, "Oh, it was nothing." They decided one day and went the next, but they did get nine and a half miles away.

I said, "Boy, that's too bad. Nine and a half miles down the Red River, that's really great, George."

He said, "I guess we could have done better if we had prepared properly."

"Well, look at it this way: if you had made it, we would never have been able to meet here."

We both laughed.

About that time, the guard was coming back. George Coker gave a bump on the wall, the danger signal that a guard was approaching. Everyone was quiet and moved away from the walls. I went to my bunk and sat down. Sure enough, in a few seconds, the trap door on my door opened. The guard looked in, squinted his eyes and pursed his lips to indicate that he was very angry. After looking around and ensuring that I saw his angry face, he slammed the small metal door to the peep hole and turned the latch.

I went to the door and looked at the metal hatch over the peephole. I saw that I could push the plate out and see the threshold to the doorway which led to our cells. We would be able to communicate when necessary and still be able to warn each other in sufficient time when the guard approached.

That night, George Coker helped me with my tapping. With my net up, I lay in the bunk, put my ear to my cup, and placed the cup to the wall. Then I propped my knees up while under the blankets. In that way, when the guard looked in the peep hole, he would be able to see me in my bunk, but with my knees up he would be unable to see my head.

The cup amplified the sound so that we could hear one another but the guard could not detect the faint sounds. I tapped to Coker, asking him how long he had been with George McKnight.

He responded, "Ever since Dirty Bird."

I asked, "What is Dirty Bird?"

He tapped, "That's the name of another small camp."

I also discovered that the Dirty Bird was near the "Plantation." Also there was another camp, called Alcatraz. They had escaped from the Dirty Bird. They had just moved from Alcatraz.

George Coker then asked where I was before coming to the Mint.

I said, "I was in a small cell called the Cubicle, and before that I spent a long time in Room 18, the torture room."

He asked, "Why were you there so long?"

"I escaped with Ed Atterberry."

"Did you say escaped?"

"Yes."

"Tell me about it."

At that moment, I decided it was time to wait until the following morning. We had been on the wall for hours, and it was wise to knock it off. During that session I found out that George Coker was also from New Jersey, he also was a wrestler, and he had attended Rutgers University. When I asked how tall he was, he replied, "Two inches taller than Napoleon." It sounded like Little George had spirit.

Very early the next day I was called out to a quiz. I walked into a room that we called the "Knobby Room." This was the Cat's quiz room. It had rough unfinished cement on all the walls and the ceiling. Probably to deaden the sound, I thought. There was again the familiar long table and blue cloth. When I entered, the Cat cordially offered me some hot tea, which I accepted.

He offered me a cigarette. I said, "No, thank you." He said, "You may smoke."

"No, I do not want a cigarette."

Smiling, he said, "I force you to have a cigarette. I force you to smoke."

I accepted and smiled. I had been "forced" to smoke a cigarette. After I puffed a few times, in an attempt to please him, the Cat asked "How are you today?" and I told him, "I am doing well."

"Perhaps soon you will have some roommates."

"That will be very much appreciated, after being alone for so long."

Being very direct, I asked, "Are you the camp commander?" He responded, "Yes, I am the camp commander here."

I said, "Well, then you must be a colonel." He said, "It is not necessary for you to call me Colonel. Call me the camp commander."

I smiled slightly. It was obvious that he enjoyed being complimented.

I said, "You are very young for a colonel. It seems that many of the people here in the camp respect you very much."

He said, "The Oriental does not show his age like an American."

"Oh, yes, that is true. You are"—I hesitated—"forty or forty-one."

He smiled and said that he was forty-seven years old. He seemed delighted that I was incapable of guessing his age and thinking that he was a colonel.

Spurred on by these compliments, he began to tell me of his days as an interrogator of the French prisoners during Dien Bien Phu. He indicated that he had been working with prisoners for a long time and was quite aware of all the tricks and attitudes of prisoners. He ended his monologue with "I know all the tricks."

I agreed, "Oh, yes, it would be stupid to try to fool you."

The Cat asked, "Do you know why you are allowed to live with other prisoners?" Yes, I know, I thought. It is because the

North Vietnamese are being forced to be lenient. I had no doubt that if it were not for our value as a psychological weapon, we would have been tortured and killed a long time ago.

But I said simply, "I do not know why I am being allowed to have two roommates." I stressed the number two.

"Today we must have a new start," the Cat said. "You must repent." The word was like a trigger. The Cat took off on the 4,000-year history of the North Vietnamese; on their lenient and humane treatment of prisoners, and on and on. Finally he asked, "What have you done to repent?"

"Done? What have I done? I have not done anything."

"You have not done anything to show your remorse? You have not done anything to repent so you can receive the lenient and humane treatment of the North Vietnamese?"

"Well," I said apologetically, "I wrote a letter to the camp commander once."

"I read that letter. It was not a good letter." I knew he was attempting to decide if he could afford to allow me to join Coker and McKnight.

I added quickly, "I am remorseful." That was one of Stack's favorite words. I suspected it would please Cat to hear me say I was remorseful. He said sternly, "But you must repent."

"I understand." Apparently that was what the Cat was waiting to hear. He sent me back to my cell.

Doors banged, bolts clanged, locks clicked; Little George was next. No doubt if the answers were right, we would join up as a threesome. George Coker came back and then George McKnight left. While George McKnight was gone, I asked George Coker, "How did your quiz go?"

He told me that the Cat had told him that the United States has made many, many mistakes.

George said, "I agreed with him, of course, the United States has made many mistakes."

Irritated, I said, "No, George, that was not the right thing to say. They will attempt to confuse a man about the facts of the war. That done, they dictate what is right and wrong—and it always adds up to the United States being all wrong."

George said, "Yes, I know what you're saying now."

George McKnight did not return to Cell Three of the Mint that day. I suspected that the Cat had probably asked George to tell the truth. I smiled, knowing George. He probably had done just that; and the Cat no doubt did not appreciate the truth.

But it seemed that at least before Christmas, we would all be together.

That evening, before going to bed, it was quiet in the Mint. I hoped George McKnight would rejoin us soon. I climbed on top of the bed. I walked back and forth, back and forth, like a caged animal. When the radio came on to play the nightly propaganda, I pulled the wires off. At times like that, silence was most welcome. I arranged the wires in small hooks. When I heard the faint sound of music from other speakers, I just hooked the wires onto the terminals and the music played. It was nice being able to turn the radio off when I pleased.

While I was walking on top of the bed, Mousey came to the door. I could tell it was Mousey because of his squeaky voice and long protruding buck teeth. Mousey had been a guard over at the Zoo. He would always run around slapping his oversized sneakers. He loved to sing. Others at the Zoo called him the Machine Gun Kid. He always carried a Russian machine gun during his guard duty. Mousey banged the door with the butt of his machine gun and grunted. I was to get off the bed. When I told Mousey there wasn't much room, he insisted that I just sit down. When Mousey shut the door, I got up again and started to walk around on top of my bed. That night, after Mousey sounded the clanger, telling everyone that it was now time to put up nets and go to sleep, I climbed up near the window, put my face to the bars, and whistled, "Put Your Dreams Away for Another Day."

Sooner or later, somewhere, Ed Atterberry would answer. But no one answered that night. Every night after the clanger would sound, I would whistle as loud as I could "Put Your Dreams Away for Another Day." Occasionally someone would clap, but I never heard what I was listening for, "Maria."

Again, George Coker called me to the wall. We both lay in bed with our cups to the wall, our ears to the backs of the cups, and began our tapping.

George Coker said, "When you want to whistle, tell me and I'll watch for you."

That was a good idea and I agreed.

Then George said, "Please tell me about your escape."

I said, "There is not much to tell."

He tapped back, "Please tell me."

I tried to explain in the broadest terms how it happened. What we did, what we prepared, and how we escaped.

But George was filled with questions. By the time we were finished, we were long into the night.

Finally, when George said, "What happened after you were recaptured?" I said, "George, that's another story. We'll have to knock off for the night. I'll give you that next time."

I finally went to sleep almost exhausted from being on the wall for so long.

Apparently, from George's story, tapping was all they ever did in Alcatraz. And Little George was very much accustomed to such long sessions.

Four days after I had moved to the Mint, the guard opened my cell and then George Coker's cell. The Cat was waiting for us in the Mint's small anteroom.

The Cat explained that he was going to allow us to live together, and, in response, we were to do something for him. He wanted us to write something about Easter. He explained he could not do anything for us if we did not explain the American ways. I did not answer.

He finished by telling us about the rules. We would be allowed out together in this small area. The door between us and the small courtyard of Vegas would be locked at all times. After the second meal, we would be locked in our individual cells for the night. In the morning we would be allowed the privilege of walking in the Mint's anteroom.

As soon as the Cat left, George Coker asked, "Are you going to write the article?"

I said, "No, I don't intend to write anything."

At that point, George began to beg, saying, "I've been solo for a long, long time in Alcatraz."

"Our obligation is not to do what he wants, whether it be to write about a tree or a mountain or Easter or whatever."

George insisted, "If we refuse, he's going to separate us."

I finally gave in. "You can write about Easter, but don't ask for anything. After you write it, I'll sign it also."

Perhaps nothing would come of it. Even if the Cat attempted to capitalize on it, I felt assured that I would be able to resist his next approach. But regardless of what happened, there was no denying it was a mistake.

It was the first time George and I had an opportunity to talk face to face. George asked, "What are those cracking noises coming from your room?"

"The bed squeaks when I walk on top of it."

"Do they allow you to do that?"

"No."

He looked a little puzzled and said, "I noticed that you don't bow to the Cat."

I said, "Even when I was in irons, I didn't bow and I don't intend to bow again until I am forced to do so."

It was interesting to note that every time we went out to either wash or get food, George Coker tried not to bow, but each time he was stopped by either Ferdinand or Big Stupe. They would give him a very stern look and say, "Bow, bow." Back in the room, red-faced, George would say, "That really pisses me off. They don't say anything to you, but they insist that I bow."

I told George that a lot of effort had been put into establishing that relationship.

When the Cat was in the hallways or yard, George would stop, look at me, and say, "Please bow." My simple reply was, "Not this time, George."

The following day, after the Cat's visit, Jeff Chandler came in with his young interpreter. He looked around the room. At first, he asked me a few words in English. I was surprised. It seemed Jeff Chandler was attempting to learn English. He said a few words and I corrected him when asked to do so. Earlier, George Coker had remarked that it was very unusual for the Cat and Jeff Chandler, the staff officer, to come to the cell rather than having us go to the Knobby Room. I knew there was just one reason for the visit.

He said, "You will not escape here."

I said, "Yes, I cannot escape from here."

"If you try again . . ." he paused, lifted his index finger, put it over his throat, and ran his finger across his throat while making a gargling sound. He continued, "If you try again, you will not live this time."

Having made his point, Jeff Chandler and his young interpreter turned and departed.

George bowed as they left.

I stood straight, watching them leave. As they departed, George asked: "How much do they know about you?"

"If they know only what I've told them, nothing."

"Do they know you have been in South Vietnam with the Army?"

I said, "No. At times I thought they did know, but every time they pressed me for an answer, I always denied it. I think in the end it paid off."

George confessed that he knew nothing of the war in South Vietnam. I told him of the other side of the propaganda he had been exposed to for over three years. When I finished, George looked at me and said, "John, you have helped me more than anyone else since I've been here. I think I'll be doing a lot better when I talk to the Cat the next time."

"Oh," I reminded him, "don't go into long explanations. The idea, when we talk to the Cat or any other interrogator is to terminate that interrogation as soon as possible. Make it difficult for him to talk to you just as it is for you to talk to him."

Once, when we were talking, George asked, "What were the best years of your life?"

I looked at him and, without hesitation, I said, "The best years of my life are those I have yet to live."

George noticed that I did not hesitate in answering and said, "Did you have that prepared? Did you know you were going to say that?"

I said, "Yes, it is one of my realized word relationships."

He said, "What are they?" He seemed quite inquisitive.

I said, "It's a mental exercise which helps you to understand yourself, to realize your weaknesses and your strengths, to formulate a relationship between yourself and those things about you. Simply pick a subject and determine in detail what it means to you. In the end, you will have developed a philosophy of life."

He was interested and said, "Well, do you know yourself now?"

I said, "George, in knowing myself, I think I am now better able to understand others. For example, I am basically honest, requiring physical work, mental exercise, and guidance. I am a

realist, an opportunist, an optimist, and at last an idealist. At
times I am inconsiderate, selfish, quick to criticize, and easily
offended. In the presence of those I respect, I am humble, respectful, attentive, and obedient. Unity, loyalty, discipline, and
orderliness are my concerted characteristics for man. Beauty is
talent, intelligence, height. I am a worldly student and an ignorant teacher. I'm American first, and by virtue of that, I am a
free man. My country, my friends, my family are my life values,
for to preserve my name the preservation of an idea must come
first. I am dogmatic about just two things—the human goal and
man's responsibility to man. My dream is not to create a revolu-
tion in thinking, simply to prepare the base. I have developed a
philosophy of life, established a goal, and selected a course which
makes agnosticism acceptable. There is no doubt about it, I'm a
product of my environment, of my teachers. I'm a product of my
experiences and proud of what I am and who I am. I am insignificant but alive."

When George regained his composure, he said, "Could I do
that?"

"Of course."

For the next three days, George sat and thought. When ready,
he recited his first word relationship. It seemed very similar to
mine. I smiled. George Coker was a very impressionable young
man.

Within four days after George and I were allowed together, we
made contact with the Stardust, where the rest of the "Alcatraz
gang" was located. We tossed notes over the walls of adjoining
shower stalls and used a coughing code devised in Alcatraz. At
times when the guards were watching this was an especially good
means of communicating, because it was no different than the
constant spitting, choking, and sneezing that the North Vietnamese
did themselves.

All of "Little Vegas" was in contact with each other except one
cell block located between the Mint and the Stardust. No one
could contact the Desert Inn, where a number of senior American
officers were located.

We learned one day that the Desert Inn was considered the
Bug's private propaganda reservoir. The Cat graced the Mint with
his presence once more. "Write of anything," he said, "mountain

climbing, road racing, anything." It sounded simple enough, but I refused. The conversation continued as George watched.

"You will not be going home now," he said. "Nixon has been elected your President, and it will be a long time before you can go home. Perhaps after the next election."

After he departed I turned to George and said disgustedly, "Isn't that stupid? It just goes to show you how much he knows about American politics. That election is three years away."

George's response was, "Hmmm."

On December 23, after the evening meal, I was sitting back on my pallet, whistling. George had said he enjoyed it. I stopped. Someone came into our anteroom and opened Cell 3. As soon as the guard had left, George McKnight said, aloud, "I'm back. I heard the whistling as I came in." Big George continued, "It's good to know there's somebody in this fucking place that's not afraid. Those bastards in the Desert Inn won't even try to communicate."

In the dismal Mint, Big George was a breath of fresh air. He was a fighter, tough and candid, probably why some people were leery of him.

George McKnight was allowed to join our exercising and conversations in the anteroom. We were allowed out to shower that Christmas. Back in the Mint, Little George laid a brightly colored towel over one of the bed pallets and put up some decorations. Our table for Christmas dinner was set. We were given a thick soup, an egg roll, turkey, green vegetables, a hard boiled egg, and a little bit of rice wine. It was easily our best meal each year. After Little George said grace, we took our time trying to enjoy our food.

The New Year's Day meal was the same except we received beer instead of rice wine.

Other than that, 1970 started off as 1969 had ended. We were allowed out once a day to wash. The Desert Inn people were the only ones allowed to eat their meals at tables set up outside.

Once, probably due to a mix-up in the routine we ended up in a shower stall next to three officers who were making tapes for the North Vietnamese. While Little George watched for guards, I boosted Big George up to the top of the wall that separated the two shower stalls. "Hey, you cocksuckers," George shouted, "the

SRO says to start acting like the soldiers you're supposed to be!"

He dropped down immediately and said, "Those bastards tried to hide from me." Our new guard heard the commotion, realized he'd made a mistake, and promptly took us back to the Mint.

On May 10, 1970, one year to the day after my second escape attempt, I was caught trying to retrieve a note we had written to the Stardust. Mousey spotted me groping for it.

The two Georges were taken off to individual cells in the Stardust while I was marched off to see the Bug in the Knobby room. It seemed already that he was angry, for his right eye began to close. Cyclops was glaring at me. There was a tremendous compulsion to bow. Having been caught redhanded by Mousey with the coded note, I felt a tendency to please the master in an attempt to ease his anger. I had to gather all the courage within me just to stand there. It seems my head wanted to nod and my shoulders wanted to dip. But this time in particular I was expected simply to do as I had preached. The Bug looked down at his papers, looked up again, and growled, "Do you know what day this is?"

I hesitated, not knowing whether to act stupid or not. I knew what day it was. Finally I said, "Yes, I know."

Immediately he jumped up, slammed the table with the palm of his hand, leaned over the table, and shouted, "Do you want me to call my guards? Do you want me to start again?"

I was startled. He had almost thrown me off guard. Pushing the crumbled piece of paper forward on the table he said, "What does that say? What does that say?"

I followed Bug as he came forward around the table and noticed with a start Ferdinand standing in a corner. In his hand was a coil of rope.

Bug unfolded the note, placed it on the table, and looked up. "Read it," he demanded. I had an urge to turn to see if Ferdinand was still there. It would have been very easy to read the note. After all, I was caught redhanded. The note contained our participation in a fast ordered by Commander Denton and our joy with the Lon Nol coup in Cambodia. I could rationalize that the fast was useless and considering the difficulty of my situation, I could very conveniently denounce the new Cambodian leaders in the presence of the master.

Knowing that Ferdinand was behind me with the ropes, it would have been easy to say after decoding the note that Lon Nol was a bandit and a traitor. Finally I said, "I cannot read it." I felt that Ferdinand would be upon me and I would feel the ropes once more. Instead, the Bug stood facing me. "I will give you one more chance, I will come back, then you will tell me what is in this paper." Bug snatched the paper from the table. Ferdinand threw the ropes in one corner and followed Bug out the door. The door was not locked. Mousey was still outside with his Russian machine gun.

Could Bug still administer torture for such infractions of the camp regulations? Would I be able to simply say no and not even feel the ropes? In the past I did not receive a second chance, but now I wondered if the situation was in our favor. When Bug returned in a few minutes, Ferdinand was not with him. The Bug looked at me and said, "I have talked to the staff. You must read what is in the paper." It was clear that he needed permission before he could apply the ropes. I wondered if this time he had that permission. I once again said, "I cannot read it." Bug angrily ordered me to stand in the corner. "You will stand there until you read." I moved into the corner with my face against the wall. Again Bug departed.

For the next two days I stood there in the heat. At times I sat down or lay down, and when I heard or saw the guard coming, I would stand up. Finally Tonto came and took me back to the Mint, but this time I went to Cell 3.

Shortly after I arrived, the Bug showed up at the peephole. Without any preliminaries, he simply said, "You will keep all your clothes on and you will sleep with your clothes on." He slammed the metal cover of the peep hole and departed. In the middle of May it was stifling in that room. Bamboo mats covered the barred windows, and I was expected to wear all my clothes. I wondered how Big George was able to live in this dirty, smelling room. The stench came from a bin between the main prison wall and Cell 3 which housed seven or eight pigs. Every other day the guards washed the area down. At that time the smell was suffocating, but even when the manure was not being agitated by splashing water or brooms, the smell was overpowering. I remembered Little George had complained about the smell and the squealing of the pigs at night. Jeff Chandler looked at him, smiled, and said, "Make friends with your neighbors."

It was time to help myself. I wore only my black shorts and little by little tore the bamboo curtains from the windows. The circulation improved slightly. That night I used the coughing code, to contact the Thunderbird, another cell of Little Vegas. "I was O.K.," I told them.

Now, what to do about the camp-wide fast that was ordered. First, I considered fasting a form of self-induced punishment, and secondly, since I was under pressure to decode the note, I would need all my strength to resist. But Commander Denton wanted 100% participation, so I started leaving my full bowl of soup and eating less than a half of a loaf of bread. The most discouraging thing came when I took my dishes to be washed. The dishes coming from the Desert Inn were clean as a whistle. There was absolutely not a single person in that cell block following the order of the recognized senior ranking officer in Little Vegas.

The fast was designed to protest our treatment. It did not do any good. As far as I could determine, no North Vietnamese officer ever asked why some of the men were not eating all their food. Though McKnight got sick from not eating, support for the plan generally was half-hearted.

After dismantling the bamboo screen over the back window I hoisted myself up to look out. During the quiet hour I examined the tower in the northeast corner of the compound. I counted the steps to the top; noted how often guards went up there and why; took note of the bars on the tower windows; projected the slant of the roof; counted the number of barbed and electrical wires on the wall; and studied the broken glass on top of the wall. Someday that information would come in handy.

XV

Days of Monotony

> Be not ashamed to look to those who elevate themselves above all others, for it is they who, knowing that indecision is the burden of man, guide the confused minds of the masses. It is they we recall when we speak of leadership, genius, the great.

I had a complete picture of the tower when I was moved, two weeks later, to a "solo" cell in the Stardust. Seconds after the guard was gone, I learned McKnight was solo in the cell across the hall from me.

"Boy, I thought you were a goner," George said. "What happened?"

I told him, "I was threatened with the ropes but ended up only having to stand in the corner for two days. For some reason, it looks like no torture anymore."

Things did seem to improve. In a few days we were all together again in another cell in the Stardust.

We started receiving hot tea and were allowed to exercise in the yard. McKnight was getting regular attention for his illness when he demanded it. But there was always the need for the North Vietnamese to make that psychological gain.

Commander Stockdale was sentenced to the hot, foul cubicle called Calcutta. After days of it, in the middle of that sweltering tropical heat, he couldn't take it anymore. After telling us of his experiences by tapping in code on the wall, Commander Stockdale relieved himself as SRO of Little Vegas until he regained his composure.

When Peg, Commander Stockdale's code name, was returned to

to the Stardust, the hard core in Little Vegas continued to look to him as their commander. Peg was willing to lead, to live by the code of conduct as much as he was physically able. To me, he had been and continued to be the leader of resistance in Hanoi. There were at least five Air Force officers in Little Vegas who outranked Commander Stockdale, but for some strange reason they were not available for command. Will it make any difference when we get back to the States? I wondered. As Ed Atterberry had once said, "When we all get back to the security of the United States with our feet up on the bar rail, they'll all be tigers again."

"No problem," said George McKnight. "Whatever happens, one thing is for sure. They'll have to look at themselves in the mirror every morning."

Prison was improving. The two Georges received packages from home. Little George received snacks and underwear from his Mom. The items Big George received from his Dad were perfect, vitamins and protein pills. The only thing Big George did not like were the letters the North Vietnamese happily gave him from his Mom. They were antiwar messages that managed only to get George mad.

One thing did not change. Guards and keepers continued to leave bamboo screens up and herd prisoners in groups of two or three, trying to keep us from seeing and talking to each other. Many times, while walking from the wash stalls to our cell, the guards would stop us and hurriedly push us to one side so that we would not be able to see the other prisoners. On many occasions the guards would make a mistake.

One day, as we were going out to exercise, we ran into three prisoners who were coming the opposite way. Immediately, without any instructions from the guard, they turned away from us so we would not meet. We were simply amazed. We wondered who would go to such lengths. Big George immediately began to grumble, "What a bunch of pimps." Finally we passed and recognized them as three officers who were cooperating completely with the North Vietnamese. That trio was very intent on satisfying their masters. They were out to please. If they were not supposed to gaze upon the others, they were not going to do it. If they were asked to make tape recordings for North Vietnamese propaganda, they did it. They looked silly and pathetic to us.

Out in the exercise area, one was capable of forgetting about such people. Little George was learning fast to do handstands. All of a sudden, we realized there were no guards around and there was a bit of giggling from the bambo enclosure next to us. We moved up to the screen and looked through to the next exercise area. There all the guards congregated. One of them was going to attempt to do a handstand. He was obviously not going to trust himself on his first try. "Step by step" is the North Vietnamese outlook for success. The guard was going to throw his feet up against the wall and support himself on his hands. One individual was designated to catch him, just in case he fell.

They all gathered around and were watching closely as the guard got into position. He placed his hands on the ground and threw his feet against the wall. As his feet hit the wall, his arms gave out, and like a pile driver his head went down into the dirt. The fellow who was to catch him stood there laughing as did everyone else. We on the other side began to giggle also.

Our exercising continued. I would flex my arms as if I held some dumbbells. I usually walked in circles while I did this exercise. As usual Mousey was watching. Shortly thereafter, Big George pointed out that Mousey was nowhere in sight. I attempted to look around the screen to locate Mousey. There, in the doorway which led to the Mint, was Mousey. He was standing with his feet spread apart, his Russian machine gun leaning up against the side of the wall, his pith helmet balanced on top of his head. He was flexing his arms, straining, gritting his teeth, and with all the determination that his face could express, he was attempting to grow muscles immediately. The only thing that seemed to be protruding from his skinny arms and hands were his knuckles as he clenched his fist attempting to duplicate my action. He did not see me, but suddenly when he realized that I was watching him, he picked his head up, stopped his pumping action, suddenly squatted slightly and smiled, showing all of his protruding teeth.

That night, back in the cell, I duplicated the antics of Mousey for the amusement of Big George and Little George. We all had a hearty laugh to the extent that the guard had to come a number of times, bang on the door with his rifle, and shout, "Be silent, be silent."

As usual, that night, the walls hummed with communications. I would do most of the clearing and Big George would be on one wall tapping to Commanders Rutledge and Jenkins, while Little George on the other wall tapped to Shumaker and Tanner.

Little George interrupted, stopped Big George, and said to me, "Stockdale has asked you to be an honorary member of Alcatraz. Do you accept?"

I told him to send back the message, "With honor."

They went back to communicating. I went back to being the sentry.

Things were definitely improving. We were even allowed to play ping-pong every once in a while. In this changing atmosphere, it was only natural that Little George fell in love. I do not know for sure whether he was in love with Zorra or whether he was in love with the flared blouse and black silk pajamas. Little George said apologetically, "Well, she is the best one of the three." Big George blurted, "That's for sure, but it's not saying much."

Zorra was the Twiggy of North Vietnam. "There is one little girl who has some shape," I told the group, "and her tight Army pants prove it. In the last weeks of my stay in Room 18, five people came in, led by the Clanger, another of the Heartbreak Courtyard players, whose sole duty, it seemed, was to pound, with a metal rod, a shell casing hanging from a tree. The Clanger was the Hanoi Hilton's timepiece. He opened the window. As I stood up, they looked around the room. In the group was one pretty, black-haired girl. I forced myself not to smile, nor did she. When they left, I was ready to hobble to the window. Naturally I wanted to get another look at the girl. But, before I could reach down and pick up my irons to shuffle to the door, the window swung open again. It was Clanger and the girl. Apparently she had a question. I looked at the Clanger and smiled and then looked at the girl. She finally smiled. We all knew. This time when the window closed I shuffled to the door to peek from my favorite hole. There, walking away from me, was a shapely Vietnamese girl with a long pony tail that went all the way down to her lovely rear end. With the tip of her pony tail swinging as if to say, 'Goodbye, John,' she turned the corner. That girl has most of the sex in North Vietnam."

Dusty, Piggy, and Zorra had a long way to go, but I could understand George's predicament. If there were three to choose from, Zorra would probably be the choice.

You could tell Mousey was interested in the kitchen girls also. When the girls passed as we did our exercises, he would look at them and shake his head and smile, wanting some comment from us as to whether they were "OK" or "No OK."

Little George would say, "OK."

Mousey was satisfied to recognize that the "beauty" of the North Vietnamese females was appreciated by the Americans.

Occasionally the guards asked questions about our personal lives. Mousey, through the keeper I called Blasé, asked, "Are you married?"

Blasé, known by others as Ichabod, was a fairly good looking boy, slim and a little taller than the average North Vietnamese. He thought he spoke very good English, but most of the time he seemed bored with his job and his surroundings.

I said, "Yes."

When Mousey found out I was married, he threw his hands up to his chest, obviously asking if my wife was well endowed.

I said, "Oh, yes, she is."

Mousey then looked at me inquisitively as Blasé asked, "Do you touch?"

I looked at Mousey and said, "Of course."

It was not necessary for Blasé to interpret. Mousey looked at me wide-eyed, placed his open hand to his mouth, and giggled. It seemed to Mousey one was fortunate to have a wife who was well endowed. If you were able to touch her, you were to be considered even more fortunate.

As I turned to look at George, I had to laugh. Big George was thoroughly disgusted with the proceedings.

As we were led back to the room, it was not uncommon that we should hear one of the "infamous three" fulfilling his daily requirements to repent, making a tape to be played later over radio Hanoi. At times it seemed I had to restrain Big George. He wanted to shout out again as he had before, or to rush through the door of the Knobby Room and shake them by the collars.

Meanwhile, the three of us in our room talked of escape. It was

Little George's plan that we should attempt to dig through the floor since the wall was only seven to ten feet away.

I said, "We have no tools, but we shouldn't necessarily give up the idea. In the meantime, let's try to get some tools."

The project seemed unlikely to me, but I certainly was not going to discourage Little George.

When we were not talking about escape, our discussions and arguments centered around such important things as hairstyles, underwear, the use of underarm deodorant, cars, wearing elevated shoes, drinking martinis, and other all-important subjects.

Although the arguments were many, there was no hell here, for as soon as that guard approached the door and banged his rifle butt and shouted, "Be silent, be silent," we were united.

Resistance was the essence of our existence. The guards sometimes banged on our door fifteen times a day, to indicate we were too loud. That did not stop us; we were not going to cower or be intimidated. We simply talked in normal tones and laughed when we had to laugh, otherwise we would have been accepting defeat.

There were two new people in the camp now. One was Dick Stratton and the other was Paul Brudino. When we were out in the stalls washing our clothes, I peeked through a crack and saw Dick Stratton. He was walking straight, very businesslike. When he passed an officer, he stopped and bowed, no more than thirty degrees. He simply went about his business in a very dignified manner.

Paul Brudino seemed to be the bustling type. He hustled here and there talking and smiling to guards and interrogators alike. That, I thought to myself, will get you nowhere. I wondered what his past performance had been.

There was no need to be disrespectful toward the guards, as perhaps George McKnight was at times, but at the same time there was still no need to be constantly groveling in the presence of the North Vietnamese.

I was surprised when I was escorted to see the Bug. Except after the escapes, rarely was I interrogated. The Bug was seated in his usual place. He looked up. I did not move. Smiling, he said, "You are not going to greet me?"

I looked at him and said, "Good morning," refusing to bow.

He continued to smile and said, "Sit down." He asked, "What is your mother's name?"

I said, truthfully, "Andriana."

"Would you like to write a letter?" I paused, thinking this was the first time he had offered me the opportunity to write a letter.

I said, "I will have to think about it."

Still smiling, he said, "When you want to write a letter, tell me. You may have the paper and a pen and you can write a letter to your family."

I said, "I will think about it."

"Would you like to receive a letter?"

My heart jumped into my throat. I was wondering if he was going to pull the same trick that our old interrogator at the Zoo Annex had pulled one day, when he asked me if I wanted to receive a letter. After the interrogation, he had just laughed at me and indicated that I had not given him the right answers.

I said, to Bug, "Yes, I would like to receive a letter."

He said, "But before you can receive a letter, you must tell me of your family. Write down the names of your family and their addresses."

I had successfully refused to give him that information.

"I do not know where they live now. It has been a long time."

Then he handed me a piece of paper and said, "Read this."

At that point I noticed a tape recorder on the corner of the table. I had not paid any attention to it until then. He said, "Read this."

This was the prelude to having something recorded. I tried to ignore the tape recorder, assuming it was there for the infamous three to make their daily propaganda broadcasts.

I read quietly a series of questions, "Do you know that Tet is coming? Do you like the Tet food? Have you enjoyed playing chess? Did you enjoy the Christmas dinner?"

There was a constant attempt by the North Vietnamese to propagandize the "lenient and humane" treatment of prisoners in North Vietnam. These questions, if answered properly, would obviously give that impression.

Bug said, "It is not difficult. Listen." When he punched a button, a cheery voice asked similar questions.

I asked him, "When I ask the questions, what will happen?"

Filled with enthusiasm, he answered, "Your fellows will answer the questions."

Again he played the tape to demonstrate the innocence of what he was requesting of me. The questions involved food, playing games, books, chess, cards, none of which we had.

The intent was to give the impression that we were enjoying ourselves here in Hanoi. There were even questions concerning eating outside, playing volleyball and basketball, things we had never done. Everyone would think that we were all together in one big happy family being able to talk to each other freely and sing or whistle any time we desired.

"You must be able to do something. Sing a little?" He smiled. "Whistle?"

I said, "I am not talented and would not be able to perform for you."

He decided again to give me an example. He pushed the button and the tape recorder played. Sure enough, there was a chorus of men, singing some Christmas songs.

A thought flashed through my mind. Here we are approaching Christmas 1970. Our whole concept of time has changed. Weeks have flipped by like days, and months like weeks, and to us a long time is no less than five years. One fellow doing an outstanding job of whistling followed my interlude of thought. What a mess, I said to myself. Finally, when it was finished, he turned and looked at me and, before he asked the question, I shook my head and said, "No." His patience was now running thin. He shouted, "Go back to your room!" And that's exactly what I wanted to hear.

When I returned I told the others what he wanted of me. Immediately the report of my visit with the Bug was tapped out on the walls of the Stardust. At that moment, I felt just as proud of being able to say no as I was of anything I had done since being captured. Unfortunately the Bug was going to get what he wanted. Someone would ask those questions and there would be others to supply the proper answers.

XVI

The Will
and the Purpose

Exercising one's will and physical strength to comply with that which is accepted as the common will is discipline. Exercising one's will and physical strength to comply with that which is recognized as one's philosophy in conjunction with the common will is self-discipline.

There was a surprise move on the night of Christmas, December 25, 1970. Commotion at night was unusual. One after another the doors in the Stardust were being opened. When our door opened we were told to stand in the hall. Each of us was searched by a team of three people. They looked in our hair, between our toes, at our fingernails, underneath our armpits, up our rear ends, and around our genitals. It was the most thorough search I experienced in captivity. They looked at our sandals and our clothing very carefully. Finally, we were told to get dressed. Outside the door of the Stardust we sat and waited, completely confused. Big George and I kiddingly chided Little George. He had been carefully doling out some sweets he had received in his last package. Now, no doubt, we would never see them again. Always, during a big move, there was hope that one day you would move and finally leave forever. But, for some reason, we felt this was not a move to go home.

We were ordered to move into the alleyway between the Golden Nugget and the shower stalls. There, all the prisoners of Little Las Vegas congregated. It was going to be a big move, and it seemed for the first time we would all be together. Most of us always thought that, sooner or later, the North Vietnamese would have to put us together to make some shabby effort of compliance with the Geneva Conventions. That meant some kind of compound situation.

It was amazing how different people looked. Some ended up being shorter than expected. Some people turned out to be older. It was always different, looking at a person in full view rather than seeing him through a crack in a wall. Many rushed from one end of the alley to the other shaking hands. Some sobbed as they hugged and pounded each other on the back.

"Are you Dramesi? Fifteen people have mistaken me for you. My name is Rob Doremus. They were telling me that they were proud to know me. Unfortunately, I had to point you out. I was not Dramesi, but Doremus."

Already many of the controversies were being settled. Who had said what, when, and where?

But there was one noticeable absence. The infamous three were not with us. They no doubt were still labeled by the North Vietnamese as requiring special attention. I met white-haired John McCain for the first time. We shook hands and hugged as though we were longtime friends. The magnetism of two men with like attitudes and respect for one another was easily felt. Most of the time he moved around on a crutch. He had a broken arm and a damaged knee, yet he was able to get up on stools and devise the most ingenious ways of communicating. He was always on the move, smiling and waving to people he knew were watching and disregarding the guards' harassment. The sight of the lively John McCain was enough to lift your spirits for the rest of the week. For the weak he was an inspiration; for the strong a constant reminder to keep trying. It was not the North Vietnamese who impelled John's smiling and laughing. He had a smile for all Americans and disdain for the North Vietnamese. He was thin and not a big man, but there was no doubt John had heart.

Speculation about what was going to happen was interrupted by Bug's appearance. "Be silent, be silent!" he shouted. We were arranged in groups, blindfolded, and led by armed guards through the kitchen into the Heartbreak Courtyard. Having made the trip many, many times, I knew where we were going. Through the

Heartbreak Courtyard, we were led through the double iron doors of Heartbreak Hotel, into the rear area of the Hanoi Hilton. Forty-seven P.O.W.s moved into Room 7 of what was to be called Camp Unity.

The room was about seventy-eight feet long by twenty-three feet. There was a raised portion in the middle on which we were to put our straw mats for sleeping. Immediately after our arrival, ten-foot bamboo fences were erected forming small yards for each building.

At one end of the room was an enclosed old French-style toilet in which you had to mount the steps and squat over a hole. In addition, a fifty-five-gallon drum held the water used to wash down the latrine. Throughout the room were placed eight buckets in which we were to urinate. On one side of the room was one large window covered by a wire mesh screen. On the opposite side were three large windows covered with bamboo screens.

I looked around wondering what all the people were going to be like. I knew all by name, but I did not know what each was like personally. Sooner or later I would be able to clarify all the stories I had heard about Colonel Jim Hughes. He had prepared his bunk at one end of the room. Commander Stockdale was bunking at the opposite end of the room. They had been roommates, but here they were trying to get as far apart as possible.

Most of us talked long into the night. Later some put their mosquito nets up and went to bed, but our group—Paul Brudino, Bud Day, John McCain, Jim Kasler, George McKnight, and myself—just stood exchanging stories. A guard came to the door bars periodically and shouted, "Be silent, shleep, shleep quickly." Finally we decided it was time to end our first day together.

The need to organize was still apparent the following day, and it was decided to have four ranking officers with Colonel Vern Ligon in command, followed by Risner, Stockdale, and Denton. Five duty flights would be formed under them, each having a flight commander. Naturally there were disagreements. Paul Brudino said we should change the rules for determining who was senior because Risner was not the senior ranking officer and he felt Ligon did not deserve to be leading us because of his long un-willingness to take command while we were in Little Vegas.

I said to Paul, "Well, it depends on what rules have been es-tablished. As far as I know, at the Zoo, it was your rule to determine seniority according to your rank at the time you were shot down." He denied giving that order and insisted that Risner should be the ranking officer. "Well, that's the way it is now," I said, "unless, of course, the criteria for determining rank or seniority are revised."

In no time at all the fences were up and our routine started. The previous routine existed except we were allowed out twice a day for baths.

The baths were the catalyst for the first crisis. We were told by the North Vietnamese that we were to bathe with our shorts on. This restriction some of us decided was unnecessary. We normally washed with our clothes off and some of us wanted to continue to do so. Others, however, wore their short pants as they were told. In these discussions over minor things which seemed to grow gigantically out of proportion someone said, "they want us to, and besides it doesn't mean anything. There is no reason to rock the boat." The phrases "rocking the boat" and "causing a flap," I realized, would be used more and more as the two factions in the camp clashed over how we should conduct ourselves in a North Vietnamese prison.

In my first discussion with Colonel Risner he decided it was time for me to talk to Colonel Ligon. A meeting was arranged. I went with Colonel Risner to meet Commander Stockdale, Commander Denton, and Colonel Ligon. With crossed legs we sat in a circle ready to discuss the problems of what to do if we were caught communicating, of washing with or without our clothes, and of talking or laughing in normal tones. Colonel Ligon gave me a short lecture, and ended up saying: "You should try to be more disciplined in your conduct."

In an attempt to justify my actions I stated, "It is not a matter of disobeying. When the rule, decision, or judgment is made, you will not find anyone more disciplined than myself in following those orders." Moved by the urge to counter his statement questioning my discipline, I said, "It is discipline that enables a person to go through the ropes or wear the jumbo irons and, in the end, say 'no' to the North Vietnamese." The conversation ended with me agreeing to accept the final decisions of Colonel Ligon and he agreeing that we should establish a policy of resistance.

Our first concern was to dig a hole through the wall to the

next cell so that communications would be easier. Each flight would take turns during the night, digging the hole with a tool I fashioned from a heavy piece of wire. It was a very uncomfortable task because it was decided that we should drill the hole in a place underneath the platform of the latrine. Needless to say, no one was anxious to work squeezed underneath that smelly place. The area itself was surrounded by a wall which prevented the guards from seeing anyone at work, and the extra margin of safety was considered imperative. Each of us did take our turn in the flight, and the flights rotated every night. No one complained openly, but one person refused to work. It was Paul Brudino. For some reason, Paul decided that it was below his dignity to assist in drilling the hole, while everybody, including the high ranking staff officers, helped.

Each flight was a unit; we worked together and ate together. On the day we were scheduled to have our turn in the "pit," as it was called, we sat together having our second meal of the day. It was our custom to say grace before each meal. The day before, Colonel Risner's gratitude for the meager meal was expressed in a ten-minute prayer. It was Al Brady's turn to say grace this day. He started as Colonel Risner had, thanking God for this and thanking God for that, asking God to help us, the President, our families, and the boys in the South, and finally, just before he ended, he said in his most serious manner, "and please, God, please make the hole be finished before it's our turn again." It was great to begin the meal with laughter.

With all of us together, there was a definite increase in tension. The guards were constantly trying to keep us quiet and attempting to lessen our activity. The order was issued: We should go to sleep during the quiet hour, and only those who were playing cards or chess were allowed to stay up. If in fact you were not doing anything, you were to be on your own bunk. You were not allowed to watch any games or engage in conversation while walking in the room. I thought that this was a North Vietnamese order. It was not. Immediately the controversy flared once more. One faction thought we should show the North Vietnamese that we could control ourselves and therefore we would be able to get better treatment and more conveniences. The opposition announced, "We should impress the North Vietnamese not by our docile ways and our willingness to accept everything they insist upon, but with the fact that we resist being disgraced and humbled. We should do everything possible to show them we want nothing but to live a normal life in these prison walls. Our objective is not to solicit greater benefits but to regain respect."

It seemed almost ridiculous. Here we were in prison, forty-seven strong, still being intimidated by the North Vietnamese, now doing to ourselves those things they had failed to force upon individuals. Could it be that those who had failed so miserably were now to determine our conduct?

On the first Sunday after being united, we held a church service. Everyone participated. I was asked by George Coker to whistle a tune to accompany the Lord's Prayer as part of the program. I could look out at all the men standing in a semicircle at one end of the room. Many were wiping away tears. It was a good service. Fortunately, we were finishing when the guards came to insist that we be quiet.

To formulate a policy of resistance a committee was established. McKnight, Crayton, Tanner and I were chosen. As always, one's view of resistance was in accordance with his own experiences. Crayton and Tanner seemed to rely on the necessity to deceive and to avoid being tortured. George McKnight was one of the best, if not the best, resistor in the camp. He had experienced far more torture and in the long run had given less than most. His basic philosophy was to try. You were obligated to try and try.

Finally, it was my turn to speak, I indicated that the Code of Conduct was still our guide, still our standard, and nobody had the authority to change it. Our only obligation was to attempt to fulfill the guidelines as they existed and that meant following the Code of Conduct.

We talked about this for a while, and soon all were in agreement, the Code of Conduct was our primary guide for resisting. It was established that one would take torture in resisting the North Vietnamese in their attempt to make a gain. This, essentially, was the backbone of what later became Plum 3 of the Wing Guidelines.

The "plum" was a code word describing the policies for Camp Unity. Although it was first, when the plums were rewritten, it became known as Plum Number 3. The object was to minimize the North Vietnamese net propaganda gain and guard the camp's secrets, utilizing physical and mental strength, moral courage, and cover stories if necessary. However, it was also recognized that one would cease resisting physically prior to the loss of one's mental senses. At that point, one would be able to continue resisting by utlizing fabricated stories that seemed reasonable.

We also decided that it was in everybody's interest to resist self-induced punishment, such as kneeling on the floor or doing something that was harassing or physically uncomfortable. Simply stated, do not torture yourself. And, in the end, it was realized that even if you were defeated, the only obligation you had when again called upon was to try and try again.

One by one, the committees were organized. Discussions were taking place in all corners of the room. All of a sudden, in one corner where a number of high-ranking officers were congregating to form other committees, there was an argument. An angered Jim Hughes walked away from his group. I found out later from some of the other people that Jim was asked to form a psychological warfare committee. This was acceptable to him and he would do it. Then he found out that he was expected not only to lead the psychological warfare committee but to take all the actions and risks alone. The hierarchy wanted to establish a committee of one to take psychological warfare action against the North Vietnamese. It seemed unusual. He certainly should have people working for him rather than attempting to do it by himself. Stories of personality conflicts were emerging, and Jim Hughes was certainly one of the most controversial individuals in the group.

Later, Colonel Risner approached me. He said he wanted to talk about escape. We sat down, apart from everyone else. Before any discussion about escape could take place there was one point to clarify. I think he realized what I was going to say. I asked frankly, "Did you give the order not to escape without outside help?"

He said, "Yes."

"Before you tell me why," I continued, "I would like to tell you that I thought it was an order probably meant to cover a specific and very short time period. I thought it certainly was not to apply to us in the Zoo and the Zoo Annex a year or so later."

He replied, "Yes, that's right." He told me the circumstances involved. Two people were thinking about escape. It was an escape of opportunity. They had no plan, no material, no preparation, and no firm destination. Colonel Risner thought it best to delay them by suggesting they acquire outside help and a better plan.

Having breathed a sigh of relief, I told him that many people had actually used that as a primary means of determining their interest in escape. It depended on the individual himself, I added. If he was enthused and ready for escape, the order probably would not have deterred him; however, if he was looking for an excuse, that was the one commonly used.

But now there was a new situation. With all the effort to organize, I knew that sooner or later I would be approached concerning the question of escape. Colonel Risner told me that Colonel Stockman would be the escape committee head. It would be necessary for me to explain to Colonel Stockman the rationale for escape. In the meantime, Colonel Risner told me that I was to cooperate with the committee in preparing for an escape. The lines of communication would be outside the normal chain of command, and if I required assistance in the preparation for the escape I was to go to him. He said he knew that the escape committee would do a good job in developing the best possible plan for escape.

I accepted the job. It was understood that we would form our own communications net and that there would be someone unknown to us who would make the final "go," "no go" decision.

With that out of the way, our conversation drifted to the question of resistance and one another's experiences. He told me that he had been very close to doing anything the North Vietnamese wanted him to do. But for some reason they stopped and gave him the opportunity to recuperate. I respected Colonel Risner, because I realized that within him was that proper attitude which demands a constant effort.

His question was as direct as mine. "How were you able to do what others were incapable of doing?"

Colonel Risner had already explained to me that, in difficult times, he looked to God for help. He wanted to know from what source I received my strength. I told him, first, that perhaps I had an advantage in the fact that I had experienced the ropes and the beatings prior to reaching Hanoi. Before reaching Hanoi, I had to understand the factors which motivated me to take the beatings. I explained that there were primarily four factors—ambition, discipline, loyalty to purpose, and physical strength. "I want to make my own way within the military," I explained. "In order to do that, I had to do those things that were expected of me. If, in fact, I signed a confession or wrote a biography, or made propaganda tapes or did anything that would later be recognized as weakness, or if I acted not as a military man, I would not be considered for promotion. Within our society we both strive to attain some authority in order to contribute. I feel most confident as a military man contributing simply as a military man and fearing not death but failure." The second factor was discipline. We discussed the influence of our relatives, our backgrounds, our childhood, our growing up in high school, our playing of sports, and, finally, the people with whom we associated ourselves. I explained to Colonel Risner there is a difference between discipline and self-discipline. Most discipline comes about through fear of something, but, later with increased understanding there is a recognition of that which is best for you and the group. Therefore, fear is no longer the motivation behind being a disciplined individual. Self-discipline is complying with the best of two philosophies, your own and society's.

The third factor was loyalty to purpose. If I can determine that the purpose is of value, then the sacrifices and the willingness to accept death will be justified. He asked if that meant we were right in fighting the war with the North Vietnamese. I answered, "It's more basic than that, its the overall struggle between that which we recognize as our way of life and a way of life which others attempt to force upon us. It was simply a definition of freedom. Although the war is being waged here, the battle is being waged all over the world." To uphold our own ideas is the valid purpose.

The fourth factor was simply physical strength. Having listened to others, and having critically reviewed my experiences, physical strength appears as an important factor in being able to resist successfully.

Colonel Risner was ready to accept what I said, perhaps because I had been talking for so long. "But that's not all," I persisted. There was a necessity to re-evaluate those motives because I knew things would become more difficult, especially after my second escape. That awareness of stark reality caused a reversal in the first and third factors. Loyalty to purpose became the greatest motivating force. Discipline remained number two, and ambition became number three. Physical strength remained number four. It was the conviction that purpose was paramount that justified the sacrifices.

I thought he would tire of this lengthy conversation, but Colonel Risner leaned forward and said, "I am very disappointed in our younger people." I was surprised to hear him say that and I inquired, "Why?" He said that he had heard stories of younger officers not putting up a sufficient battle in order to resist the enemy's attempt to gain propaganda at their expense.

I said, "That may be so. We both know that most of us were acting as individuals or in small groups, but it should be remembered that the performance of the younger people is simply a reflection of the leadership. If they do well, it can be said that the leadership was good, but if they do poorly, I think the only conclusion is that the leadership or the example is absent. That is the test for however long we are here. We can determine if the leadership is good or bad by witnessing the performance of all; one is proportionate with the other. Good leadership offers good performance and poor performance will invariably reflect poor leadership."

We studied each other momentarily. "We'll see. Thank you, John."

I respectfully replied, "Yes, sir. I thank you." As I walked away I wondered if he would have the opportunity to lead.

Colonel Hervey Stockman approached me the day after I had my discussion with Colonel Risner.

"John, do you have a few minutes?"

"Yes, sir."

And as we sat down he looked around, insuring that no one was within hearing distance. He said, "I noticed you were talking with Colonel Risner yesterday. I suppose you know I have been appointed head of the escape committee."

I said, "Yes, sir."

Colonel Stockman said, "I don't know what Colonel Risner

told you, but I would like to assure you that I was not put here to discourage any escape."

I said, "Yes, sir. . . . I understand."

For some reason he thought it necessary to repeat, "I am not here to dampen the idea of escape. We are going to try to do the best we can. I would like your philosophy on escape. Do you think it can be done?" Before I could answer he continued, "Just give me your ideas so I can form some opinions. Perhaps we can go about this properly and succeed."

I said, "Yes, sir. I'd be glad to talk it over with you. What would you like to know first?"

"Well, give me the philosophy behind escape. I'm not sure I understand why we must escape."

I said immediately, "It's not a matter of why we must escape but a matter of why we should want to escape."

He said, "Good, go ahead."

I began, "First of all, there's the Code of Conduct. Let's first consider that. I, as we all do, regard the Code of Conduct as our main guide. I do not have it memorized, but there are a few lines I do remember. The first, of course, is 'I am an American fighting man.' I do not know really what follows, but I think that is sufficient for starters. The one thing that I do know and that I have memorized is this—I believe it is the third article of the Code of Conduct—'If I am captured, I will continue to resist by all means available. I will make every effort to escape and aid others to escape.' "

"It's not the most important thing," he said.

"Yes, I agree."

"We have to take care of ourselves first," he said.

I said, "Yes, that's right and I think we've done that. When our physical or mental health is jeopardized, that will be our primary concern. But at the present time, we are all healthy enough to accomplish that which is specified for us in the Code of Conduct. The Code ends, I believe, in the same manner—'I will never forget that I am an American fighting man.' Considering that, I would imagine that our only obligation is to attempt to fulfill the Code of Conduct."

"But can it be done?" he asked.

"Yes, I think it can, but it depends on the effort we're willing to expend. With all the brain power, with all the possible help available in this room, we can increase our chances of success. Even with the limited resources that we had in the Zoo Annex, Ed and I were able to walk past any number of North Vietnamese and get four miles away. The reason we were not able to get any farther than that was our mistake."

"What was that?"

"We simply did not know how to tell time. We stopped before we were able to get out of a five-mile security circle. I know," I said, "the next thing you're going to say is that there are millions of people out there. The fact is we can be a couple or three or five or whatever of those millions. You see, it has already been done."

"You know, a lot of people don't agree with you."

"Yes, sir, I am aware of that, but if you look at the record, you'll find only one expert. For success, there are two most important considerations, but the purpose of escape is so basic that it can not be denied. There must be leadership and the will."

"What is the purpose, John?"

"Freedom! Realizing the complexity and uncertainty of our situation, can we deny anyone the opportunity of attempting to gain freedom?"

There was a long pause. It seemed as if Colonel Stockman was groping for the answer. Finally he said, "You know, John, the conditions are improving in the camp, as we can well see. Do you think that we would be jeopardizing that situation by escape?"

"That's very possible," I said. "But it all depends on which is more important to us, honor and respect or an extra bowl of green soup. You know," I added, "gaining recognition for our leadership should be our number one objective. How fast do you think the North Vietnamese Camp commander would start talking with our leaders if there was an escape from this Camp? The respect for ourselves and the leadership is gained only through resistance."

"Well, as far as I know now," he said, "our leaders are backing the escape effort."

As he rose to leave, Colonel Stockman said, "If you do not know already, the committee is already formed. I'm heading that committee. There's you, Coker, George McKnight, Bud Day, and Jim Kasler. We'll get together and hash this thing out. I'm sure we'll be able to accomplish something."

"Yes, sir. I think we can, as I said, only if we want to."

George Coker came hustling up to me. "I guess we're in business again."

"It certainly seems that way," I answered.

He said, "You know, I've been talking to a bunch of people. They all have a hell of a lot of respect for you. You shouldn't judge some of them so harshly."

I said, "What do you mean by that?"

"Well, for example, I remember what you were saying about Dick Stratton. You know, that guy's gone through hell."

I said, "I'm sure he's a good man."

"Oh, yes, he is, and I wish you'd talk to him."

I said, "Well, the time will come."

"Oh, there's another guy who wants to talk to you," George said.

"Who's that?" I replied.

"Jim Hughes," he said.

I said, "Oh, that's interesting. You know, a lot of people don't particularly care for him."

"Yeah, well, you ought to give him a chance to talk to you," George said.

"Well, what's the problem?" I asked.

"Well, I think the biggest problem," George explained, "is that in your case, you did not break, so you can push many of the things you talk about. In his case, he says some of the same things but people don't appreciate it because his record isn't as good as yours."

"By the way, what was the trouble between him and Stockdale?" I inquired.

"Oh, I think it was over communications. Hughes didn't want Stockdale to communicate. He was afraid of reprisals. They just got at each other's nerves to such an extent that now they hate each other's guts."

"Well, Little George, this next year ought to be very interesting."

After hours of conversation with Tom Kirk I walked away

with only one of Tom's comments churning in my mind: "All I wanted to do was to sit in the corner of the cell, and I didn't give a damn if that door never opened. All I wanted them to do was to leave me alone." It was a common syndrome of those who attempted to regress and forget their imprisonment.

Late that night, I talked to John McCain when most of the others were asleep. John McCain's story was a little different. Here is one of the true heroes, I thought. He was crippled, as severely as anyone in that camp, yet, when given the opportunity to accept parole he refused.

Others before him had accepted certain privileges and had fulfilled the requirements demanded by their captors, but by refusing to abandon his ideals, principles, and strengths John McCain had retained his identity.

Finally, it was time to go to bed, and the "Prince" departed. That was the name given to John by the North Vietnamese. His Dad was Commander in Chief of the Pacific Forces, and in the outlook of the North Vietnamese, the son of such a high-ranking officer must be a prince. And I believed them. Although John limped, he walked with an air of dignity.

After the dishes were washed and the guards locked us in for the last time, on Tuesday, February 3, Commander Stockdale approached me as I walked up and down one of the aisles. I had always admired Commander Jim Stockdale. He was one of those rare individuals who had resistance foremost in his mind. He asked me if I was going to attend the church services to be held the coming Sunday. It was expected that the guards would again try to stop us. This time, we had a plan.

"Yes, sir, of course," I answered.

Commander Stockdale and I agreed that it was not the church service that was at stake. We were in fact, fighting for permission to live. We agreed that the church service was the lever which we were going to use, to attempt to pry additional privileges from our captors.

He said, "It is necessary to have one-hundred percent participation."

I asked, "Is the intention to carry it through?"

Both of us realized that any privilege gained would be lost if there was not the willingness to carry through with the planned program. If one of the senior ranking officers was pulled out of the room, that should not stop us from having church services in the future. We were also required, according to the plan, to make some display of discontent when a senior officer was removed from the room. Persistence was the key to success. As always, before the discussion ended, the subject of resistance was raised.

Inquisitively he asked, "Did you make some news tapes?"

I answered, "No."

He gave me a doubting smile and looked at me as if to say, "You're really kidding, aren't you?"

Knowing what he was thinking without saying the words, I said, "No, sir, I did *not* make any tapes."

He replied, "You know they can get anything they want out of you."

I said, "That may be true for most. However, I do not think so. I think if mentally prepared, some may accept death before disgrace."

He nodded his head and, without carrying the discussion any further, departed.

Everyone views resistance in the light of his own experience of imprisonment, I thought. For Commander Stockdale, who felt he was a very strong soldier, it was difficult to believe that some were capable of sustaining themselves in the torturous situations in which so many had succumbed.

I wondered if it was a coincidence that later that night Jim Hughes approached me and asked if I would like to play chess. We sat down, cross-legged opposite one another, and began to play, not saying very much. In a short time I announced "checkmate."

While the pieces remained on the board, Jim Hughes began what he had set out to do—engage in a conversation that involved letters, resistance, signing for soap, and a number of other things. He first wanted to know if I had received any letters from home.

I said, "No, I have not."

He asked if I had written any letters.

I said, "No, I have not written any letters. Up until recently I was never offered the opportunity to write."

He asked, "Do you intend to write?"

"I do not know, Jim. It depends on the situation at the time. You see, I have strong feelings about this. It is my opinion that the letters are being used by the North Vietnamese possibly to make inroads into our own families at home. I am certainly not going to help the North Vietnamese propagandize our own people."

Over the long run letters caused more anguish for those who participated in that program than any other single issue. Some were angered because they could not write what they wanted to write. Others wrote and were angry because there would not be any return mail for six months or eight months, in some cases a year or more. Knowing that the letters were a gain for the enemy, the rationale presented for writing was "My family needs it." I wondered.

"As a matter of fact," I said, "our only responsibility is to take care of ourselves. I am sure there are many good people attempting to help our families at home. They certainly would not want us to jeopardize our own situation in an attempt to help them."

I suspected that most of the letters and pictures found their way to various agencies and files in North Vietnam.

I thought I had answered his question, but again Jim asked me, "Are you going to write?"

I said, "It depends on the situation, Jim."

Once Jim started to talk, I understood why I was asked to play chess, to listen. Did Jim think that resistance was now meaningful because of our strength in numbers, or was he compensating for his own past performance? I couldn't tell.

There were two points he wanted to make. In reference to himself he said, "As long as there is one man there is hope." And later he said, "When the time comes you will not be able to rely on many people." Continuing his talk, he likened the situation to the GI's in World War II, and explained that many times in order to get their way and pacify the populace in Germany, the GI's gave the people Hershey bars. He said seriously, "Now do you know what those Hershey bars have turned into?"

I said, "No."

He said sharply, "Milk." As he waved his finger around the room, he said, "Watch them in the morning. We are getting warm milk in the morning from the North Vietnamese. The North Vietnamese are doing what we were doing in World War II with the Hershey bars." Sneering, he said, "They are buying their way. It worked in Germany, and you will see it work here." In an even more contemptuous manner he said, "We will not give up our milk to resist. Resistance will become a dirty word."

I interrupted, "Jim, you can't say that. You know damn right well there are people here who have gone through hell."

At this point, Hughes was perturbed. He said, "Now you are playing conversational ping-pong."

The conversation ended. I walked away annoyed. I certainly did not intend our conversation to end on that note. Later I became aware that most of my discussions with Jim Hughes ended with my "playing conversational ping-pong."

It was not easy to dismiss a man like Jim Hughes from my mind. I wondered if what he said would be true, that "resistance will become a dirty word." In time is it possible that hot milk in the morning would become more important than the Code of Conduct?

After Jim Kasler told a number of stories about shooting down MIG's during the Korean War, I found myself sitting next to Paul Brudino. He asked if I was ever at Myrtle Beach Air Force Base.

I said, "Yes, I was there for quite some time."

The next question he asked was rather surprising. He said, "Did you ever hear of me?"

I hesitated for a moment and said, "Yes, of course, you were the senior ranking officer at the Zoo."

Chuckling, he said, "Oh, no, no, before we were shot down."

I thought for a moment, embarrassed because I could not remember where I had known Paul Brudino. Finally I said no.

He said, "You mean you never heard of me? I was at Myrtle Beach one time."

I said, "Well, it's possible, but perhaps I was in Turkey at that time."

"Did you know that I shot down two airplanes in World War II?"

"No," I said, repeating his statement, "I did not know you shot down two airplanes in World War II."

I thought his questions were a bit unusual. He seemed like a two-bit performer acting coy and trying, I imagine, in one way or another, to be modest. But I sat there listening, interested in the next surprise.

He said, "Of course, you know that I was the S.R.O. of the Zoo."

I nodded my head.

"Why didn't you tell me that you were going to escape?"

Apologizing, I said, "That really was not my decision." Regaining my confidence, I said, "As a matter of fact, I thought it was a good decision. The communications were not really that good, and apparently Trautman felt that it was best to keep it within the Zoo Annex."

Paul puckered his large lips, wrinkled his brow, cocked his head, and said, "Well, I would have given you the O.K. to go anyway."

I thought that interesting also, since the question as to whether he would have given Ed and me permission to escape was not raised.

Then he put his arm around me and said, "You know, I have a son in the Air Force. I think he is in South Vietnam now."

I said, "I hope he makes it all right."

Paul drew me close, looked at me, and said, "I wish my son would be like you."

Feeling self-conscious, I said again, "I'm sure he'll make out all right."

Paul pressed my shoulder and said, "No, no, I'm not kidding. I've heard what you went through and I think that they killed Ed Atterberry. A lot of guys have talked about escaping but you did it. I want you to know that I really love you, I love you like a son and if there is anything that I can ever do for you—" He paused and said, "I can do it."

"Thank you very much, Paul, and I'm thankful for the fact that you are not angry with me considering what happened after the escape."

He said, "Oh no, that wasn't your fault at all."

I lowered my head so that the tears in my eyes were not noticed and I said, "I am relieved that you feel that way." I said, "Goodnight, see you tomorrow."

Paul patted me on the back and said, "Goodnight."

I wiped the tears away with the back of my hand, hoping no one was watching. One could make great sacrifices for people like Paul, I thought.

I felt bad that we had not told him about the escape so that he could be part of it. He said that during the time he was trying to convince the North Vietnamese that he had nothing to do with the escape they told him that he did very well, that they were surprised that there was such a chain of communications, and that we were able to prepare, organize, plan, and execute such an escape.

It seemed that he was genuinely proud of it all, and I felt good that he did not feel any animosity toward me because of the torture he had experienced as a result of the escape. I went to sleep that night thinking about Paul Brudino and looking forward to the next time we could sit down and talk. He'll be a nice guy to know, I thought.

In the first week in February the tension seemed to be mounting. The guards were being harassed by some of the prisoners as they came into the cell to make their daily count. We were simply expected to stay in place as the guard moved around the room to ensure that his count was correct. Usually Bud Day, John McCain, and Jack Fellowes were the ones who snickered and made snide remarks as the guards made their rounds. Things really have changed, I thought; the prisoners now harass the guards.

One day, after being locked in for the last time, one of the guards decided to get up on a ladder, poke his head through the bars of one of the large windows, and shout, "Be silent, be silent!"

Suddenly Jim Lamar, Hervey Stockman, and Pete Schoeffel jumped up and began shouting, cursing and threatening the guard with their fists. The guard was utterly amazed. I was dumbfounded also, because such behavior was totally out of character for these men. I was wondering what in the world are they trying to do. I was especially astonished to see Hervey Stockman, head of the escape committee. If he was attempting to plan an escape, he certainly was not going about it in the right manner.

That night I had a talk with Jim Kasler. I regarded Jim as one of the strongest. He was badly banged up when he ejected from his airplane and refused to submit to the North Vietnamese.

On one occasion he explained that Fidel, a notorious Cuban interrogator, insisted that he choose between Ho Chi Minh and President Johnson. Each time Jim chose President Johnson, he would be beaten severely. Time and time again he suffered the beatings until finally Jim chose Ho Chi Minh. The real test came the next time Fidel asked, "Ho Chi Minh or President Johnson?" When Jim Kasler said "President Johnson," Fidel realized he had won a battle but not the war.

As we parted I hoped Jim would be able to influence some of the others. As a Korean ace and a well-known tactical fighter pilot, he commanded a great deal of respect.

On Saturday, February 6, we were briefed by our flight commanders. Colonel Risner, George Coker, and Howie Rutledge would lead the church program. We would attempt to continue the program to the end. If anyone was pulled out, then we were to show our disenchantment by singing "God Bless America." We would continue having church services and continue singing as long as people were pulled out. If necessary we were to continue until the last man was pulled out of the room.

On February 7, 1971, we had our church service. While the service was in progress I could hear the scurrying outside. There were no loud noises, and the singing was normal, but the guards were excited. It was apparent they did not know what to do.

Ladders appeared and guards climbed up into the windows to look down into the large cell. As the church service continued, some guards scribbled on pads of paper. Colonel Risner, Howie Rutledge, and George Coker were leading the service. That was not difficult to determine.

When the services were finished, guards gathered, the doors opened and Colonel Risner, Howie Rutledge, and George Coker were removed to Heartbreak Hotel. As they left the room there was a loud cheer, "Hip hip hurray! hip hip hurray! hip hip hurray!" As the door clanged closed, everyone joined in with "God Bless America . . ."

The day's routine continued but with increased harassing of the guards, more shouting, and defiant singing out at times. The day dragged on with the tension rising as the hours passed.

Outside the guards were stirring again. They seemed confused. Many of the prisoners inside the room stood there with wide-eyed amazement, being carried along by the tide of emotion. I could tell as I stood near the door listening that the whole camp was quiet, listening, waiting, wondering what Room 7 would do next.

That night the tension rose even more. Guards stationed themselves on ladders in the windows. No one among us was willing or able to grasp the reins of leadership. Sporadically the singing and shouting continued by first one person, then a small group, and then picked up by another group on the other side of the room.

Then all of a sudden, Paul Brudino, seemingly electrified into action, shouted in a high-pitched voice, "This is Room Number 7, where the hell is 6? This is Room Number 7, where the hell is 6?"

When Room Number 6 picked up the chant, the walls in Room 7 amplified the sudden roar of satisfaction. A cheer accompanied each room's entry.

"This is Room Number 6, where the hell is 5?"

"This is Room Number 5, where the hell is 4?"

"This is Room Number 4, where the hell is 3?"

"This is Room Number 3, where the hell is 2?"

"This is Room Number 2, where the hell is 1?"

"This is Room Number 1, where the hell is Zero?"

Suddenly there was complete silence. Room Zero housed our high ranking colonels. The guards looked at one another, not knowing what to expect. First they were enclosed in sound, and now the camp was hushed. I could feel my muscles tighten. Everyone stopped breathing and listened.

Faintly at first, from the far corner of the camp we heard, "This is Room Number Zero, where the hell is 7?" Our roar of approval must have alerted all of Hanoi. The riot was on. The Marine song, the Navy song, the Air Force song, college songs, fight songs, every cheer that one could think of was heard that night. Bedlam reigned but sleep conquered, and finally it was quiet.

When the first rays of light streaked through the bars, we knew what the North Vietnamese had decided. Soldiers with fixed bayonets, gas masks, and hand grenades strapped to their sides assembled outside our cell. I counted 25 soldiers in our courtyard. What was next?

As the soldiers stood ready outside, Bug entered the room. Calmly he said, "Be quiet, sit down and listen to me." Immediately everybody did exactly that, and I knew we were on the road to defeat, for it had been decided that we would acknowledge only the orders of the acting S.R.O., thereby forcing the interrogator or guard to seek our seniors. Of course, the plan also required that the S.R.O. be available to relay any orders. Colonel Ligon was in the middle of the group as the Bug motioned everyone to move to the far end of the cell.

I mentioned to one of the Flight Commanders standing next to me, "We are not supposed to be moving; we are not supposed to be reacting."

The reply was, "Shh, forget it." Everybody moved to the rear of the room. Jim Lamar, quiet John Finlay, Hervey Stockman, and Pete Schoeffel were removed at bayonet point.

For the rest of the day, one by one, most of us were questioned. There were two rooms being used as interrogating rooms. The guards with their fixed bayonets lined a corridor to each room. The treatment was the same for all of us. We were told that we were criminals. We were to obey the camp regulations and any violation of the camp regulations would bring severe punishment.

I simply stated, "I understand," and was permitted back into the room.

In the moves that followed Harry Jenkins emerged as the senior ranking officer in the room. Harry was one of the old Alcatraz Gang. According to George McKnight, not the strongest of the Alcatraz Gang, but in any case he was recognized as a good resistor, having been associated with that group. He was very tall and skinny, with a long thin face and a large jaw. Perhaps fearing the aftermath of other alternatives, Harry decided it was now time to fast.

This had been Jerry Denton's idea. He believed in dieting and fasting to gain attention. I did not. Jerry Denton was as tough as they come, but to me, fasting was not resisting.

Looking up at Harry, I said, "We are going to require every bit of strength to continue our resistance. Fasting is no option, its simply a program of self-induced torture."

He explained, "Back in Alcatraz, it always helped. When we needed some medical treatment we went into a fast and it worked."

I said, "If I recall the story correctly you also shouted *Poxy*, the North Vietnamese word for doctor, a number of times. So you really can't tell whether it was the fast or whether it was the shouting that got results."

It was decided, the fast was the way to lodge our protest. On the first day the effects of the fast were noticeable. There were those who required their day-to-day rations just to keep them going. The rations were not much and any reduction would certainly be disastrous. People began to be listless and a little more argumentative. Most just lay down and did nothing, waiting.

I looked outside. The guards were all there sitting on a large cement bench we usually sat on when we were outside.

On the second day the Bug removed the barrel of water we used to wash the latrine. His next move was to diminish our drinking water.

During my discussion with Harry I explained, "The worst thing that we could do is to beg for relief from our own mistake."

It now seemed inevitable. People became more irritable, some stood up, became light-headed, and fell over. Others said nothing and began to retreat into their own little worlds. And then, as the conditions became more difficult, the verbal battles increased. "Why should we do it? What are we accomplishing? What are we resisting?" These were the questions that were asked. Others complained, "Things were getting better. We screwed it up for ourselves." Another common statement was "Little by little the North Vietnamese will make concessions." Yes, that was true, but only at a price.

If we did as we were told, little by little we could expect a chair, a radio, or a loudspeaker in our courtyard. Many in the room were now willing to do as the Bug told me once before, "sit on the end of your bunk and do nothing." And that's exactly what they wanted us to do. Do nothing, be fed, and receive what was coming "step by step." On the third day Harry Jenkins decided to ask for food and water.

The doors clanged, the guards threw open the doors, and Bug strutted into the room with a couple of his armed guards. His little smile of confidence was the herald of our defeat. He said that he would give us some food and water, but because our stomachs would not be able to take the "good food," we would have only rice soup for the next two meals. Bug accepted the room's groan with a wider smile. Everyone ate the watery rice soup eagerly and looked forward to regular rations the next day. The regular rations probably would be greens, a loaf of bread, and a small side dish consisting of fried squash, but anything would be welcome after rice soup.

The disappointing thing about the fast was that no one was "quizzed." The North Vietnamese had not the faintest idea why we were not eating. Their only concern was that it was over. If we had been able to persist, perhaps we would have been able to air our grievances. As it was now, they were not heard.

Things settled down into what could be called a normal routine. People began playing chess and bridge—and I decided to make an

American flag. It seemed to me there was a necessity to reaffirm our identity, to be able to see and touch that which was American, to again be reminded that we were American fighting men. Red Wilson gave me the idea when I recalled his words, "Do we need a symbol?" I thought, perhaps in normal times Red was right but in difficult times, when all you hold of value is being threatened, that is the time to hold symbols high. What better symbol would there be than the flag of the United States of America.

Because the North Vietnamese did not allow me to receive packages and letters from home, many shared with me their news and gifts. Likable Norland Daughtery gave me a bright red nylon set of underwear he had received from his wife. This was the material used for the red stripes.

On a brick I sharpened a soft piece of copper wire found in the yard. The other end was flattened and pierced with a sharp nail. I now had an excellent needle.

From a blue sweater provided me by the North Vietnamese I cut out a small rectangular patch. The thread which was used to embroider the stars onto the blue field was pulled from a small white towel, and heavier yellow thread pulled from a blanket made a perfect gold border. All my bits and pieces were carefully stitched onto a white handkerchief so that white stripes showed through the properly placed red strips of cloth.

Each evening for a week and a half, sitting with crossed legs and my back toward the windows to hide my work from the guards, I fashioned the symbol of freedom, the freedom flag. When I finished, I sewed it inside my mosquito net to hide it during the cell inspections by the North Vietnamese.

This symbol of freedom was my most prized possession. It was the most beautiful thing in all of communist North Vietnam.

A small committee was formed to arrange for Bob Shumaker's sixth anniversary in prison. Bob Shumaker was shot down on February 11, 1966. He had been a captive longer than any other American prisoner except Everett Alvarez, another Navy pilot. I was asked to give a toast to honor Bob. Naturally there were some who protested, fearing reprisals by the Bug. But Harry said that he would simply explain to Bug that it was only an anniversary party and nothing more. I was glad that we were going through with the anniversary but disappointed in the motive.

After the meal that evening, I stood up and announced to everyone, "A soldier is a man, aware of the cause and willing to make the necessary sacrifices. I know a man who is aware of the cause and continues to make the sacrifices. My toast is to a soldier, a fine man, and a great American—Bob Shumaker."

That started off our party. Jack Fellowes presented a skit and Harry Jenkins read a poem. Immediately, the guards were up in the windows, but they did not come in to stop us. When it was over the guards came in and escorted Harry Jenkins, Jack Fellowes, and me to "the Bug's house," a small interrogation shack in our courtyard. Under a bare lightbulb, the Bug was waiting with his head lowered. We walked into the room, stood behind his table, and waited for him to address us.

Finally, he asked what we were doing. With his long neck stretched forward, Harry nervously launched into a long monologue, telling Bug that we were simply celebrating Shumaker's sixth anniversary. I could see that the Bug was becoming bored and mad with Harry's chatter. His right eye began to close, transforming the Bug into Cyclops. Bug's head suddenly snapped up. Glaring at Harry, he shouted, "Shut your mouth, shut your mouth!" Harry tried to persist, and at this the Bug jumped from his chair and screamed, "Shut your mouth!" More calmly he said, "You will do nothing. If you want, you must ask the camp authority's permission."

That, indeed, was the crux of the whole matter. Asking for everything that they very well knew we needed is tantamount to complete domination and our total defeat.

The Bug turned his attention to Jack Fellowes and accused him of being a troublemaker. We were dismissed.

On February 12, Harry Jenkins and Mulligan were removed from the room. They were the next two highest ranking officers. Bill Franke was now the senior ranking officer in cell Number 7 of the Hanoi Hilton.

Thanks to internal pressures and assistance, Bill Franke did well as a leader. The guards would seek him before attempting to issue instructions. In turn, Franke would ask the group to sit so that the head count could be taken. The impression was that the North Vietnamese did not want to cause us any difficulties. Perhaps the rules governing our treatment were changing to our favor.

But we were always pushing Bill for a number of things, to salute an American flag that I made, to have choir practice, to have church services, and finally to go no further than to simply sit of the edge of our bunks for the head count.

Sometime in the first week of March a committee was formed to write and post on a wall inside the cell as much of the Geneva Conventions as could be recalled. Part of the scheme was to allow the guards to find it so that the North Vietnamese would be aware of our wanting treatment in accordance with the Geneva Conventions.

While the Geneva Conventions were being drafted, there were other things to occupy one's mind—our first chess tournament; Ben Pollard, who was the radar operator for my old cellmate, Don Heiliger, taught thermodynamics; French and Spanish classes started; and Dick Stratton began a series of talks on government and American history.

It was after one of these talks by Dick Stratton that I had an opportunity to talk to Mel Moore, a Navy pilot. I knew that before the move to Camp Unity, Mel had disassociated himself from the Bug's Desert Inn propaganda group. Bug removed him so that he would not be able to influence the others in the Desert Inn. I considered any self-made decision to resist a tremendous boost for morale. Now having had the opportunity to talk with Mel I found him to be an interesting, intelligent, kind, and very honest person.

Mel and I decided to play one game of chess before turning in that night. As we played the game, Jim Hughes squatted nearby to watch. Hughes slept next to Moore, and I slept head to head with Hughes on the other side of the cement sleeping platform.

When the game was finished I walked for a while observing our little world. Here within this single room was probably a microcosm of American society. The ramifications and psychological forces at play within a normal society could probably be found right here. Motivations could easily be distinguished because they were stripped of complex social trappings and accentuated by the constant pressure of uncertainty.

I sat down and listened to Bud Day's story of his escape and evasion when he was first captured. It was a fascinating story told by a fascinating character. He had one arm that was mutilated. He looked like a man who at one time had the strength and determination of an ox, but right now he was something less. However, when the time came, I thought, he would be able to provide some leadership, because certainly a good portion of the men respected Bud Day. Where some had not shown the wear and tear, Bud Day had. He had a rugged face to begin with, but now it looked even more rugged from the beatings he had absorbed.

When the story ended and conversation drifted to other subjects, Paul Brudino turned to me and said, "Hey, what's wrong with you?"

I replied, "What do you mean?"

He said, "You know you are hanging around with the wrong people."

"I still do not know what you are referring to."

"I saw you yesterday talking to Jim Hughes and today you're talking to Mel Moore. Those guys are bad, bad guys."

Smiling, I said, "Hell, Paul, there is no reason to cut off conversation with those people. Mel is a pretty smart guy and it always helps to know what the heck Jim Hughes is thinking."

Paul persisted, saying, "Listen, John, you've got a great future. There's no sense in hanging around with the wrong people now."

I smiled again and said, "Well, I don't think you have to worry about that."

I was ready to say that I in fact respected Mel Moore when Paul interrupted and said, "Do you know that guy is going to adopt some North Vietnamese brat when he gets back to the States?"

To go along with Paul and even more amused than I was at the start of our conversation, I said, "No," as if astonished by something that was a totally unthinkable act by a P.O.W.

Encouraged by my pseudo-enthusiasm, Paul eagerly continued, "Not only that, the guy is a fucking socialist."

I gasped, "Nooo kidding! Well," I said, "I'll try to be more careful."

Satisfied, Paul changed the subject and asked, "Have you ever been to Japan?"

"No, I've never been stationed there."

"That's too bad. I'll have to tell you some stories about that place. It's a great place."

Just then John McCain grabbed me from behind. Every once in a while he would come up from behind me and tackle me or jump on my back. We struggled with each other, rolling over rice mats. Our wrestling bout had started.

It was a lot of fun grappling like kids with John. Talking seriously, joking, or now with a little roughhouse, John McCain was always great company.

One morning I was awake before dawn. Often pans rattled as the kitchen help began to prepare the first meal of the day. So there was usually quite a bit of noise before the gong would ring. Then we were expected to get up, fold our nets, and put them in place.

While I was awake listening to all the noise, I noticed that John McCain climbed out of his net and staggered to the end of the room to find a bucket. I thought this was an opportune time to play a little joke on him. I climbed out of my net and into his. Pulling the covers up over my head so that he would not be able to see me, I waited. Still sleepy-eyed, John walked right up to his net and was ready to climb in when he noticed that there was someone under the blankets. I peeked up over the covers watching him. He hesitated, rubbed his face, and moved to the next bunk. Realizing that one was not his, he went to the net on the other side of his own. That one was not his either. He went down to mine, two places away from his own. It was empty but he knew it was not his. Confused, he returned to his own, stood there scratching his head, looking from one mosquito net to another. Finally, he heard me giggling. He charged in under the net, ripped the blankets off and yelled, "Get out! Get out of my bed, you Wop!"

I scrambled out of bed laughing and yelling back at him, "You dumb Irishman, you don't even know your own bed."

Finally, the gong sounded, and as usual, Jim Hughes reared and yelled out as loud as he could, "Ahh ha, Santa Fe!" Immediately someone imitated his cry, shouting "Ahh ha, loony bin!" I did not like Jim's early morning outbursts, but if they made him feel better that was fine with me. I could see already that it was going to be an interesting day. It was March 17, 1971.

The Geneva Conventions were printed and had been posted for the last two days.

The first thing for most of us was to do some exercises. John McCain, two bunks down, hopped on his one good leg attempting to run-in-place. At his side I would imitate his awkward exercise. He'd come hopping over on his crippled leg and tap me on the head for my insolence. While we were there, he turned, still running-in-place, and said, "Just look, look at it."

"Look at what, John?"

"Look from one end of this room to the other. This place is a madhouse, look at it." And so I did. A Marine officer very carefully folded his things, straightening out corners, patting this and patting that. Render Crayton, a ghostly looking fellow, was slowly stacking his unused hoard of soap. At one end Rob Doremus "exercised." Lying on his back with his legs elevated he wiggled his toes and fingers. Some were jumping, some were running-in-place, others were doing push-ups, and a small group practiced their handstands. The communicators were writing notes to be passed later in the day. And some scribbled on toilet paper preparing for the Spanish or French lessons.

John McCain shook his head saying, "The folks back home will never believe it!" For such a small group the variety of ideas, activities, and personalities was fantastic. No two people did anything the same way. And in the middle of it all, Jim Hughes strolled up and down the aisles, looking like a ragpicker.

John was right. If someone looked in for the first time, he wouldn't believe his eyes.

After the preliminary chores, we were allowed outside to bathe. In his usual walk-around inspection, Hawk spotted the printed Geneva Conventions and calmly tore the piece of paper from the wall. As he walked out of the room and past the bathing area, Bud Day created a commotion by badgering Hawk for his actions. Jim Hughes was in the process of bathing when he heard that the document was ripped off the wall. Caught up in the confusion and excitement, he suddenly startled everyone by screaming at the top of his lungs, "Fuck Ho Chi Minh!" Everyone turned in astonishment, not sure what had happened.

The guards probably heard Ho Chi Minh's name but were equally confused. Perhaps his cry might have gone unnoticed, but with overwrought emotion he bellowed again, "Fuck Ho Chi Minh, fuck Ho Chi Minh!" That did it. The Bug and his armed guards rushed into our yard. As soon as we were inside the guards heavily pounced upon Jim, bound his hands, and dragged him off to Heartbreak.

The reactions were mixed throughout the cellblock. Paul Brudino was calling him a "fucking crazy bastard"; others exclaimed "that nut." Most everyone was in agreement that Jim had brought it on himself, that he should not have done it, and he would have to pay for it, but the big question now was: What are we going to do if they begin to torture him?

On one side, "He deserves what he is going to get."

On the other side, "That makes no difference. The fact is, he is still one of us."

I talked to Mel Moore. He said, "John, you are wasting your time. Most of the people in here think Jim is a nut anyway, and if you expect anybody to make any effort over him you're wrong."

As it turned out, that is exactly the way it was. No one was willing to make an effort for an American, especially a crazy American.

Late that afternoon we heard the screams and moans. Jim Hughes was being whipped and beaten in a Heartbreak cell right next to ours. We did nothing.

It was a dismal day. Everyone was mad at Jim Hughes and a few of us were mad at everyone else because we did nothing. We were allowing an American to be tortured right in front of us without even reacting or lifting an eyebrow. Unity before self, I thought, hogwash.

On the next day, March 18, all lieutenant colonels and Navy commanders were removed; that included Bill Franke and Mel Moore. I was really sorry to see Mel go for a number of reasons. He was a good conversationalist, and he was my Spanish teacher.

The following day, on March 19, 37 men were moved from Camp Unity, including John McCain, Bud Day, and Jack Fellowes from our room. The North Vietnamese had kept careful notes over the last month and had identified McCain, Day, and Fellowes as obvious troublemakers.

Paul Brudino was in command of Room 7. Also in the month of March 1971, Colonel Flynn took command of what was referred to as Camp Unity in the Hanoi Hilton. With him, Colonel Winn, Colonel Gaddis, Colonel Bean, all the lieutenant colonels and Navy commanders were now located on the south side of the camp. Rumors began to fly when it was announced that Colonel Flynn was now in command. At one time prior to his taking command, we had received the message, "Don't trust Colonel Flynn with camp secrets."

McKnight, Coker, and I knew that we tried every possible way to make contact with the four colonels when they were in Little Vegas. We were unsuccessful and not because of a lack of effort. We went out of our way, taking far greater risks than should have been necessary. At times it seemed that George McKnight was going to batter down the wall in an attempt to communicate with them while we emptied our buckets in the latrine next to their room. Never did they attempt to answer or acknowledge. We sent them notes, opened their peephole to talk, told them where there were bottles and places to drop notes, all to no avail. It seemed at times that the four colonels just were not interested in communicating or taking over command of Little Vegas. But now when communications were easy, when the pressure was off, when it seemed like there was no torture, except for the Jim Hughes incident, it was safe to take command.

I remember John McCain prophesying, "You wait, wait until these guys start crawling out of the woodwork when things get a little easier, there will be a whole new concept for resisting."

Now a steady flow of directives was being received from the colonels' side of the camp. The camp was named Camp Unity and everyone was organized along Air Force lines. One of the first campaigns was a "letter moratorium." Everyone was to stop writing letters. The idea was to focus attention on the American POWs in Hanoi. It was interesting to note that once the decision was made, everyone claimed to have initiated the idea. People who had argued with me to write were now agreeing that we should not write. It seemed like a good thing, and if this was the type of leadership that was available in Colonel Flynn, then I was all for him. It was the first campwide project. It was also agreed that even if people were separated, they would not write until September. Everyone, even those who had left the camp on March 19, knew that they were not to write until September 1971.

One of the announced primary reasons for the program was to bring the letter writing situation into perspective—that is, at least to be able to receive one letter for every one written. This whole effort, according to some, was an attempt to improve our conditions here. We had received a number of reports that there was a tremendous effort by the people at home to force the North Vietnamese to improve our situation here. I was always amused with that approach, to improve our conditions. To me, that was irrelevant.

There was unity in reference to the letter moratorium, but there was still an argument going on concerning our conduct in the event another person was pulled out and beaten. Already another situation presented itself in which that question was relevant. Quincey Collins had been pulled out of the Room 6 next door. We did not know why, but during the interrogation we heard cries of pain. Again the question was raised—what do we do? What do we do in an attempt to relieve the pressure on another American while he is being beaten or tortured by the North Vietnamese?

In a discussion that night over that very subject, Paul Brudino presented a little bit of his philosophy. He announced, "There is nothing worth going to Heartbreak." He said also that if he was taken out he did not expect anybody to do anything for him if he was beaten outside. The implication was obvious to everyone—if anyone else was taken outside, no one was to lift a hand to help.

Howie Dunn, the Marine, took exception to this. He raised his hand and when he was permitted to speak, he asked, "What about unity before self?"

Whether Paul Brudino realized the full implication of what Howie was saying or whether he just took exception to the fact that Howie was questioning or rejecting his approach, he became irritated and shouted, "What's this unity before self shit? That's gone out a long time ago."

I sat stunned, amazed by what had been said. Was Paul envious of the fact that "unity before self" originated with Commander Stockdale, or was he ensuring that he, as the senior officer, would not have to take action if, in fact, someone else was taken out and beaten? And if nothing was worth going to Heartbreak, why resist?

But Howie Dunn persisted, saying, "There is such a policy, it's 'unity before self' and we still recognize it."

Immediately Paul was on his feet. "It's just another one of those goddamned stupid phrases made up by Stockdale and Denton. We are not going to bang our heads against the wall just because some son of a bitch says fuck Ho Chi Minh."

By this time everyone was tense. Howie got up and began to walk away. Thoroughly disgusted, he turned and said, "You don't know what you're saying." Unexpectedly, Paul jumped off the platform and started after Howie with closed fists. He had to be restrained by Sam Johnson and others; otherwise, Paul Brudino, the senior ranking officer in the room, would have attacked the Marine major who was a Flight Commander.

Dick Stratton, sitting next to me, looked at Paul, shook his head, and said, "Bad show, that's a bad show."

I wanted to go to Howie and tell him that he was absolutely correct, but I did not, knowing that Paul's support was required for what was being planned—escape.

XVII

The Real Hell of Hanoi

> The strongest bond between men is common sacrifice and great achievement.

In the weeks that followed we found out more about Paul's outlook. After a meeting of the Staff and Flight Commanders, the word was brought to us by Sam Johnson. Our group listened to Sam as Paul's May plan unfolded before us. We were to bathe as quickly as possible. We were to complete our bathing, ready to return to our cell in ten minutes, before the gong was to ring. I asked Sam why this was necessary. According to Paul Brudino, this was the manner in which he would be able to show the North Vietnamese that he had control of the group. It was Paul's opinion that in this way the guards would not have to wait for us while some were still bathing or drying themselves after the gong rang, requiring us to return to our cell. A program of shifts was set up so that one shift would bathe early one day and second the following day. Our bathing was now needlessly regulated, not by the North Vietnamese but by our own commander.

The next order of business concerned "greetings." For years the North Vietnamese had been wanting us to bow or "salute" all North Vietnamese. Some prisoners had been forced on occasion to bow or greet North Vietnamese cows. Now, according to Paul, we were "to greet the guards and greet the Bug and greet the interrogators with a nod and a 'Good morning, Sir!'" When we heard this, George McKnight howled like a wounded bear. I wondered what could possibly be going through Paul's head. For years they had been trying to get us to do this, and now our own people were

223

going to enforce the North Vietnamese greeting rule. Again, the explanation was that this was a way that Paul Brudino could show the North Vietnamese that he had control of the group, and then they would acknowledge him as the senior ranking officer.

The next point was concerning people being pulled out of the room. The rule was, according to Paul Brudino, that we were to do nothing if someone was pulled out of the room and beaten. There was nothing new here; he had already stated, "Nothing is worth going to Heartbreak."

Now the controversy over my handmade American flag. There was always a discussion as to whether the flag would be discovered and what would happen if in fact it was discovered. This was reason enough for many not wanting the flag in the room. It was now determined that if the flag was found and if it was trampled upon or mutilated, we would do nothing. At that point I objected: "Sam, you cannot expect us to stand by doing nothing while some North Vietnamese throws our flag to the ground and stomps on it. I tell you that I will react."

Sam Johnson nodded his head and said, "It has already been decided, but if you feel so strongly about it, I'll try to get clarification."

After all the moves there were only four of us left in the escape committee—Jim Kasler, myself, George McKnight, and George Coker. Jim Kasler took over as head of the committee. At our first meeting it was decided that we would continue the planning and organize a communications net to include the covert operations officer under Colonel Flynn. The line of communications to the wing commander would be called the Stockholder Net. The "Chairman" in room 7 would be Kasler. The rest of us would be referred to as the Stockholders. In each room in the camp there would be a designated Stockholder in charge of communications.

There were two things that were of immediate concern: to find a place where we could hide our materials, and to steal from the guards some of the items from our own packages that were received from home.

During one of our meetings Jim Kasler said, "It's not going to happen."

I asked, "Why?"

"Those people on the South side are not going to allow this plan to get very far."

But I thought Paul was going to be our greatest obstacle because in one of his emotional tirades he blurted out, "There's not going to be an escape from this room as long as I am the SRO."

Jim said, "I don't think we are going to be able to convince Paul of anything."

"Well," I said, "approach him and talk to him. I'm sure you can. See if you can set up a time when we can give him a briefing on what we expect as far as support."

Jim replied, "I'll try, but I don't think it will work. He simply does not want to talk about escape."

"Somehow we've got to convince him. At least we've got to try to convince him. We've been given a job to do and we will have to try to do it the best we can. We are going to need everybody's help, and the only way we can get that help is to ensure that we have Paul's cooperation."

As Jim left, George McKnight turned to me and asked, "What do you think?"

I said, "It'll be tough."

"No," George said. "I mean what do you think of Jim Kasler?"

"Right now, it looks like he's going to give it a try."

George McKnight said, "I think he can do a lot. A lot of people respect him and a lot depends on how much he's willing to push."

I nodded, "Jim told me once, 'If you go again, you sure as hell are not going to leave me behind!'"

Before we separated I reviewed the proposed schedule of events. March would be devoted to planning. In April we would do our communicating and coordinating. In May we would attempt to gather materials, including food, iodine, anything that we could use. June would be the month we would make things such as hats, rope, clothes, and shoes. In July we would dig a hole through the ceiling and camouflage it. In August we would make our practice runs, be prepared to go that month during the flood season, and if necessary, according to Jim's plan, make a reconnaissance run on the roof.

Immediately the most important thing was to find a place to hide our contraband. In searching the walls and banging and listening,

I came across three large drain holes which were cemented closed by the North Vietnamese. These were the drain holes near the Bug house. I examined them over and over again, banging and listening. I was satisfied, those holes were hollow. All that was necessary was to dig out the plaster plugs and then make a false patch to cover it again.

I started immediately. My first inclination, of course, was to ask permission to dig in the wall, but I knew darn well that if I asked permission, especially if it involved escape, it would be refused. Besides, the way the system was set up, I did not require permission from the SRO in matters of escape. According to the initial development of the organization, our committee was directly responsible to the covert operations officer working for Colonel Flynn.

One evening I gathered all my materials while Big George watched for guards. I started digging out the three holes. In no time I removed a small amount of plaster that covered a number of broken bricks that plugged up the holes. I crushed the plaster and re-mixed it with water and some cement that I stole from the workmen when they enlarged our bathing tub. I cleaned the holes out and put what few things we had gathered into the hole. It was a better hiding place than I had suspected. I replastered the holes. In no time at all it looked as if the wall had never been touched.

Big George was elated. We now had some place to hide everything that we could collect, and it also proved that we could prepare an undetectable plug for any hole, in the wall or in the ceiling.

While I was working, the bridge players would look up from time to time and wonder what Dramesi was doing now. But no one, except Bob Shumaker, came over to offer his help. He too was enthused with the fact that we now had a place to hide some of our supplies.

That evening Paul Brudino, Kasler, myself, and George McKnight sat down for a meeting to discuss the possibilities of escape. I could tell already that Paul was not enthusiastic. His face was hard and he glared at George McKnight and me. Apparently he felt that he was defeated in allowing us to talk to him, but somewhere in his mind he felt that he had to at least listen, especially when the Code of Conduct says "I will make every effort to escape and aid others to escape."

Paul did not say anything but just looked. Finally Kasler said, "Go ahead, John, explain the plan as we know it."

I started explaining that we would be able to hide any hole that we made in the ceiling, either with a bamboo matting or by gluing our brown sheets of toilet paper together with rice glue. The paper hardened into a cardboard and I had already experimented with a three-foot square. After it was painted with whitewash, it was perfect. In many places the ceiling had already fallen through or was ragged. Even if we didn't do a perfect job, a little irregular line would not show up as being unusual.

I explained that the wire and cloth were available for forty feet of rope. We had already made and tested a seven-foot section. The rope would support two of us at one time.

I explained that we had the tools to cut through the ceiling, and we would emerge on the roof in a place which was not visible to any part of the camp. The only place that anyone could see us was from a far portion of the Heartbreak courtyard, and even then the grapevines would help block the view. The place where we were going out did not have a light on the roof and most of the lights that were on the roofs did not work. We would also be going out at night when it was raining, an additional cover. I told him that we had figured the moon cycles, and it would be a black night.

The materials—food, clothing, everything that we had, including accurate information, was more than Ed and I had during the Party in 1969. If we wanted to make the effort, I explained, we could almost eliminate the possibility of being caught.

We would move over the roofs of the darkened portions of the camp where there were no guards at night. The northeast corner of the prison was our objective. There we would be on the roof of the Mint. I had carefully studied that area. I knew we could go from the roof of the Mint to the roof of the northeast corner tower.

Paul asked, "You're going on the tower roof?"

"Yes, sir," I replied. "The reason is that no one ever uses that tower except to hang clothes to dry during the day. I've watched it day and night. They did not even man the tower when we were over there in Little Vegas." It was a perfect place for us, not only to avoid the electrical wires and glass on top of the walls, but also because we would be able to rest on top of the tower roof prior to descending.

Apparently not even listening, Paul said again, "You can't go on the tower." Kasler said, "We have asked some of the other rooms. As far as they can tell, the tower is not manned."

"How are you going to get up on the tower roof?" Paul asked.

I said, "As you know, we have two poles within our reach immediately outside our prison door." We placed them there when the guards were repairing one of the fences. I simply walked over, picked two poles, and wired them into the corner. Later one guard was puzzled, wondering why it took three poles to hold up that portion of the fence, but he did not realize that the wire was easily removed and that the poles were within our reach from inside the cell.

Paul grunted, "So you get over the wall. Then what? You are in the middle of a million people."

"Yes, sir, but I have made my way through towns before and we can make ourselves up to look just like the North Vietnamese. We've already proven that."

"You got away with it one time," he said, "but that doesn't mean you can do it again."

"Twice," I corrected. "It all depends on the effort. We can do it."

We talked about dimly lit streets, proper disguises, bread baskets, carrying poles, the surgical masks, skin coloring, hats, peasant clothing, and finally I concluded, "I think we can make it to the river."

"What are you going to do when you get to the river, steal a boat?"

"No," I answered. "If we steal a boat too soon, we will be pinpointing our position. Instead we will use plastic bags as life preservers. We have a sufficient number of bags so that if we put them inside a roll of cloth we will have adequate floatation. The Red River would carry us at a speed of perhaps five knots. In August during the heavy rains as much as seven knots. The food would be waterproof, either in plastic bottles or plastic bags. If necessary, we could carry a little bit of fresh water with us. In any case, we would have some iodine for purifying water.

"The only time we would steal a boat," I explained, "is when we're ready to go to sea, and this is the only time that we would, if necessary, attack anyone who attempted to stop us."

We wanted to avoid contact with the North Vietnamese as long as possible, but if we felt that someone was standing between us and freedom, then we would fight if necessary.

"It's a damn big ocean," snapped Paul.

"Yes, sir, but we can make plans for that also. If we get out that far, let's just say that it's up to the Navy then. There are ways that we can help the Navy to find us."

"Bullshit," Paul growled.

So that was it. He wasn't arguing with anything or any particular point. He simply was saying in his mind, "You are not going to do it."

"But, Paul," I said, afraid I was losing ground rapidly, "we were asked to organize and plan. The decision has already been made and you're expected to help us." Paul interrupted and said, "I'm the S.R.O. in this room."

At this point it seemed that the best thing to do was to stop talking and let higher authority do the convincing.

George McKnight spoke up. "I think we can make it if you'll let us try."

"If you did make it over the wall," Paul said, "you'd never make it through the city."

"Perhaps," George said, "but I'd rather give that a try than to rot here for the next five years."

It looked like we were headed for an argument. I interjected, "Let's put it this way, Paul: if we get permission to go, will you give us your help?"

Paul's face was turning red, and it looked like he was ready to explode, but he smiled a wicked smile and said, "Sure, sure, I'll help you."

When we were alone, George said, "You know damn right well that he isn't going to help us."

"I think you're right, George, but in the end I think also it will be said that we did our part. We were asked to try to plan an escape from this place, and it won't be because of us if there is no try or it fails."

Later, Sam Johnson approached me and said, "I talked to

Paul about the flag. Paul said that there was some confusion, and that if they mutilate or stomp on the flag before us, Paul will protest." Sam quickly added, "But only Paul will protest."

I looked at Sam and said, "Did he really say there was a bit of confusion?"

"Yes, that's correct."

I said, "You know darn well he knew exactly what he was saying when he gave you that order, Sam."

Sam knew he had been used and was embarrassed about it.

"Anyway," Sam said, "there was some confusion."

"Thanks, Sam, at least that's something."

That night Paul signaled to me to sit down and have a talk with him. We sat on the end of the cement island. He moved very close to me, slapped me on the thigh, and said, "John, listen, I like you; I want to be your friend." He squeezed my leg, grinned, and said, "You know us Italians—we've got to stick together. You don't want to do this thing. Think about this escape business. Listen, I don't want to have to go through the same thing again, and I'm sure you don't either. Think of Dorothy. I know you have a nice wife. She doesn't want you home without a leg or arm. Don't do that to her."

"Paul, it's not my business to think of her. We have to think of ourselves. If we don't help ourselves, we may just as well throw in the towel."

"Listen, John, you've been lucky so far. If you try it again, who knows what's going to happen the next time?" He waved his arm in the direction of the other cellblocks and said, "Give someone else a chance, let them do it."

"Paul, if somebody else wants to go you know darn well that they are going to come looking for me; and as soon as they come into this room, that means that you are involved also. We can't avoid it, so let's do it right, and give it the best chance to succeed."

Disgusted, he said, "Well, they're not going to do it anyway. Don't fool yourself. Nobody wants an escape, and those guys over there," pointing to the South side, where the senior officers were quartered, "are not going to let you do anything."

"Paul, if the decision is finally 'no,' fine, if they say 'yes,' then, by golly, we'll be ready."

"Listen, John." He leaned a little closer and squeezed my thigh again. "We are going to get out of here soon, and besides, no matter what you do, it isn't going to be appreciated by those bastards over there."

Again he glanced to where the full colonels were imprisoned. "Just take it easy and think it over, okay?" He smiled again, a little less confident now. "Think it over," he said. He patted my knee and stood up. "Think it over, John," he said.

As Paul walked away I wondered what Ed Atterberry would have thought about that conversation. I thought to myself, damn, if it's worth it for someone else to do it, then it certainly should be worth it for us. We have the experience and the know-how and more of everything in this room than in any of the others.

It seems so many just want to sit on the ends of their bunks and do nothing. I thought of that pacified huge black bull with the brass ring through his nose. Must we accept another five years in this rat trap? I guess there are differences between men, just as there are differences between some wild animals. Some wild animals cannot be kept in captivity and others can be domesticated and kept in cages all their lives. Some animals are content to die in their cages and some animals will die trying to get out.

It was getting hot. The summer was always my most uncomfortable season. This summer could be worse, considering the bathing rules now in effect.

I walked up and down the courtyard just meditating. I walked to the bamboo gate of our yard, then turned and started to walk back the other way. I walked past Ray Vohden seated on the large cement bench. Ray had a terribly mutilated leg and spent all his time on crutches. He was one of the few introverts. He seemed always to have a cigarette although he received no more than the others. What irritated many was his constant hacking cough. He looked up and said, "Good morning," and nodded. I looked at him, surprised, and said, "Hi, Ray." Puzzled, I continued my walk, thinking that's nice, that's the first time Ray ever tried to be friendly with me.

I was approaching Paul Brudino. He stopped in his tracks, nodded, and said, "Good morning, Sir." I knew something was wrong.

I turned around. The Bug was following me. I did not realize that he had entered the courtyard when I turned to walk back toward our cell.

Needless to say, Bug was grinning from ear to ear. He was enjoying his newfound power and probably wondering what he would do next to test our attitude and to dominate our lives even more.

Hawk shortly followed Bug into the yard carrying a big board, upon which were pasted a number of newspaper clippings and photographs. Hawk hung the board on the wall for us to read at our leisure and departed with Bug.

As I walked by after the small crowd around the board had dissipated, I noticed a picture of President Nixon. I walked over to take a closer look at it. On the bulletin board was an 8 x 10 picture of President Nixon. Underneath the picture was printed, "Murderer," his name, height, and age. He was depicted in a black and white striped prison uniform. I calmly reached up, grasped the picture, ripped it off the billboard, crumpled it up, and threw it into the open sewer drain. When we were inside, Paul approached and asked excitedly, "What did you do?"

I asked in return, "When?"

"To the billboard, what did you do?"

I said, "There was a picture of President Nixon saying he was a criminal and murderer. I just ripped it off and threw it away."

"Don't do that again."

"Why not, Paul? Hell, all we have to do is mention Ho Chi Minh and we get the hell kicked out of us, and now you want me to stand there and look at something that is degrading our own President."

"That's just bullshit," he said. "Don't do it again."

"Are you kidding? It may be bullshit to you, but it's disgraceful to me."

"Don't you touch anything on that board without asking me first." He turned and walked away.

It was my group's turn to bathe first. I stood outside with Duffy Hutton listening to some of his jokes.

We stood there and already we were perspiring from the summer heat, watching the water in the half full tank glisten in the summer sun. Although the gong would not ring for at least another twenty minutes, we were not allowed to cool ourselves. We became hotter and perspired as the water splashed into the tank. It was now almost full but no one used the water. To distract us from our discomfort, Duffy was telling some jokes, and we laughed.

In the past when we laughed loudly the Hawk would look sternly at George McKnight or me and say, "No, no." At other times he would send us back into the room for the remainder of the period. This time Hawk motioned to us to go into the room. Duffy Hutton, Kasler, and I returned to the room.

In the meantime, Paul Brudino was called out for a quiz. While he was in the interrogation room with Bug, we continued to laugh at Duffy's jokes.

Sam Johnson came to the door, which was locked by the Hawk so we could not get out again, and yelled, "Shut up in there, shut up."

"Who said so?"

"Sam Johnson."

"Okay, Sam, we'll keep quiet, but I can't understand why in hell you are asking us not to laugh in this place."

He yelled back, "Just keep quiet."

And so the jokes stopped.

In a short while the gong rang and the rest of the group came in the room, but Paul was not with them. He was still with the Bug. Twenty minutes later the door clanged open and Paul quickly marched down the aisle toward his corner. He was furious, shouting, "I'm going to kill that bastard, Dramesi! I tell you, I will get that son of a bitch!"

I was standing on the platform talking to Bob Craner when Windy Rivers, who was second in command, looked up to me and said, "Dramesi, from now on, don't laugh."

I looked down at him and said, "Are you kidding?"

He said, "No, and don't whistle, either."

"You really must be joking."

He said, "From now on, you are to keep your mouth shut."

No doubt the Bug had told Paul to keep me quiet, and he had passed the order on to Rivers. The Bug for years had been trying to keep me from whistling and laughing. I felt a pain in my chest. I did not know whether to cry or strike at the face in front of me.

With the ropes, the jumbo irons and the heat, Bug was ineffective, and now it seemed he had found an even more effective means to break my spirit,

Rivers was ready to leave. But either from stupidity or delight, he twisted the dagger and said once more, "From now on, you are to keep your mouth shut, and that's an order."

Anger swelled within me. I looked down and said, "What specifically is the order?"

Less sure of himself now, Windy said, "From now on, keep your mouth shut." The words "from now on" and "keep your mouth shut" were both favorite expressions of Bug. My hands clinched, I was about to unload all of my frustration and anger on Rivers when I heard, "John, that's enough, that's enough."

I looked around. It was Dick Stratton.

I turned to Windy Rivers and said, "I understand what you have said, but I am going to live as normal a life as possible."

I looked at Dick Stratton. Our eyes met, but we said nothing.

I walked off and met George McKnight. He told me that he wanted to wring Rivers' neck like a chicken's. More quietly, George said, "There is one other thing. I think you should lay off a little bit. Just be quiet and go along with all this crap, we've got more important things to think about."

Calmly I said, "You're right, I'll give it a try. Thanks, George."

I guess when meek, softspoken Lou Makowski approached, his intention was to help me somehow. But it was not appreciated, probably because my preconceived picture of Lou was that of a nervous, nonentity who would sway whichever way the wind was blowing.

As he stood there swaying back and forth, gesturing unnecessarily with his hands, he said, "You don't have to laugh loud. Why, if I wanted, I could be heard clear down to the next block."

"Lou," I said, "if you are normally heard clear down to the next block when you laugh and here you are not heard clear down to the next block, friend, let me give you some advice. Watch out—you're conditioned." I abruptly walked off, thinking: Can you imagine what's going to happen to some of these guys when they get home? One of the kids will laugh and he'll fly into a rage, and the wife will constantly plead, "Speak up, dear, you're whispering again."

One disappointment followed another. Howie Dunn delivered a message:

1. Don't push the SRO;

2. There is a personality conflict between John Dramesi and the SRO;

3. There will be no escape from this room;

4. Dramesi is to stop causing trouble with the others in the room.

The ultimate disappointment came one evening a short time after I had ripped President Nixon's picture from the bulletin board. Five people were called before a board composed of Paul Brudino, Windy Rivers, Sam Johnson, and Ray Vohden. Duffy Hutton's crime was telling funny jokes; Jim Kasler and George McKnight's obvious crime was being on the escape committee, and Bob Craner's crime was eating his meals with John Dramesi. Bob Craner was a quiet but tough New Yorker. His only comment when he returned after being reprimanded was "I can take a lecture on discipline from anybody except Paul Brudino."

I was the last to appear. After being seated, I looked up to examine my judges. Paul Brudino stood there, spread-legged, with his hands behind his back. He started talking. With bloodshot eyes, he gazed over my head, never turning or looking at me. This, I thought, will be part of the story that will never be told. Attempting to pronounce his words properly, and act official, Paul listed my crimes:

"You whistled too loud. You laughed too loud. You talked too loud."

These were ridiculous enough, but I was stupefied by my last offense: "You ripped President Nixon's picture from the bulletin board."

How could I combat this insane fantasy? Yet it must be real, for the others saw nothing funny in what was happening.

Still acting out his part, Paul asked: "Will you accept punishment?"

"What is the punishment?"

"Will you accept the punishment?" he repeated.

"I will not accept it until I know what it is," I said firmly.

"You will not be allowed outside for two weeks, and you will not be allowed to take part in any of the formal activities in the room. Also during that time, you will not teach the beginners Spanish course."

After a pause I said, "Yes, I will accept the punishment," thinking it was the quickest way to terminate the crazy scene.

For the next two weeks I stayed inside. Hawk looked in every day and smiled. He knew what had happened.

This whole mad sequence of events had two results, planned or otherwise; one, I was discredited, and two, the escape effort was destroyed. A message was sent forward to the colonels on the south side: the undisciplined troublemaker, John Dramesi, had to be punished. Shortly thereafter Jim Kasler told me that the escape committee was dissolved. I asked the communications officer to confirm that the escape committee was disbanded. I was told, "You are not allowed to send any messages, John." The whole organization and communications system was changed. Everything was funneled through one man—Paul Brudino.

On a moonless, stormy Saturday night in August, I experienced my greatest slump. That was the night of the planned escape, and I was still here watching the lizards on the ceiling race after mosquitoes.

XVIII

The Return
of the Prodigal

Tell me not of the adventures of others or what
you have seen, but of your participation. Have you
played the game? What respect do you command?
Can you be called man?

In early November 1971, the door rattled and when the guard finally
got it open, a tall, handsome individual walked into the cell.
He was well tanned, and fairly well proportioned. There was a
smile on his face and he appeared confident. His clothes were
noticeably clean and well-pressed. By far the most dapper looking
prisoner I ever saw.

Jim Kasler was near the door and as soon as the stranger
walked in, Jim put out his hand and said, "I'm Jim Kasler, welcome."

"I'm Bob Schweitzer, it's great to be here."

Involuntarily, Jim Kasler withdrew his hand.

There were others there who shook his hand, made him feel
at home and started asking him questions. Immediately Bob
Schweitzer began his monologue.

Because he had refused to cooperate with the North Vietnamese
in preparing this year's coming Christmas program, the North
Vietnamese expelled him from what was now referred to as the
good guy camp, The Zoo. Bob Schweitzer was one of forty or
fifty men who moved out in late September and early October.
Now he was returned to the Hanoi Hilton because as he ex-

plained, "I wouldn't do a damned thing for them." George Mc-Knight almost choked.

Bob Schweitzer was a guy who, many vowed, would be on the receiving end of a punch in the mouth. For a long time he had lived with two officers widely believed to be cooperating with the North Vietnamese. Schweitzer had just recently been reinstated by the wing commander, when his cellmates were denied their command. Not too long ago, he had told us over the radio that the Code of Conduct was meaningless; and his voice was so familiar that we had long since stopped counting the number of times he went to the "Knobby room" to pay tribute to the Bug. I was convinced that his was one of the voices the Bug referred to as "a good reporter."

Bob Schweitzer knew exactly what he was doing, for now he was talking about the subjects most dear to everyone's heart, promotions and pay. The scene was so utterly ridiculous I started laughing to myself. Schweitzer didn't have a snowball's chance in hell of being promoted when he got out; and there he was talking about promotions. But, I had to give Schweitzer credit, he had everyone intently listening to every word he had to say. It was not difficult to determine what was most important. Uppermost in the minds of his audience was not resistance but when they would receive their next promotion and how much was the last pay raise.

I happened to glance to the other side of the room. Walking back and forth, glaring at the group listening to Bob Schweitzer, was Paul Brudino.

Suddenly I realized why Paul was in such an emotional state: Bob Schweitzer outranked him. Interesting, I thought. The only stupid people here were those who thought the North Vietnamese were stupid. Moving Bob Schweitzer to Room 7 was another good move by the North Vietnamese. They were satisfied with Paul Brudino as the ranking officer. Now, I thought, they can be more satisfied with Bob Schweitzer as number one and Paul Brudino as number two man in Room 7.

It would be interesting to see how Paul Brudino handled the situation. Would he undermine Bob Schweitzer's influence, would he dominate him, or would he subtly use Bob Schweitzer?

The next day Paul Brudino's advice to Schweitzer was: stay

away from some people here, and secondly, definitely do not tell everyone all about your own experiences. But Schweitzer had some ideas of his own. There was among the P.O.W.s a tried and true method of attempting to elevate yourself—simply degrade someone who has performed more poorly. Schweitzer's two ex-cellmates provided the means by which he could elevate himself.

In speaking of his ex-cellmates, and in an attempt to justify his own actions, Schweitzer said, "I tried for years to get away from them."

That is simple, I thought; you simply refuse to continue doing what the North Vietnamese ask of you, and if the others continue, eventually they will separate you. Other officers had used this tactic successfully. When an officer decided to stop helping the North Vietnamese, they simply removed him from the group so that he would not have a bad influence upon the others.

I wondered now what tactics Bob Schweitzer used to get away from his undesirable roommates. Schweitzer's solution was either naive or an attempt to be funny. "For years," he said, "I wrote letters to the North Vietnamese Camp Commander. I wrote seven letters to the camp commander requesting that he remove me from the room with those two."

Schweitzer's letters had simply played into the hands of the North Vietnamese. Such letters, which were the official channel for all personal requests, provided the North Vietnamese with important information about attitudes, relationships, and morale among the prisoners.

I realized that all the failures of Bob Schweitzer were indicative of his reaction to future situations here. I could not understand why Colonel Flynn would allow him to command. But then, there were new attitudes prevailing. New attitudes that were totally unfamiliar as far as my experience in the military was concerned. "Forgive and forget, live and let live!" Why was it necessary for us to forgive? Were we so lacking in our leadership? And why was it necessary to forget? Unless you wanted the other person to forget what you had done also.

In less than a month after Bob Schweitzer took command, we were called together to listen to a very important briefing. The subject of this briefing was how we should conduct ourselves when faced with an interrogation by our own people after being released. I thought I was hearing things, but by the time the briefing was finished, I was thoroughly disgusted with what I had heard. In essence, what we were being told was, "You don't have to tell the US debriefers anything," and secondly, "If you do have to talk to them, make sure you have a good lawyer." And, most important of all, "Don't sign a thing."

Here we are, I thought, in a North Vietnamese prison with some people incapable of resisting interrogations properly, yet there has never been an open command sponsored discussion on the methods of resisting the enemy. We were talking instead about how to resist our own debriefers upon our release. In essence, Bob Schweitzer was telling us that the Code of Conduct was meaningless and that it was not necessary to follow it.

A decision had to be made—whether the letter moratorium would be carried over into December. Most were behind the letter moratorium, and as the months passed the North Vietnamese were constantly after us to write letters. They were even willing to give us more letters, so that we would write. It looked like the plan was working.

But now, with Christmas approaching, attitudes changed. For months men like Ben Pollard and Lou Makowski were praising the letter moratorium and its effectiveness. The logical conclusion obviously, if it was effective, was to continue the moratorium.

But now there was a different factor to consider, Christmas. As enthusiastic as many were with the letter moratorium in the beginning, men like Ben Pollard and Lou Makowski were just as adamant over the fact that we should write before Christmas. I talked to Ben specifically and asked him, "If we are doing so well, why not pursue it?"

But Ben refused to listen. His only comment was, "I have to write to my wife on Christmas."

Lou's comment was simply, "It's been long enough, my wife will be expecting a letter."

In the two months after the moratorium ended, over one thousand letters left the camp. During that period, the North Vietnamese guards and interrogators ran around with pencils, pen, paper, and big smiles on their faces. They obviously were happy. And we were once again helping them.

The letter moratorium, at this point, seemed to be a total farce.

George McKnight came up and asked me, "Are you going to write?"

I said, "No, nothing has really changed, the letters are still being used and probably more so now."

There were a number of inner-camp and inner-room moves that were made in the last months of 1971. I noticed that there were many new faces in Room 7. These certainly could not be the young men that Colonel Risner had referred to. Next to me was Leroy Stutz, a graduate of the Air Force Academy, a football player, a strong and intelligent individual. "We are here as soldiers," he used to say, "and if nothing else, we're here to cause trouble for the North Vietnamese. The more trouble we can cause for them, the more they have to watch us, and the more they have to watch us, the less they have to use in South Vietnam. It may be a small amount, but at least it's our contribution. We're not dead yet."

John Pitchford was another strong soldier. He was an Air Force tactical fighter pilot and knew one thing, to fight. He was badly banged up. Regardless of his misfortune, John's attitude was "that is my unfortunate situation, but that does not relieve me of my responsibility to fight."

Soon after Ted Kopfman arrived in Room 7, he told me that while at the Zoo, Paul Brudino had refused him the opportunity to escape. There was no escape committee in the "Zoo" at the time that the escape from the Zoo Annex took place in 1969. While we sat eating, Bob Craner told me why I disliked Ted Kopfman. "Why is that?" I asked Bob. "I'm really not sure I know myself."

"Oh, it's very simple," he replied. "When you beat him at chess, each time he gets up and pats you on the head as if to say, 'Not bad for a young fellow.'"

I looked at Bob and laughed. He was probably right.

Since the escape committee had been "dissolved" there was no talk of escape. In a friendly manner, Paul approached me and asked, "Do you know Ted Kopfman?"

"Only since he has been in the room," I answered.

"Don't listen to him," Paul said, "about this business of escape. I told him that there was a policy of no escape without outside help."

It was interesting to note that on this occasion he was telling me that there was no escape without outside help, yet when we talked previously he told me that he would surely have given the order permitting Ed and me to escape in 1969. If Paul had known of the "Party" in 1969, I now knew what his answer for permission to go over the wall would have been—the same he gave Ted Kopfman.

On December 15 Lou Makowski was caught redhanded attempting to pass a coded note to the colonels. The question was: what to do? It was thought that either Lou or Bob Schweitzer would have to answer for our error.

I went to Lou first and told him, "Lou, I was caught with a coded note back in '70 in Little Vegas. If the situation is the same, you won't have to admit anything. The only thing I had to do was stand in a corner for two days. Just tell them you don't know anything about it."

"I can't do that," Lou insisted. "They caught me redhanded with the note, they know that I was trying to pass it. We're going to have to tell them what is in it."

"Don't be silly, Lou. What I'm trying to tell you is that exactly the same thing happened to me at a time when we did not know the torture had stopped for such things. I was able to get away with it. You can do exactly the same."

But Lou was not listening to a word I was saying. All he could do was repeat over and over, "They found the note, they saw me, they know that I tried to pass it. We're going to have to tell them."

Lou was furious when no one would tell him what was in the coded note.

Sam Johnson said, "If they don't pull Lou out, you know that Bob Schweitzer will be the first one on their list."

I said, "Yes, I figured as much. What do you want me to do?"

"Go to Bob and tell him about your experience in Little Vegas, and try to convince him that he doesn't have to say anything."

"Okay, Sam."

I explained to Bob Schweitzer the same thing that I told Lou and concluded by saying, "The best thing is simply to say you are not aware of it and deny the incident altogether. You may have to persist perhaps for a couple of days but that is the best approach."

"Paul just said go ahead and tell them about the damned thing, they know we communicate and it doesn't mean a damn thing."

I got up and walked away, scratching my head, knowing Bob Schweitzer obviously was not going to listen to me. After admitting he knows all about the note, the next demand will be: "Read it." Where will he stop?

Fortunately, no one was pulled out, no one was questioned, and no one was pressured to decode the note. Things were even better than I had thought, and I almost went up to Lou Makowski to say, "See, I told you."

The next crisis involved Toastmasters.

Paul Brudino had established a number of rules and regulations which I totally opposed. This was the reason Dick Stratton asked me not to leave Toastmasters, because if I did, most likely, a few others would follow and the club would disintegrate. Our practice speech making was enjoyable and beneficial to all who participated.

Little by little the rules that Paul imposed upon us conformed with those posted by the North Vietnamese. If we spoke loudly, we would be forced to terminate the speech by someone appointed to monitor the noise level.

Now we were not allowed to talk about Americanism. If we wanted to show our appreciation by clapping, we could not; if we wanted to laugh we simply smiled unnaturally, afraid not of the North Vietnamese, but of our own leaders. We were not even allowed to talk about resistance, for that would be inciting the guards to take action. The object of our whole existence was not to anger the Bug.

A short time after our speeches were finished on December 16, 1971, the doors opened unexpectedly. The guards came in to remove Paul Brudino, Windy Rivers, Bob Schweitzer, Collie Haines, Howie Dunn, and Ron Webb. All of them except Paul belonged to Toastmasters.

XIX

The Third Escape

> Let us continue to do as we are expected to do, and
> to be the men we are expected to be. What is ex-
> pected is to be expected. What must be endured
> will be endured.

A note was received one day by the communications people. They
did not know how to handle it. It was for Tiger. The leader of
the camp covert committee wanted to know why Tiger was not
communicating. I tried to put the pieces of the puzzle together.
Apparently someone, thinking that we should still be communicating with them, is calling us Tiger. Somewhere along the line
our committee changed from the Stockholders to Tiger. How about
that, I thought; we're back in business.

In Brudino's absence the escape committee was again formed,
only this time Jim Kasler, Ted Kopfman, and I were called Tiger.
The communications links were reestablished, with "Rosebud"
the coordinator on our side of the camp. Rosebud would recom-
mend a go or no go. The final go or no go would still rest with
Colonel Flynn, the Wing Commander. Rosebud informed us that
Room 3 was now in the plan. They had what was called a "Mole
Plan." There were options Alpha, Bravo, Charlie, and Delta. The
plan was to dig out of Room 3 and under the wall. The Mole Plan
had three secret destinations. If "Mole Plan" was refused or if
something went wrong, option Delta would back it up. That was
our Tiger plan. Immediately we established communications with
Room 3.

George McKnight and Render Crayton moved from Room 7 to
"Mayo," a small hospital cell on the south side, George usually

got sick in the winter, but he was a picture of health compared to Render, who was slowly starving himself. "Mayo" was no better than the rest of the cells, but they could get a little more attention there from the guards.

Big George was now the communications link between the colonels over on his side and Room 7. He had accomplished what no one else was able to do. And why? Because he tried.

I wondered how Render Crayton was getting along. Render had some queer ideas about food. He would eat absolutely no sugar and no fats. He was the skinniest person in camp. His buttocks began to sag, his eyes began to look like deep holes, and his bones showed all over. He would go so far as to wash the fat off his meat and pick threads of meat from the tiny portions that remained after completing his processing. He ate no grease and when the bread was served he would pick the crust off, the dark portions only. Each loaf of bread that he examined had certain portions that he would eat. He would carefully pick at these select areas with bony fingers. After an hour of examining and picking, he probably consumed as much crust as one small sparrow could eat. When he was finished it looked like a flock of birds had descended upon many loaves of bread and only pecked at them until finally there were piles of crumbs all over the place. No one was attempting to help Render Crayton.

His feet swelled and week after week he lost more weight. I had mentioned it a number of times to Paul that something should be done, but Paul insisted that it was just his way and that nothing could be done.

I surmised that this was what was happening to a number of other people who had started on that road. They had denied themselves food in an attempt to gain sympathy from the enemy. If they were weak or incapable, they would not be able to do the things that the North Vietnamese wanted them to do. This was their method of resisting. It was self-induced and wrong. Day after day they became weaker mentally and physically.

People who had adopted this peculiar method, I felt, would not fare well because as they attempted to remove themselves from reality in their physically weakened state, they would be less able and willing to return to their ever-increasing misery.

One time when Render was picking through the basket of bread,

I asked him, "Do you realize what you are doing? Do you understand what you are doing? Just look." He had gone through eight loaves of bread, picking tiny bits of charred crust from each one.

But the advice of Paul Brudino was simply, "Don't bother him," "leave him alone," "he's not bothering anybody." I hoped that George McKnight might be able to pound a little sense into his head while they were in Mayo. At least George would do something, because Render Crayton at this point was incapable of helping himself.

In the evening on December 21, five days after the Toastmasters incident, the first of the six officers removed by the North Vietnamese returned to Room 7 of the Hanoi Hilton. We all crowded around him near the door. Many of us stood on the bunks, looking down at him as he stood there. His haggard appearance and trembling hands caused me to think—torture.

Somebody asked the officer, "Well, what happened? What happened?" He said that they wanted to know about Toastmasters and our organizations.

"What did you tell them?" someone asked. He started to talk. At times it seemed he was mumbling to himself. He said he told the North Vietnamese about Toastmasters. He told them who were the organizers, who were the presidents, who were the officers, how often we spoke and about what. He told them everything anyone could possibly think about Toastmasters. But then he continued. It seemed that he had forgotten what the question was. Now he said he told them about our organization, who the S.R.O.'s were, how we were organized in the room, the flight commanders, what our duties were, the committees that we had, and so forth and so on. By the time the officer had finished, I knew more about our organization than I had known previously. Someone in the crowd murmured, "The poor guy must have had the shit kicked out of him." Feeling sorry for the man, I nodded my agreement.

From another part of the room someone asked, "Well, what did they do?" When the officer was finished talking, it finally occurred to everyone that the North Vietnamese did absolutely nothing except threaten him. He was convinced that they were going to torture him, and that was enough to start him talking.

"Why did they take you out in the first place?"

Revived, the officers said angrily, "Because of Toastmasters."

They found some Toastmasters' material during last week's inspection and they did not understand it. They wanted to know about our practice speaking sessions.

Because of the episode Toastmasters was cancelled for the next three weeks.

"Why the cancellation?" I asked. "So they did take you out, and they did ask you about Toastmasters, but they did not touch you. Is that any reason to cancel Toastmasters?" I added.

"They're going to torture us next week."

"What are you talking about? Torturing us next week! What makes you think they're going to torture us?"

The officer hesitated a moment and then said, "I think they're going to torture us next week."

"But they didn't do anything to you while you were out there."

"I know, but they're going to torture us next week."

The physical and mental torture that this officer had experienced was far less than many others I knew. I was still looking for that common fiber that good men possess. It certainly was not the military academies. Denton, whom I respected, was an academy graduate. This officer was also. It was not the fact that you were a pilot. It was not the fact that you were a college graduate. It was not the fact that you were from a rich family or a poor family. It was not the fact that you were a jet ace, and it certainly was not the fact that you were a fighter pilot.

As I talked to various people, the similarity between those who provided the leadership and example emerged—the awareness of a purpose and the willingness to make sacrifices to uphold that purpose.

Two days later, on the twenty-third, a second officer returned. His story was the same. No pressure, but he signed an apology.

A day later, another officer returned. His story was entirely different. He joked, laughed, and said, "I charmed the pants right off them."

Having always been against Toastmasters, this was an opportunity. He said, "Was all that goddamn Toastmasters fault. All they wanted to know was Toastmasters, Toastmasters, Toastmasters."

The other three returned also, but they had gone to Heartbreak. Howie Dunn, Collie Haines, and Ron Webb were in Heartbreak for two weeks. It was understandable. Many said the same thing, "If you ever want to know how a person does or how good a resister he is, just watch the Vietnamese. They'll identify the tough guys for you." In this particular case, the North Vietnamese were telling us that half of the officers removed from the room had failed miserably. And no doubt there was a reason for Collie, Ron and Howie being in Heartbreak. They tried.

After Paul's return, his good humor did not last very long. Suddenly there was a loud "What?" that came from his corner. Somebody was briefing Brudino on the past events. He was angry about something. When he approached me the next day, without preliminaries, he said, "That bastard told a bunch of lies."

I said, "What are you talking about?"

"George is over at Mayo and he's telling those guys lies about me."

I said, calmly, "How do you know, Paul? You don't know what he's told the colonels. It seems to me they want an escape plan."

"You guys are pushing me; watch it."

Our 1971 Christmas party started off pretty good. The guards continued to harass us from the door. Each time Bob Schweitzer would go to acknowledge their presence, listen, and then interrupt the program to repeat what the guard said. We tried to enjoy ourselves. But after the third interruption, the enthusiasm for the party waned. People did not clap, and they restrained their laughter.

By chance I had a short talk with Dick Stratton. "John, you have a lot of friends here, but I don't envy you. You've accepted the responsibility of being a 'gadfly.' I know what's going on, but for the next couple of months, see if you can help lower the tension in the room."

"What is a gadfly?" I asked.

He told me that it was a big horsefly that flies around stinging the rumps of horses. "A gadfly," he continued, "is someone that irritates others, and when you irritate Paul, you have a tendency to annoy everyone. But I'm not telling you to stop what you're doing. I'm just glad it's you and not me. I'd hate to be the one to have to try to keep this group honest with itself."

I tried. But when George McKnight returned from Mayo, that did not reduce the level of tension in the room. Paul Brudino at times stared at him, wanting, no doubt, to pound him into the ground. But Paul knew that he could not tangle with George Mc-Knight. Perhaps Howie Dunn, but not George McKnight.

It seemed as the months passed that the excitement in the air increased instead of decreasing. The guards were busy preparing—perhaps the bombing was going to start again. We could not tell definitely, but the exercises that the guards were going through certainly indicated that they expected airplanes any day.

One night, just before the "go to sleep" gong rang, we heard the clanging of doors on the other side of the camp. Then we heard it. The cries and moans told us someone was being beaten.

George and I were standing in the aisle talking. We looked at one another and at the same time we said, "That's an American." The grunts and shouts did not stop.

Paul Brudino was passing us, oblivious to what was going on. I stopped him and asked, "Do you hear that?" He said, "Yes, I hear it. So what?"

"But that's an American they're beating."

"You don't know that," he snarled.

"Ah, c'mon, Paul, you know damn right well that's an American. Just listen, listen to him."

"But we don't know why he's being beaten," Paul said.

"What difference does it make?" I snapped.

"How the fuck do you know it's an American?" he said angrily.

"Paul, there are only two kinds of people in this camp—Americans and North Vietnamese, and it certainly isn't a North Vietnamese that's being kicked."

Paul Brudino found his excuse. He muttered angrily, "It could be a Thai." I was stunned.

Most people seemed relieved when the screams finally stopped. They could play bridge in peace now, and not be bothered with the annoying cries for help. I thought at times that I had reached rock bottom, but this by far was the Hell, the real Hell, of Hanoi.

In April most of the P.O.W.'s were in Camp Unity, but on May 13, 1972, 209 were moved out of the camp. Our South Vietnamese and Thai prisoners reported that they overheard guards saying that the prisoners were moving to one of two northern camps, very near to the Chinese border.

On April 16, 1972, the bombing again began. For some it was

a joy that the bombing started again. For others it was a gloomy day, for the bombing indicated the beginning of another period of indecision, to bomb or not to bomb, to wage war or pull out.

Things were going well as far as the escape was concerned. Room 3 had floated a map down the gutter. It was wrapped in plastic and placed inside a twig. When the guard wasn't looking, I was able to pick it out of the water.

It was a perfect map of Hanoi. It showed the places to avoid, streets, buildings, the river, and the exact location of the prison in Hanoi. We now knew exactly what streets were heavy with traffic and which ones to use to get easily to the river.

Big, black-haired Ron Webb noticed that there was a Russian-English textbook on top of a cabinet in the Bug house. Ron asked me one day if I could get it. It seemed I would be able to reach it from inside the cell with a long pole and a wire loop. I could insert the pole through the bars and into the Bug house, loop the wire around the book, pull the wire tight, then lift the book into the room. I gathered the material—the long bamboo pole and the wire —fixed up the loop at the end of the pole, and was prepared to go fishing. But first we needed permission.

Ron asked his flight commander and his flight commander went to Schweitzer for permission to get the book. It was decided that Ron could have permission. In the course of making the decision, the comment was overheard, "Go ahead and let them try it. They're not going to be able to get it, anyway."

But the fishing expedition was a success. Jaws dropped and eyes popped when I dropped the book on Dick Stratton's bunk.

A few cheered. We had the book. A. J. Myers, our philosopher and intellect, handled it with loving care. It was the best educational item we ever had in our captivity. Those attempting to study Russian practically drooled. We had a real book. Russian was presented on one side, English on the other. It had poems and stories, and it looked like it would be something that would keep everyone's interest for quite some time.

While most were marveling about the book, and realizing that we would be able to keep it because we were locked in at the time of its disappearance, others were frightened. The fear was that it might be found, and someone might be sentenced to Heartbreak. And, of course, nothing was worth going to Heartbreak.

When Ron had asked for permission to fish for the book, he had also been told that if he got the book he could keep it. But now a new decision was made by Schweitzer and company, fifteen minutes after the book was in our possession. We were ordered to return it to its exact, original place. Ron and A. J. Myers were seething with anger.

But Big George and I were determined to get a six-inch shaving mirror, for it was the last item that we required to complete our inventory for escape. Unlike the Russian book, the mirror was a piece of escape equipment, and so it did not come within the jurisdiction of the normal chain of command. With George clearing to insure that no one was there, I went up again on the windowsill, hung on to the bars, put the fishing pole through the bars into the Bug house, and came up with the mirror. I put it in our concealed storage hole for safekeeping. No one said anything. Now we had everything for escape, including a detailed map and two mirrors for signaling. Our plans were complete.

The ironic thing about the book was that it stayed there in position for the next two weeks. Finally it disappeared. Either the true owner picked it up, or another guard stole it. Who knows, but we were never questioned about its disappearance.

Unexpectedly, in the month of May, we received a note from the colonels. It said, "No go for options Alpha, Bravo, and Charlie." The "Mole Plan" was canceled. Jim Kasler immediately sent out a note to our contact on the south side saying that we felt Rosebud would give us a go, that there was a 75 percent chance that our plan would be approved.

On May 2, at twelve o'clock, we were to receive a signal from Rosebud. It happened. There was a loud clang like that of a symbol exactly at twelve o'clock. According to the prearranged signals, there was another clang ten seconds after the first. Our plan had been approved.

Kasler was playing bridge at the time it happened.

He asked me, "What was that?" I nodded my head, "yes," trying not to be obvious.

Paul Brudino and Bob Schweitzer were aware that something unusual was happening. We sent our request to the colonels on the south side, asking permission to go—saying Rosebud had approved option Delta of Tiger plan. A few minutes later I was called to the wall. On the other side was an old friend from the "Zoo Annex" who was on the Room 6 communications team. He informed me that Bob Schweitzer sent a message to another S.R.O. requesting that they urge Colonel Flynn to refuse any escape attempt.

"How did Schweitzer know the signals?"

Projecting my voice through the small hole, I said, "He probably didn't know, he guessed."

The next day we received a note from Colonel Flynn. Tiger plan was canceled. There was no need to talk to Jim Kasler. His only appropriate comment would be: I told you it was all for show. It could always be said we planned for escape.

We received another note from the south side a few days later. It explained the criteria for escape. It said that if the chances for escape were over 50 percent, then the escape would be permitted. If the chances for success were determined to be between 25 to 50 percent, it was up to the S.R.O. If they were less than 25 percent, there would be a no go. It was ridiculous to think that anyone could accurately compute the chances for a successful escape attempt, or that we could guarantee ourselves a 50 percent chance at success. We looked at one another when we read the message and finally realized that someone, someplace, was just playing with us. In the most dishonest and insincere manner, we were used.

George McKnight summed up our experience. He said, "John, when we get out of here, if someone were to ask me, 'What was the greatest obstacle to escape?' my only reply can be, 'Our own leaders.'"

XX

Fireworks
and Our Release

Of all those selected for leadership, only a few will emerge. The great leader is one who is capable of instilling within the people an attitude of understanding and a feeling of love.

On May 14, minus the younger officers who departed the day before, thirty-five of us moved from Room 7 across what was known as Camp Unity to Room 1. Room 1 was smaller than Room 7; it was dirtier; it smelled worse; and not only that, bothersome pigs lived on the other side of the wall. When the wind was right, it smelled, and when the soldiers cleaned the pens in the morning, it smelled even worse. The room was so small that some had to sleep on the floor. Sometimes when A. J. Myers tried to get a breath of air through one of the large drainage holes, he came nose to nose and eye to eye with a hog on the other side of our cell wall.

We were losing ground fast. There were no more singing rehearsals, and now there was talk again about discontinuing Toastmasters. As the new president of Toastmasters, I had decided we were either going to have it as it should be or we were not going to have it at all.

I went to Bob Schweitzer and told him that I objected to the rules as they existed and that, as president, I could not associate myself with anything which denied us the opportunity of speaking of Americanism, patriotism, or resistance. "That is why the hell we're here fighting," I said. "I am going to declare the rules void. If we want to clap because the speech is good, we should be able to clap. If we want to laugh aloud at some humor, we should be able to laugh aloud." I also said there would be no restriction on the volume used by the speaker; that was the prerogative of the speaker. I said that if I could not change these rules, I felt I could no longer be associated with such weakness.

Surprisingly enough, Bob Schweitzer said, "I think we can do that."

Without waiting for his explanation, I said, "Thank you," and left him.

Toastmasters meetings went on as usual. Our final meetings were with new rules, and we went on to complete Toastmasters in a fine manner.

Just before we switched rooms and after the April bombing started, there was a good deal of talk of the chances of the people in Hanoi storming the prison, or the guards attempting to take revenge on the prisoners because of the bombing. The guards could very easily throw grenades in the windows or shoot through the barred windows. There was also the annual flood scare and the possibility of being trapped inside the cell when a flood hit Hanoi. There was the possibility of a rescue attempt by the United States Forces, and there was the possibility of being bombed by our own pilots. All these things had to be taken into consideration and appropriate plans developed. Through the persistence of Collie Haines and myself we convinced Bob Schweitzer that a Disaster Control Committee should be established. Finally, it was organized, but every recommendation requiring action was turned down.

For example, in the new Room 1 we were now no more than seven feet away from the wall. It was possible to dig a tunnel from our room under the small alleyway and underneath the wall.

We proposed this as a hedge against any disaster situation; but we were refused permission by the S.R.O. The reason? We could be caught.

On one hand we were attempting to save our lives, and on the other we were willing to do nothing because we feared being beaten.

When an angry guard poked his Russian machine gun in the window during one of the bombing raids, I moved next to the wall where the guard could neither see nor shoot me in case he pulled the trigger.

I was later told to stand still in such a situation, because during bombing raids the guards were irritated, and an action such as mine might cause them to act irrationally. To my mind nothing could be more irrational than to stand in front of an automatic weapon held by an angry or possibly emotional North Vietnamese guard.

On no issue were our leaders willing to make a stand. If you argued with the guard, it was called a flap. No matter what happened it was always the P.O.W.'s fault. The Bug entered one day to announce, "Everyone must salute the guards." That meant when the guards entered the door we must stand up. And that's exactly what we did. By standing up we were now saluting the guards when they entered. Bob Schweitzer decided it was okay for all of us to stand up in the aisle by our sleeping places. Then the flight commander standing at the door would give us the order to sit down while we were counted.

On one occasion when the guard came in we all stood up as we were ordered. Then Ken Simonet, one of the flight commanders, gave the order to sit down. We all sat down, but the guard was not ready for us to sit down and insisted that we stand up again. Ken stood his ground and refused to give the order to stand up. The guard became furious. We were doing great until Bob Schweitzer gave the order to stand up for the guard and wait for him to give us the order to sit down.

In 1971 we sat anywhere while the count was completed. In 1972 we saluted the guards by standing up when they entered. In 1971 we saluted the American flag. In 1972 we conveniently forgot about it.

That night A. J. Myers announced that he would no longer volunteer or do anything in the room unless he was specifically ordered. He made no bones about telling Bob Schweitzer that if we were incapable of standing up for our own kind, or making at least some effort to resist the North Vietnamese, he was not going to do anything except what he was specifically ordered to do.

Many of us felt the same way. If we were going to lose our self-respect, perhaps we could maintain our dignity some other way.

I told Dick Stratton, who was sleeping next to me, that I was

going to put up the flag. I asked Dick, "Will you join me in saluting the flag every night?" He said, "I certainly will." The next
step was to inform Bob Schweitzer that I was going to put up the
flag. The night after I put the flag up, the room was called to attention and the flag was saluted for the first time in many, many
months. Paul Brudino was overheard saying, "To satisfy Dramesi,
we'll salute the damn thing."

The routine was once again established. In the evening, the room
was called to attention and we would salute our flag. In the morning, again the room was called to attention and we would salute the
flag before the day's activities began. During the day I concealed
the flag inside my mosquito net. We simply reversed the cycle—the
flag flew at night and was covered in the daytime.

A number of times at night I had to leap across people lying on
their beds and playing cards, and dash across the room to get the
flag before the door was opened. I always made it and our beautiful American flag was never discovered.

The tension in the room eased considerably. Ted Kopfman had
made one last attempt to form an escape committee and was refused. That now seemed to be a dead issue. There was no organized escape effort in Camp Unity.

Paul Brudino and Bob Schweitzer were talking. As I walked by,
Paul said, "How're you doing, John? Sit down." I sat down and he
asked, "Are you okay?"

I said, "Fine, everything is going just fine." I guess he was looking for some kind of congratulations for saluting the flag again.

He asked me, "Are you happy?"

I said, smiling, "Of course, of course."

Although I was far from happy with the whole situation, at least
the tensions had been relaxed. We were talking to each other, and I
was doing my best to get along with everyone in our tiny world.

Finally I had a long talk with Dick Stratton. We had always
talked very briefly at times and just recently we talked about Toastmasters. Our businesslike relationship had warmed slightly, but I
wanted to better understand the man, Dick Stratton.

"Dick, I have to apologize to you."

He looked up, puzzled, and asked why.

"Do you remember last year when I made a toast to Paul
Brudino on his birthday, and I told about seeing this fellow walk

through the Vegas courtyard with his chest out, proud to be an American?"

He said, "Yes—yes, I remember that."

"Well, Dick, I have to apologize because at the time I said that about Paul I was hoping to win his friendship so that I might be able to influence him concerning escape. If he thought that I viewed him as being a strong American, then perhaps when the question of escape came up, he would try to act like one. I must confess that the fellow I saw walking through the courtyard that time was not Paul Brudino, but Dick Stratton. It was you that I was admiring."

Dick looked at me and said, "Thank you."

I told him I was sorry; it was a stupid thing to try, but I guess I was desperate. His smile broke the ice, the conversation began.

I asked him about the "plantation," and I warned him ahead of time that I had heard so many conflicting stories about that camp that I was now confused. But I added that I had heard from John McCain and Ron Webb that it was Dick Stratton who, time and time again, tried to organize and establish communications throughout the camp and provide the necessary leadership. I said, "It was too bad you were forced to appear before the cameras."

I guess Dick realized what I was trying to say. He cut me off, saying, "John, that's one of your problems. You just don't realize that everybody isn't as strong as you."

"That's all over with now," I said. "By the way, I have to thank you."

"For what?"

"On the few occasions we talked, you gave me some good advice. You cautioned me against quitting Toastmasters and you stopped me from punching Windy Rivers in the nose. You may not have realized it." Dick nodded his head. He had the knack of being able to advise and yet not appear to criticize or lecture.

In an attempt to turn the conversation to something a little lighter, I asked, "Did you straighten out your buddy, George Coker, before he went North?"

"According to George," Dick said laughing, "everything I have learned about religion is all wrong, and everything George Coker learned about religion is right. The amazing thing is that we're both Catholic."

Getting serious for a moment, I said, "I'm afraid your gadfly has not been too successful. I have failed on all counts. It's pretty damned difficult to talk about resisting when people are unwilling to accept abstracts such as honor, respect, and pride."

"In another place and another time," Dick said, "they would agree with you, but here it's just too difficult to make the effort."

"But don't you think we're all going to have to account for our actions while we're here, Dick? That's why we resist—that's why we try to keep our self-respect."

"John, let me tell you—when we get out of this place, you'll be surprised who the good soldiers are going to be. *Everybody*'s going to be a good soldier. And everybody will be so tired of the Vietnam war and the P.O.W. issue that the question of resistance won't even be brought up. We'll all be part of one big group."

"Not if some of the people I know are still around. And if that happens the way you say it will, it won't be the military I'm familiar with. We can forgive and forget here, but out there it's a different world. If this whole situation isn't examined to determine the proper attitudes, then how in the world are we going to benefit from this experience? Somebody, somewhere along the line has to determine whether you do attempt to escape or you don't—whether you try to resist and limit the enemy's psychological weapon or you don't."

"I'm afraid we're going to be in for quite a few surprises when we get back," Dick commented.

"Well, there may be changes when we get back," I said, "but there is one truth. If we as a nation find ourselves without the will to play the game right, we're really going to be in trouble."

The gong went off and it was time to call it quits. I thanked Dick.

"For what?"

"Thank you for your honesty. In my book, you're one of the real heroes of this place."

He smiled. "And I admire the persistence and consistency of the gadfly."

I guess it was automatic now, but as soon as we moved into Room 1, I began looking around. As always, I examined all the bars and all the large drain holes, the toilet area, and the roof and the walls. Then I found it—the door in this room was the weakest point.

For the next few days I very closely watched the guard as he came in and out, inserting his key into the keyhole and opening the door. There was no doubt in my mind that I would be able to get out through that door.

There were two actions to the lock. One lifted a locking mechanism out of the sliding bolt, and the other simply pushed the sliding bolt to the unlocked position. To lock the door, one simply had to slide the bolt into position and the spring-loaded locking mechanism would fall into place and lock the bolt.

The key was a large old colonial type. One day before Hawk started giving haircuts, he had placed his keys on top of the small wall that surrounded our bathing area. When Hawk had his back to me, I gingerly picked up his keys and made a soap impression of the large key to our door. I was very careful not to make any noise, but as I set the keys down again, there was a faint jingle.

Hawk turned around, looked at me, and walked to the low wall. Standing nude before him, I began to soap myself with the piece of soap. As always, he very suspiciously looked at me. Sometimes I had the impression that Hawk thought I was either a magician or a superman, especially after the lock incident in 1969.

He pointed at the keys and grunted, "Umph. Umph." I gave him a blank stare and continued washing. Finally he picked up the keys, walked off, and continued cutting hair.

I looked through my assortment of rods, nails, and pieces of metal and came up with the proper piece. It was a small piece of rod about a quarter of an inch in diameter. With some filing and twisting I finally was able to make a crude key, using the soap impression as my guide. I also twisted the rod to form a fair handle for my new prized possession.

Most of the other prisoners did not know what I was doing. Some, as usual, looked and wondered what mischief I was up to next. When we were outside to bathe and the guards were busy handing out to some of us the crushed contents of the packages received from home, I gave a loud cough and simultaneously pushed the bolt into its locked position. I inserted my key and lifted the locking mechanism. At the same time I pushed the bolt from its locking position. The bolt very easily slid out of position. The door was again unlocked. I was ready. From inside the cell I knew it would require two people, one to insert the key and lift the locking mechanism and someone else with long arms to reach out through the bars and over my arm to push the bolt out of place.

The biggest hurdle, I thought, would be to obtain permission to unlock the door from inside the cell. I went to Collie Haines, who was responsible for our disaster control plan. I told him that I was positive I could get the door open, but to be absolutely sure, we had to try from the inside. I explained that it was necessary to know if we could get out of the room to satisfy contingencies of our disaster control plan. I emphasized, "Saving our lives is certainly more important than being beaten or harassed for attempting to open a door."

I was doubtful Bob Schweitzer and Paul would approve the plan, but two days later Collie approached and said, "Permission granted." I guessed they felt they could not refute the rationale for attempting to unlock the door.

The next day, with George McKnight hanging up in the windows, watching for guards, and stocky Ken Simonet peeping through the drain holes to clear where George was not able to see, Bob Craner and I went to the door. I was going to depress the locking mechanism with the key and Bob was going to put his fingers through the eye bolt and push the locking bolt aside. For the next two or three minutes, huddled next to the door, Bob tried but could not budge the bolt. Finally we gave up. By watching the guard the next day, I realized that there was a bit of pressure on the door once it was closed.

The next morning, with fat from our meal that day, I greased the sliding bolt and the eye bolt. During the quiet hour, we tried again.

This time I included Ted Kopfman. He was to reach between Bob and me and grasp the door. When I gave him the signal, he was to pull inward hard. I looked at Ken. Big George was again hanging in the window. They nodded, no guards were in sight. We went to work.

I pushed the locking mechanism down and kicked Ted. "Pull," I whispered. He braced his foot against the wall and pulled the door inward. I looked up to Bob.

"Did it go? Did it go?" I asked.

He looked at me, smiling. "Like a breeze," he said.

"Let go, Ted, let go," I said. Ted released the door. I slowly pushed the door open.

I turned and looked into the room. Everyone was dead silent, facing the door. Those sitting on their bunks with crossed legs, playing bridge and other games, looked up, stretching their necks to see. They looked like a family of prairie dogs sitting upright in the desert.

"Okay," I said, "we have no time to waste. Let's lock this thing." Bob stepped out of the way. Ted pulled on the door and I tried to push the bolt into place. It wouldn't go. I told Ted, "Pull harder!" He pulled harder. I tried again. I could not push the bolt into its locked position. "Get on that thing and pull!" I told Bob. "Sometimes the guard has to push hard to close this damn thing." Bob grasped the bars above Ted. They pulled harder. The bolt suddenly slammed into place. I forgot to cough.

The guard never showed up to investigate the noise. We relaxed, knowing we could get out anytime.

I already knew where I was going to hide the key. I climbed up on the back window. There were a couple of metal plates soldered onto the bars in a place where apparently they were weak. The two braces formed a small pocket. I laid the key between two bars. Then I covered it with some dust and dirt that I gathered from the windowsill. It was impossible to see the key. One would have to know it was there and then make a definite effort to get it out. As I walked back to my bunk to lie down for a while, I received a number of congratulations from those who were playing bridge. I flopped down on my rice mat, put my hands behind my head, looked up to the ceiling, and said, "It's a nice feeling to know you can get out anytime you want to. Right, Dick?"

He turned toward me, smiled, and said, "Yes, that is, if you want to get out. But how many people want to get out?"

"I guess you're right," I answered. "Sometimes success is only as easy as making up one's mind to make the effort. It's the all-important will to do it that is the key."

I looked around the room. It was my opinion that fewer than ten people of the thirty-seven, if given the guarantee that they could be on the other side of the wall with an airplane waiting for them just a few miles away, would make the effort.

Two days after the successful attempt to open the door, we received a lengthy note from the colonels on the south side telling us that only Bob Schweitzer had permission or authority to use the key to open our door. The note also specified that only escapes of opportunity were allowed. That meant that only if you were alone and if your effort did not affect any others, could you attempt to escape.

Big George McKnight looked at me and laughed. We laughed about the ridiculous situation that had developed over this escape business. Big George said sarcastically, "Yes, if you're alone in Heartbreak, you can escape."

I said to George: "Even then, it affects everybody. No matter who escapes—when, where, or how, it's going to affect everybody else. That's what these people can't get through their thick skulls."

"I think they understand that," George said. "That's why no one is going to escape."

For years we had discouraged escapes of opportunity. Now they were permitted. Fear dominates those who cannot master it. The motivation was clear.

The last part of the message reemphasized the necessity for a 50 percent chance of success. It was an impossible situation which Jim Kasler recognized a long time ago when he told me that no one in command here was going to allow an escape from this prison.

I did not totally agree with his statement. Neither did George McKnight. We knew strong military men like Denton and Stockdale were there on the south side, but unfortunately our situations were probably identical with respect to the prevailing attitudes among the prisoners.

Some time later George McKnight and I received a coded note, personally addressed to G.M. and J.D. When we finished decoding the note, we realized it was from Peg—Commander Stockdale.

The note read: "I have done everything I could to help you. Sorry I could not swing it. I know you tigers deserve that opportunity." Then it went on to say: "I have keys. I can open our door and get to the roof. Signed, Peg."

We looked at one another. We had analyzed correctly what had happened over on the south side. There were probably just as many arguments over escape among the senior officers as there were over here, and we knew who was on what side.

"Why is he telling us that he can get on the roof?" I asked.

George shrugged his shoulders.

I said, "Hmm, I wonder . . ."

Twice, sometimes three times a day, the radio spewed its propaganda. Most amazing was the fact that we were expected to be quiet so that everyone could listen to the propaganda. "It does not affect us," we were told by the SRO. Supposedly, it did not affect us, but from various corners of the room we would hear a loud "bullshit, bullshit" and people would become angry with what they heard.

The propaganda did not affect us, but in conversations among the prisoners one could hear mentioned the "Saigon government," the fact that the North Vietnamese had a right to treat us the way they did, the rotten government and the corruption in South Vietnam, and, of course, the concern over why the United States did not end the war.

There were supposedly two reasons why we did not tamper with the radio or simply turn it off: (1) because we could be caught and (2) because we had to glean some intelligence from the radio. I was told that there might be two percent truth in what the North Vietnamese told us. My only comment was "Two percent bullshit is still bullshit." When the music came on, it was no longer necessary to be quiet.

When the children's music played on Sunday, Ken Simonet actually was instructed to climb up the bars and disconnect the radio. Meddling with the radio was now justified. The children's music was disturbing to those who were playing bridge.

There were times when our world revolved around the fan in the ceiling, the radio, and the single bare bulb hanging from a steel beam. We were settling down to playing bridge and chess when a new guard, playing with the switches like the others, turned the light on but switched the fan off.

Paul Brudino called out, "Bao Cao, Bao Cao," the North Vietnamese words used to attract the guards' attention. The guard came by and Paul pointed up to the ceiling, telling him to turn on the fan. As far as the guard was concerned, Paul was pointing to the light and the fan. The guard went back to the switch box and turned off the light and turned on the fan. "Bao Cao, Bao Cao," Paul yelled and the charade was repeated. Again the guard went back to the box, turned on the light, but the fan slowly stopped its whirling. By this time everyone was being entertained.

Some began to hiss and to boo and to harass Paul by saying, "Way to go, Paul, you did it again," or "Can't you speak Vietnamese, Paul?"

It was all in fun, but to Paul Brudino it was very serious. The boos and the hisses continued until he became flushed. With all his might he screamed, "Bao Cao, Bao Cao." The guard came rushing back, but this time with an English-speaking interrogator. The English-speaking officer climbed up the ladder, pushed his face against the bars of the window, and demanded angrily, "Who Bao Cao?"

Finally the light, the fan, and the radio pacified the group.

But I had other things on my mind. There was another rainy season coming up. Another inspection was not expected for at least a month. I wondered just how much I could accomplish in one month. And Stockdale's phrase kept running over and over in my mind. "We can get on the roof—we can get on the roof." What did he want? What did he mean?

When everyone was outside, Ron Webb helped me to get the key. I relocated it in the toilet area. During that month, I stripped a mat and made a hat. It was better than any hat that I had ever made. I also was able to put out the lights by "accidentally" moving a ladder and knocking the wires out of place. Both lights outside were now out. It was completely dark within our courtyard. I had rubber straps and my shoes would be easily prepared to look like North Vietnamese shoes. I collected iodine for water purification and to darken my skin. I had a number of plastic bags available also. In a few weeks I fashioned a girl's North Vietnamese blouse, slitted skirt, and a pair of black baggy pants. The pregnant typist across from Room 18 gave me the idea. I was thinking I would disguise myself as a pregnant woman.

Before the end of July I had from John Pitchford, Larry Friese, Ron Webb, and Dick Stratton more food than I could possibly use. The small breakfast cereal bars we were now getting were perfect for what I intended. They were in plastic bags and waterproof.

With a couple of white handkerchiefs and some string, I made a white surgical mask. There was one final touch. I gathered all the hair that was cut during our last haircuts. The guard, thinking that I was doing a good job of cleaning the yard, paid no attention

to me. I carried it all into the room. When I was finished, I had
two long black braids of real hair. Then I attached my long pig-
tails to a skullcap I made from a sock. By now it was obvious
to everyone what I was doing. Everything I needed was available,
including at least forty feet of copper wire that could support my
weight. I made some alterations in my clothes with the needle that
I had used to make the flag.

Then one night when everyone was asleep, I put everything on
and stuffed a towel underneath my blouse. Now I had a protruding stomach. I picked up one of the bread baskets and walked
down to the end of the cellblock to where John Pitchford was
sleeping. "John, John," I whispered. "Wake up." He looked up in
amazement. He was not quite sure what he was seeing. Finally
when he realized that it was me, he said, "Christ, look at that!"

I leaned over and said, "Shh—how does it look?"

"Great! I can't believe it!" He whispered, "Are you going tonight?"

"No, not tonight! I just wanted you to see what I looked like.
See you later. Good night, amigo."

The next day I told Dick Stratton that I wanted to speak to
him that night.

After the door closed for the last time that day, we drifted
apart from the group. "You must have guessed what I've been
doing this last month," I said.

Dick said, "Well, there's no doubt about that, especially when
you knocked out the lights."

I smiled. "Of course, that was just an accident."

"Of course."

Seriously, I said, "Dick, you know that I can get out of this
camp. I have a detailed map. The Red River will rise again in
August. If everything goes properly, traveling only at night,
it's possible to be out to sea in forty-eight hours. And if things
don't go well, then let's say it takes four days. I've got a perfect
disguise, and I'm confident it can be done. No one can really say
how much longer we're going to be here, and I guess what I'm
asking is: will you help me if I decide to go?"

"Yes, I'll help you."

"Thanks, Dick," I said. "Seven other people have already told
me that they will help me. If I don't go, we'll have a ball eating up

all these breakfast bars that I've accumulated. I have one other question. I think I can make it, but do you think I should go?"

"That is your decision. But I can say this for sure—you're bucking a lot of people."

"I know that."

"There is a big question mark as to who is right and who is wrong here. A higher authority that says you will, and you should, but here the people are afraid—afraid of what could happen. But the only one putting his life on the line is you. We may be bounced around a bit, but I don't think anyone here will be killed. There is one other aspect. You have a hell of a lot to lose and the chances are you're not going to make it. If you make it, you'll be a hero, and if you don't make it, well, you know how the military is. . . ."

"But that can't be the basis for deciding," I said.

"I know," Dick said. "You're going to talk about the Code of Conduct and words we have a tough time defining here, but just once in your life be practical. You've been slapped down at every turn. Maybe you should take the hint."

The next morning I returned all the food bars and dismantled everything I had prepared in the last month. But every time it rained in the month of August, there was one burning question in my mind: "Did I make the right decision or did I let Ed Atterberry down?" There would be a clap of thunder, some lightning, and the lights would go out in the camp. The rain made loud noises as it hit the cement in the courtyard and the shingles on the roof. I pictured the water moving fast toward the sea. I finally fell asleep thinking: the perfect night; the perfect night; the perfect night.

By the end of August most of the old-time POWs were in Camp Unity, and all the new POWs who were shot down as a result of the April bombing were housed in Room 5. In late September and early October there was increased activity in the courtyard. The fences were being torn down and replaced by tarpaper fences. Also it looked like there was going to be a volleyball and basketball court. Recreation buildings were being built also.

As the work gang from Room 3 moved close to our building, tearing down the fences and putting new fences up, one of the senior officers suddenly jumped up on the beds, stood on his toes to look out the windows, and shouted to the group that was working outside our window: "Hey you cocksucking gook lovers, what are you doing?" There was a low moan in the room.

Paul Brudino was once more on the rampage. This time it was against Render Crayton, one of the flight commanders. Paul rushed over to Bob Schweitzer and said excitedly, "He lied—he lied!"

Bob said, "Wait a minute, Paul, who lied about what?"

"Render told me he was going to eat his food and he lied. He's hiding it and when he does eat some of his food he goes into the john and puts his finger in his throat and throws it up."

Bob had been making an effort to get Render to eat, and it looked like it was working, but now Paul Brudino was personally offended. So Bob, forced by Paul to take action, stripped Render of his command and told Render that if he did not start to eat, he would be denied the right to command his flight permanently.

The way it all happened was disgusting, but the fact that something was now being done to help Render and to force him to eat was encouraging.

There were a number of other encouraging events. After a redistribution of people we only had twenty in the room. On October 17 we were given some chairs and tables. By mid-October we had physical examinations, dental checks, and X-rays. By late October all the fences separating the courtyards of the cells were down.

With no escape planned I attempted to normalize my relationship with Paul Brudino over the next few months.

Each evening after the dishes were washed, the gong would ring indicating it was time for us to return to the room.

Often I would stand by the barred door and look out at the sky. A change had taken place in my outlook. I had never appreciated the combination of blue and green, but now as I looked through the leaves to the blue sky I realized that I had a liking for that combination of colors. The green of the leaves and the pale blue of the sky represented the freedom we all yearned for as we searched through cracks and small windows for glimpses of the outer world.

After the shadowy darkness dominated my picture, I focused my attention on the uncomprehensible multitudes of our minute view of the universe.

On nights like this Paul Brudino would come over after the

others were under their mosquito nets and lean against the bars. One night I said, "Do you know, Paul, that there are stars out there that are bigger than our whole solar system?" I turned to him.

He tilted his head, dropped his jaw, wrinkled his brow, and said "Yeah?"

I guess such magnitudes reminded Paul of God, and he started to tell me the story of how, when he was shot down, he saw God. He would go through the act of how he was bending over and taking off his parachute. He said he could see God's big feet right at his eye level standing in midair. Paul re-enacted the scene saying, "O God, O God, help me—help me."

His efforts to withstand the torture was another of his favorite stories. In an attempt to escape the agony he ran a piece of broken glass over his arm to cut his wrist. "It was a miracle," he explained. "As hard as I tried, I could not cut myself."

At times we would talk about resistance. He would ask me to give him my support in asking the colonels to lower the standards so that a prisoner could apologize and sign a written statement when accused by the North Vietnamese of defying a camp regulation. "Then everybody would be able to follow our rules of conduct," he said, "but as they stand now, no one can follow them."

I said, "Paul, you may be right when the time comes and there is a re-examination, but right now we don't have that authority. No one has told us that we can change the Code of Conduct. The guidelines stand as they exist. Our only obligation is to try to live up to those standards."

Then he would say, "You'll see—you'll see that I'm right when the time comes."

Paul enjoyed telling stories of his love adventures. I'm not quite sure whether it was an attempt to impress me or to reassure himself. He would go on and on. Sometimes I would be half listening and half watching for a comet or looking for the Big Dipper.

When I finally got back to my bunk and crawled under my mosquito net, Stratton whispered, "What did your Italian friend have to say?"

I whispered, "He really thinks I'm interested in his lousy sex stories."

The door was my favorite place to meditate after being locked

in for the night. The blare of propaganda over the radio interrupted my thoughts. As usual, an American voice told of the
righteousness of the North Vietnamese.

Bob Schweitzer was standing at the door.

I asked, "Who was talking?"

He said, "An old roommate. I could recognize that voice anywhere."

Naively, I said, "You were living with those two, weren't you?"

That started Bob Schweitzer off talking about his favorite
subject. He said that he thought that one of his ex-cellmates really
believed in what he was saying. "But the other," he said, "he's
something else."

Bob Schweitzer told me of the many times he and this prisoner
engaged in verbal battles over trivialities. "He always insisted that
he get the last word in or demand that I keep quiet." One example followed another depicting Schweitzer's conflict with his
cellmate. After 20 minutes, I realized that Bob Schweitzer's hatred
for this man and his desire to get out of the cell had nothing to
do with the question of resistance or with prison conduct; it was the
fact that his cellmate was an overbearing personality and totally
dominated Bob Schweitzer.

In that situation, Bob Schweitzer had lost his individuality.
Here he regained it. But only momentarily. A note which surprised
everyone, was received from Colonel Flynn, the camp S.R.O.
Paul Brudino was now the senior ranking officer in Room 1.
Brudino chalked up another success. He had badgered Colonel
Flynn into submission and verbally battered Bob Schweitzer into
surrendering his authority.

There was a nebulous cloud of confusion just below Colonel
Flynn, the wing commander. No one was ever positive who was
second in command. Our professed objective was to fight the
enemy and to resist in accordance with the Code of Conduct—to
escape, if possible. In the Hanoi Hilton, it seemed our objective
was to maintain one's prestige.

Paul Brudino did not stay around very long to enjoy his new-
found power. On October 27, 1972, we were told that there was a
breakdown in the Paris-Vietnam peace negotiations. The foxholes
began to be cleaned out and again it looked like they were preparing for air raids. On that day, Paul Brudino moved to the south

side and Jim Lamar moved to Building 1. As he walked in the door, George McKnight said, "The North Vietnamese know how to pick 'em." The senior officer in Room 1 of the Hanoi Hilton was Jim Lamar.

The North Vietnamese anticipated something, but they never expected what happened on December 18, 1972. When the guns started firing and the bombs started falling, there was no doubt in our minds that the United States was using B-52 bombers over North Vietnam.

The building shook and dust rose from the floor. As the bombs came closer, we cheered. At times we dived under our bedboards to hide from the falling plaster. The tremendous thunder of exploding bombs was accompanied by great bursts of flame in the distance.

Someone yelled, "It's the greatest show on earth!" Another shouted, "Kill 'em, kill 'em!"

It happened. What we suspected would have to happen finally was here. It was the most exciting, exhilarating, most encouraging thing that had happened in the last six years. Sometimes there would be hysterical laughter. Somebody shouted, "Go get 'em, Tricky Dick!"

"Pack your bags, pack your bags!"

"San Francisco, here I come . . ."

"Pack my bags? Hell, I'm ready!"

After nine days the smoke and dust settled. On January 21, 1973, 141 POWs returned from the northern prison camp called "Dogpatch." The whole prison was rearranged into groups according to the dates we were shot down. I moved into Room 3.

And on January 29, 1973, we were called out into the courtyard. The agreements of the release were read to us.

I walked back to Room 3 thinking, "After over seven years of indecision they finally got around to it."

On February 12, 1973, the first group left the Hanoi Hilton. That was a good day. It was Lincoln's birthday and it was my birthday also.

Now we were free to wander in the yard. I headed across the yard to old Room 7, thinking and remembering the first time the whole camp was allowed to congregate in the yard of Camp Unity. A tall prisoner came up to me and said, "I know what some people think, but I still think you did what was right." I smiled as I walked along thinking it was like telling a girl that she's ugly but you love her anyway.

I walked through the entrance of Room 7 and stopped, momentarily expecting something that was not there. I was recalling that great buzzing of mosquitoes in the torture room. Now this room was empty and silent.

I walked down to the other end of the room, and as I came closer to the wall that separated Room 7 and Heartbreak Hotel it seemed like it was throbbing. I recalled the time when American prisoners were packed four and five to a room in Heartbreak. In one week there were six and the next week there were seventeen sick men. The walls were attempting to help the men. Each was sending the signal, "Help us—help us." But as I looked around, no one lifted their heads. They continued to play bridge, and Paul Brudino's reply to the desperate plea for help was, "Eat crow."

I walked out of Room 7 for the last time and started across the courtyard to Room 1. On my way I met the Bug. He was trying to avoid me, but I caught up with him and asked, "Do you remember my friend, Captain Atterberry?" Bug was ready to turn, but I insisted and asked again, "My friend—do you remember my friend, Captain Atterberry?"

He wanted to move on but with invisible hands I held him there. Finally he answered, "He died—of a serious disease."

"When? When?" I asked.

Bug replied, "May 18—May 18." He turned and walked away from me.

I stared at the back of his head, wanting to reach out, grab him about the neck, and shake him like a rag doll, but I turned and walked toward Room 1, mumbling to myself, "I'm sorry, Ed —I'm sorry, Ed." Were we right? Did we do the right thing? Have we been right all these years?

Before I could answer my own questions, the gong rang.

Please send all correspondence to The Image Factory, Inc., P.O. Box 1827, Trenton, New Jersey 08607 to the attention of John D. Warwick.

"I would like to engage your services."

"You're getting married." Tiffany couldn't keep the shock from her voice. Jafar was a playboy desert sheikh who made no secret of the many women he'd loved and left. She'd found out the type of man he was when she'd looked him up. Sheikh Jafar Al-Shehri had surpassed every other best man she'd worked alongside. Ruler of a desert kingdom, a reformed playboy prince after unexpectedly inheriting the title, he was the ultimate incarnation of everything she wanted to avoid in a man.

He was also everything she'd been searching for in a man, yet had never expected to find. Ever since her only steady boyfriend dumped her because she'd wanted to wait until they were married to share intimacies, she'd been cautious about getting involved again. The idea that the desert sheikh could be the man to have a wild, passionate one-night stand with to shake off her past was a step too far.

"I am." His deep, commanding voice crashed through her wild train of thought. How could she be having such ideas about this man?

She forced herself to look into those sexy eyes, and her heart began to thump harder in her chest. Was it his sudden closeness or her thoughts? "And you want me to organize your wedding and be bridesmaid to your bride?"

He looked at her, assessing her, an air of calculation lingering around them. "No, I want to hire you—as my bride."

Rachael Thomas has always loved reading romance and is thrilled to be a Harlequin author. She lives and works on a farm in Wales—a far cry from the glamour of a Harlequin Presents story—but that makes slipping into her characters' worlds all the more appealing. When she's not writing or working on the farm, she enjoys photography and visiting historical castles and grand houses. Visit her at rachaelthomas.co.uk.

Books by Rachael Thomas

Harlequin Presents

The Sheikh's Last Mistress
New Year at the Boss's Bidding

Convenient Christmas Brides

Valdez's Bartered Bride
Martinez's Pregnant Wife

The Secret Billionaires

Di Marcello's Secret Son

One Night With Consequences

A Child Claimed by Gold
From One Night to Wife

Brides for Billionaires

Married for the Italian's Heir

The Billionaire's Legacy

To Blackmail a Di Sione

Visit the Author Profile page
at Harlequin.com for more titles.

Rachael Thomas

HIRED TO WEAR THE
SHEIKH'S RING

Recycling programs
for this product may
not exist in your area.

ISBN-13: 978-1-335-50435-7

Hired to Wear the Sheikh's Ring

First North American publication 2018

Copyright © 2018 by Rachael Thomas

Printed in U.S.A.

HIRED TO WEAR THE
SHEIKH'S RING

To Joanna Brown, who sowed the seeds of an idea, which grew into *Hired to Wear the Sheikh's Ring*.

Thanks!

xx

CHAPTER ONE

EVERYONE HAD A PRICE. Jafar Al-Shehri knew that better than most. He also knew exactly what that price was as far as bridesmaid Tiffany Chapelle was concerned.

It was a price he was more than prepared to pay in order to get what he wanted. He would do anything to prevent the increasingly hostile claim from his cousin Simdan on the kingdom he'd inherited after his brother's unexpected death. Ruling Shamsumara had never been his ambition, but duty to his people and kingdom, as well as to his brother, was something he would take very seriously. After hearing about Ms Chapelle's unconventional business as a hired bridesmaid, he knew she was exactly what he needed to stave off Simdan's latest attempt to overthrow him.

Jafar's gaze locked with that of the tall slender woman dressed in a bridesmaid gown of pale blue. She raised her brows in question, then continued with her duties at his friend and business partner Damian Cole's wedding. Her glossy dark brown hair was piled high on her head and dainty white flowers within the style matched the 'English country garden' setting of the wedding. She had a dusting of freckles on her face, which only added to her beauty, to the allure she unwittingly created. The thought of kissing her full lips had remained irritatingly close to the forefront of his mind since they had been introduced as best man and bridesmaid yesterday afternoon at rehearsals.

Ever since she'd smiled up at him, the stunning bridesmaid had unsettled him. He tried to convince himself it was because of the business deal he intended to put to Ms Chapelle and not the sparkling sizzle that had rocketed through him as she'd shook his hand.

When his friend had first announced he was marrying his childhood sweetheart, Jafar hadn't been at all surprised. What had shocked him was that the chief bridesmaid was not a close friend or relative of his bride, but a woman hired to do the job. Tiffany Chapelle made her living from hiring herself to brides as not just a wedding planner, but the chief bridesmaid. Damian had laughed when he'd quizzed him about hiring a stranger, saying every bride should hire their chief bridesmaid, especially if she had overzealous friends like his wife-to-be. Since then, Jafar had done his research on Tiffany thoroughly. Very thoroughly.

She was a woman who appeared to live romance vicariously through other brides' weddings and surprisingly had been hired by many rich and famous names. The fact that she was prepared to hire herself as a bridesmaid made her the perfect candidate for what he had in mind. Added to that, she didn't have any obvious signs of a man in her life but, most importantly for him, she was in considerable debt and had recently given up her rented apartment and moved in with her sister. He hadn't yet discovered what the debt was from but was confident he could strike a deal with her. To him, the debt was nothing and he intended to offer her far more to take on a role that would require her total commitment for the next three months.

The orchestra began to play and Jafar had attended enough Western weddings to know that the bride and groom would now dance alone and that he, as the best man, would be expected to lead the chief bridesmaid to the dance floor to join the happy couple a short time later. His best-man role was a duty he intended to perform with the same exacting standards he did everything, especially as it would give him the opportunity to begin subtle negotiations with the delightful woman fate had delivered into his path as the answer to his problems.

He focused his attention on the bride then his friend. He clenched his teeth together as he watched the commanding man he knew his friend to be, a lethal businessman who took no prisoners, looking adoringly into the eyes of the woman he'd married. He should be happy for Damian but witnessing such devotion, such love, served only to remind him of all he'd lost when he'd discovered Niesha's true colours. They had been promised to one another since they were children and he'd always had a fondness for her that had turned into what he'd then assumed was love. He'd been more than ready to enter into the marriage and make it work. Niesha, however, had set her sights on someone far superior to the spare heir of Shamsumara, as he was then.

The trail of his thoughts led back to his brother and the overwhelming sense of loss for a man who'd been both brother and father to him, shielding him from the wrath of their father's power-hungry ways, which had almost brought the kingdom to its knees. Malek had worked hard to regain the trust of the people and now that duty fell to him. He would not and could not fail his brother.

'I think this is where you come in.' The sultry and somewhat chastising voice of the bridesmaid jilted him from the gathering storm of thoughts as she came to stand next to him.

'I was merely allowing the happy couple time to enjoy the spotlight.' He looked down into blue eyes. They were as pale as her dress but rimmed with deep blue and full of an intensity that did more than hint at her passionate side. That sizzle he'd experienced at yesterday's introduction strengthened, becoming more like a bolt of lightning across the desert sky of his homeland.

Was it excitement at finally being able to put in motion his plan to save the people of his kingdom, Shamsumara, from his cousin's hostile claim on the country that bordered his own? Or was it the thought of being able to hold this particular woman in his arms as they danced?

'And there I was thinking you were avoiding me.' There was a teasing note to her voice, one that suggested a playful nature. A woman who was able to enjoy life.

'I hardly think allowing you time to complete the duties you have been hired for is avoiding you. That is your role, is it not? *Hired* bridesmaid?' His response was swift and the ferocity behind his words surprised him as much as the sizzle of tension around them, but the deal he intended to put to her was far too important to allow himself to be distracted by a pretty face and a sexy figure—or the challenge that lingered in the depths of those sexy eyes.

'You don't approve of me, do you, Mr Al-Shehri?' Her full lips pressed together in annoyance as she stood, one hand on her hip, glaring up at him, her eyes sparking like the icicles he'd always been fascinated with during those long cold winters at boarding school in England. 'Or is it the fact that I charge women to be not only their wedding planner but their bridesmaid too? It may be unconventional but Bridesmaid Services isn't the only business offering such services.'

'Having had the somewhat dubious pleasure of meeting the bride's best friend this afternoon, I can see how there is a need for hiring a bridesmaid who will do all that is required without any dramatics.' He'd soon discovered just what Damian had meant when he'd met the woman in question.

'So it must be me you don't approve of.' She teased him again with a smile and that underlying provocation in her voice, daring him to agree.

Challenge fired in her eyes but, instead of engaging her further in a battle of words, he gently but firmly took her hand from her hip, stifling a smile as her eyes widened in surprise. Before she could protest he led her onto the dance floor, fully aware she had no choice but to do his bidding unless she was prepared to risk drawing unwanted attention to them.

The gathered wedding guests applauded as he pulled her gently towards him, taking her in his arms until he could feel her slender body pressed against his. His body responded instantly to hers, to her scent, light and floral like the classic English garden flowers of the hotel. The movement of her waist beneath his hand as she began to move slowly in time to the music only intensified the surge of lust that hurtled through him.

What the hell was happening? It was as if this dark-haired beauty was sapping his strength, diminishing the control he was renowned for. She was making him want things he'd long ago learnt were not possible. He desired her, of that there was no doubt, but it was much more intense than his usual need of a woman. She was unlocking the man within him who long ago had put aside the need for the companionship of a woman. He knew precisely how destructive needs such as that could be. He shut down the train of thought, banished it from his mind, allowing heated lust to fill his mind and body in its place.

'Are you going to tell me?' The haughty rising of her brows and the challenge in her voice helped to snap him from the edge of somewhere he hadn't been for a long time. Somewhere he had no wish to venture ever again—memories of his past, of the life he could have led with the young girl he'd grown up with, the woman who should have become his bride. He pushed them savagely away. Now was not the time to complicate the future with the past and what he'd hoped for.

'It is not that I disapprove of you,' he said softly, holding her gaze as other couples now joined them on the dance floor. 'Quite the reverse.'

'You approve?' There was genuine shock in those lovely eyes now and despite the memories she'd almost cracked open he laughed softly.

'I do, yes.' He smiled at her increasing shock. 'You are the first woman I have met who doesn't attach sentimental nonsense to a wedding.'

She tilted her head to one side and looked up at him, her eyes narrowing slightly with suspicion. 'This is my job, Mr Al-Shehri. I am merely doing what I have been hired to do, which is to make it the best day of the bride's life.'

'So your sense of duty is strong?' He engaged willingly in the conversation, pleased that he could discover all the finer details about this woman from her, not second-hand through someone else. Private investigators could only glean so much, but they could never inform him of what made a person tick and it was important he got all the answers he needed before he put his deal to her. A deal that would secure his kingdom, Shamsumara, and maybe even set to rest the ghosts of his past once and for all.

'I'm dancing with you, aren't I?' Laughter sparked in her eyes and even though he wanted to keep their discussion on track and on a businesslike footing, he couldn't help but laugh too.

'I had no idea it would be such an arduous task for you.' He propelled them to the edge of the dance floor and towards the exit from the grand marquee, decked out in white and pale pink. The flower arrangements were all of the same white and pink flowers; only the bridesmaids in pale blue deviated from the colour scheme. 'Shall we enjoy the late-afternoon sunshine?'

'Are you taking me away from my duties, Mr Al-Shehri?' She was testing him, of that there was no doubt.

Jafar glanced at Damian and his bride, dancing as if they were one being. 'I think your duties are over for now. The bride and groom look blissfully unaware of anything except each other.'

Tiffany didn't miss the undertone of steely irritation in the best man's accented voice. All day she'd felt his gaze on her. She'd been acutely aware of him since their first meeting yesterday, in a way that unsettled her, tugging at dreams of love and happiness she'd long since given up on. As she'd sizzled beneath his scrutiny she had tried hard to ignore the disapproving set of his mouth, which had only increased each time they'd had to spend any amount of time together.

She'd also tried to ignore the fact that he was extremely handsome, tall and, with his dark skin, had an exotic appeal she knew had captured the attention of many female guests at the wedding—married and single alike. If circumstances were different, if she weren't here to work, then maybe he would be just the distraction from life she needed right now. Shocked at the direction her thoughts had wandered, she forced herself back to the present, wishing her best friend, Lilly, hadn't planted the idea of a casual fling, a one-night stand, as the best way to rid herself of the bad memories of her ex-boyfriend. She just wasn't that kind of girl. That was why she'd been dumped.

'Now I do detect a note of cynicism,' she said as she looked up at him, shielding her eyes from the glare of the late-afternoon summer sun with her hand as they stopped at the edge of the rose terrace. It was obvious this man was as against the idea of marriage as she now was but it was men like him who had shattered her illusion of true love.

'Do you believe in love and happiness, Miss Chapelle?' His gaze pierced hers and the vivid green of his eyes was in total contrast to his inky black hair and not at all what she'd expected when she'd been told the best man was a desert sheikh, ruler of a kingdom far away.

Tiffany reeled at the direct question, at his scathing tone. It proved her thoughts of moments ago—he most certainly didn't. She also was well aware of his reputation with women after listening to the bride chatter with the other three bridesmaids, all of whom were friends and one very obviously smitten with the dark desert stranger.

'As a matter of fact, I don't.' She pushed back her long-held dreams of finding the kind of love her parents had never managed to, standing taller in the face of this man's challenge. 'Not that I would ever let any bride I work with know that.'

He looked into her eyes, the connection so intense she could hardly breathe, but she wouldn't give him the satisfaction of looking away, of fluttering her eyelashes and enticing him to make her his next conquest. She almost gasped at the thought. What on earth made her think a man like him would want anything to do with her, a woman who, at the age of twenty-five, was yet to experience the touch of a man's caress and the pleasure of that ultimate intimacy between a man and woman? She'd been adamant she wanted to wait until her wedding night, until she'd found that fairy-tale happy ending.

'I like you, Miss Chapelle.' He turned from her, leaving her visibly weak after being under the spotlight of his gaze, but his next words sent her back into the spiral of confusion he'd had her in since he'd taken her hand and led her to the dance floor. 'I think it's important to like the person you are married to.'

She looked at his broad shoulders, encased in the dark charcoal-grey suit he wore, and wondered why such a self-assured, bordering on arrogant man couldn't face her and say the words.

She touched a nearby pink rose, the softness of its petals strangely calming. 'Yes, I think you are right. After all, if you don't like the person you marry, the odds of the marriage lasting are pretty slim.'

Her parents were testament to that. As were the arguments followed by stony silence she'd grown up thinking were normal. It was only when they'd split up and she'd been old enough to stay over at friends' that she'd realised it was far from normal. Those volatile early years of her life had made her resolute in her determination that she would have a happy, love-filled marriage.

He turned to face her. 'We agree on that, at least.'

'We do?' He confused her, one minute talking as if referring to marriage and friendship in general, then as if the discussion were directly related to them. As if they were a couple about to be married.

'Indeed, yes.' He moved towards her and the scent of his aftershave, exotic and wild, hit her as it had done on the dance floor. At least this time she wasn't pressed against his body, feeling every move he made, igniting sensations—hot, burning sensations—she'd never felt before. 'And therefore I would like to engage your services.'

'You're getting married.' She couldn't keep the shock from her voice. This man was a playboy desert sheikh who made no secret of the many women he'd loved and left. She'd found that out very easily when she'd looked him up on the Internet, just as she always did with every best man she was paired with. At least then she was able to find out the type of man he was, but Sheikh Jafar Al-Shehri had surpassed every other best man she'd worked alongside. Ruler of a desert kingdom, a reformed playboy prince after unexpectedly inheriting the title, he was the ultimate incarnation of everything she wanted to avoid in a man.

He was also everything she'd been searching for in a man, yet had never expected to find. Ever since her only steady boyfriend had dumped her because she'd wanted to wait until they were married to share intimacies, she'd been very cautious about getting involved again. The idea that the desert sheikh could be the man to have a wild, passionate one-night stand with in order to shake off her past, as her friend Lilly had put it, was a step too far.

'I am.' His deep and commanding voice crashed through her wild train of thoughts, bringing her sharply back to the present. How could she be having such thoughts about this man?

She forced herself to look into those sexy eyes, to appear in control even though her heart began to thump harder in her chest. Was it his sudden closeness or her thoughts? 'And you want me to organise your wedding and be bridesmaid to your bride?'

He looked at her, assessing her; an air of calculation lingered around them. 'No, I want to hire you—as my bride.'

She blinked and looked up at him, unable to say anything, then to her utter embarrassment she laughed.

Jafar inhaled deeply and waited while the prim and proper Miss Chapelle's laughter subsided. How dared she laugh at him? Nobody but his closest friends would dare to do such a thing. Didn't she know who he was?

'I think you have had too much champagne, Mr Al-Shehri.' Her voice still rang with laughter and a smile twitched at the edges of his mouth as she teased him, showing him a light-hearted side to her he found intriguing, but he forced it down.

'I am in full and total control,' he said as he prepared to play his ultimate ace. 'I have need of a bride and you, I believe, have need of a large sum of money to cover debts.'

Silence sliced between them as she looked at him suspiciously, all trace of laughter suddenly gone. The dark rims of blue around her eyes reminding him of the ocean that formed one border to his kingdom, but the paler centres had become hostile, like the heat of the desert. 'I see I am not the only one to have been doing some research.'

The tartness of her voice warned him he was

pushing her too far but, as ever, the challenge of getting *exactly* what he wanted pushed him on. 'I never enter into anything, not even being a best man to my childhood friend, without doing my research, Miss Chapelle.'

'So, do enlighten me, what has your research turned up?' She folded her right arm across her, beneath her breasts, placing the elbow of the other arm in her hand. Then, in a sexily tormenting gesture, she placed her thumb under her chin and her finger on her lips, sending a bolt of hot desire surging through him.

Her eyes blazed like the purest of gems, and her full lips snagged his attention as a bright red fingernail pushed into their plumpness. The late-afternoon sunlight danced in her hair, turning it to fiery bronze, highlighting the freckles sprinkled over her face. All he could think about was pulling her hard against his body, pressing her curves into him and kissing her. There was nothing gentle about the heat in his body, the need to touch her, kiss her, possess her. Without a doubt, he knew that if he gave in to the demands of his body now, it would be fierce, savage and wild. It would be total possession and if he weren't putting such an outlandish deal to her, he might already be taking her to his suite here in the hotel.

'I think you are bluffing, Mr Al-Shehri.' Her words dragged him from the erotic images of just what he'd like to do to her, sharply focusing his attention once more.

'You are in debt and you also need more, much more, thanks to your brother-in-law, who has left your sister in a very precarious financial situation.' He'd discovered that useful bit of information at almost the eleventh hour.

She gasped, her eyes becoming wide with shock. 'How do you know that?'

'I made it my business to know, Miss Chapelle.' He moved towards her, unintentionally breathing in her delicate scent, serving only to stir his body's needs once more. 'Everybody has a price and I now know yours.'

'So you want to pay me to be your bride?'

'Yes, Miss Chapelle, I do.' He'd just heard Damian say those words to his bride, but they'd been said with love, with hope for the future. Now he was saying them to this woman who stirred his senses in a way no other woman had; even Niesha, the woman he should have married if his life hadn't careered off course, hadn't ever roused in him such intense passion.

'And what makes you think I would agree to such a bizarre request?' Both her arms were folded protectively in front of her now, one hand pulling firmly on the other arm, serving only to press her breasts together in a way the pale blue dress couldn't disguise. Lust throbbed through him but he pushed it aside. This was not one of his casual affairs; this was a woman who held the future of his kingdom in her hands. The answer she gave him decided the fate of his people—and his.

If she declined, then his cousin, Simdan, would have every right to challenge his ability to rule. He didn't have the time to find a wife in the conventional way of his country. Besides, with his sister expecting her first child, which he intended to name as his heir, he didn't require a wife, merely a bride.

'As I intend our marriage to take place in two weeks' time you will be financially rewarded and therefore able to settle all your debts, and those of your sister. I will also ensure you have a substantial amount of money once our agreement is complete.'

'No,' she said, shaking her head. 'I have absolutely no intention of getting married for any sum of money and certainly not in two weeks.'

Jafar hadn't expected her to say yes instantly. Indeed, he would have worried that she saw him as some kind of knight in shining armour, the answer to a woman's dreams of happy ever afters, if she had. But in light of her current financial situation, he hadn't expected an outright no.

'So what has happened to the bridesmaid who ensures a bride's dream comes true to make her so against marriage?' He taunted her and satisfaction filled him as he saw her visible blanch at his question. It seemed she too had issues with the state of matrimony.

'What makes you sure something has happened?' She flung the question straight back at him.

'A woman who prefers to always be the bridesmaid and not the bride is definitely hiding from something.' He resisted the urge to tuck a stray strand of hair behind her ear as it slipped from the confines of her bridal hairdo, but had to clench his fist tightly in order to do that.

'This is my job, Mr Al-Shehri.' She glared at him and once again the need to kiss away the angry tension in those lips lurched forwards. 'Only a man like you could seriously contemplate buying a bride.'

Irritation spiked at the desire. She dared to challenge him? 'And what kind of man is that, Miss Chapelle?'

* * *

Tiffany could hardly contain her anger. How dared he offer to buy her? What kind of country did he rule over if he thought he could simply buy a bride when the need arose? Even worse than that, she had actually contemplated accepting because right now she'd do anything to free her sister, Bethany, of that abusive, gambling man she'd married seven years ago, and sort out the financial mess he'd created then walked away and left her in.

'The kind of man who can buy just about anything he wants, even, it seems, a bride.' She hurled the accusation at him and turned quickly, intent on walking away from him, from the lure of the answer to Bethany's financial problems and the almost irresistible draw of the man himself.

'Can you really afford to walk away from such an offer?' His words were hard and full of determination. Her steps faltered and she stood with her back to him, breathing deeply, still shocked by the way being close to him had made her feel as well as the outrageous proposition he'd put to her. 'Can you really deny your sister?'

She whirled round. 'I have no idea how you have managed to find out so much about me and my family, Mr Al-Shehri, but I will not be bought.'

He moved towards her, his long strides closing the gap between them. 'I have no intention of buying *you*, Miss Chapelle. I merely wish to hire you to accompany me to Shamsumara and become my bride. Beyond that we can remain exactly as we are. Strangers.'

'Your audacity almost makes me speechless,' she hurled at him. 'You even expect me to go to your country.'

'I doubt there is much that can make you speechless.' The tormenting laughter in his voice was clear, and as he smiled and raised his brows at her she wanted to stamp her foot and scream in frustration, but before she could do anything he continued the onslaught. 'Just as I know you will do anything you can for your sister—and her little girl.'

Now he'd hit her Achilles heel. Four-year-old Kelly didn't deserve to be caught up in the mess her parents had created. The acrimonious divorce had turned her from a bright happy child to an anxious little girl who barely spoke and Tiffany would do absolutely anything to rectify that, especially as she knew what it felt like to be that little girl.

'This has nothing to do with my niece.'

She could barely control her anger now. How dared he bring an innocent child into this absurd deal?

'Think about it, Tiffany.' The sound of her name on his lips shocked her, not least because of the dart of pleasure it sent coursing through her. 'Meet me here after breakfast tomorrow, when I am sure you will have come to realise this deal is the answer to all your problems.'

CHAPTER TWO

TIFFANY HAD TOSSED and turned all night, the usual buzz of having created another perfect day for a bride obliterated by Sheikh Jafar Al-Shehri's outrageous suggestion. It wasn't any kind of normal contract. He didn't want a bridesmaid. He wanted a *bride*. He wanted to buy her and that had unsettled her almost as much as the reaction of her body whenever he was close. Not to mention the steamy images, which had raced into her mind, of being kissed by him. A kiss she instinctively knew would be earth-shattering and dangerous.

As dawn had crept into the room she'd given up on sleep and left her hotel room and gone for a walk. It always helped to clear her mind and by the time she returned she knew she would accept the deal—but on her terms.

She changed into a short black summer dress and slipped on her black leather jacket, the only other outfit she had with her other than jeans and jumper, not having expected to have to be negotiating any kind of deal this morning. She made her way to the terrace with purpose in her step, intent on putting to him her terms for acceptance of his deal. The morning air was fragrant with roses but there was no sign of the man himself. She looked at her watch. She was late and she guessed he was the kind of man who didn't tolerate tardy timekeeping. A flutter of panic threatened. This was the chance she needed, and probably the only one she'd get, to make things right for Bethany and Kelly, and she'd thrown it away.

She turned to check she hadn't missed him. Not that anyone could miss noticing a man like that. With a flash of relief she saw Sheikh Jafar Al-Shehri striding across the terrace, the morning sunlight behind him as he came towards her. Just as she expected, he was dressed immaculately in a suit that had definitely been made for him if the way it hugged his long legs, hips and shoulders was anything to go by. Handsome didn't even go halfway to describing him. Sexy was the word that came to mind, but she slammed it back, refusing to accept she was in any way attracted to him.

'Good morning,' she said brightly, as if

meeting with a man to thrash out the finer details of a marriage contract were something she did every day.

'Would you like to walk or have coffee?' His fiercely alert gaze travelled down her, taking in the dress, which was probably too short to meet with a man who ruled a desert kingdom, finally resting on her white high-heeled sandals.

Again she'd earnt his disapproval. 'I'm not really dressed for walking. Coffee would be better.'

'Indeed,' he said as he gestured with an outstretched hand that she should precede him to the tables outside set for breakfast.

A thrill of something she'd never known before skipped up her spine as she became acutely aware of his eyes on her. The intensity of his scrutiny burned through her leather jacket and the fine fabric of the dress, making her shiver as if she were cold. In contrast the kind of heat from sipping fine brandy flooded through her.

As they neared the terrace of the restaurant a member of staff appeared instantly, eager to please the sheikh, and she realised for the first time just what his life must be like. He was much wealthier than any of the couples she had been hired by in the past, although plenty of them had given her a window into the world of wealth and luxury. This man, however, far surpassed that.

'A quiet table for two.' He spoke firmly, demanding precisely what he wanted without so much as a please or thank you.

'This way, Sheikh Al-Shehri.' The waiter led them to a secluded table at the edge of the terrace, where a mass of climbing roses clung to a trellis forming the perfect private area. The view from the table across the rolling English landscape was unrivalled, but, with her nerves like that of a young colt, she wasn't in the mood to appreciate it.

Tiffany allowed herself to be seated, as if waiting for such a thing were normal, and then tried to focus her attention on the view instead of the formidably brooding presence of the man she was about to strike the most bizarre deal with. A deal that, given the imminent repossession of Bethany's home, was now the only option she had.

'I'll come straight to the point, Mr Al-Shehri.' She paused for a moment to gather herself as he fixed his attention on her, wanting to word this right, but before she could say any more he filled that pause.

'Decisive. That is good. I like a woman who knows what she wants.' She looked at him, into those green eyes, and wondered if he was mocking her, but there wasn't even the smallest hint of a smile. In fact there was very little trace of any emotion. Only severe control.

She began again before her nerve failed her. 'Providing my terms are met, I will accept your deal. I will be your hired bride.'

Those last two words almost choked her. After the mess and complications of her parents' divorce, she'd longed to find true love and happiness. Her ex-boyfriend hadn't understood her need to wait to take their relationship to the next level and now she accepted her reluctance to do so was because she hadn't loved him. Not in the deep and intense way she'd always dreamt it would be when she met the man she would spend the rest of her life with.

'Terms?' He sat back, his elbow resting on the arm of the chair, his thumb and finger moving over his chin, the subtle sound of the hint of dark stubble snagging her attention.

'Yes, my terms,' she fired back at him, defiantly lifting her chin, determined to stand up for herself. 'You didn't think I would just accept whatever conditions you put forward, did you?'

'Very well.' He folded his arms across his chest and fixed her with the searing heat of his gaze and an explosion of fire erupted within her. 'What are your terms?'

This time there was a hint of amusement in his voice, the slightest movement upwards of his lips. She almost laughed out loud when she realised he'd probably never had anyone set out their terms to him for anything. He must be used to getting precisely what he wanted all the time. Well, she wasn't about to make this easy for him. Yes, she needed the money, and needed it now, but she had to keep some dignity, had to demand at least something for herself. After all, marrying anyone was a big deal, let alone a stranger.

'Before we discuss that, I want to know why you need a bride in such a hurry and why me?' She looked at him, using the fire to boost her confidence, to show him she was a woman who could hold her own. 'Why not a woman from your country? In fact, I think you are hiding something, Mr Al-Shehri.'

'Jafar,' he said calmly. Completely unruffled by her questions. 'I'd much prefer to be on first-name terms with the woman I am negotiating a marriage contract with. It's so much more personal, don't you agree?'

Her fierce response to that question was halted by the arrival of coffee and for a moment she allowed herself to believe this wasn't happening, that none of this was real as the strong aroma of coffee fired her senses.

'Well?' he demanded as they were once more left alone. 'Do you agree, Tiffany?'

The emphasis he put into her name, his exotic accent caressing every syllable, made her pulse leap and she had to force herself to look into his eyes, to meet the power of this man head-on without flinching, without showing any fear or doubt. 'Absolutely, Jafar.'

His name seemed strangely familiar to her tongue as she sat straight and tall in the chair in a bid to appear as in control as he was. She almost achieved that until he smiled. It happened so suddenly she quite literally forgot to breathe as she became the focus of his attention. Heat sizzled over her at an alarming rate.

Jafar watched as a charming blush bloomed on Tiffany's cheeks, knocking the confident businesswoman sideways and allowing him to glimpse the woman he believed she never wanted him to find. The passionate, yet shy woman who lived beneath her toughened exterior. That was precisely why he wouldn't be giving in to the urge to kiss her that he'd had since the moment they had been introduced. She was wrong for him on so many levels, but right in only one. She needed him as much as he needed her, not that he'd ever allow her to know just how much.

'What exactly do you want to know, Tiffany?' She looked at him, then away, that shyness coming to the fore once more. It intrigued him. Maybe the time they would have to be together as man and wife was going to be far more interesting than he'd anticipated.

'Why a man such as yourself has to marry a complete stranger within two weeks?' Her blunt question fired directly at him and he admired her honesty, even if it meant he would have to share part of himself, part of his past with her. Something he never did with women.

He looked away across the fields of green grass as he thought of his brother, Malek, and the accident that had claimed him and his wife. That tragic day had made Jafar the ruler of Shamsumara. He'd always had the good of the country at heart, but never once in recent years, when he'd been sharing the burden of bringing the kingdom back to a good place to live after the tough years his father had ruled with hardness and cruelty, had he imagined himself the ruler. Jafar had never considered the possibility that one day that responsibility would lie solely with him.

'I became the ruler of the kingdom of Shamsumara after a sudden family death. One which has left the country in a vulnerable position, open to the challenge of leadership from a man who rules his own kingdom with the same fear and dominance my father had ruled with. It is not the way I rule and I will not allow my people to live through that again.'

He looked at her face, saw the confusion in her eyes and knew this must be sounding so far-fetched to her. A dart of doubt shot through him. Was he doing the right thing, involving this woman in the affairs of his country? She might be in need of the sort of funds he could easily provide, but would she be able to fulfil the duties that would be required of her as his Queen? Even if it was only for a short time?

'It seems to me that you need far more than a bride,' she said as she sipped her coffee. He looked at his, but knew he wouldn't taste it, that the memory of his brother and the threat posed by his cousin, the one man he truly hated, would obliterate all sense of taste. 'You need a wife, a *proper* wife, a woman to give you heirs. That woman would be your Queen, wouldn't she?'

He couldn't help the shock that slammed into him. Maybe he'd misjudged this alluring woman. She was far more astute than he'd given her credit for. 'Yes, my bride will be my Queen and in normal terms an heir is exactly what I would need, but, on this occasion, no. My sister married last year and is expecting her first child. The usual order of things in our country is that *her* child will become my heir until such a time as I have my own child, which of course I don't plan to do. So producing an heir myself isn't necessary.'

She narrowed her eyes at him. 'I'm confused. If you don't need an heir why not marry a woman from your own country?'

'Because I have no wish to be married in the true sense of the word.' How the hell did he put the last two years into a few concise sentences that would make sense to her? 'As an unmarried ruler, I am open to challenge. That challenge would come from my cousin Simdan, who rules harshly over a small country which borders Shamsumara. He wants my kingdom for the power it would bring him—and the wealth. Shamsumara is rich in oil.'

'And if you were married?' The question lingered in the air like the threat of thunder.

'My cousin has recently become a father and as a married ruler with an heir he can challenge my rule. If I married, his immediate ability to challenge me would become less and once my sister's child is born and declared my heir, his claim on my throne is no longer valid.'

She put down her coffee cup with a clatter, spilling the dark liquid into the saucer. 'When is the baby due?'

'At the end of October.' It was this very fact and the possibility that things could even now go wrong in his sister's pregnancy that necessitated Jafar's marriage. He was well aware that Simdan was already making moves to launch a claim for Shamsumara. If the unthinkable happened and his sister lost her baby, he would at least be the married ruler tradition demanded.

'So where exactly do I come into all this?' The panic in her voice was clear and he quickly realised where his explanation had taken her thoughts.

'I only require you to be my bride. I have no intention of making a real marriage or having my own children, not when my nephew or niece will soon be born.' He saw those expressive eyes widen and knew exactly what she was thinking. Three months was a long time and anything could happen. It was his aide's main concern too.

'If that is the case, why do you need to marry at all?' Was that a hint of relief he detected in her voice? She pushed her coffee cup away as if the conversation was coming to an end, as if she'd already decided she would not take him up on the deal. He couldn't allow that. He had much to lose and so did she. Something he would remind her of. 'Can't you name the baby now as your heir?'

'In order to continue to rule in my brother's place I must be married the day after the feast of Shams, which is two weeks from now, or my cousin has every right to claim the kingdom.' Just as she had done yesterday, she laughed. He bit down hard against the irritation. How dared she when her own life was in such a mess? 'I must then remain for two years.'

'Two years?'

'You would only be required to remain in Shamsumara as my wife and Queen for three months or until my sister's baby is born. We will have to remain legally married for two years, but after that a divorce will be easy to procure. And, of course, you will have a very substantial settlement.'

'And because of my job and my financial situation you thought I would be desperate enough to be your hired bride?' The amusement in her voice held no malice but it didn't soften his mood. He was not used to having to cajole women around to his way of thinking.

'I would rate imminent repossession of your sister's home desperate, but, of course, if you don't...' He left the sentence unfinished, his withdrawal of the deal, which he knew full well she needed, hang in the morning air between them. It felt like the biggest gamble he'd ever made. She looked at him in silence, something other than strained tension zapping between them. Raw desire.

'I find it alarming that you know so much about me, Mr Al-Shehri.' The curtness of her tone when she finally spoke left him in no doubt he'd touched a raw nerve.

'I thought we were on more informal terms now, Tiffany.' He added her name, enjoying the flash of anger in the depths of her eyes. He leant forward in his chair and lowered his voice. 'We are, after all, almost engaged.'

'Not so fast. Not until you have agreed to my terms—all of them.' He admired the fire of defiance burning within her, revelled in the challenge she was unwittingly creating. He thrived on challenge, hated meek-willed individuals who would agree to anything he said just because of who he was.

At last he'd met a woman who was more than a match for him. The next three months of living as man and wife would prove very interesting indeed. 'I think it's about time you told me just what they are.'

She sat back as she looked at him, the haughty lift of her chin showing her spirit, reminding him of an unbroken horse. She had as much spirit as a stallion and, just as he did with his horses, he looked forward to harnessing that spirit, to turning her into one of his graceful falcons that would fly at his bequest and return willingly to his arm.

The thought shocked him. Did he want a woman to return to him, to want to be with him? It was something he'd never sought before so why now? Because she would be his wife, his hired bride?

'First of all I want a payment up front. Today.' She looked at him, as if waiting for his objection, but he merely sat and studied her. 'I want a quarter of a million pounds in my account before the end of the day and a second payment the day we marry.'

Was that all? He'd planned on offering her much more than that. 'Consider that done. Anything else?'

Tiffany looked at Jafar, at the handsome and very regal figure he cut sitting opposite her. Had he really agreed to that amount of money without so much as a flicker of a reaction? Was he that used to buying everything he needed he didn't care what it cost?

She still couldn't believe that by her simply agreeing to stand beside this man and become his wife, all Bethany's problems would be over. It was almost too good to be true. The saying of looking a gift horse in the mouth drifted through her mind as she looked at the firm line of his full lips. Was it really going to be this easy to help her sister and secure a future for her niece, Kelly?

'I will need to continue my business.' His frown slashed her confidence and her words stalled.

'You have other bridesmaid contracts such as yesterday's?'

She hadn't taken any bookings for the next six weeks because Kelly was about to finish nursery school for summer holidays. It was her chance to give Bethany a break and really be there for Kelly as she prepared to start big girl school in September. It was also a reminder that being an aunt could well be the closest she'd ever come to being a mother herself, with her dreams of finding true love and a happy marriage sabotaged by this man's deal. She would put aside her dream for her sister and niece because she could never be happy knowing she'd walked away from the only chance to sort things out for them.

'The next wedding is booked for early September and I will need to visit the bride between now and then.'

'You will remain in Shamsumara for the full three months specified unless I accompany you.' The harshness of his tone shouldn't have surprised her, but it did. She was helping him out as much as he was helping her. Maybe it was time to remind him of that.

'In that case you will have to do exactly that.'

'No, that is out of the question.'

She pushed her chair back and stood up, slowly and full of poise and dignity. 'In that case, Mr Al-Shehri, we will not be able to strike a deal.' She was calling his bluff and he damn well knew it, but she didn't care. This was her stand. If he'd managed to find out all about Bethany's financial situation, then he knew just how desperate she was, but there was no way she would ever act it in front of him.

'I don't think for one minute you intend to walk away from this deal.' The vibrancy of his eyes pierced into her, dragging her secrets from the depths she'd hidden them. 'And while I do applaud your honour to your business commitments I insist you stay in Shamsumara for three months. My cousin must see our marriage as real if it is to achieve its objective.'

'And what does that mean?' Irrational anger bubbled away within her like a hot spring. 'I can't continue my business? That I can't return to England and make arrangements for my client?'

'It means that you can continue with your business but I would prefer you to remain in Shamsumara. How many other weddings do you have to attend to?' There was a brittle harshness in his tone, which only served to anger her further.

'There are others in later months, but our three-month deal will be over by then and no concern of yours.' His brows rose at her tone and that sexy hint of a smile made her tummy

somersault and to hide her embarrassment she
sat back down, wondering if Bethany could
stand in for her and visit her client.

'As it is just the one client, then I am happy
to support that.' There was a mischievous glint
in his eyes and she wondered if he was toying
with her, but now was not the time to test it
out. She needed that incredible sum of money
he was prepared to pay if she was going to secure Bethany's and Kelly's future, keep a roof
over their heads. She'd even be able to set herself up once this bizarre marriage was over and
three months wasn't that long.

'In that case, Mr Al-Shehri, we have a deal.'
She stood up and put her hand out to shake
on the deal. He stood and looked down at her,
then finally took her hand in his, but not in the
way she'd expected. He held her fingertips and
lifted her hand to his lips, his gaze locked on
hers all the time, and then kissed the backs of
her fingers.

The spark of fire that kiss evoked rushed
up her arm, making her heart flutter as if she
were a teenager. Shyness crept over her and
she lowered her lashes, blocking out the intensity of his eyes.

'I will send my car for you next Friday.' If
she didn't know any better she'd say that the

moment had affected him too, his voice was more of a hoarse whisper, but surely not. A playboy sheikh who had the pick of all the glamorous women he wanted would never be affected by a woman like her. Did he have any idea just how inexperienced she was with such things? 'Is that sufficient time for you to put things in order?'

Put things in order. Could that ever really be achieved? At least the payment he'd agreed on would take away the threat of repossession for her sister.

'Yes, perfectly sufficient,' she said, keeping her voice brisk and businesslike, trying not to think of the implications of accepting his proposal. After all, it wasn't a real proposal and certainly wouldn't be a real marriage.

'Good, then it is settled. You will accompany me to Paris, where we shall make it obvious to anyone who sees us that we are not only a couple in love, but engaged to be married.' His bold confidence almost knocked hers, but she held her ground, kept her composure.

'If arranged marriages are acceptable in your country, why do we need to do that?'

'Because this is not a conventional arrangement and I do not wish to give anyone, least of all my cousin, the chance to challenge it.

We will act out our engagement in Paris for one week. In private I will instruct you on all you need to know and provide you with everything necessary for your role. After that we will travel to Shamsumara and arrive in time for the feast of Shams—and our wedding ceremony.'

'So soon?' The hesitation in her voice brought his scrutiny to her once more.

'I trust you are not getting cold feet?'

'Absolutely not. This is a deal that will enable us both to get what we want and for my sister and her daughter I will go to Paris with you, then to your country to become your wife.'

CHAPTER THREE

FIVE DAYS LATER Tiffany was waiting for the car Jafar had told her would collect her. She had put her life in order, at least as much as she possibly could, given the bizarre deal she'd agreed to. She pushed the implications of marriage to a man like Jafar Al-Shehri to the back of her mind as a sleek black and very luxurious-looking car pulled up outside her sister's house. At least Bethany wasn't here to try one last time to talk her out of it, having left early to go with Kelly on her nursery school trip.

Tiffany took hold of the handle of her suitcase and looked around the living room one last time. Kelly's toys, as usual, were scattered around everywhere and the book Bethany was reading was face down on the coffee table. Shock crashed over Tiffany like angry waves. She wouldn't be here to see the book finished or the toys played with. She would be in a country she barely knew anything about, married to a man she knew even less about.

Was she doing the right thing?

'Stop it,' she berated herself. It wasn't as if she'd be away for ever. Just three months. She had to do this, for Bethany and Kelly, and there wasn't really any other option left to them. With a determinedly inhaled breath, she turned and walked out of the house to the waiting car, its darkened windows making it impossible to see inside.

The driver's door opened and Jafar got out. The burst of determination that had filled her just moments ago vanished as his eyes met hers. He looked sexy and incredibly powerful. The black suit, over which he wore an expensive camel-coloured coat to ward off the unusual chill in the summer air, only elevated his aura of command.

A skitter of apprehension raced down her spine, excitement hot in pursuit. How could just one look from this man have such a profound effect on her? 'I wasn't expecting you.'

The words were out before she could stop them or give herself the chance to act as calmly and in control as he so effortlessly did. He remained tall and straight as he stood next to the car.

'We have much to do once we arrive in Paris before we begin the act of a whirlwind romance.' There was a new depth to his voice. Was it more command or more determination?

She moved closer to the car and as he came to take her case from her she could see the determination in his eyes too. The fierce spark of power that only a man in complete control of his destiny could have.

He's also in control of your destiny and will be for the next two years.

'Such as?' she demanded fiercely as that thought lingered in her mind like the ash after a fire.

It was the first time she'd thought beyond the three months he had stipulated she spend in his country. She'd been so wrapped up in being able to help Bethany she hadn't thought of what would happen for the remainder of their so-called marriage and it was now one of the things she intended to sort out in Paris.

Jafar opened the passenger door for her and stood looking down at her. Was it possible that he suddenly seemed taller than she remembered or was it because she was losing control rapidly? She could still back out. She looked at the house she'd moved into with Bethany and Kelly several months ago and knew she couldn't, not if she wanted to help them keep a roof over their heads, and now that Bethany knew all about this deal she definitely couldn't.

She met the suspicion in his eyes and spoke again before he had a chance to say anything. 'All the trimmings that come with such a whirlwind romance?'

'One thing you will learn about me, Tiffany, is that if I do something, I do it properly.' He paused and stepped a fraction closer so that she caught the exotic scent of his aftershave. It was wild and free, like the air itself—or the desert. As she tried to halt those thoughts he spoke again. 'And making you my wife will be no exception.'

No response to that statement came to mind and instead she got into the car, trying to ignore the sensation of overwhelming wealth and luxury that assaulted her senses as she did so as wildly as the man himself. Jafar got into the driver's seat and soon they were heading towards London for their flight to Paris. She watched the countryside she'd grown up in rush past, her thoughts crammed with just how he was going to make their engagement and subsequent marriage appear real. She was thankful when music began to play gently against the hum of the car engine. She forced her mind to relax, to go with the absurd deal she'd struck with this man. A man who had the ability to make her wish for things she'd vowed never to want. He made her want to be desired and even loved.

The full extent of the contract she would sign with the desert sheikh became apparent later that day, as she entered the suite of one of Paris's most prestigious hotels to find the room full of designer dresses, shoes, handbags. Everything the kind of woman she was expected to be could want.

'Now I am beginning to understand what you said to me earlier.' She was determined to keep the complete shock and wonderment from her voice. There was no way she was going to allow him to know he was playing into the kind of Cinderella moment almost every girl dreamt of. 'You certainly seem intent on kitting me out properly.'

'As I have said, we need to be seen having a whirlwind affair while we are here in Paris and you need to look the part.'

This was confirmation that she was not at all like the kind of woman he usually associated with. She didn't have the experience of men like him to start with. What if he realised that and backed out of their deal? She couldn't allow that to happen. She would have to ensure she played her part well, be what he wanted her to be.

'I had all this arranged.' He gestured around him at the rails of clothes. 'To provide you with all you will need.'

His deep voice was silky, his words gentle, but there was no mistaking the undertone of icy determination in them. Or the accusation that she was far from suitable and it hurt. For some strange reason it mattered to Tiffany what this man thought of her. She hid her confusion at that revelation behind sharp-edged words.

'If I am so very unsuitable, then why are we even doing this?' She couldn't help but test him, push him to the limits.

She saw his jaw clench as he looked at her from across the luxurious surroundings he was so obviously used to. 'Our arrangement serves us both well. I am in need of a wife and you are in need of money, part of which you have already received.'

'You make it sound so cold.' He glared at her and she hid the smile of satisfaction that she had riled him, rattled his gilded cage a little.

'Not getting sentimental on me, are you?' He moved closer to her, his steps silenced by the thick carpet of the room. Now he was testing her.

She could feel his presence invading her, feel him taking over the very air she breathed. 'No way.' She lifted her chin to look into those fierce eyes and tried to ignore the jolt of something unidentifiable, yet exceedingly powerful, that zapped through her as if he had actually touched her. 'This is merely another contract as far as I am concerned.'

'Good.' The word was strong, forceful. 'I wouldn't want you to get the wrong idea when I begin to wine and dine you and act like a lover who wants nothing more than to seduce you.'

She swallowed hard against the sizzle that held both fear and excitement as images raced into her mind of this man doing exactly that. 'You are not my type, Mr Al-Shehri. There is no need to worry about that.'

The fire in her voice sent a thunderbolt of lust-filled desire streaking through him. Tiffany Chapelle was as good as issuing him a challenge. The challenge of seducing her and right at this moment it was all he could think of doing. He wanted her naked beneath him as she writhed in ecstasy, begging him for more.

A knock on the hotel-suite door hammered through him as if he'd been slapped in the face. What the hell was he thinking, wanting this woman? All he needed to do was marry her, make her his wife in name only and then live with her for three months. Once his sister's child was born, they could return to their lives and divorce in two years' time. If he made love to her, either before or after they were married, it would turn their deal into something so much more. Not to mention harder to extricate himself from.

'Come,' he snapped as the control began to return to his body, even though his mind still reeled with images of Tiffany naked beneath him as he looked down at her. He never allowed women to get to him like this and he was damn sure Tiffany wouldn't be any different. It must be the bizarre situation they were now in. A primal need to claim her as his wife in every way.

He had no time to indulge in such thoughts now. He had a job to do and that was to supply Tiffany with all she would need to carry out her role as his bride-to-be. Whatever else he thought of the state of matrimony and no matter how close he'd come to it once, he had to ensure the woman he'd selected for the role of his bride looked the part, both here and in his kingdom of Shamsumara—the very reason all this was even happening.

'This is Madame Rousseau.' He introduced the world-renowned designer and was pleased to see a moment of surprise on Tiffany's face. 'She will provide you with all you will need for our week in Paris and, of course, your wedding dress.'

Tiffany turned to the older woman and spoke to her in French. 'I am honoured, *madame*.'

Instantly the woman he'd chosen for a bride was winning over the designer and a dart of admiration filled him. It appeared there was much more to Tiffany Chapelle than he'd first thought. Again that need to know more, to find out more, to explore in unchartered waters surfaced.

'You will be the most beautiful bride,' Madame Rousseau praised, obviously pleased to be able to converse in her mother tongue. 'And you will make a fine queen for His Highness.'

Jafar's body stilled. He had not yet explained to Tiffany that her role would entail much more than being his bride, that she would have to assume the role of his Queen for the duration of her stay in Shamsumara.

'She will indeed make a fine queen.' He smiled at her, aware of her scrutiny.

'It's a role I intend to take very seriously,' she said with the biggest smile he'd yet seen on those very kissable lips. Confidence oozed from her, making him sure she could carry it off perfectly and letting him know she accepted the challenge.

'So you have kept your romance secret for the last few months.' Madame Rousseau continued in that wonderfully passionately way she was known for, obviously buying into the story he'd told her. 'How very clever of you both.'

Madame Rousseau instructed with the wave of a pointed finger for Tiffany to turn, and as she did so Tiffany's gaze met his and the sparks of annoyance in her eyes were so powerful and incredibly sexy he had to curtail the need to send the designer away and kiss Tiffany until she begged to be his.

He pushed that urge to one side as he sat waiting while Tiffany was fitted with the first dress, which he'd instructed to be simple but elegant for daytime in Paris, but his mind kept returning to the memory of her last Sunday morning in the short dress with a black leather jacket. Far from expensive, he was sure, but it had made her look a million dollars.

'This one is perfect.'

Madame Rousseau's voice ruptured his thoughts and he looked up to see Tiffany in a black dress, loosely cut yet somehow incredibly sexy. To complete the look she had a black clutch bag and dark sunglasses. The whole look showed off her glorious hair colouring and pale complexion to perfection.

'I agree,' he said, not liking the hard gravelly tone to his voice, and if the expression on Tiffany's face was anything to go by, neither did she. There was that challenge again.

He kept that steely control as Tiffany paraded in many different outfits, some of which he rejected, but most of which he agreed with Madame Rousseau that they would be perfect for her role as his bride-to-be.

'There is one more gown,' Madame Rousseau said. 'The evening dress for the charity event.'

'Charity event?' Tiffany questioned and looked at him, her lovely blue eyes wide, like a captured animal who didn't know whether it should run or stay.

'We have been invited to World Water charity dinner, attended by many famous names.' He had a twinge of guilt as she suddenly looked completely out of her depth. Surely she'd mixed with the rich and famous before as part of her job? She'd certainly sold her business to him as that, which had been one of the main reasons for going through with his plans; he'd been sure she wouldn't be fazed by such occasions.

'Come, come,' the designer said quickly, and Tiffany turned her back on him. He watched her as she walked back into the other room and listened to the delighted sounds from Madame Rousseau.

Even so, he wasn't prepared for the way Tiffany looked as she came into the room again, chin held regally high, her hair quickly pulled up roughly into a chignon. Her pale skin showed the beauty of the black lace, set with black gems, but it was the slit to the top of her thigh he couldn't stop looking at. One pale, slender leg was showcased to perfection as she stood there, taking his appraisal as if she'd been born into the role of a princess to be his Queen. In that moment she was exactly what he wanted in a wife—a real wife. She was desirable and aloof, competent and confident.

What was he doing entertaining such thoughts?

He pushed them roughly aside. 'I agree.' He looked at Madame Rousseau, unsure if he could look into the blue depths of Tiffany's eyes and be able to disguise the powerfully raw desire pounding through him.

Later that evening, after having her hair, nails and make-up professionally done, Tiffany stepped into one of the evening dresses Jafar had selected. Tonight they were to have a romantic dinner at one of the city's top hotels, frequented by rich and famous people from around the world. The bright green fabric of the dress was soft and luxurious against her skin and she couldn't help but admire it, even though she felt like a bought woman.

That is exactly what you are. The words taunted her as they played over in her mind. She was Sheikh Jafar Al-Shehri's bought bride.

Jafar's expression as she'd stood waiting for his approval this afternoon had been cold and detached, which only backed up her anxious thoughts. He had been merely approving the items of clothing, ensuring they fitted in with the plans he'd made for the announcement of their engagement.

She looked down at her left hand, where the biggest diamond she'd ever seen glittered on her third finger. It was rose pink and so unusual that, despite the way he'd given it to her after Madame Rousseau had left, as if having it at all was an afterthought, she had been stunned by its beauty.

'You look perfect.' Jafar's voice, the harsh tones of earlier still lingering, dragged her mind back to the present. 'Perfectly beautiful.'

She looked at him, wanting to return the compliment, if that was what it was. His dark suit fitted his tall, athletic body, accentuating his muscular contours that could only come from regular workouts, but as he came closer her words dried on her lips.

'The colour shows your glorious hair off.' He reached out and took the ends of her loose hair between his thumb and fingers and her breath caught audibly in her throat, her gaze meeting the vibrant colour of his. What was this power he had over her? Every nerve cell in her body was on high alert when he was near, waiting for his touch—wanting it.

She should step back, away from his power, but she couldn't. Something dangerous simmered around them but still she couldn't move. Just what was it this man possessed that made her act so differently from normal? Usually she wouldn't entertain anything that was even remotely like flirting. This wasn't flirting. Instinctively she knew this was much deeper, much more primitive, and it excited and scared her at the same time.

'Madame Rousseau's choices are amazing,' she enthused, desperate to talk of neutral things, needing to calm the erratic thump of her heart.

'I told you,' he practically purred, but she knew this jungle cat was far from docile, 'that when I do something, I do it properly, which is why I always hire Madame Rousseau when I am in Paris.'

'You do?' The question was out before she could stop it. So too was the hurt that she was not the first woman to have been paraded before him like this, kitted out with everything to meet his demanding requirements.

The urge to throw a tantrum, to stamp her foot and march out rushed through her, but the memory of Bethany's face as she'd told her what she was about to do calmed the need to run, the need to be away from this man—as far as possible. It was the hope that had mixed with the shock in her sister's eyes that had convinced her she was doing the right thing and recalling that now would help to keep her focused on what she had to be. A woman of quality that could grace the arm of a man such as Jafar Al-Shehri.

He looked into her eyes and moved closer and for one heart-stopping moment she thought he was going to kiss her. Properly kiss her. Her lips parted and softened even though panic rushed through her. She did want to be kissed. It wasn't part of their deal but right at that moment she didn't care about the deal or the money. All she cared about was tasting this man on her lips, feeling his breath mix with hers and, most of all, responding in a way she'd never, ever, wanted to do with any man.

Jafar's control had almost slipped. He hadn't even left the hotel suite and all he wanted was to take Tiffany to his bed. Never had a woman had such a profound effect on him, not even his childhood sweetheart, Niesha. But then she had never been forbidden fruit and even if she had her centre would have been poisoned by her greedy ambition, which had showed itself in time to stop him making the biggest mistake of his life and marrying her.

The familiar stab of rage that accompanied thoughts of Niesha was a welcome relief to the hot, searing passion of need coursing through him right now. 'We should go,' he said coldly, swallowing down the taste of betrayal that always reared its head at the thought of just how low Niesha had stooped when she'd married his cousin.

'I think that is best.' The supercilious tone of her voice didn't hide her embarrassment at what had almost happened. There was no denying the blush on her pale skin, which the sexy dusting of freckles couldn't hide.

Had she wanted the kiss? Had she wanted more? He gritted his teeth against the questions, determined to remain in control. All he had to do was remind himself why Tiffany Chapelle was here with him, why she'd agreed to the deal. She was as motivated by money and position as Niesha was. Were all women the same?

The question had hung over him as they dined in the finest restaurant Paris could offer, with views of the Eiffel Tower as it shimmered like gold in the night, then lit up with glimmering lights for the first five minutes of every hour. He'd thought, having seen it now three times during their meal, that his need, the insatiable desire to kiss Tiffany, would have eased—but it hadn't.

Time to talk business. Maybe that would remind him that she wasn't here for his pleasure, but for the stability of his kingdom. 'When we arrive in Shamsumara there will be a feast.

One that is celebrated every year, but this time it will be bigger than normal in honour of your arrival.'

'My arrival? Why?' Had she really thought she could hide herself away from his people?

'You are my bride, Tiffany, and my country has been in a state of upheaval since my brother's death. Your arrival is causing much excitement.'

Her eyes widened in surprise and he fought hard against the urge to smile. Better she thought he was cold and detached.

'Even though I am not from your country?' The doubt and hesitation in her voice were endearing.

'Especially because of that, and also because you will be my Queen.' He sensed her reservations.

'And what is expected of your Queen?' The question darted back at him.

'There will be times when we must be seen together during the three months you are in Shamsumara and that is all I ask of you. To be at my side and show an interest in the kingdom and its people.'

'How can I best do that?'

Her question gave him hope of successfully acting out the marriage in public. 'My aide informs me that you are seen as a new hope and it has been suggested you should build on that, create a project to occupy your time while in Shamsumara. One to call your own.'

He thought of the discussion he'd had with his aide in the days after he and Tiffany had agreed on the deal. He was the only other person who knew that the marriage was a business deal, not just out of the necessity of drawing up the contract, but because he would be best able to serve both Jafar and Tiffany knowing the truth—especially when it came to getting a divorce in two years.

'Like what?' She frowned at him, her lips forming a pout that was so seductive, but with the air of innocence about her right now, he was sure she had no idea just what it did to him.

'There must be a cause which is close to your heart.'

'Well, yes,' she said, suddenly shy, which only enhanced that innocence he found so appealing. 'I'd like to help women who for whatever reason are struggling to bring up children on their own.'

The fact that she didn't have to think about it spoke volumes about the kind of woman she was and he questioned his earlier opinion of her. When he and Niesha had had a similar conversation, many years ago when he'd thought his future would be very different, she'd been unable to instantly come up with anything. That should have been all the warning he needed that she hadn't been suitable princess material, let alone queen, that despite all her so-called suitability she was far from capable of the role.

'A very worthy cause.' He knew it was her sister's plight that had instigated the suggestion, but it made him see her in a different light. She hadn't accepted the deal because it was going to financially benefit her directly. She'd accepted in order to help her sister. 'I shall have my aide put things in motion for you, so that you can take over once the honeymoon is over.'

'I didn't expect us to have a honeymoon.' He watched her swallow, watched the movement of her throat and wanted nothing more than to kiss her there, to feel the softness of her skin.

'It is tradition in my kingdom that a bride and groom spend seven days alone, with only each other for company after the wedding feast.'

'Seven days,' she exclaimed loudly, a little

too loudly if the turn of other diners' heads was anything to go by.

'We will be expected to be on our own for the duration of the honeymoon, after which there will be another feast and guests will bring gifts.' He sensed her nerves once again. Why did she not want to be alone with him? Was it because he'd misread the signals, misinterpreted the desire in her eyes? Did she really dislike him?

'It all seems very drawn out. Do we really need to adhere to all that tradition?'

'The tradition comes from the need to ensure the arrival of an heir and as we are taking on the role of lovers wanting to marry, then I am afraid it will have to be observed.'

She sat back, her delicate brows pulled together. 'What about an heir? Will your sister's child really be accepted as your heir?'

She doubted what he'd told her and a flurry of irritation rushed over him. 'I didn't ever want to rule Shamsumara but fate has decreed that I should and I will not let my brother down or turn away from my duty. However, being a father is not something I have ever envisaged for myself and my sister's child will be accepted by the people of my kingdom. I will ensure that.'

'So let me get this straight.' She sat forward, confidence suddenly oozing from her. 'We have to spend seven days locked away, pretending to be newly-wed lovers? How are we going to achieve that?'

Did she not feel the increasing sexual tension between them? Right now he would give anything for her to want him as much as he wanted her. He slammed the idea aside. He could not truly make this woman his wife. If he did, all he'd grown up believing in, the honour and tradition that went with the position of ruler of Shamsumara, would mean that he would be going against it all by divorcing her. He could only do that knowing he'd never consummated the marriage. His beliefs were everything to him.

He was already in turmoil just by going through with the deal with Tiffany but he couldn't stand by and allow Simdan to claim his title, his throne. Just as he couldn't ever drag a woman into the situation of his kingdom by letting her think the marriage meant anything to him. At least Tiffany was well aware of what was expected of her and she'd signed a contract to that effect.

'Our palace quarters will be vast. You will have your own rooms.' He dragged his mind back to the conversation. 'That will ensure the ease of your departure once my sister's baby is born.'

'And what will you tell your people, your officials?' There was accusation in her voice.

'I will state how unhappy you were, how homesick and unsettled. It will be merely a formality.'

'Good,' she replied officiously. 'I have no intention of making this marriage any harder to get out of than it already is.'

'In that case, we understand one another well.'

CHAPTER FOUR

FOR THE LAST six days Tiffany had tried to avoid being with Jafar as much as possible, which had been far easier than she'd ever imagined, as he too seemed to have had the same idea, especially when they were alone. If they had been together, it was in public, and when they were in the suite it was so big she could easily hide herself away. It was also exactly how she hoped it would be once they were in Shamsumara and not at all like her recent dreams, which had been full of images of Jafar in the desert, white robes blowing in the warm wind. He was fast becoming her fantasy and that was the last thing she wanted or needed right now.

To counteract these sensual dreams, during the day, when she had been on her own, she'd thought back to his almost callous use of his sister and her child. The fact that he'd calmly told her his sister's child would be his heir made her view him in a different light. He was powerful and more than prepared to exert that power to get what he wanted. No matter how outrageously sexy he had been in her dreams, by day he was the epitome of all she hated in a man—just wrapped up in a very sexy package. And it was this sexy packaging that was causing her the most concern. She'd never been so affected by a man before. She felt trapped in a web of desire she had no idea how to escape from and was totally unprepared for how to deal with a man like the Sheikh of Shamsumara.

On her finger was the biggest diamond she'd ever seen and in her mind Bethany's words of shock continued to play.

'He is hiring you as his bride? Why are you agreeing to it? Why are you going off to some far-flung country? Please don't do it—not for us.'

Tiffany had remained firm, knowing that there was no other way she or Bethany could ever find enough money to keep a roof over their heads. It wasn't just for Bethany and her daughter now, it was for herself too after she'd given up renting her apartment and moved in with her sister to help out with loan payments.

It had been enough to keep the wolf from howling at the door, but it wouldn't last long. Jafar's offer had come at the right time and there was no way she was going to let it pass.

With a sigh of regret for all that had happened over the last few years she looked out over the city of Paris, the glow of yellow lights giving it a surreal feel. It was the most perfect place and she'd longed to visit it for many years, but if someone had told her she would be here engaged to a desert sheikh, about to become his wife as part of a deal, she would have said they were crazy.

'He is hiring you as his bride?'

Again Bethany's words careered into all other thoughts and she took a deep breath, trying to compose herself. She was dressed in the most exquisite black lace dress and she felt like a princess on the outside. But inside she was a complete mess.

'The city is beautiful tonight, is it not?' Jafar's voice paused the words in her mind as they looped again and again. She turned to look at him, instantly wishing she hadn't.

He was dressed in his usual suit, but there was something different about him. He looked powerful and commanding and devastatingly handsome. The black suit over a pastel lavender shirt made him appear much taller, much more powerful. Or was it her nerves that did that?

'I wish I could be up there,' she said as she looked towards the Eiffel Tower, lit up in the darkness. 'Paris is so lovely I don't want to leave.'

She had expected him to brush off her comment with yet another of his harsh comments. They'd been coming thick and fast all week and she was seriously wondering how she would be able to spend another week ensconced with him after their marriage. The sooner that part of their deal was over, the better.

'If it makes you feel any better, neither do I.' She looked up at him, into his handsome face, and into eyes that seemed full of emotions she couldn't read. 'I appreciate this week has been tough, but you have proved many times over you are more than capable of being my Queen. I have no doubt you will be perfect, but if you do want to back out, now is the time—the last chance you will have.'

'I'm not going to back out.' She forgot the amazing view, the romance of a city she longed to explore better, rising to the challenge he was most certainly throwing her way. 'Whatever else you think of me, Jafar, I honour my promise.'

'That is all I need to know,' he said as if gentling a startled animal. 'Because once we arrive in Shamsumara tomorrow there will be no going back.'

He moved towards her and the warm evening air became charged with that same spark she'd tried to ignore on their first night in Paris. The night when she had been fool enough to think he might actually kiss her. He had spoken softly then too, lured her into a false sense of security, bringing down almost all her barriers even if only for the briefest time.

'Don't we have to be somewhere?' She moved quickly past him and into the room, away from the romance of the view, the balcony, the open window with lace rippling in the breeze.

'We do indeed.' The words had hardened. The Jafar she'd come to know over the last week was back. A man in control, a man for whom sentiments were not something he indulged in. So who was the man who had just slipped to the surface? Which was the real Jafar?

'I'd like to go, get it over with.' He frowned at her comment. 'Arriving in front of the press, that is. It might be normal for you, but I have not experienced such a thing, not when the attention is thrown at me.'

* * *

Jafar had never seen such a pack of photographers, all vying for the best shot. Tiffany had been right to worry. The car stopped outside the hotel entrance where a red carpet led the guests into the World Water charity dinner he attended most years, but news of their engagement was spreading fast and now the press were ferociously hungry for a story.

He should have known better. His playboy reputation, together with his wealth and now the speculation as to what would happen to his country after his brother's death, was not just creating interest in his own kingdom, but worldwide. It was sure to become worse now that his chosen bride had been revealed, mostly due to the fact that she was English. Now more than ever it was important to show a façade of lovers eager to be married.

Beside him he sensed Tiffany tense, sensed not only her reservations, but fear. Again he wondered why, when she'd told him her work brought her into contact with the rich and famous. Surely she'd been in the thick of something like this before as a bridesmaid. She must at least be used to media attention.

He took her hand, momentarily taken aback by the smallness of hers as he turned to face the press who looked more like baying wolves. 'Just be yourself.' He moved closer to her and spoke softly in her ear but in doing so inhaled the scent of bergamot and rosewood. It made him think of home as yet more Eastern scents invaded his senses. Was this her usual perfume or had she changed to one he would recognise and react to? Was it to tempt him, to lay down another challenge?

'So who will be your bridesmaid?' one of the photographers shouted as she lifted her chin and smiled at the cameras, again making him think that, whatever else she was, she was born to the role he'd created for her for the next three months. She could easily put on the show of confidence even though he could sense her reservations, her fear.

'All will be revealed very soon, gentlemen.' This was a discussion he needed to have with her this evening. He had his own plans, which he'd put in motion as part of a thank-you gesture to her, but he still needed to ensure she was happy with the idea.

He looked down as she glanced up at him, surprise in the depths of her eyes. In that moment he knew he would do all he could to ensure that her sister and niece filled those roles as he'd planned. That spark of fire he'd felt the first night in Paris shot through him once more and as her lips parted he couldn't help himself. He had to kiss her.

The noise of everything else subsided into nothingness as he lowered his head and, meeting no resistance from her, he brushed his lips over hers, testing and teasing. What he hadn't expected was the sigh of pleasure from her, or for her to move her lips against his, to respond and demand. What was she trying to do to him? Just when he thought he might lose his mind, his control and his ability to think, camera flashes popped all around him, bringing him startlingly back to reality and he pulled away from her, but didn't miss the confusion in her eyes.

She had been playing out the role he'd instructed her to. Why else would she have spent all week avoiding being with him unless they were out in company and then kiss him like that?

'Finally the bride,' another photographer taunted.

'Not the bridesmaid this time,' one said in heavily accented English, making it clear they knew all about her.

He was sure Tiffany shrank back a little, making him want to ram the camera down the man's throat. The need to protect this woman was fierce and distinctly primal. It was also one he'd never experienced before.

'That's enough,' he growled as he turned and led Tiffany into the hotel. 'Damn pack of wolves.'

'I had no idea it was so intense being the centre of their attention,' she said as they moved into the sanctuary of the hotel lobby. 'And you just made it worse when you kissed me.'

The censure in her voice was clear and the image she created, standing against the backdrop of luxury within the hotel, was overwhelmingly beautiful and he found himself thinking how stunning she would look dressed in the Eastern wardrobe he'd had prepared for her arrival at his palace.

'Only to ensure there is no doubt about our relationship.' Who was he trying to fool? It was simply because he'd wanted to, had been unable to resist the temptation those soft, full, lipstick-covered lips had presented. 'And you played your part admirably.'

'Just like you, Jafar, when I do something I do it properly.' His earlier words came back at him like a bolt of lightning.

'Then may I suggest you take my arm and

accompany me into the charity dinner where we can both play our parts to perfection?'

The next few hours passed slowly and all he could think about was the woman sitting next to him and the brief but powerful kiss they'd shared. Because they had shared it. She had kissed him back, had wanted it to go on, to become something else as much as he had. Whatever it was between them it was mutual—just as the resistance was.

Each time he looked at her, the elegance of the black lace dress begged him to remove it, begged him to reveal all that pale skin. What would it look like next to the darkness of his? Erotic images surged forward like a tidal wave and he pressed his thumb and one finger on each temple, his hand covering his eyes. What the hell was wrong with him? Maybe he should just kiss her and get it out of his system?

No, one kiss would unleash more need, more fire and desire. He was in no doubt of that.

'Let's go,' he said as the speeches finished, not caring what their early departure would look like. He just wanted her for himself.

'Where are we going now?'

As she become embroiled in goodbyes with those at their table, he took the opportunity and made the call to put in motion a plan to spend time with just Tiffany, to indulge her in the one thing she wanted to do in Paris but hadn't been able to. *It's just a token of thanks*, he told himself, but deep down knew it was much more, just as flying her sister and niece to the wedding was. He wanted to make her happy.

'To the restaurant in the tower,' he said, sliding his phone back into his inside pocket.

'But we've eaten.' The alarm in her voice made him smile.

'I want to show you Paris, take you to the one place you said you wanted to visit, as a thank-you. Once we are in my homeland we will be busy with feasts and celebrations. Tonight will be for us.'

She looked at him with big eyes, making her appear vulnerable and sexy at the same time, and for a moment he thought he was drowning and that she was the only woman who could save him.

'I'd like that.' Her breathy whisper sent the spark of lust throbbing through him afresh and he was thankful his car had arrived.

Tiffany wanted to look away from the intensity in his eyes but she couldn't. He might not be physically close to her but the overpowering pull of attraction between them was becom-

ing harder to ignore—and much more difficult to resist.

'So would I.' Jafar's voice was deep and
husky, his unmistakable accent more pronounced, and it sent shivers of awareness down
her spine. When he took her hand and led her
to the waiting car she almost pulled back, the
fire of his touch so hot.

Was this too just an act, like that intense yet
very light kiss he'd brushed over her lips earlier? Was he continuing the act of lovers in the
grip of a whirlwind romance? She pushed the
questions away, refusing to think too much,
only knowing that she intended to enjoy this
night, make the most of the romance that was
unexpectedly lingering in the air—real or not.
Lilly's suggestion that she have a fling to get
over her ex came to the fore. Could Jafar be
that man to help her heal her wounds? Maybe it
was just being in Paris, the city for lovers, but
right now she wanted him to be exactly that.

Jafar's car negotiated the busy Parisian traffic and Tiffany focused her attention on the
tower as they approached it—anything other
than look at the man beside her. The air inside
the car sparked with something so unfamiliar
that her heart pounded. At last the car stopped
and within minutes she and Jafar were inside

the elevator on their way up to the restaurant. Except that was worse than the car—far more confined. This time she focused on watching the iconic gold-coloured metal structure of the tower as they went higher, praying that it wouldn't be much longer before they were at the restaurant.

'I thought it would be busier.' Her words trailed off in wonder as they stepped out of the elevator. She looked around the restaurant and beyond the wall of windows to the city of Paris. It was breathtakingly beautiful.

'The final service of the evening is almost over, but they have agreed to cater to our special occasion and I have arranged for a table with the best view.' The command in his voice was clear and the implications that he could just arrange whatever he pleased wasn't lost on her.

'I didn't expect this,' she said and fixed her attention on the view because she couldn't look at him, not when she could still feel the heat of his lips on hers.

As they were seated at the table with an unrivalled view of the Palais de Chaillot, Tiffany could feel herself falling under the spell of romance. She fought it, but it was all too much to resist, the soft music playing in the background, the view, but most of all the man himself.

'I need to know who you would like to attend the wedding.' Jafar dropped the question between them, shattering the illusion of romance she'd allowed to build up inside her. 'What about your sister and your niece to be your bridesmaids?'

Was this an afterthought because of what the reporters had asked as they'd arrived? Did he see their attendance as a way of validating the marriage, making it appear more real? 'Do we really need to involve them? It's not as if the marriage is for real.'

'I thought you would welcome a friendly face.'

'Or give the whole thing the appearance of being more real.' She couldn't keep the hurt from her voice, but at least that stab of pain was more preferable than the soft, romantic notions it had just replaced. 'Do whatever you want. I doubt Bethany will come anyway.'

After the way her sister had pleaded with her not to go through with the marriage, that they would find another way to sort out the financial mess they were in, she doubted Bethany would have anything to do with the actual marriage ceremony—especially if it meant travelling to another country. There was no way she could afford a plane ticket anywhere right now.

'What about your best friend?' His question surprised her and she tried to think if she'd spoken to him of Lilly.

'How do you know about Lilly?'

'I don't.' There was a hint of amusement in his voice and it confused her. She was trying to be irritated with him and all these questions were just pushing her back to the notion that he cared, that there was an undercurrent of something romantic between them. 'I just know every woman has one.'

'I haven't told Lilly yet.' She knew full well that Lilly knew after the texts she'd received this last week. Bethany must have told her and she owed her friend a call to explain just what it was she was doing and why. All she needed was the confidence to actually tell her with conviction.

'I'd like your parents to be there too. I want to make sure you feel comfortable on your wedding day, Tiffany—and happy.' His voice had softened, as if he really did care, and she recalled the shock on her mother's and father's faces as she'd told them she was in love and getting married. She hadn't been able to tell either of them the truth.

'You are making a good show of it.' She threw the hot words back at him, needing to cover up the flutter of attraction that was threatening once more to erupt and overflow.

He took her hand across the table. She should pull back, shouldn't look into his eyes, but she couldn't do anything she thought she should do. She was once again well and truly under his spell.

'Nothing about tonight has been for show.' There was fierceness to his words, as if he too was fighting the growing attraction between them. The fact that he wanted her, found her attractive, only heightened hers for him. She wanted to be desired by him—and so much more.

'But we agreed nothing would happen between us.' Her voice was a whisper and there was a glint of satisfaction in his eyes. Had she walked into a trap of her own making? Right now she didn't care. She wanted to be caught by this man.

'We can also agree to enjoy this moment for what it is.' His thumb and finger were caressing her hand, making thought impossible.

Her breath hitched noticeably. 'What is this moment, Jafar?'

'The moment when a man and woman who

are attracted to one another forget all else and
live just for the moment.' His poetic words
sealed her fate and she was eternally grateful they were in a restaurant where nothing
other than holding hands across the table
could happen.

He let her hand go and stood up, towering
over her and the table, dominating every bit
of space, every bit of air she breathed. 'Let us
make the most of the impressive view.'

'But what of other diners?'

'They have all gone.' That self-assured satisfaction was back in his voice. 'As have the
staff.'

'We are alone?'

'Alone enough to enjoy the romantic view,
yes. I have paid well for this and want to share
this moment in Paris with you.'

He held out his hand for her and she took
it, placed her napkin on the table and stood
up, but as he didn't move it brought her very
close to him. Close enough to kiss him if she
had the courage.

She lowered her chin, averted her eyes from
that powerful gaze, but with his free hand he
lifted her chin back up, forced her to look into
his eyes. His sparked with gold as they bored

into her soul, dragging her from her corner of self-doubt.

'I want to kiss you, Tiffany.'

Now she couldn't move, couldn't look away. He'd successfully snared her, catching her in his trap, and all she wanted was release. The kind of release that would only come from feeling his lips on hers, not for show because cameras were flashing, but for real.

'I want that too. I want you to kiss me,' she whispered, her heart thumping so hard it sounded in her head like a drum.

He moved his fingers from her chin and stroked the side of his thumb over her cheek and her eyelashes fluttered and closed at the sensation of fire and heat that bubbled up from deep within her. She shouldn't be doing this at all, but everything felt so right, so real, how could she not?

'You are so beautiful.' His hoarse whisper only stoked that fire higher and she opened her eyes. He moved closer, his hand sliding round to the back of her head, holding her right where he wanted her.

Her breath was deep and hard and she knew her breasts were rising and falling rapidly as desire began to consume her. She parted her lips as he moved closer still, his eyes locked on hers. Should she close hers, block out the image of his swirling with hot passion?

His lips touched hers and she closed her eyes, pulling herself against him, snagging in a breath as her body made contact with his. He pulled her hard against him with his free arm. She could feel the muscled contours of his chest, the strength in his arm and, more potently, the hardness of his arousal as her body responded, moulding her to him in a way that set loose the fire of desire she'd been hoping to control.

He murmured something against her lips and she sank deeper into the desire that was now flooding through her. The kiss hardened, became more demanding, but instead of pulling back, instead of ending it as she knew she should do, she returned the kiss with a fever she'd never thought possible. His hand gripped her harder at the back of her neck, angling her head so that he could force her lips apart and plunder her mouth with his tongue. She gasped her pleasure into his mouth, which only made him demand more from her.

Then as suddenly as it all started he stopped, let her go and she staggered backwards, gasping for breath as she clutched at the back of the chair. His desire-heavy gaze travelled down her body as if he were physically removing the black lace dress from her and, although it was so wrong, right now it was precisely what she wanted him to do.

'Perhaps we should return to our suite.' The firmness of his voice shocked her. Didn't he feel the same wild passion thumping through him? 'To sleep alone, as the tradition of my country dictates.'

'I think in light of our deal that is the best thing to do.' Inside she was crying out for him, wanting his kiss and more. Thankfully her head was once more ruling the situation, crushing down the passion he'd evoked with that kiss, the like of which she'd never before experienced. She'd only ever kissed her previous boyfriend and that had always been a chaste affair, but what she'd just shared with Jafar had been dangerous yet wildly exciting.

'As you wish.' He turned from her and she knew the moment was gone, that they were back on track, back to being two people entering a business deal. The lovers that had surfaced briefly were well and truly suppressed.

CHAPTER FIVE

THE SEARING INTENSITY of the kiss last night in Paris soon became overshadowed by the reality of being in the desert kingdom of Shamsumara, where Jafar was obviously respected by his people. Tiffany had a twinge of guilt for deceiving them, but determinedly she pushed it aside. The fake marriage had never been her idea and, yes, she would be benefitting, but it was all about Jafar getting what he wanted, preventing his cousin from claiming the kingdom as his own. Would she meet this cousin now she was here?

The palace was beautifully striking and the early evening sun was casting a gold glow over all the intricately decorated archways they were walking through. She followed her husband-to-be, his long purposeful strides hard to keep up with as she tried to look around her too.

This would be her home for the next three

months. Jafar paused outside a set of ornate doors. The thought hit her that tomorrow he would be her husband and for the next three months they would be expected to live together as man and wife. She thought again of the kiss in Paris. Could she be with him for that time and not want to be kissed again?

'This will be our suite, but for this evening I will be at the opposite end of the palace as tradition dictates.' The velvety tones of his voice were still evident despite the authority in his words and relief rushed through her; she was thankful that she wouldn't have to spend time alone with him tonight when all she could think about was last night. Her body still ached for him, her lips desperate to feel his claiming hers once more.

Last night had been a reckless mistake and she couldn't allow it to happen again.

'Of course, I wouldn't have expected any-thing less.' She walked into the room, stunned at the height of the ceilings. Through an arch-way that was almost key-shaped she could see a bed draped in gold silks and much big-ger than any she'd ever seen. Gold lace hung from a frame above the bed and rested behind the array of pillows and cushions. It was opulent, luxurious and totally beyond anything she could have imagined.

It also signified exactly what their marriage was to be about as far as his kingdom was concerned. Tiffany was shocked at the regret that fluttered after that thought. She wanted to be in that bed, with Jafar. She wanted to explore what it was her body was begging for whenever he was close.

'The bridal bed,' Jafar said, coming to stand directly behind her, and she blushed at her wayward thoughts. He lowered his voice to a whisper, making her breath catch, her body heat. 'We will be expected to share it tomorrow night. Or at least make it appear as if we are, but for this evening you can enjoy it alone.'

'It's quite beautiful and the perfect place for a desert king and his bride to be ensconced for a week—if it were all for real.' She had to set some boundaries for herself as much as him, because if she didn't she was sure she would want to be kissed like last night again and she had to remember this wasn't a real marriage. This was a deal. He'd paid her and paid her well. Whatever else was between them, it meant nothing.

'Don't be fooled that this isn't for real, Tiffany. This time tomorrow you *will* be my wife.'

She turned to face him and instantly wished she hadn't. His eyes darkened, becoming like the depths of the forest where the sun didn't reach even at the height of the day. 'The ceremony will be real, as will the three months I am to remain here, but nothing else. Our *marriage* is a deal, nothing more.'

How was she going to spend a whole week in his company, in a setting as blissfully romantic as this, and not want him to kiss her—or more? Last night she'd tasted the kind of paradise she'd thought only existed in dreams, the kind of passion and desire she'd never thought herself capable of. She should never have given into the need her body had suddenly craved. A need only this man could meet. She was losing control fast and needed to find it again if she stood any chance of making it through the next week, let alone the next three months.

'We understand one another well, I think,' he said as several women slipped in through the open door behind them. 'Now that your maids have arrived to be your chaperones, I will leave you in their capable hands and you can be assured that you will not have to be alone with me at all until after tomorrow's celebrations.'

Tiffany watched him go, aware of the speculation of the young women watching her. Would they speak English? How was she going to manage without Jafar to guide her? The urge to call him back almost made her rush from the room; instead she pulled off the black headscarf she'd been instructed to wear for their arrival. She was in the company of only women now and could relax—a little at least.

'Your hair is so beautiful.' One of the maids stepped forward with a friendly smile, making Tiffany suddenly shy and so pleased too that she could at least talk to someone in English. 'My name is Aaleyah and we are here to serve you. A bath is drawn and your clothes for the feast this evening are ready.'

Relief filled Tiffany as she instantly sensed she might have an ally in Aaleyah. 'I'd like to ensure I do things right,' she said, hoping to instil authority into her voice instead of the nerves fluttering through her. 'I hope that you will help me.'

'Of course,' Aaleyah said, her English very good. 'That is what we are here for.'

Jafar had been anxious for Tiffany as he'd walked away from the Royal Suite. He was glad now he'd put in motion the idea of her sister, friend and parents attending the wedding tomorrow before he'd even mentioned it to her. It would be a fitting surprise for her and at least she would have familiar faces around her. It was no different from what he would have done if they had been embarking on a real marriage.

The idea of a real marriage with Tiffany, of truly making her his wife, sent a rush of throbbing lust through him. If this were a real marriage, then tomorrow night they would be together in the bridal bed, exploring the passion that sparked between them. Passion he knew she felt too, despite her words of bravado.

Now he waited for her arrival at the feast. Her first public appearance. When she finally arrived, nerves were clearly etched onto her beautiful face but as she entered the banqueting hall, her entourage of women following closely, he let a breath of relief escape him. She looked absolutely stunning and completely regal.

Beneath the black silk *abaya*, which she wore open, he could see her silver dress, fitting her sensually curvy body yet conforming to the traditions expected of his bride-to-be on the feast before their wedding. Her lovely deep brown hair was piled up on her head, which was covered in fine black chiffon. He imagined removing the chiffon and unpinning her hair, letting it tumble down her back.

He'd seriously have to get better control of his libido before tomorrow evening. He had no intention of making the marriage a true marriage by consummating it and his aide's words of caution came back to him like a spirit on the desert wind.

'You will have no choice, sire, but to remain married to your English bride for two years. Your ability to rule will be brought into question if the marriage is not seen to be real—just as it will if you are not seen to be spending the first week of marriage alone with your bride.'

The only thing in jeopardy if he gave into the building desire for the woman he'd hired as his bride was his honour—and honour was everything to him.

He focused his mind elsewhere. There was nothing he wanted less than any questions over his claim as the rightful ruler of Shamsumara. If it hadn't been for his cousin's underhand attempts at taking over the kingdom after his brother's death, he would never have had to find a bride and do the one thing he really didn't want to do.

Tiffany took her place at his side as he sat

on the raised platform at the top of the banqueting hall. She settled onto the large red and gold cushions, not at all fazed by how unfamiliar such an arrangement must be to her, and it struck him that she too was as calculated in accepting his offer as Niesha, the woman he'd always believed would one day be his wife, had been.

'How was your evening?' He was well aware that she would have been bathed in scented water and then pampered before being helped into her dress and tomorrow it would be even more of a ritual. Tomorrow she would be being prepared for him—his pleasure. He shoved the thought aside, angry at his lack of control yet again as his body heated at the thought of holding her again, kissing. Was it so wrong to desire the woman you were about to marry, even if only for convenience?

'A little daunting. I am beginning to wonder why I'm here, if I can do it,' she confessed and he didn't miss the fact that she wouldn't look him in the eye. Was it because she was trying to be sensitive to his kingdom's culture or because she trusted herself as little as he did? Part of him hoped it was the latter.

'It's too late for that now.' His fierce tone was born out of the need to be totally in control, something which, if he was honest, he'd barely been around this woman. Especially last night. Memories of the kiss, of her lips against his for a second time, obliterated the tenuous grip on his control. It was a kiss that had felt very real, not at all like the staged one as they'd arrived at the charity event.

'I have no intention of backing out. I need the money. Remember?'

As if he needed reminding of the terms of their deal—his marriage. Irritated by her aloofness, even though it was probably for the best, he turned his attention to the newly arrived guests.

His cousin Simdan's perfectly timed arrival, just after Tiffany, only highlighted how much of a threat this man was to Shamsumara. He was as threatening to the success of what he and Tiffany were doing as his wife, Niesha, and their young son were. She was the woman he himself should have married if her need to do better than the spare heir of Shamsumara, as he was then, hadn't forced her to break their long-standing engagement and marry Simdan. He had grown up knowing he was to marry Niesha, but Simdan was more than welcome to such a scheming woman. Whatever his cousin thought, Jafar was adamant that Simdan wasn't going to take his kingdom with the same ease he'd taken his promised bride—or at all.

'Good, because my cousin and his wife have just arrived. As the closest members of my family other than my sister, they will be joining us here.'

'The cousin who is threatening to take over your country?' She looked at him now that the attention was not directly on them or the simmering sexual tension that was threatening to explode in the most spectacular fashion. Disbelief filled her eyes.

'The very same.' He just had time to confirm her question before Simdan sat beside him. He spoke in his own language, the undertone of warning to his cousin clear whatever any bystander understood and he was aware of Niesha's cold, curious gaze on Tiffany. How could he ever have thought he could come to love Niesha, to want to spend the rest of his life with such a woman at his side? She was as wrong for him as Tiffany was.

'Simdan, Niesha, may I introduce my bride, Tiffany?' He spoke in English as knowing that Niesha understood the language made saying those words all the more satisfying. His cousin's eyes narrowed and he glared hostilely at Tiffany, but it was Niesha's angry eyes that rang alarm bells in his head. She had married his cousin and that fact alone made her capable of just about anything. Would she pose a threat to Tiffany or was he allowing irrational thoughts to get the better of him?

'I am honoured to be joining your bridal entourage,' Niesha said silkily, and already he was having misgivings about allowing the traditions of extended female family members attending the bride. He should have insisted Niesha couldn't be part of that, but had been wary of alerting his cousin to anything that might lead him to the fact that the marriage was merely a deal brokered in an English hotel garden with a woman who made a living out of being a professional bridesmaid.

'I'd be grateful for your guidance,' Tiffany said firmly and he had the distinct impression that she had already assessed Niesha.

'It is time we men withdrew.' He looked at Tiffany and again that sensation that he was abandoning her came over him. 'Your ladies will take care of you and tomorrow, when I see you, it will be to become your husband.'

Tiffany looked up into his eyes as he took her hand and helped her to stand. The warmth of Jafar's touch sent a tingle of awareness all through her, swiftly followed by the realisation that tomorrow her life would change. It didn't matter that the marriage wasn't for love and that they would lead separate lives in three months, tomorrow still changed everything—for her and for Bethany.

'And is everything in place for all my requests to be met?' She kept her voice low, aware that some members of their party spoke very good English, but also needed to refer to their deal. It was the only thing that would serve as a much-needed reminder for her that this was a business deal, one that would gain each of them what they needed. It would be all too easy to slip into the fake world of affection and, even more so, the illusion of desire. Except, for her, that desire was very real. It was powerful and threatened to consume her. 'Do I have all I asked for?'

His jaw clenched and his lips drew into a severe line. He looked formidable, his eyes sparking a warning at her as he let go of her hand. 'Everything is as planned.'

She wished now she'd insisted on Bethany being with her tomorrow. She wanted reassurance from her sister that he'd kept his part of the deal, because there was no way she was going to tie herself in the legal bindings of marriage to a man who upset her equilibrium so completely she lost all sense of reason unless the money had been transferred. She had to keep the money at the forefront of her mind. Remind herself why she was here.

'Good.' The word sounded cold and officious and from the quick rise of his brows he'd noticed it too. 'So I can call Bethany tomorrow and tell her everything is sorted?'

'She knows the full details of our arrangement?' His voice lowered and his eyes narrowed in suspicion, then he looked around them, checking to see who was paying them any attention.

'Only Bethany. I had to tell her something.' A sense of triumph sluiced over her. In this one thing at least she had some power.

'Make sure it stays that way.' The deep, almost feral growl of his voice dragged her attention back to him and she smiled sweetly, uneasy as she became aware of Niesha watching them closely. She wasn't a fool. She hadn't missed the undercurrent of tension between the man she was to marry and the beautiful Niesha.

'I do things properly,' she quoted his words back at him once more and got the same satisfaction as last time.

'Sorry to break you two up.' Niesha's words cut through the air like a knife and she saw Jafar inhale deeply. 'It's time for the ladies to go. There is much preparation still to do for tomorrow.'

Tiffany looked at Jafar, seeking some sort of guidance or reassurance, the thought of being abandoned to this woman again unsettling. Was Tiffany overreacting to feel threatened by her, by something between her and Jafar?

'There is one more thing.' Jafar pointedly ignored Niesha's intrusion. 'I have arranged a surprise for you, which should by now be waiting in your suite.'

'A surprise?'

'Isn't a man allowed to give gifts to the woman he is to marry?' There was jest in his voice, but Tiffany had the distinct impression it was for Niesha's benefit, all part of the act of a couple madly in love. Maybe there wasn't even a surprise at all.

'Thank you,' she said softly, wanting only to escape the undercurrent of attraction that still sizzled between her and Jafar.

'Then I bid you goodnight.' He looked into her eyes as if he was sending her a special message—but what? 'I will be waiting for you tomorrow.'

Tiffany entered her suite, Jafar's last words ringing in her mind. Niesha and one other lady followed her in, apparently to be her chaperones for the night. She was tired from travelling and fighting the deepening attraction for the man she would marry tomorrow and didn't feel in the mood for any kind of surprise.

'Tiffany. You look amazing. Different, but amazing.' At the sound of her sister's voice she whirled round to see, not only Bethany, but her niece, Kelly, looking so excited to be part of the surprise Jafar had arranged to be waiting here for her. He'd done this for her? Her heart softened a bit more towards the formidable desert sheikh who'd bought the next two years of her life.

'Oh, my goodness. When did you get here?' She rushed over and scooped up Kelly, whirling the little girl around and then stopping to look at her as she held her in her arms.

'You look like a princess.' Kelly's voice was full of awe.

'She is a princess now.' Bethany moved towards them and together they all hugged one another. Then she stepped back. 'There is one more surprise.'

Tiffany looked at her sister, unable to fathom out what that could be. 'What can be better than my two most favourite people in the world?'

'Your best friend?' Lilly's voice sounded from behind and she turned, still holding Kelly, to look at her friend, guilt rushing over her for not having responded to her texts.

'I had to come and see for myself if you really wanted to go through with this and why.' Lilly moved to join them, a teasing smile on her face. 'Of course, I know the supposed real reason, but have also realised there is another very valid reason.'

'There is?' Tiffany was stunned. What other reason could there be other than to help Bethany and Kelly?

'Your groom.' Lilly looked at Kelly, appearing to search for suitable words. 'He is very handsome, not to mention caring for his bride. He arranged all this. He flew us here in secret, as a surprise for you. That tells me a lot—as does your blush.'

'I am not blushing,' Tiffany said quickly, knowing full well she was doing exactly that.

'I think I will put Kelly to bed now.' Bethany touched Tiffany's arm and smiled. 'You two must have lots to catch up on.'

'Before you go…' She halted, not sure how to ask. 'Have all the funds been paid in?'

Bethany looked at her, relief in her eyes. 'Yes.' The word was a whisper and then she silently turned and walked away with a tired Kelly in her arms.

Tiffany watched her sister go, smiling as Kelly waved at her over her shoulder, and she knew that, whatever else Lilly was reading into her motives for accepting this deal with Jafar, she'd done the right thing. Already there was lightness in Bethany's step, a hint of hope in her eyes. Jafar had kept his part of their deal and now she had to keep hers.

'As you have your sister and friend here now, we will leave you and return in the morning to begin the bridal preparations.' Niesha slipped from the shadows of the room, startling Tiffany. She'd completely forgotten about them. Had Niesha just heard that exchange?

'Yes, thank you.' She managed to project calmness as she spoke but didn't miss the look on Niesha's face and wondered again just what it was that had been—or even was—between her and Jafar.

As the two Shamsumarian women left the suite Tiffany looked at Lilly. It was time for the difficult explanation she'd been avoiding.

'Right, Miss Arabian Princess.' Lilly took her arm and propelled her to the living area of the suite, which had looked out over the sculpted sand dunes during the day, but now showcased a velvety blackness full of sparkling stars. 'I need to know everything that is going on and I mean everything.'

After Tiffany had relayed the story, from the moment at the last wedding when she was a bridesmaid for his friend Damian Cole, to the moment at the charity dinner in Paris, she sat back and looked at her friend.

'So let me get this straight.' Lilly's expression of disbelief echoed all she felt as she'd told her almost everything that had happened in the last two weeks. 'He kissed you, in front of the cameras as part of the deal, and you can honestly say you felt nothing?'

Tiffany sighed. 'No and that's the problem.'

'No, it's not. The problem is that you won't let go, can't allow yourself a bit of fun. This could be the perfect opportunity to bury the past, have a fling, prove you don't need your dream of happy ever afters to enjoy yourself.'

'I don't call a two-year marriage contract enjoying myself.' Tiffany bounced out of the chair and began to pace the room, pausing to look out of the window at the beauty of the night.

'Are you kidding?' Lilly said from behind

her. 'It's the perfect excuse and Jafar is exactly the right man to fool around with, have some fun, forget about your ex and live a little.'

'I'm not sure.' Tiffany turned and looked at Lilly unable to hide the truth much longer, and that wasn't the truth about her lack of sexual experience that even Lilly didn't know, but the truth about her deepening feelings and strengthening attraction for Jafar.

'You're blushing,' Lilly said as she rushed over to her, grasping her arms and looking into her face. 'You like him, don't you? A lot?'

'If he kissed me like he did after the party I don't think I could resist him.'

'Hold up. *After* the party?'

Tiffany recounted the kiss that had unlocked all the emotions she'd been trying to hide as well as opening the door for the woman she wanted to be, enabling her to set herself free if she just took the chance.

'Tomorrow night is your wedding night,' Lilly said, looking at her earnestly. 'You are going to be married to him for two years whatever happens, so make the most of it—and the week you have to shut yourself away from the world, which, by the way, I'd gladly do with him.'

To make the most of the week with Jafar, to

enjoy his company, to explore the attraction, was what Tiffany wanted more than anything else. She was falling for Jafar, falling for a man who'd struck a deal with her, bought her for a huge sum of money, but none of that mattered when he looked at her with dark desire in his eyes.

Tomorrow she would be his wife and shockingly, she finally admitted to herself, she wanted to be his wife in the truest sense of the word. 'I told him it was to be a marriage in name only.'

'He's a hot-blooded male, Tiff, and you are an attractive woman.'

'I'm his bought bride. Hired to do the job.' Tiffany tried to talk reason into herself as much as her friend. The admission that she wanted Jafar, wanted to be his wife in every sense, suddenly changed everything for her. After all the resistance she'd put up, could she really change the goalposts now?

CHAPTER SIX

THE BRIDAL PREPARATION Niesha had referred to last night at the feast had been far more intensive than anything Tiffany had encountered before. She'd seen brides pampered but never to the extent that she had been in the last twelve hours. Now she stood in her white gown, encrusted with an intricate pattern of the tiniest diamonds down the front of the full skirt, and on the fitted bodice they were set against what she suspected was real gold. A sense of panic rushed over her as at any moment the tall doors of the palace banqueting hall would be opened and she would walk towards the man she was to marry.

Nerves raced through her. Could she really do this?

You are doing it for Bethany.

Her ladies fussed around her one last time, adjusting the white veil clipped in her hair, which had been scented and elaborately piled on top of her head. Her full skirt was arranged around her one last time. There wasn't a detail they missed, even checking the gold and diamond band at her waist, which showed off her figure while maintaining the modesty of being covered as tradition dictated.

And you are doing this for Kelly.

She looked at her niece as she and Bethany were treated to the same attention. She smiled at Kelly, who was having a wonderful time being a little princess. The little girl's laughter made her smile and chased away the doubts that had been building since the moment she'd opened her eyes early this morning. As did Bethany's carefree smile.

Tiffany's attention fell on Lilly, who was less than enamoured with the long-sleeved bridesmaid dresses Madame Rousseau had arranged. The very fact that there were bridesmaids' dresses prepared for them by the designer meant Jafar must have planned from the day they agreed on their deal to have Lilly, Bethany and Kelly at the wedding, as her bridesmaids.

He had mentioned her parents on that night in Paris and she wondered how he'd fared with her mother and father, who hadn't spoken to one another for many years. Jafar was a man who relished a challenge so she wouldn't be at all surprised to see her parents here. She remembered how her father had tried to talk her out of it, believing she was simply rushing into a marriage, having no idea why or that Bethany and Kelly would benefit. As far as her mother and father were concerned it was a real marriage in every sense. Would they really want to miss that?

'It is time,' Niesha said, coming to stand before her, and Tiffany still couldn't shake off that feeling that this woman knew something about the marriage deal. She always had a superior expression on her beautiful face. Had Jafar told anyone other than his aide that this was a business deal? Did anyone else know it was an arranged marriage with a difference? That he'd hired his bride?

'It is.' Tiffany took a deep breath, reassuring herself that all brides were nervous as they were about to walk down the aisle to their future husband and these woman would expect nothing less.

'There is one more essential item.' Niesha's voice had hardened with disapproval. 'A final surprise from your soon-to-be husband.'

Niesha turned and gestured someone forward. Her father. Guilt rushed over her again for not having told anyone other than Bethany and Lilly the truth about the marriage, but she was so pleased to see him and her feelings towards the man she was to marry softened a little more.

'So you are going through with it?' The tone of her father's voice left her in no doubt he hadn't changed his mind. As far as he was concerned, she was making a big mistake.

'I am, yes.' She kept her tone firm. She had to make him think this was the real thing for her. 'This is what I want, Dad.'

'And nobody is pressuring you into this?' Had he any idea just how close he was coming to the truth?

'No,' she laughed softly, hoping to distract him, for Bethany's sake. 'Nobody is making me do anything I don't want to do.'

'In that case, you have my blessing.' He smiled and offered her his arm.

Tiffany looked at Niesha, who was watching them closely, eyes narrowed with suspicion, and she tried to derail the conversation before it deepened. 'Thank you.'

'Your mother is here too, I'm told.' Her father's lips set into a firm line once he'd informed her of his ex-wife's presence, reminding Tiffany of another reason why she'd never wanted to get married. At least not for real. If her parents could barely be civil to one another since their divorce, what was the future for her and Jafar in three months' time?

'We must not keep His Highness waiting any longer.' Niesha cut the conversation quickly. 'Nobody *ever* keeps the ruler of Shamsumara waiting.'

'Then I am ready.' Tiffany took a deep breath and looked ahead of her at the tall, ornate doors, behind which guests were assembled—and Jafar waited.

Slowly the doors opened and she stood looking into a room filled with women in black *abayas* over colourful dresses on one side and men dressed in white robes on another. Jafar stood waiting for her on a raised dais and all eyes in the hall were on her as she walked towards him on her father's arm. She, however, couldn't take her eyes from Jafar.

Dressed from head to foot in a subtle gold colour, he looked like a warrior prince. At his side hung a sword and from either side of the shoulders of his clothing, which had hints of Western influence, were fine gold chains and diamonds. As she drew closer the fine gold fabric of his headdress shone in the shaft of light that slanted down from the highest windows of the banqueting hall.

Was it a good omen or a bad one?

Her step faltered but she couldn't take her gaze from the handsome man in front of her, now so very close yet so utterly unreachable. His stubble-covered jaw flexed and she knew he was biting down hard in that way she'd already seen him do many times. Was he having the same misgivings as she was? The same doubt?

He smiled and relief surged through her as it reached his eyes, softening the hard lines of his face—and her heart. It thumped wildly and a host of butterflies took flight inside her, making her light-headed.

She let go of her father's arm and began to walk towards him again and as she reached the steps up to the dais, he moved towards her, took her hand and drew her up. Behind her there were a few gasps and she wondered if he should have done that, if he should have touched her before they were legally married.

It was then that she noticed he held a single flower. Large and white like an exotic orchid. Just as she was wondering why, he held it out to her with a smile. Once again, he was so good at acting the role of enamoured bridegroom that she could almost believe the smile was real. She took the orchid in her free hand, glad that her small but exquisite bouquet wasn't large, and lifted it up, wanting to smell the scent of the flower.

'You must put it in your bouquet,' he said softly, as if he only wanted her to hear.

She did as he asked and slipped it among her flowers, many of which she'd never seen before, and then looked back up at him, trying to chase away the nerves that were rampaging through her right now. Behind her were Lilly, Bethany and Kelly and in the assembled guests, she now knew, was her mother. What would she have to say about this arrangement? Not that it mattered now; Tiffany had gone too far, committed herself completely. She was doing this for her sister and right now nothing else mattered. She'd been paid a large sum of money for these three months and that would ensure that, not only were Bethany and Kelly free of all the threat of financial ruin, but she could set herself up again.

Lilly's advice rushed back at her as Jafar smiled at her, making her heart leap wildly. Was it the thought that she wanted more than the kiss they'd shared at the Eiffel Tower restaurant? That other than Jafar refusing her, reminding her she'd stated the marriage was in name only, there was no reason she couldn't be his true wife? That she could enjoy this time with him without the worry of future commitment or false promises?

The idea of being his sent a ripple of awareness all over her and she blushed at the thought.

'Now we can be married.' Jafar's words wiped out all those thoughts and she looked at the two ornately carved gold chairs, placed like a medieval banquet in the centre of the dais overlooking the assembled guests. The chanting of a man, dressed in white robes with a gold sash adorning them, was the official words that would join them in marriage and once the rings were exchanged the deal would be sealed in the most unbreakable way.

She would be Jafar's wife.

He led her to the chairs and she took her place as best she could in the voluminous folds of white diamond-encrusted silk. She tried hard to remember all she'd been told about what was now happening and watched as drinks were passed out to the guests in preparation for the toasting of the bride and groom.

Then Jafar took her hand. 'Now the rings.'

Tiffany looked down at her right hand, onto which Niesha had told her to put her engagement ring in readiness. Once Jafar took the ring and placed it on her left hand and she had done the same to the gold ring he wore on his right hand, they would be married. A hired bride but a legal wife.

His fingers were warm as he slid the pink diamond from her finger and she looked up, instantly realising it was a mistake. That spark arced between them again and, together with memories of the kiss at the Eiffel Tower, heated her body. Try as she might she couldn't look away, not even when his eyes became the darkest of greens. He took her left hand without breaking eye contact and she felt the ring being slid onto her third finger.

She was so enrapt by his heady gaze that she forgot what should happen next. He prompted her, his voice deep and husky. 'Now you must do the same.'

She blushed beneath the intensity in his eyes and focused her attention on doing what was expected. She took his right hand and eased the gold ring from his finger. Foolishly she looked up at him. The spark of desire in his eyes made her breath catch and for a moment all she could do was look at him. Then she felt him remove his right hand and replace it with the other.

She blinked back her confusion, caused by the swell of heady desire and passion tossing her around like a small ship on a stormy sea. There was the promise of quieter waters, of gentleness if she was brave enough to take it. Lilly's advice floated through her mind once more and she swallowed down the cocktail of emotions and concentrated on completing the ritual that would bind them together in marriage.

The man in the white robes chanted more loudly and applause came from the guests. 'We are now married. You are my Queen.'

Jafar had called on all his control and stayed firm against the powerful surge of desire that had raged inside him as Tiffany had slid his ring from his right hand and onto his left, making her legally his wife—his Queen.

Right now, as he looked at her, oblivious to anyone around them, he wanted to kiss her, to taste her lips against his. He wanted to feel the same heated passion as he had in Paris and he wished now he'd insisted on inserting many more Western influences into their ceremony, because then he'd have had an excuse to kiss her. Instead he would have to wait until they were alone in their suite, and after the kiss in the Eiffel Tower he wasn't sure he could risk kissing her. Not when she'd made it clear, despite the attraction between them, that she didn't want a physical relationship. As much as he wanted to kiss her again he couldn't, not when she threatened his control so completely it was unnerving and exciting at the same time.

Her lips parted as she looked up at him, inviting him with eyes as blue as the depths of the ocean, currents of passion swirling in them. Would she welcome his kiss again? The darkening of her eyes told him one thing but the tenseness of her body told him the opposite. Was that because she was fighting the desire or because she wished she weren't here doing this, that there had been some other way to help out her sister?

'We are now married.' He kept his voice firm, shutting down the desire that pulsed inside him, demanding satisfaction. 'The celebrations will continue for a few hours, then most guests will leave and we will be escorted to the Royal Suite and, as the tradition of Shamsumara dictates when a ruler marries, we will be shut in and guards will be placed at the main doors to the suite.'

'We were alone for a week in Paris. We coped then,' she said, her lashes lowering and a hint of a blush creeping over her cheeks, making her freckles, or sun kisses as he now thought of them, stand out. 'I am sure we can manage in the vastness of our suite here in the palace.'

Right at this moment he didn't think he could manage to ignore the desire even if he banished her to another country. He wanted her, desired her. His body craved hers in a way that heated his blood, pushing his legendry control to new limits, testing his honour. She looked up at him, so cool, so aloof that he would give anything to find the passionate woman he'd kissed as they'd viewed Paris from the Eiffel Tower and this time he wanted more than a kiss—much more.

'You do not find it strange?'

'That we will effectively be locked in? No. I accept that your country will do many things differently and, after all, nobody needs to know what happens—or doesn't happen between us.'

The noise level of the celebrations increased, giving him the opportunity to talk more without being overheard. 'Being shut away in our suite, with a guard at the door, is part of a long-standing tradition to secure the future heir for the kingdom. The flower I gave you is a symbol of fertility and, as part of the service, was blessed before you entered the hall. It is these traditions that mean we will have to remain married for two years, as the marriage will be assumed to have been consummated.'

'What about your word as leader of the kingdom? Wouldn't that be good enough?'

'Nobody will believe otherwise, Tiffany. Not when you are a beautiful woman and especially not with my reputation.' There was amusement in his voice and she followed his lead, allowing herself to relax.

'Ah, yes, the playboy prince,' she teased. Jafar was pleased to see the light-hearted girl he'd talked with in the English garden on a Sunday morning was beginning to emerge.

'Precisely and on top of that we have acted the part of lovers since the engagement was announced. Two years is what we agreed, but you only need to stay in Shamsumara for three months, or until my sister's baby is born.'

'No pressure, then.' She laughed and something softened inside him. He liked her sense of humour, liked how she handled all that was being thrown at her. Just as she had done in Paris, when she'd been instructed in the many traditions that she would have to adhere to while living as his wife, the Queen of Shamsumara.

* * *

Behind them there was movement as the door closed and the key turned in the lock. She was alone with her husband and the attraction and desire Tiffany had for him threatened everything she'd promised herself since she'd agreed to be his hired bride. The bridal suite was in almost subdued darkness, lit by many lanterns, their flickering flames creating a romantic ambiance, which was reflected in the Eastern music subtly filling the warm night air. The scent of incense completed the mood perfectly.

This was her wedding night. The night she'd always thought she'd give her virginity to the man she'd spend the rest of her life with. Instead she was with a man she would only spend three months with, yet that made no difference to the heady desire she had for him and she found herself wishing this could truly be her wedding night—the night she gave herself to the desert sheikh. A night of complete fantasy.

'Do you require help with your dress?' Jafar spoke, shattering her thoughts until they resembled the hundreds of sparkling stars in the night sky beyond the ornate arched windows.

'That would be a good idea if one of the

ladies is available. Or Lilly?' The thought of being able to speak with her friend fired a jolt of excitement through her. Lilly would know just what advice to give. It might not be what she herself wanted to hear, but she would tell her straight exactly what she thought she should do.

He raised his brows in amused disbelief, taking away that hardened expression he'd worn for most of the wedding celebrations. 'We are totally alone, Tiffany, and you will have to make do with me.'

'Oh.' Shock jolted her from her thoughts. As she moved across the marble floor the silk of her dress rustled and she knew there was no way she was ever coming out of it without some help.

Her heart pounded hard. Could she trust herself to allow him close, to touch her?

'You have my word that nothing will happen.' His voice lowered, becoming silky smooth. 'Unless you want it to.'

Unless you want it to.

Did he know that was her deepest and most secret wish? That she wanted something to happen—wanted him?

'I just want to take this dress off.' She reached up to unpin the veil.

'No, wait.' He crossed the room, bringing him unbearably close. 'I have wanted to do this since you stepped up onto the dais with me.'

She held her breath as he raised his hands and unpinned the veil from her hair. His gaze locked with hers as he let it float to the floor. Had she imagined the crackle of the spark that jumped between them?

'And this too.' He pulled the few pins from her hair and it tumbled around her shoulders, the music swaying her mind into a turmoil of passion-infused thoughts.

She should back away from the temptation he was putting before her. She wanted to be kissed again as she had been in Paris. Only this time she knew she wouldn't want it to stop. She wanted to forget everything for tonight— every bit of their deal. Was he just entertaining himself and tormenting her or did he want her as much as she wanted him?

He held her hair, focusing on it, and she backed away a little, forcing him to let go. She should ask him to unbutton the back of her dress, then she could slip away, go and hide in one of the other rooms of the suite. Get as far away from the temptation of this man as she could.

She turned her back on him. 'Can you unbut-

ton the dress, please?' With a flutter of anticipation she lifted her hair in readiness. Seconds
ticked by and the tension in the air ratcheted
up to unbearable levels until eventually she
heard Jafar move closer again. His touch was
gentle as he began to unbutton the first of the
many small buttons down her back.

Tiffany's breathing deepened as she waited,
head lowered, holding her hair against her
neck. As more of the buttons were opened her
nerves rose and her heart thumped, nearly skit-
tering out of control when his fingers brushed
her bare back.

Jafar paused.

She waited. The anticipation of the moment
was almost too much, then he continued his
task until the bodice of the dress loosened
slightly around her and she became acutely
aware of the fact that she was braless.

'I can manage now.' Her voice had become
a husky whisper and she didn't dare move in
case his fingers touched her skin again. She
didn't think she could tolerate this much more.
It was sheer torture.

'There are more yet.' His cracked whisper
only added to the sensation of being close to
him, feeling his touch on her skin or the pres-

sure as the bodice of the dress moved when he unbuttoned yet another small white button.

Lilly's advice was all she could think about now. Would he reject her, push her away as he had done in Paris, if she told him she wanted to be kissed again or would he kiss her—and more?

'Do you feel it too?' The whispered question was out before she could stop it.

Again he paused in his task, this time holding the bodice of the dress taut at her lower back. 'The desire?'

'Yes.' That one word was so husky, so full of emotion she hardly recognised it as coming from her lips.

'More than you can imagine.'

'Would it be so wrong to give in to it?' Her nerves almost failed her as she asked the question in a whisper. 'When tonight is like a fantasy?'

Silence came back at her and she was glad she couldn't see him, see the expression on his face. What kind of fool was she? He'd been acting the part of lover all along in order to portray their marriage as real. He wasn't really interested in her.

'Is it what you really want?' The deep sen-

sual tone of his voice sent a ripple of awareness cascading over her.

'I'm sorry.' She pulled away from him and
walked towards the window, desperate not to
look into his face, to see the shock in his handsome features. 'I shouldn't have said anything.
I'm not used to being in situations like this.'

'Are you referring to wedding nights or seducing a man?' Was that a hint of amusement
in his tone?

She turned to face him, a shy smile on her
lips. 'Both.'

'That pleases me.' He moved towards her
again, coming to stand next to her at the window, looking out at the night sky as if it held
the answer to her question.

She looked up at him just as he turned to
her. There was no mistaking the desire that
darkened his eyes, even for a woman as inexperienced as she was. 'It does?'

'Tiffany, you must know I want nothing
more than to make love to you—tonight. Our
wedding night. I want this night to be real in
every sense of the word.'

Her heart thumped so hard she had to lean
against the cool marble of the arched window.
He wanted her—really wanted her.

'You need to know—' she began, aware that

she had to tell him now she was a virgin. She wasn't, after all, his true bride and if he was expecting experience he would be very disappointed.

'There is nothing I need to know.' He cut across her nervous words as he moved closer, pulling her to him. 'Other than you want me to make love to you, to make you truly my wife, my Queen.'

'I want that.' Those words were a husky whisper, but he didn't wait to hear more as his lips claimed hers in a kiss that was gentle yet demanding in equal measures. The desire she'd tried so hard to ignore leapt to life, sending heat spiralling through her.

She wound her arms around his neck, pulling herself against the gold silk fabric of his wedding outfit, and as his hand slipped inside the open back of her dress to caress her skin she gasped in pleasure. He kissed down her neck as the passion increased and she knew she had to try again to tell him she had no idea what to expect or what to do to please him.

'Jafar,' she gasped, which had the effect of increasing his desire, his assault on her senses. 'Jafar, I need to tell you…'

His lips trailed kisses back to her face, back to her lips and he whispered against them.

'Then tell me, because very soon I will be incapable of processing anything. You are driving me wild.'

'I'm—' she began but his kiss smothered the word. She pushed her hands against his chest and forced him to look at her. 'I'm a virgin, Jafar.'

Jafar's senses reeled. His bride, his wife, the woman he wanted to claim in a passionate frenzy was a virgin? Had he heard correctly? It should have doused the desire, calmed the passion, but it only intensified it.

She was giving herself, her most precious gift, to him and on their wedding night—their fake wedding night. It should change everything. He couldn't knowingly take her virginity, then divorce her in two years' time. *This isn't a conventional marriage*, he reminded himself, his sense of honour slipping away into the mists of desire. *This is a business deal*. A contract they had both willingly entered into and, more than that, she was as attracted to him as he was to her.

'I'm not the kind of man who takes a woman's virginity. I'm not worthy of such a gift.' Harshness had entered his voice but the tension in his body softened when she looked up at him and smiled.

'It's very chivalrous that you care enough to try and dissuade me, but it's not going to change my mind. This is my wedding night, after all.' There was an element of coyness in her voice, which barely concealed the steely determination.

He touched his hand to her face, a stab of lust shooting through him as she closed her eyes and sighed. She was so beautiful, so incredibly sexy, and the fact that she now wanted the marriage to be real, tonight at least, filled him with hope. Maybe their time together would be much more pleasurable than he'd ever imagined.

Lust and desire careered around him and he couldn't take much more. His body was almost exploding with need for this woman and the fact that she would be completely his only intensified that. 'Are you certain this is what you want?'

'Tonight, with you, is everything I want.' She moved towards him, reaching up and placing her lips on his in a gentle, teasing way. 'I want the fantasy of you, this room, everything.'

He wanted to deepen the kiss, to demand so

much from her, but he had a duty to her. He wanted to make sure this first experience of sex was the most pleasurable she'd ever experienced and he couldn't do that if he lost control now.

CHAPTER SEVEN

THE SOFTNESS OF Jafar's kiss was so intoxicating Tiffany's mind spun, leaving her light-headed, and she leant against his lean, hard body. There was no question in her mind that she was doing the right thing. She wanted his kiss, his touch, his total possession in a way she'd never known before. The need inside her for this man, her husband, was all-consuming.

When he stopped kissing her she looked up at him, wondering if he was about to tell her he didn't want her, that a woman without any sexual experience didn't interest him. She searched his eyes, now so dark, looking for some hint to what he was feeling.

'I am honoured that you have chosen me as your first lover.' His voice was as soft as the silk dress she wore and it caressed her senses so gently, easing the nerves that surely went with such a momentous event. 'I want to make this night special for you.'

'Being here, with you, in this wonderful palace, it is already a special night.' She looked beyond him towards the large bed, draped in gold silk. A trail of lanterns created the ultimate romantic bedroom for a bride and groom while the remainder of the room was shrouded in darkness.

Without a word, he took her hand and led her away from the window and the warm night air, through the archway that led to the bedroom. The vastness of the domed ceiling was overpowering—or was it the enormity of what she was doing? She hesitated and he turned to her.

'It is a tradition that those attending the bride leave suitable gifts to be opened after the ceremony and your friend and sister have done that.' The gentleness in his voice wasn't reflected in his eyes as the passion and desire she'd seen before she'd told him she was a virgin returned, obliterating everything. He gestured to the ornately decorated table that stood alone at one side of the room.

She could see several gifts, all neatly packaged with white tissue paper and gold ribbon. 'Should I open them now?'

'You may do if you so wish, but I would rather continue with the task I started a few moments ago.' The suggestive rise of his brows made a heavy sensation deep inside her at the thought of him not only unbuttoning her dress, but removing it.

She moved towards him, lulled by the soft music, the heady scent on the warm night air. Everything was all so perfect. How could she not want to make the most of this moment? He watched her intently as she smiled coyly at him, then slowly she turned her back to him, waiting for him to unbutton the remainder of the buttons, only this time she longed for his fingers to brush over her skin, to set her alight with desire.

She pulled her loose hair over her shoulder and waited with building anticipation to feel the bodice of her dress move as he dealt with the buttons. His touch when it came was the sensual trail of his fingers down her spine, making her shudder with pleasure.

'You are so beautiful.' His husky whisper was filled with desire and she closed her eyes against the onslaught of sensations she'd never felt before. 'I want to explore all of you. Slowly. Very slowly.'

She clutched her hair tighter as her control slipped away, thawing her virginal body like the sun rising over a frost-covered landscape of England, bathing it in the heat of the desert sun. She sensed him move closer, her body tuned into his every move, anticipating his touch. The kiss he pressed against her bare shoulder forced a sigh of pleasure from her lips and she moved her head to one side as he kissed up her neck.

'I want to show you the wonders of making love,' he whispered in her ear before kissing back down her neck.

'Show me,' she responded in a throaty whisper, wondering if that seductive voice was really her.

He pulled her against him, her partially bare back pressing against the gold silk of his wedding robes, feeling the hardness of the diamonds that decorated them. She turned to look at him as his arms circled her waist. Then his lips claimed hers and she stretched her body, needing to deepen the kiss, to show him how much she wanted him, wanted this.

A harsh stream of words tore from him as he broke the kiss and she could feel his chest rising and falling as rapidly as hers. Was he angry? Uncertainty threatened. 'What's wrong?'

'How can anything be wrong with a woman like you in my arms?' He gently pushed her forward, turned her round and she was about to step away when she felt him working on the last of the bodice buttons.

Jafar forced himself to control the fierce passion surging through him. The need to rip the dress from her, take her to the bed and claim her was so fierce, so intense, he'd had to focus hard on those damn buttons. Who the hell put so many buttons on a wedding dress?

'Now I will finish what I started.' As the last of the buttons were freed he stood and looked at her back, his gaze trailing down her sexy spine as he willed his body to slow the pace, forced his needs back under control.

He slid his hands inside the dress and around her waist, feeling the silk begin to move, to slip away. In a slow purposeful move his hands massaged up her sides, then up over her shoulder blades and finally he pushed away the shoulders of the modest wedding dress that had never really concealed her fabulous figure from him.

Tiffany pressed her arms against her, allowing the sleeves to slide downwards, exposing the full glory of her naked back. His breathing was hard and laboured and he took a deep controlling breath, resisting the urge to push the silk away from her hips to reveal more of her.

Patience.

In a bid to hold onto his control, to take things slowly, he moved his fingertips down her back. The shudder of pleasure and soft sigh she gave was almost too much, but he held onto his control. Instead he put his arms around her waist, spreading his palms over her bare stomach before moving upwards to her naked breasts. He caressed the swell of them, desire throbbing through him as she leant back against him, gasping in pleasure. He circled the hardness of her nipples with his fingertips, lowering his head to kiss her neck once more.

Her scent, the same intoxicating one he'd noticed before, pushed his desire higher, as did the taste of her skin on his lips.

'Jafar,' she sighed his name as he kissed up her neck, his fingers still teasing her nipples.

Slowly.

The word pulsed through him and again he moved away from her, his hands lingering on her waist briefly before he pushed the silk dress down until it billowed out around her legs in a mass of white and sparkling diamonds. The white panties she wore accentuated her pert bottom.

'So beautiful.' His throaty words warned him again he was in danger of losing control, of giving into passion far too quickly. 'Turn round.'

Slowly she turned, the silk of the dress still around her lower legs, the brightness of the white reminding him of her virginal body, waiting to be claimed—by him. He took her hand, helping her to step out from the dress, unable to take his eyes off her long, slender legs as she did so.

Without breaking eye contact he led her away from the puffed-up silk of the dress and towards the vast bed. The sound of her heeled shoes on the marble floor was wonderfully erotic. She was naked apart from the white panties and heeled shoes and so sexy, so beautiful.

'I don't know where to begin with your robes.' The demure tone of her voice was in complete contrast to the image she created as she stood next to the silk-covered bed, the glow of the candles caressing her pale skin.

She wanted to undress him? The idea sent his body into overdrive and all he could think about was lying naked with her, seeing her pale skin next to the darkness of his. He unclipped the gold decorations at the collar of his wedding robe.

'It is much easier than removing you from your gown,' he teased as he moved towards her, his robe open at the neck. He held the fabric towards her. 'Pull this.'

Her eyes were wide and full of desire, her delicious breasts rising and falling with each breath as she reached out to take the gold fabric from him, her fingers brushing his. 'Like this?'

The question was teasing and slowly she pulled, a provocative smile of satisfaction on her lips as she exposed his chest, her gaze lingering on him, scorching his skin. He pointed to the fastening inside the robe at his waist. 'And then this here.'

She pulled the fastening and the gold robes slithered down him like a serpent so that he too now wore only underwear. Unlike Tiffany, he didn't stand in the gold silk robe, but kicked it casually aside, along with the soft leather sandals fashioned especially for his wedding.

'Now we are equal.' She bit her lower lip and looked at him coyly from beneath long lashes.

'Not quite.' Jafar lowered himself to his knees at her feet and ran his hands down her legs, over her knees and to her shapely ankles. 'These need to go.'

She lifted her foot and he slid the shoe from her, placing it on the floor as he looked up at her. Then, before his lust got the better of him, he let her foot go and did the same again, this time tossing the shoe aside as he began to stand up, pausing to press a kiss, first on her thigh, then on her stomach, then upwards to her breasts. Wild fire erupted in him as he took one nipple in his mouth, nipping at it.

'Oh,' Tiffany cried as she pressed her fingers into his hair and he moved to the other breast and began the torment once more.

He moved his kisses lower again and looked up at her, knowing he couldn't take much more of this. His control was slipping rapidly away. He took the fine lace of her panties and pulled them down her legs, resisting the urge to rip them from her and push her back onto the bed and cover her body with his. She stepped out of the skimpy lace and he kissed her thigh, moving upwards towards the very centre of her femininity, lingering there as he kissed the softness of her skin. Wanting more, wanting to taste her.

Not yet, he told himself.

Tiffany dragged in a deep and ragged breath as the warmth of Jafar's caressed her skin where moments ago the soft white lace of her panties had been. She stood breathing hard, wanting more than his breath on her skin. She was completely naked and so incredibly aroused she could hardly think.

Just as her legs weakened, threatening to buckle her knees, Jafar stood up, so close to her that the soft dark hair on his chest grazed her sensitised nipples. How could anyone stand this? It was exquisite and torturous at the same time. She wanted it to stop but at the same time she didn't want it to ever end.

'Lie down,' he demanded, his eyes so dark with desire they were almost black. She did as he'd bid, sitting on the edge of the massive bed, then leaning back on her elbows, watching him as if she'd been waiting for this moment with this man all her life.

He didn't take his eyes from her as he divested himself of his underwear, leaving him powerfully and wonderfully naked. His skin was olive dark, the candlelight seeming to illuminate every contour of every muscle. Hungrily she drank him in, her gaze sliding down the light covering of dark hair on his muscled chest, down over an incredibly defined flat stomach to the length of his erection.

She bit at her bottom lip, a dart of uncertainty soon chased away by the increasing beat of desire deep within her, the need to feel him intimately against her, feel him inside her, possessing her in the most natural way. Instinctively she moved herself backwards on the bed, looking directly into his eyes as he joined her, bracing the strength of his body over hers.

He kissed her, holding himself away from her, and she kissed him back, demanding more from him as she slipped her tongue inside his mouth. A wild sensation erupted within her and her hips lifted to him, seeking the release she knew only he could give, the release she wanted so badly that she was losing her mind, losing her ability to think.

A wild flurry of words she didn't understand unleashed from him as he broke the kiss, looking almost out of control as his body remained tantalisingly over hers. What had he just said? The question flew from her mind as he began the torment on her nipple again and she let her head fall back onto the silk covers, sighing softly and giving herself up to the pleasure of his kisses. He moved to the other nipple, making her body wriggle, then he moved lower again.

She gasped out loud, her eyes flying wide as she felt his tongue caress her intimately. His fingers gripped her thighs as he continued the torment, making her body buck and writhe, taking her to heights of pleasure she'd never imagined possible.

Just when she thought she was going to break apart, to shatter into hundreds of tiny pieces, he began kissing his way back up her body. This time his was much closer to her and as if her body had taken over she pulled up her knees, wrapping her ankles around his legs as she clung to his back. The heated hardness of his erection pressed against her, but it wasn't enough and she lifted her hips, gasping as she felt him slowly possess her.

She pressed herself provocatively up to him, drawing him deeper inside her until he completely filled her and his name came to her lips. 'Jafar.'

He looked down at her and before he could say anything, or stop, she kissed him hard, demanding more from him, from this moment. She wanted to live the fantasy to the full.

She caught the deep guttural growl that tore from him as he kissed her back, setting her on fire as he began to move inside her, deeper and harder. Everything turned wild, as she gasped against his lips, lifting herself up to him, digging her nails into his back. He thrust deeper and harder, taking her to a height of wild pleasure she'd never imagined possible.

'Tiffany.' He growled her name, followed by a rush of words she had no hope of understanding, but it only intensified the experience and she clung to him as her body began to float among the stars.

It was pure ecstasy and as she floated back down to earth, she became aware of his body, sweat slicked and hot, against hers as he lay on top of her.

With a thud of her heart the words I love you tried to force themselves past her lips, but she bit down hard to keep them in. It was just the wildness of the moment. She'd lost her virginity to a man she found compellingly attractive. It was nothing more than heated lust of the moment. It could never be more than that. She was just being fanciful.

Jafar woke as dawn stretched her fingers of soft orange light across the desert sky. His body was heavy with the effects of last night and with a smile of satisfaction he recalled the moment Tiffany had kissed him from his sleep in the early hours and they had once more enjoyed one another's bodies as hot passion had ruled over them.

He moved in the vastness of the bed, expecting to find her naked body, but the bed was empty. He sat up and looked around the almost dark room, the candles having long since gone out. She was standing by the ornate table, dressed in one of the two gold robes left for them and holding one of the gifts he'd suggested her sister and friend leave for her, as would normally happen to a bride in Shamsumara—especially a royal bride.

'According to our tradition you should have opened them last night,' he said, a teasing note in his voice as he flung back the covers, got out of bed, pulled on the other pale gold robe and walked over to her.

She turned to face him and smiled. She looked different. A night spent in his bed had given a glow to her pale skin, accentuating the freckles he found so irresistible. 'I was otherwise occupied last night.'

Her bashful words made him smile, as did the memory of just how occupied they had been. When he'd agreed to this deal with her, he'd never expected his wedding night would have been what it became. A hot passionate night, the like of which he'd never known before—ever.

He moved behind her, pulling her against

him as his body stirred, demanding satisfaction from this woman once more. 'We could be occupied again. In fact, we have a whole week in which to occupy ourselves.'

She laughed softly, a very sexy sound, and he pressed a kiss to the side of her neck, feeling the zing of passion rising between them. 'I have gifts to open first.'

First? He liked the sound of that, the promise of once again taking her to his bed. He watched as she opened the first gift, a beautiful necklace with a heart pendant. Her slender fingers trembled slightly as she opened the heart locket to reveal a small photo of her sister and niece.

'Shall I fasten it on for you?' He could feel the mood dip. She must be thinking of home and all she'd left behind.

'Yes, please.' Her soft whisper was almost too much for him as he took the necklace from her and she lifted her hair, just as she had done last night when he unbuttoned her wedding dress. After he'd fastened it he stroked his fingers down her neck and along her shoulders, feeling the heat of her skin beneath the silk wrap.

'Open the other and then I will call for breakfast.' What he really wanted was to pick

her up and take her back to his bed, but sense
prevailed.

She leant forward and picked up the remaining gift from the ornate table, pulling at the
gold ribbon and then opening the white tissue
to reveal a beautiful box. He kissed her neck
as she opened the box, the idea of breakfast
slipping to the back of his mind. Indulging in
a more passionate activity would be far more
satisfying.

Tiffany gasped with shock, snapped the box
shut and pulled away from him, leaving him
momentarily wondering what was happening.
'Is it not a suitable gift?'

He had made it clear to her sister and her
friend it was tradition for the bridesmaids to
leave gifts for the bride that would help her
in her new role as a wife. The necklace was
perfect, forming a connection with her homeland. What was in the box that would upset
her so much?

Her beautifully arched brows pulled together
and the look on her face was one of genuine
fear. What the hell was in that box?

'It's a very suitable gift. I only wish I had
opened it last night.'

'What is it?' he demanded sharply.

She looked down at the box clutched in her

hand, then handed it to him, her expression wary, as if she was expecting an explosion of fury from him at any minute. He took it roughly from her, opened it and swore savagely in his own tongue. Inside was a box of condoms with a note attached.

Have some fun! Xx

'Condoms?' The word was fired out from him and a cold slick of dread crept over him. He *never* slept with a woman without using protection. Even if she told me she was on the pill, he always used condoms. *Always*, damn it.

'I didn't think…' Her words trailed away as she pushed her hands through her hair in frustration. He wanted to be angry, with her, with himself, but the distress she showed made that impossible—especially after last night.

'It is my fault. I should have been more responsible. You told me you were a virgin. I should have made sure I looked after you—in every way.'

He moved to take her in his arms and held her against him, inhaling the scent of her hair as the ramifications of what could happen settled over him. Last night they could have done the one thing he'd sworn never to do. They could have created a new life.

'But what if...?' she said as her breath shuddered from her. 'What if I'm pregnant?'

He closed his eyes against the word, knowing full well that if this had happened in Paris they could have averted an unwanted pregnancy. Things were very different here in Shamsumara, especially for the Sheikh and his Queen in the days after their wedding. 'There is nothing we can do now. We must spend the week together, as tradition dictates. We cannot be apart for any reason.'

'But a baby, Jafar,' she implored, looking so frightened his heart constricted. 'That would change everything.'

He took a deep breath, silently acknowledging the truth of what she'd just said. 'It was one night, Tiffany. Your first time.'

He didn't believe a word of what he'd just said, but put as much conviction into it as he could. The blame for this lay firmly at his feet and if anyone was going to spend the next few weeks worrying, it was him.

Tiffany tried to eat the delicious breakfast that had been prepared for them, and the fragrant tea smelt amazing, but the worry of last night wouldn't go away, despite Jafar's apparent lack of concern. She might have been a virgin when she'd walked in this room last night, but she knew that one time was all it took.

Had his subtle yet persistent seduction been part of a bigger plan? Had she fallen into the trap of believing all he'd told her about his family situation? What if his plan had been to seduce her, create the heir he needed? If so, what would happen to her now?

'You should try and eat something.' He spoke firmly as he looked across at her, the lover of last night disappearing as the sun rose higher in the bright blue sky.

'Why didn't your sister come to our wedding?' The question rushed from her as doubts stacked up along with the realisation that his sister hadn't been present at yesterday's ceremony. Did she really exist? And, if so, did she really carry the heir Jafar needed to rule his kingdom?

'She is heavily pregnant, carrying the heir not only for her husband's kingdom but for Shamsumara. Travelling was out of the question.' He poured the tea from the most ornate gold pot she'd ever seen into small glasses, also lavishly decorated with gold. 'Once our week of observing the tradition of being alone has passed, I will escort you to meet her.'

Tiffany took the tea from him, inhaling the delicate scent, and sipped at the sweetness of the liquid, still trying to decide if last night had been planned or if they had both been taken by surprise by the strength of the desire between them. It had certainly been that way for her and, with her feelings towards Jafar deepening, despite knowing it was foolish, she'd hoped it was the same for him.

'But our marriage isn't real. Wouldn't that just complicate everything?' Why had she said that? Meeting his sister would be the perfect way to discover if she'd fallen into some bizarre scheme to rule his kingdom.

'You're right.' The sharpness of the declaration cut through her unease, causing more doubt to rise in her mind. 'In the circumstances, maybe it would be better if I went alone?'

If that didn't confirm she was nothing more than a temporary and necessary addition to his life, then nothing did. Whatever misguided affection she was beginning to feel for him, it was not reciprocated in any way.

Tiffany had to remind herself of this every night for the next week. As soon as the sun slipped down behind the sand dunes, Jafar became the passionate lover he'd been on their wedding night once again and, just like that first night, she was powerless to resist. He confused her and made her fall deeper and harder for him every night.

Last night, their final night together as newlyweds, the passion had been more powerful than ever and the lovemaking so intense, but, just as they had been doing since she'd opened Lilly's gift, they had used protection. Not that it lessened the worry that she might already be carrying his child—a child he'd claimed he didn't ever want. A child that would complicate everything in a way she couldn't bear to consider.

Now the sun was rising, heating the cool palace rooms in which she had been shut away from the world with this man for seven days and nights. She had no idea what to expect when he resumed his normal daily life, or even what that would be for her.

'I have duties to return to today,' he said, as if he'd read her mind, and she turned to see him fully robed in white, looking as magnificent as ever. 'You too will have duties to learn and my aide will help with these. He has been setting up your suggested charity since our wedding.'

There was no mistaking the aloofness in his voice, or the tense way he stood, as if he couldn't wait to leave her, to go back to his life. A kick of pain shot through her. They'd just enjoyed the most amazing week, where passion had ruled everything, and now he was going to turn his back on her.

'Good,' she said sharply. 'I will need something to do for the next, what is it now, eleven weeks?' If that didn't serve as a reminder of their deal, then nothing would.

He scowled at her and his anger simmered across the increasing heat in the room. 'You are counting the weeks until you leave so exactly?'

'Of course, I am.' Her flippant tone helped to instil confidence in her, to give her the same carefree attitude he had adopted.

He came to stand before her, his eyes vibrant, sparking with anger. 'Have you not found pleasure in your first week?'

Pleasure. She'd found far more than pleasure. She'd become ensnared in the web of passion he'd weaved every night and had no idea how she was ever going to sleep alone again.

Already her body longed for his, longed for his touch and so much more.

Jafar looked at Tiffany as she stood in the fine silk clothes he'd ordered for her arrival. The matching headscarf clutched in her hand, the tightness of her fingers giving away so much more than her blasé words. He knew then that whatever it was they'd shared, that undeniable spark of sexual attraction would now have to come to an end. This was the business side of their deal, and the distraction they'd found in one another, while adhering to the tradition of remaining solely in each other's company for a week, now had to be put aside. He had to do all he could to prevent Simdan from making a claim on Shamsumara and until his sister's child, his heir, was born, that claim could come at any time.

He seriously doubted that he would be able to resist Tiffany each night, but it must be done. This wasn't a real marriage. It was a deal to save his kingdom and nothing more. She was a bride he'd hired at considerable cost. She wasn't even one of his affairs. Passion and desire must be put aside.

You took her virginity.

The accusing words thrashed around his

mind. Not least of all because he should never have done that and, worse still, should have ensured that the necessary precautions were used. How the hell had he been remiss about such a thing, when every other time he'd had sex with a woman he'd always been obsessively careful? After the example of marriage he'd witnessed growing up between his cold father and his fragile mother, he'd vowed he would never have a child unless it was born into a loving union. That was, of course, when he'd been nothing more than the spare heir, before he'd inherited the right to rule over Shamsumara after his brother's tragic death. Would his plans to make his sister's child his heir be enough to keep Simdan at bay?

'Pleasure was not part of our deal, Jafar.' Her determined tone forced his mind from the tragedy of the past, back to the present, back to the situation they now found themselves in.

'Neither was a child.' The hurt expression on her face jolted him and he schooled his frustration at the situation he was now in. 'Forgive me. That was uncalled for.'

He reached out to her, but she pulled back. 'I hope that very soon I can reassure you that will not be an issue. In the meantime, I would like to sleep alone from now on.'

'As you wish.' A fierce sense of rejection rushed over him. Never before had a woman made it so blatantly clear that she no longer desired him. He'd always called time on his affairs. 'I have much to keep me from our marital bed and, as you will be leaving after the agreed three months, it will convincingly build the story that you are unhappy here with me.'

CHAPTER EIGHT

THE LAST THING Tiffany wanted to do was parade herself in front of the guests assembled at the gift ceremony, especially when she discovered that Niesha would once again be attending. There was still that feeling there was something, some kind of history, between Niesha and Jafar. Whatever had happened between them, Tiffany was sure that Niesha believed it wasn't over.

The hours passed slowly and Tiffany could barely recall the food she'd eaten or half of the gifts she'd been given. Most of the guests had now left, leaving her and Jafar with his aide and those who appeared to be part of his team of assistants and the ever-present Niesha and Simdan.

The music still filled the great hall and the dancers continued with their exotic entertainment, and as she watched Tiffany became acutely aware of Niesha's scrutiny. The dark-haired woman ended her conversation with another guest and made her way towards where Tiffany sat on the large red and gold cushions. Before she joined her, Niesha looked across the hall at her husband, now deep in conversation with Jafar.

Tiffany looked at Jafar and frowned. Whatever it was that he and Simdan were discussing appeared to be getting heated. Not that they were raising their voices—quite the opposite. Tiffany could tell from their body language that they were hissing and snarling at one another like jungle cats fighting over territory. She looked again at Niesha, only to find she was the object of the other woman's scrutiny and not whatever was happening between the cousins.

'I have a special gift for you.' Niesha's voice dragged her attention away from the two men, but she couldn't shake off the thought that their discussion was a direct threat to the deal she and Jafar had struck. A deal that, if she didn't honour it, would mean Jafar had the right to call back in the money he'd paid her, money that Bethany needed.

Tiffany looked at Niesha, unease spreading over her as if the woman had said or done something to threaten her. 'That is very kind of you. I'm quite overwhelmed by everyone's generosity.'

She kept her voice neutral, sure it would be unwise to let her suspicion show. Niesha smiled brightly and settled herself on the cushions next to her, presenting from the folds of her *abaya* a beautifully wrapped gift. Tiffany took it, shocked to see her hands were trembling. She opened it, to reveal a key-like object, made from gold and studded with jewels. It was most definitely not an imitation tourist trinket and she had no idea what it was or what it might represent. All she knew was that it was as real as the sun that was setting beyond the palace.

'It is the deity of love.' The smile on Niesha's lips didn't reflect in her eyes. Only cold malice showed in their inky black depths and Tiffany began to fear that her discussion with Bethany on the eve of her wedding had been overheard. Was that why she was now being given such a gift? To show that, although the full details of the deal she'd made with Jafar weren't known, the fact that she was here as a hired bride was most certainly known. How could she have been so remiss to talk about it like that in front of others?

'It is very beautiful.' The gold was cold to the touch, but not as frosty as Niesha's expression or her icy tone. Tiffany had suspected there was once something between this woman and the man she now called her husband and somehow this gift confirmed that. Or was she being fanciful? Reading too much into things as she always did?

'It is what I would have wanted.' Niesha let the words, veiled in threat, linger between them, and the music that still played in the background suddenly seemed incredibly loud and overpowering. 'Had I been Jafar's bride.'

So that was it. Niesha and Jafar had been lovers and, judging by the venom in Niesha's words, she was still very much in love with Jafar. Tiffany's gaze darted to her husband and his cousin, who had now moved away from the remaining guests, to stand together under the archway that led to the formal palace gardens. There was no mistaking the hostility between the two men. Was it because of Niesha? She was, after all, Simdan's wife.

'The gift or love?' The response fired from Tiffany in an uncharacteristic need to protect herself, to stand her ground. She had no idea what from, she just sensed she needed to.

Niesha laughed. A cold splintering sound

like iced puddles cracking in winter. The image made Tiffany momentarily homesick. She'd never see that here, but Niesha wasn't done yet. 'Love is not something Jafar will ever give a woman. He made that very clear to me, as I am sure he has to you also.'

As the warning in those words sank in, Tiffany recalled exactly what she'd wanted to say to him as the heights of passion had claimed her on her wedding night and was eternally grateful she'd bitten down on the words, kept them from tumbling out in a passionate frenzy.

What would have happened if she'd said *I love you*? It would have been too late to change the mistake they'd both made, a mistake she was still waiting to find out the consequences of. Tiffany swallowed back the nausea of that thought. She couldn't be pregnant, she just couldn't, and she tried hard to take comfort in Jafar's reassurance that it had been her first time and unlikely.

As the fear of what could be lingered over her like a storm cloud ready to burst, she felt Niesha's scrutiny once more. The last thing she needed to let her see was just how unsettled the gift had made her.

'Then I thank you for your gift and hope it brings all that it should.' She kept her voice light as she looked at Jafar, who chose that moment to look across the room at her. Even from that distance her body heated and she dragged in a deep breath, forcing her emotions back under control.

Jafar had been angry beyond words as Simdan had insisted they talk about his claim to Shamsumara and had taken the conversation away from everyone. He'd been aware of the exchange between Tiffany and Niesha, seen the gift given; he had no idea what it was, but knowing Niesha it would have to be something to make her appear superior to Tiffany. As he wondered how he'd ever thought he could be married to her, he forced his mind back onto the conversation he was having with his cousin.

His cousin wanted to rule Shamsumara and still thought he had a claim on the throne. All Jafar could do now was hope all he'd put into action would be enough to stave off that threat. His marriage to Tiffany just needed to hold this man at bay until his heir was born.

'There is no claim for you to make now, Simdan,' he snapped out coldly, determined to do right by his brother's memory and retain the rule of the kingdom of Shamsumara. It might not be what he had ever envisaged for himself, but it was now his duty—and honour. 'My sister's child will provide the heir required by our laws for me to rule and my new marital status satisfies all the necessary conditions for ruler of Shamsumara.'

'Why do you need to name your sister's child as heir?' Simdan snarled at him, his black eyes fierce with undisguised power.

'After my brother's untimely death, I want to ensure the kingdom has a successor named, one who deserves to be the ruler of Shamsumara.' He looked at the man he despised, more certain than ever that he'd had something to do with the accident that had claimed his brother's life and that of his wife. It was too much of a coincidence that he'd launched a challenge to rule over Shamsumara within days of his brother's death. Soon after that he'd ensured his claim to the throne couldn't be ignored and had married Niesha, the most calculating woman Jafar had ever had the misfortune to know, although that wasn't how he remembered her from his youth.

'And what of your charming new wife?' The threat in Simdan's voice was clear. 'Will she not provide you with your heir?'

Jafar sensed he was being toyed with, that for some reason Simdan believed he had the upper hand. 'Our marriage happened only a week ago. It is too soon to know if our union has brought about an heir.'

He couldn't believe he was saying those words to Simdan, of all people, or how much truth was in them. What was he going to do if Tiffany was carrying his child? He'd never wanted to be a father, not after the indifference he'd known from his own while his brother, older by one year, had basked in the sunshine of his approval. He didn't ever want to be in that position. Now it seemed a very real possibility.

'You consummated your marriage?' The leer on Simdan's face made his blood run cold. 'You got more than you bargained for from your hired bride?'

Jafar clenched his fists in an effort not to grab Simdan's robes and threaten him. The disrespect he had for Tiffany was out of order, but it was the fierce need to protect the woman he'd married that alarmed him more than anything else. 'I have no idea what you are talking about.'

Simdan folded his arms across his chest and raised his chin in a display of power that would rival any of the exotic birds of Shamsumara. 'Make the most of your days as ruler, cousin, for they are numbered. I will prove your marriage is a sham.'

'If you will excuse me, I have a gift to present to my wife.' He looked across at Tiffany, to see her holding her own in conversation with Niesha. Alarm chased down his spine. If Simdan had challenged him, then almost certainly Niesha would be challenging his wife.

His wife.

Twice within the last few seconds she'd come to his mind as that. Not Tiffany, or his hired bride, but his wife. The week spent solely in her company must have made him weak, softened his emotions. That would have to change if he was to hold onto his position as ruler. He would never succumb to such power-reducing emotions as affection and most definitely not love. Lust and desire were all he needed.

'I am intrigued,' Simdan said as he stood by his side, watching Tiffany in a way that made Jafar's anger boil up. 'What gift will you give to a bride who will be gone within months?'

A pang of guilt shot through Jafar. The gift he intended to present her with would cast aside any doubt that their marriage was real. It would mock Simdan's meddling words that suggested his bride would be gone within

months and that was exactly what he'd intended when he'd organised what had become
a traditional gift for Al-Shehri men to present
to their brides.

'I know what you are doing, Simdan.' Jafar's
cold words slid out slowly, control and calculation in every one, but he didn't look at his
cousin. 'You will never overthrow my rule no
matter what wild stories you fabricate.'

As he strode away Simdan's cruel laughter followed him, but right now he had other
things to worry about. Whatever it was Niesha
was up to needed to be cut off. Tiffany didn't
deserve to be in the firing line of his problems.

As Jafar marched across the marble floor towards her Tiffany couldn't help the sense of
foreboding that filled her. The air had become
heavy and tense as the few remaining guests
stepped back to allow him past. It was as if a
storm were brewing.

'I have one last gift for my bride,' he pro-
claimed to anyone who would listen, and
around them curious glances were cast their
way. He raised his hand in signal and a door
opened to reveal Aaleyah and the most beautiful dog Tiffany had ever seen.

Then she realised what was happening. The

dog was for her. Aaleyah smiled as she handed the lead to Tiffany, and even though she didn't want to, she took it and stroked the softness of the dog's head. It was a tall, lean animal, with sleek fur the colour of sand and the kindest eyes she'd ever seen. The eyes of a true friend.

'I can't have a dog.' She looked up at Jafar, imploring him to understand. She wouldn't be here long enough. It wasn't fair to the dog.

'It is a tradition started by my grandfather and one I have kept. It is a gift to show my commitment to my wife.'

She couldn't do anything but accept the gift with everyone's attention on her. Worse than that, there was that clause in the contract she'd signed, that if she revealed the truth about their marriage their deal would end. He'd have every right to take back all he'd given to Bethany and she couldn't let that happen, not now her sister was finally looking more like herself again.

The giving of the gift also seemed to be the cue for everyone to leave and, after a long day of smiling and pretending, she was once more alone with Jafar with only the dog, who had settled at her feet as if they had known each other for years.

'Her name is Leah.' Jafar spoke as she looked down at the resting dog.

'I can't keep her, Jafar.' She looked up at him as he stood over her, determined to resist the urge to stand so as not to allow him to know he intimidated her. 'What will happen when I leave? It's not fair to her.'

'That is why I opted for an adult dog, not a puppy that would bond with you.' His explanation didn't help. It ripped her fragile heart to pieces. Was it the thought of the dog not missing her or Jafar planning for her departure?

'You shouldn't have got her at all.'

'It is tradition. One I wish to continue. My grandfather gave my grandmother a Saluki.'

She stood up quickly, causing the dog to look up with questioning eyes. 'If tradition is so important and forms such a part of our deal, I think you need to tell me a lot more than you did when we spoke in England.'

'There is nothing more you need to know.'

'If I am to keep accepting fertility gifts and symbols of love, then I think I need to know what is really going on. I need to know the truth of what is happening here between you and your cousin.'

Jafar sighed. 'Very well, but not here.'

Jafar knew, now more than ever, he owed Tiffany the full story. She had become his wife in the true sense of the word and while their deal still stood she deserved to know everything, from the part she was playing to the threat Simdan posed to Shamsumara.

He took her hand and led her into the private royal gardens, aware that already Leah was following her new mistress. This discussion should really be done in complete privacy, but he didn't trust himself not to give into the desire he still had for her, desire that should long ago have been sated but most definitely wasn't. The next best place for a private discussion was his own gardens.

'This is so beautiful.' Her voice was a silky whisper of wonder and he clenched down on the desire he had to fight if he stood any chance of achieving what their deal had been about in the first place.

The lights from the palace reflected in the still waters of the pool and around the gardens lanterns burned, casting a soft yellow light. He ignored the image she created in her cream silk dress, which clung to her body, reminding him of how it had looked in the light from the lanterns on their wedding night. Leah stood calmly beside Tiffany, completing the picture of a Shamsumarian queen.

His Queen. His wife.

Enough.

'This is where I always come to relax,' he said as he walked beneath the tall arches and into the luxurious garden room.

'I'm not here to relax,' she said as she joined him, Leah at her heel. 'I need to know what all this is about—this need to retain your kingdom.'

'Sit,' he commanded, smiling at the defiant tilt of her chin before she joined him on the array of colourful cushions. He was about to open himself up to a woman, to share his story with her, something he'd never done before, but after she'd shared something much more precious with him, he owed it to her.

'What happened to your brother?' Her question went right to the heart of his turmoil, threw open the door he'd tried to keep shut and brought back all the pain. He steadfastly refused to feel it and instead focused his attention on the woman he'd married as part of a deal.

He looked at her face, at the soulful expression in her blue eyes, and tried to deal with the memory of the day he'd learnt, not only had his brother lost his life, but his wife too. 'Malek was a pilot and he and his wife were on their way to her homeland when a sandstorm brought them down.'

'That is so sad.' She lowered her gaze and he didn't say anything about Simdan's part in it, how he'd failed to let anyone know even though he'd heard of the disaster. If they had found them sooner maybe none of this would be happening, but then Tiffany would never have come into his life. He'd never have known the intense desire and pleasure from making her truly his wife.

He couldn't think like that. It was a dangerous path to travel. 'They were on their way to tell her parents they were to be grandparents. Their child would have secured Malek's rule and Shamsumara's future.'

Tiffany gasped and looked at him. 'That is why you need to name your heir? To secure the future of your kingdom?'

'In part, but also because now Simdan has a son, he could make a claim for my title if I had remained unmarried. Even though I am now married, that claim is still possible as I am without an heir. In three months' time I will have an heir for the kingdom and his claim will no longer be possible.'

He wouldn't say anything about the delicate situation they too were now in after their wedding night. He had no wish to distress her further. He would follow her lead and not mention the subject—at least until sufficient time had passed to be able to determine if she was expecting his child. He sincerely hoped it was not the case. He had no wish to be responsible for a child that would one day have to follow in his footsteps and become the ruler of Shamsumara. He knew only too well what it was to be brought up with that legacy hanging over you. If he'd felt that pressure as the spare heir, how must his brother have felt?

'And if I remain here for three months, this will ensure your cousin can't do anything to claim the throne.'

'That is correct, but more importantly my people, my advisers, must believe the marriage is real. They must believe that you intend to remain my wife. That is why I gave you Leah. To add credibility to our union.'

At the mention of her name, Leah looked up at him, then, deciding there wasn't anything to gain, laid her head on her paws once more and closed her eyes. Already she was faithful to her mistress.

'There is one more thing I need to know.' He sensed Tiffany's trepidation.

'Which is?'

'What is between you and Niesha?'

Her question touched a raw nerve, and the

sense of rejection after Niesha had shunned him for a better prospect came back to him. 'Niesha and I were promised to one another from a young age, as is customary in Shamsumara. As the younger son, the one who was free to build his own business instead of ruling a country, I wasn't good enough for her and she very quickly became engaged to my cousin when he became the ruler of Mirtiesa two years ago.'

'There isn't any history between you?' He could tell from the way she asked that she'd picked up on the tension between them, tension that had been caused by one weak moment when he'd kissed Niesha soon after his brother's death. She had consoled him, returned to being the sweet girl he'd always known and in a moment of weakness he'd taken her into his arms and kissed her. Niesha had responded but then his sense of duty had reared up like an angry stallion. He'd held her back from him and the smile on her face had told him it hadn't been about any kind of desire for him; she'd been playing with him, seeing just how far he'd go against his sense of duty.

That kiss with Niesha had been nothing like the kisses he and Tiffany had shared either here in his palace or in Paris. Those kisses had been full of genuine desire and hot passion, not at all like the kiss that had proved beyond doubt just how scheming Niesha was and that he'd had a lucky escape.

'No, there isn't any history other than having been promised to one another by our respective families.' It was pointless to enlarge on a kiss that had meant nothing, a kiss that should never have happened. He'd been at his lowest point and she'd used that to her advantage, suddenly seeing him as much more than a spare heir, a way to raise her own star.

'So you don't love her?'

'Love is not a sentiment I have any need of, Tiffany. It is what weakens a man, takes his focus off life. My brother loved his wife.' He cut the word off before he could say any more; her shocked expression left him in no doubt that, despite her claims as they'd talked at Damian's wedding, she wanted love and happy ever afters. He'd have to dispel that notion. 'Before I became the ruler of Shamsumara I put all my time and energy into my business. Women were just a pleasant distraction—and will remain so.'

'What was your business?'

He looked at her for a moment, not able to work out if his change of topic, his harsh remark that implied she was nothing more than a distraction, had been warning enough to her that she shouldn't expect any kind of love or affection from him. Her question showed him she could play the game of evasion every bit as well as him. 'You said you were the younger son who was free to build his own business.'

'I run a civil engineering company. Or rather it is currently in the capable hands of my newly appointed CEO.'

'Sounds impressive.'

'That discussion is for another day. It's getting late,' he said softly, and again the need to kiss her, to hold her close, rushed over him. He needed to send her away before he gave into the urge and gave her the wrong idea about them and their marriage. 'I will bid you goodnight.'

CHAPTER NINE

FOR THE LAST two weeks, Tiffany had absorbed herself in the work she was expected to do while living in Shamsumara as Jafar's Queen, desperate to push aside her ever deepening feelings for a man who just saw her as a convenient bride. On the night she and Jafar had talked after the feast of gifts, he'd made it perfectly clear love was not an emotion he wanted in his life. Lust and desire were all he needed, which was exactly what Niesha had alluded to.

Since that night, Jafar had been noticeable by his absence in her new daily routine, but the process of helping women who were struggling to bring up children alone, for whatever reason, made her feel closer to Bethany. She'd talked on the phone, even had video calls, but she missed her and little Kelly terribly. Maybe she was much more homesick than she'd anticipated. It would certainly explain how emotional she'd become over the last few days.

She missed Jafar and it was more than missing the intimacy of the sex they'd shared. She missed him, missed talking with him, laughing with him. She missed the man he became when he let his guard drop in the privacy of their suite, missed him so much it made her heart ache.

She'd fallen for him. It was far more than attraction, deeper than desire. It was love. She'd fallen in love with a man who openly confessed to, not only being unable to love, but not wanting love in his life. It was an emotion he scorned.

Why had she allowed herself to fall for him, to get emotionally close to him? It was this increasing emotion, the deepening of her love, which had made her insist she slept alone from now on. The sooner she cut the tie of attraction between them, the better. She didn't mean anything to him and it would be unwise to get more involved. The only thing that mattered was the deal they'd struck.

Even the charity work she'd chosen to do while in Shamsumara didn't matter to Jafar and he had warned her about becoming too involved with those she was helping. It was almost a double standard when he'd given her the gift of a beautiful dog, which now lay at the side of her bed, waiting for her to start the day. Apart from Leah's presence, she had been alone in this bedroom since she'd rashly declared a desire to sleep alone. For two weeks her body had longed for the pleasure that Jafar's could give, as if they were made to be as one. Two whole weeks without him. Two whole weeks of torture.

A sinking realisation slipped over her and with a gasp she sat up, frantically running dates through her mind, but each time she came to the same shocking conclusion. She was late. She covered her face with her hands, beating back the tears that threatened. Was that why her emotions were all over the place?

She was pregnant.

She was pregnant with the child of a man who'd openly admitted he had no intention of ever being a father and had gone to extreme lengths to ensure he retained the kingdom he'd inherited from his late brother. He'd made sure he had the heir he required to safeguard that kingdom without the need to become a father himself, then he had hired her as his bride, negating the need to commit himself long-term to marriage.

She thought of all she'd learnt about him the night they'd talked openly, the night she'd fallen a little more in love with the man who hid behind the tough exterior of control. He'd never allowed her that close again, never let her see his guard down since that night. He had already distanced himself from the bride he'd hired, the bride he wanted to leave Shamsumara once they had been married for three months.

Could it be possible that she now carried his child? His heir?

Then the full horror of the situation hit her. Where did that leave her now? Alone and pregnant back in England? Forced to stay here with a man who'd never intended their marriage to last beyond two years? What if he sent her away after the baby was born but insisted the baby grew up in Shamsumara? Fearful thoughts made her weak, made her unsure if she wanted to cry or scream in frustration.

What she needed to do was establish if her fears were true. She needed a pregnancy test, but how did the Queen of a desert kingdom obtain that? Could she confide in Aaleyah? As soon as that idea had come to her, she dismissed it. Sweet as she seemed, Aaleyah was loyal to Jafar and her homeland. If she told her maid, then very soon Jafar would know and right now she needed to keep her suspicions from him— until she'd decided what to do. Her mind spun, making her feel light-headed with worry.

How could she have compromised herself so easily?

Passion, desire and growing love for Jafar.

The answer drifted around in her increasingly dizzy head but she couldn't think about that now; she had to find out if she was expecting Jafar's child.

Beyond the archway to her room, she heard the doors to their suite burst open and guilt rushed through her at the secret she'd just realised as she heard Jafar call out her name. He never did that. Panic rushed over her. Did he know? Was there some way he'd found out already? She leapt from the bed and grabbed the silk wrap just as he strode into the room, his handsome face as dark as thunderclouds.

'What's wrong?'

'My sister has fallen.'

'Fallen?' She struggled to piece the information together, her mind still splintered after acknowledging that she was almost definitely carrying his child. She could barely process her own news, but this just scrambled her mind further.

'Down the palace steps.' He snapped the words at her as he flung off his white robes of office and put on darker ones, more suitable for an everyday man. Already he was preparing to go to her, worried about his heir.

'What about the baby?' Tiffany asked tentatively, resisting the urge to place her palm against her stomach. If the palace steps were anything like those here, it would have been a bad fall.

'That is exactly what I intend to find out. The message didn't go into detail before the signal failed.' He looked directly at her and she sensed his fear, knowing it must be bringing back memories of losing his brother. 'I must go now.'

He strode across the room to look out at the small private garden and the pale cream walls of the palace, agitation in every step, but he couldn't look at her. If he went to his sister it would give her the opportunity to find the answer to her own problems. 'Of course, you must.'

Tiffany's heart thudded. She, of course, felt for Jafar's sister, and for what she must be going through, but she also worried for what this might mean for her own situation. If his sister lost the baby, then what would become of her, of the three-month deal she'd made with Jafar? Worse than that, if she was pregnant would he allow her to leave? She had to keep her newfound secret from him. Certainly until they knew the fate of his sister and her baby.

'I need to go.' For a moment she thought she saw regret in his eyes as he looked at her. His shoulders loosened, as if he could no longer carry the weight of his kingdom, or the duties he'd inherited. A pang of sympathy rushed through her and she involuntarily moved towards him. It was that action, that hint of thought for him, that had the barriers rushing back up, until he stood tall before her, beautifully commanding and incredibly powerful. 'I must see for myself that my sister and her child are well.'

'Then go.' Her new secret burned inside her as she spoke, as did the guilt of hatching a plan to find a way to know for certain if she was carrying his child. The unspoken meaning to his words burned in her mind.

He must have an heir.

He adjusted his robe and picked up his headdress. 'I will return once I am satisfied my heir is safe.'

Those words ploughed into her, confirming

she was right to fear his reaction if he discovered she was pregnant. How could she have been so stupid, so foolish? This wasn't an ordinary man, leading an ordinary life. This was a powerful desert sheikh who put duty to his kingdom above even his own needs—and his kingdom needed an heir.

Attack was her instant defence against that fear. 'Is that all you can think about? Satisfying yourself that your heir is safe? What about your sister? Do you not care for her?'

Anger filled his eyes as he put on his headdress and moved towards her, his voice low and threatening. 'The safety of my heir is something you should also be worried about, Tiffany. If my sister loses this baby, our marriage cannot be ended.'

The harshness he'd used as he'd said her name chased away memories of the soft, seductive way he'd said it as they'd made love on their wedding night. Then it had been a caress—a seductive caress. Now it was full of undisguised threat.

'Why?' She stood her ground even though she was seriously underdressed in only the flimsy gold silk dressing gown.

He looked at her, but his eyes didn't soften as they slipped down her body and she folded her arms around her, needing a shield from his cold scrutiny. 'You signed a contract to stay in Shamsumara for three months or until my heir was born.'

'But that was because you knew your sister would give you the heir you needed.' She tried to defend herself, tried to remember exactly what had been in the contract but the waves of nausea were becoming ever stronger.

'The contract stated clearly that you would remain here, as my wife, my Queen, until my sister gave birth to my heir, but for a minimum of three months to validate the marriage in the eyes of my people.'

She frowned at him, her emotion-muddled mind not able to clearly follow. 'But what if the worst happens? What if she loses her baby?'

'You are my wife and, if the worst happens for my sister, you will be the only thing standing between Simdan and his challenge to my leadership of the kingdom. I cannot allow you to expose our deal by leaving—not until my sister is safely delivered of my heir.'

'And if she doesn't want more children?' Tiffany's mouth was almost too dry to speak. She needed to sit down but refused to show any kind of weakness to Jafar.

'My sister will have more children. She is a

queen in her own right and needs to produce heirs for her husband's kingdom.' The calm, matter-of-fact words only intensified the heavy ache in Tiffany's heart.

'But that could take a year—or more.'

Jafar moved towards her, his voice becoming gentle, as if the panic of the news he'd just received had subsided into nothing, as if it was just the two of them once again. 'Unless our wedding night has been blessed with a child.'

Tiffany gasped. Did he know? Was this all pretence to force her to admit the truth? She hesitated a moment before speaking. 'Thankfully I am not pregnant.' She hurled the unwise words at him and stood glaring, hurt slashing into the tenderness she'd been carrying in her heart for him since he'd claimed her as his wife, become her first lover, then lowered his guard and showed her the true Jafar.

Was it just the shadows cast by the morning sunlight or was there disappointment in his eyes? She closed her eyes against the fanciful notion as the dizziness threatened once more, making her mind sway like the dancers at their celebration feast. The reality of his words made her body weaken. She was trapped. If his sister lost her baby her fate was sealed; whether she admitted that she might be carrying his child or not, she could no longer leave. Her head spun with the seriousness of her situation and the knowledge she couldn't keep her secret from him for ever.

'Tiffany?' Concern filled his voice and she looked at Jafar as his handsome face blurred, her ability to focus slipping away, then nothing but blissfully silent darkness.

Jafar called out for Aaleyah as Tiffany slipped to the floor in front of him. Her face was pale as he scooped her into his arms and carried her to the large bed they'd shared with much passion on their wedding night, three weeks ago. Just as then, desire and lust forged through him as he touched her. He held her close against his body, painfully aware of the flimsy silk doing very little to conceal the fullness of her breasts.

Beside him Leah whimpered and nuzzled Tiffany's hand as he laid Tiffany on the bed. What was the matter with her? He'd been guilty of neglecting her for the two weeks since they'd resumed normal life, but it had been the only way to stop himself from wanting her. Was she now so homesick she didn't eat? Was that why she'd fainted so spectacularly?

It was your threat to force her to stay.

His conscience screamed the answer to his question and it seemed to echo around the velvety silence of the room. 'I'm so sorry, Tiffany, for dragging you into my battles. I never wanted to hurt you.'

He stroked her hair as he sat on the edge of the bed next to her, the need to care for and protect her overwhelmingly strong. If he had a normal life, if he was able to want normal things, then he would want Tiffany. He'd want her to remain in his life, to care for her and maybe he might even be able to let go of his past and allow love into his heart.

You don't have a normal life.

Aaleyah rushed to the bedside, thankfully cutting off his unthinkable train of thought, and he looked up at her, a sensation of total helplessness almost suffocating him. Tiffany and his sister. The two women he cared deeply about and they were both in need of his presence. He refused to analyse that thought right now. The fact that he considered Tiffany a woman he cared about was almost too much on top of the events of this morning.

'What is the matter with her?' Jafar demanded of his wife's maid.

A smile slipped to Aaleyah's lips. Not at all the reaction he had anticipated. Not at all the sense of panic and loss of control that had him in its grip. 'I have suspected for a few days, even perhaps before Her Majesty.'

'Suspected what, damn it?' Jafar snapped as he sat beside Tiffany's limp body. He didn't want guessing games. He wanted to make things right for Tiffany, make her smile and laugh as she had done during their week alone. Despite everything he'd promised himself, he cared for her—deeply. 'Is she ill? Is it the heat?'

'You are to be a father, sire.'

Jafar froze as the maid's words sank in and he looked down at Tiffany as she groaned softly and stirred. His beautiful wife, the woman who'd made him think happiness could be possible, was pregnant? He was going to be a father? Elation poured through him but as he looked again at Aaleyah, who still seemed remarkably unconcerned for her mistress, all he could hear was Tiffany's words before she'd collapsed ringing in his mind. 'Are you sure?'

'Yes, sire. I have been watching for signs that your bride is with child. That is my job.' The maid looked satisfied with the explanation for her mistress passing out. He, however, felt only concern. He'd never wanted Tiffany to suffer. That had never been part of his deal.

Tiffany stirred once more, this time struggling to sit up. Cold hardness filled him, pushing away the gentle affection and concern of moments ago. Tiffany had lied. His pregnant wife had told him she wasn't carrying his child—only a few moments ago. What could she possibly hope to gain from keeping such news from him? Her freedom?

'Leave us.' He snapped the command at the maid without taking his eyes from the beauty of Tiffany's treacherous face, unable to deal with the revelations of the last few minutes and certainly not with the emotions that had surged through him for his Tiffany. He adopted the only stance he knew and sat rigid with anger on the bed beside her as Aaleyah called to the dog and left the room. For the first time in two weeks he and Tiffany were alone. Totally alone.

Jafar's breath was deep and hard as Tiffany looked up at him and he reeled in the shock of all that had just happened. Less than an hour ago, he'd learnt his sister's child, his planned heir, was in danger. Now this. *His* child had been conceived with great passion during the hottest night of sex he'd ever had. His hired bride, the woman he'd brought to his country as a temporary measure, carried his child. His heir.

'You lied.' Guilt slashed at him as he inwardly cursed his position, the duty his brother had left him. Since their wedding night he'd wished for more, wished it hadn't been part of a deal, but his duty meant that could never be possible.

Sparks of angry fire leapt from her eyes as she looked directly into his, refusing to break eye contact. The vulnerability of moments ago, when she'd lain pale and asleep on the bed, had gone, chasing away those unfamiliar gentle feelings for her. This was a woman intent on fighting her corner.

Tiffany fought to keep her breathing calm, to keep looking into the wildness of her husband's eyes. They had once held nothing but desire and passion for her; now they were hard, glittering with anger.

'You lied to me.' The glacial words cooled the air around them until she visibly shivered as Jafar spoke again.

She knew what he was talking about. She had no idea how, but he knew she was almost certainly pregnant. From the foggy recesses of her mind she recalled Aaleyah's voice, coming through the darkness that had claimed her, how she'd calmly told Jafar he was to be a father. How did her maid know before she did?

Shame burned over her. She was so innocent, so unaware of sex she hadn't even considered the need for protection on their wedding night. She'd just been swept away with the fantasy of the magical room, lit by lanterns. Transported on the warm desert wind that had come in through the archways, entwining with the soft music and totally seducing her. She'd been a victim of her own dreams, dreams of love and happiness she'd long ago thought buried. She'd been completely under his spell.

Was that why Lilly had left such an obscure present? To remind her not to get carried away with things that could never be, as well as protect her from the consequences of the attraction she'd admitted she had for Jafar?

'Why, Tiffany?' Jafar glared at her, his eyes sparking with anger in a way that would put a priceless gem to shame.

'I did not lie,' she snapped at Jafar, her emotions running high, making her ever more vulnerable to this man, even in his current angry mood.

'You clearly told me that you were not expecting my child. *Thankfully I am not preg-*

nant." Those were your exact words, yet just moments later you are on the floor at my feet. Aaleyah informed me she has suspected for several days. How long have you known?'

The sharpness of the accusation in his voice cut deep into her. She hadn't kept anything from him. 'I don't know for sure. It was only this morning I realised it was possible.'

'It's been possible since our wedding night, Tiffany.'

Was he trying to make her look stupid? 'I can hardly go to the local pharmacy and buy a pregnancy test, can I?'

She swung her legs from the bed, needing to get away from him, away from the pain and hurt of his obvious disgust at the idea of being, not only a father, but the father of her child. As soon as she stood up she wished she hadn't as the room spun once more.

She put her hand to her head, pressing her fingers to her temple, wishing she didn't feel so weak, so at this man's mercy. She heard the bed move as she stood, her body sensing his behind her, and she closed her eyes as her body begged for his touch.

'Hadn't you better go?' She was desperate to deflect the attention from herself. 'Your sister needs you.'

'As do you—and my child.'

She turned to face him. 'I am not sure, Jafar, that I am pregnant, despite what Aaleyah said.'

'I would believe the wise ways of a woman such as Aaleyah over a doctor any day.' His voice had become gentle, his eyes softening, and all that she'd been trying to hide from herself burst back into the open. She loved this man and had done from the day she'd become his wife—maybe sooner if she was really honest with herself.

He touched the backs of his fingers over her cheeks and she began to melt, her promise to never let him touch her again slipping by the wayside. This was why it was dangerous to be alone with him. She couldn't trust herself. 'I will arrange for a doctor to visit to confirm if you are pregnant.'

'And if I am?' Even to her, the words were a tremulous whisper that gave away so much. Panic rushed through her like a tidal wave, sweeping away to softer emotions she'd foolishly allowed back into her heart. It changed everything—for both of them, putting them in a situation neither had ever wanted.

He trailed the backs of his fingers down her face, her throat, over the exposed skin of her chest, down between her breasts and then placed his palm against her stomach. She didn't move. Couldn't move. Her breath became fast and shallow as his gaze pierced into her, seemingly reading every thought in her mind.

'If you are pregnant, I will do everything in my power to convince you to remain in Shamsumara as my wife and Queen.'

CHAPTER TEN

JAFAR PACED THE room beyond the bedroom where the doctor he'd summoned was attending his wife. There it was again. He'd never wanted to think of Tiffany as his wife. She'd always only ever been his bride—his hired bride, but somehow in his thoughts she'd become his wife.

Firm footsteps alerted him to the doctor and he turned expectantly to face him, realising with a jolt he wanted Aaleyah's diagnosis of Tiffany's fainting to be true. He wanted his wife to be expecting his child. The thought slammed into him like a sandstorm, taking his breath away. How had everything he'd ever wanted changed so much? He'd never wanted to father a child, never wanted to inflict that same censure he'd received on his child.

'Her Highness is indeed expecting. Congratulations, Your Highness.' The doctor's words seemed to come from far away, reaching him as if on the wings of his falcon. If he never wanted a child, why did this news fill him with such elation?

He thanked the older man and returned to his bedchamber to see that Tiffany was now up and dressed in a deep blue silk dress, adorned with diamonds. She looked stunning and his chest tightened.

As if sensing her presence wouldn't be needed, Aaleyah slipped discreetly away, but Leah remained lying on the cool marble floor close to her mistress. Tiffany turned and looked at him. He saw her throat move delicately as she swallowed, giving away her nerves.

Did she fear the situation they were now in as parents-to-be? Was it possible she didn't want his child? He moved towards her, her eyes watchful, mirroring all the doubt, all the questions that were racing through his mind.

'It is confirmed.' His voice was hard with controlled anger, the only way he knew how to deal with situations that evoked deep emotions within him that he didn't want. 'You carry the heir of Shamsumara.'

'And what exactly do you propose to do about that?' The starkness of that question was in sharp contrast to the soft image she created in a blue gown. Her long brown hair loose, framing her face, accentuating her freckles. He ignored the effect she had on him, pushed it savagely away. Instead he drew on the curtness of her words, the blame laced within them, blame that lay firmly at his feet.

'You are my legal wife. There is nothing to be done.'

'I am your hired bride. You paid me to come here for three months. Surely that goes against one of your traditions. There must be a way out of this.'

'The night we came to this very bedchamber after our wedding you were a virgin, untouched by any man, and in taking that from you I broke one of the most sacred beliefs of my country.' He'd spent many hours dwelling on this fact. He'd married a virgin bride—unknowingly, but that changed nothing. Not when he'd allowed desire to consume him so intensely that he'd refused to adhere to the sacred tradition of the rules of Shamsumara, that a virgin bride could never be cast aside.

'There are so many beliefs, so many traditions. We must have broken most of them just by signing the contract.'

'That is true, but even though it wasn't a

real marriage I took something that was not rightfully mine to take.' He moved closer to her and she looked up at him, her eyes searching his. 'We could have lived with that secret, but now that you are carrying my child, it is very different.'

She pushed her way past him, exasperation in every move she made, and he watched, a helpless sensation rushing over him. All he wanted to do was take away her pain, soothe her troubled mind.

'It must have been that stupid flower.' She flopped down to sit on the bed, her hands covering her face in a gesture of despair.

Jafar had that sensation tight around his chest again and sat down next to her, pulling her hand gently from her face. 'The flower is nothing more than a tradition. I hold myself totally responsible for the situation we are in now. I should have taken care of contraception—especially when you told me you were a virgin.'

Her lips lifted into a sad smile. 'It's not all your fault. I wanted that night with you. I'm as much to blame.'

'No.' He could never allow her to take any blame. She might have driven him mad with desire, seduced him with her soft words of wanting one night, but she was inexperienced, he was not.

'I just wish I had opened Lilly's gift sooner.' The regret and turmoil in her voice dragged his guilt further out into the open.

'But you didn't.' He laid his hand over hers, shocked to feel how cool it was and eager to take away the blame she was pouring over herself. 'Have you thought that fate has conspired to bring us together, to give us the baby that was created that night with such passion?'

She blushed and that familiar rush of lust hurtled through him. Would he ever stop wanting this woman? 'It wasn't fate, Jafar. It was my innocence—or maybe ignorance.'

He cupped her face in his hands, forcing her to look at him. 'I am honoured to have been the man you chose to be your first.'

She pulled away from him. 'I should never have done that. I don't know what happened to me. Maybe it was the total fantasy of being in a desert kingdom, maybe I was trying to live the fairy tale. I'd longed for the perfect fairy-tale wedding and then here I was, with a man like you—on my wedding night.'

'What are your true thoughts on marriage?' He had to ask, had to know. He hadn't told her yet that there was almost no way out of their marriage now that she carried his child and most certainly wouldn't be if anything happened to his sister's baby. He pressed that thought away, not daring to tempt fate by thinking it any more. His sister and her baby would be fine; they had to be.

'My parents married because my mother fell pregnant with Bethany. Five years later I arrived but by then the marriage was already in trouble. I always thought I was a last-ditch attempt at making it work but love had turned sour and I don't remember any affection between my parents. It was a relief when they finally split up and later divorced.'

'It just proves there is no such thing as true love or one that lasts a lifetime. What brings a man and woman together is more basic than that.'

Her brows furrowed together and the look of sadness in her eyes was almost unbearable. 'Sex. It's all about sex. I know. I had several boyfriends but never let them get close—in any way. I was searching for the impossible dream and being here with you on our wedding night was it, but I was wrong. I guess I just got carried away with the fantasy when really it was just sex.'

Was she too hiding from her feelings towards him? 'It was more than just sex. It was desire. Hot passion.'

Tiffany jumped up as if she couldn't bear being near him. 'Whatever it was, it was wrong. It should never have happened. I just hope everything is all right with your sister and her baby. Then I can leave here and forget all this ever happened.'

'Leave?'

'Yes, leave, Jafar. I have to go back to my life.'

'And what of my child?'

'It's a child you don't want. You made that very clear and I will never bother you, never darken your door and demand anything from you emotionally or financially, you don't have to worry about that, but I am leaving.'

'I have a duty to my child, one that I intend to take very seriously.' He stood up and inhaled deeply, instilling control back into him, blocking out the way he felt towards this woman.

'I don't want my baby to grow up as I did, Jafar.' She looked at him, imploring him to understand, and he did, but he didn't want her to leave, not now she carried his baby.

'I will never allow that.' His passionate response shocked him to the core. Already he was protective over the child their night of passion had created. It was far deeper than the need to protect his heir in a way he couldn't yet understand. He needed time and space to deal with all he'd just discovered and the best way to get that was to go and see his sister. 'I must go and see my sister. See for myself what has happened. You will remain here with Aaleyah until I return and only then will we discuss our marriage.'

Jafar's threat had remained in the charged atmosphere of their suite long after the doctor had left, having declared the new Queen to be with child. Tiffany had been relieved when Jafar had told her he had to go to his sister, but that had been short-lived as he had called in Aaleyah, instructing her to remain with his wife every moment of the day and night while he was away.

Aaleyah had done exactly as instructed and had remained with Tiffany throughout the day and night while Jafar had gone to see his sister. Now they had received word of his imminent return and her maid had left her alone to prepare yet another fragrant bath for her, although Tiffany secretly wondered if it wasn't more for her ruler. The notion of that old-fashioned view still didn't detract from the pleasure of the scented baths and all the pampering that went with it.

Tiffany slipped out of one of the exquisite silk dresses she'd found waiting for her on arrival in Shamsumara and pulled on a white cotton dressing gown, preferring it to the gold silk she'd worn on her first morning of marriage. That seemed far too decadent now.

She tied the belt at her waist, looking forward to soaking in the deep warm waters of the bath. It would soothe not only her troubled mind, but her weakened body. She looked in the mirror and rested her hands on her stomach, hardly able to believe she was pregnant with Jafar's child, much less the way he'd calmly told her he would do anything to convince her to stay.

Behind her she heard movement from the arch that led onto the small plant-filled garden set aside for her use alone. By day it was a cool shady place, a haven from the heat of the sun. By night it was lit by lanterns near the archway, but shrouded in darkness beyond.

'Jafar?' His name slipped from her lips even though she knew he hadn't ever used this way into their suite. When no response came, fear slithered down her spine, but she reassured herself it must be Aaleyah. She tried not to let her imagination run riot, tried not to think of what or who could be in the darkness beyond the light from the lanterns. She was just being fanciful yet again and it had to stop.

She turned back to the mirror and pulled her long hair from the pins that held it firmly away from her face and as it tumbled down her back she looked again in the mirror. How could she ever believe Jafar, a desert ruler, could fall in love with a pale-faced English girl when there were beautiful women around him like Niesha?

She took in a deep breath as the woman who made no secret of her dislike for the English bride Jafar had returned home with forced her way back into Tiffany's thoughts. She was in no doubt that something had happened between her husband and Niesha, although she knew enough of her husband's view of honour to know it would not be happening now that they were both married.

The rustling of leaves from the garden made her turn once again. 'Who's there?'

She waited, holding her breath, but nothing. Slowly she walked towards the arch, stepping out beyond the soft yellow light of the lanterns into the darkness of the garden. Jafar wouldn't torment her like this, wouldn't send fear through her. She placed her hand on the cool marble of the arch and leant into the darkness, about to ask again.

The hand that caught her face, pressing hard over her lips as the assailant stood behind her, was hard and calloused, a large ring pressing into her cheek. She tried to scream but the hand smothered her mouth.

'Screaming will get you nowhere, Your Royal Highness.' Simdan. She'd recognise that deep and menacing voice anywhere.

She stopped struggling and stood, hating the smell of his hand on her face, but knowing that to show fear would be the worst thing possible with this man. She resisted the urge to struggle as he pushed her into the garden, into the darkness as menacing as the man who held his hand over her mouth. He forced her through a gateway and into a tunnel that was so black she had no idea where they were, then she saw stars high in the night sky as they emerged into the desert beyond the palace walls.

Was he kidnapping her?

'I have brought you here to strike a deal with you,' Simdan said, putting his face close to hers. 'And we both know how much you like to make deals.'

'I think you should let me go.' Tiffany forced

the words from her, adamant this horrible man wouldn't know just how terrified she was.

He moved towards her and she backed up against the wall, realising very quickly how wrong that was. 'Do you indeed?'

'Yes, Jafar will return any moment now.'

'How can you be so sure when he has gone to the mother of his heir.' The laugh that erupted from Simdan turned Tiffany's stomach over and she felt sick.

'What do you want?'

'To buy you just as easily as my cousin did.' He laughed again. A cold sound that made her heart thud with fear as adrenalin raced around her. 'I will pay you three times what he did—if you leave now.'

'If I go anywhere it will not be because you have paid me.' The reply rushed from her before she'd even thought if it was wise. As far as she was concerned she would be leaving because she wanted to, not because either of the desert Kings had paid her to do so.

'If you stay, Your Royal Highness, I will expose your deal to the people of Shamsumara. I wonder how they will view their new Queen then. A hired bride. A bought woman.'

She knew full well it was nothing to do with how the people thought of her, it was how they viewed their ruler. Jafar would lose their support and, without an heir, Simdan could make his claim to be ruler of the kingdom. She couldn't stand by and allow the man she'd fallen in love with, the man whose child she now carried, be so completely destroyed.

Jafar returned to his marital suite to find it empty. Something was wrong. He could feel it on the warm breeze, sense it deep within him as if a connection had long ago been forged with Tiffany, a connection he'd fought hard against. His sister was well and her pregnancy was unthreatened and all he wanted to do was tell Tiffany he wanted her, wanted his child, that he wanted to try and fulfil her dreams.

Aaleyah entered the suite and looked at Jafar. 'Where is Her Highness?'

'I assumed you were following orders and that you hadn't left her alone?' He'd known Simdan would try something to discredit his and Tiffany's marriage, but had never expected him to stoop so low and take advantage of his sister's fall and kidnap Tiffany.

If she had left the suite by the main doors, the guards he'd thankfully had the foresight to place there would have seen her. There was only one other way out of the palace. The secret tunnel.

Without a moment to lose Jafar rushed through the garden, the trickle of the water from the fountain now an ominous sound. He pushed open the wooden door in the archway with ease and then stepped into the tunnel. Tiffany's scent that he knew so well lingered like a trail in the darkness.

How could he have put her at such risk? How could he have done this to the woman he loved?

He stopped in the tunnel. The echo of that thought made all the more powerful in the heavy darkness. He loved Tiffany. The bride he'd hired had found her way past every barrier he'd put around his heart. She'd unlocked the door to emotions he'd vowed never to succumb to.

He swore savagely in his native language as he strode on through the darkness, pausing when he heard Simdan's voice beyond the opening to the desert, low and threatening—and speaking in English, confirming his suspicions.

'What else did Jafar get for his money?' The suggestive snarl that followed this remark turned Jafar to ice and he gritted his teeth against the building hatred for his cousin. 'Did he get this?'

Jafar had no idea what *this* was, but from the protesting gasps Tiffany made he could well guess and, like a panther that had been stalking its prey, waiting for the opportune moment, he stealthily moved out of the darkness, finally ready to confront his enemy.

'Take your hands off her.' Jafar's hard voice filled the silence of the night and Tiffany's relief was intense.

Simdan backed away, his hands held up, proving he had no intention of touching her again. Revulsion filled her as he leered at her. 'I was only taking from you what you took from me.' He turned his attention back to Jafar. 'You kissed Niesha. You couldn't take it that she'd chosen me instead of you. You tried to seduce her, tried to break our union apart.'

'What I took from Niesha was given gladly,' Jafar fired back at his cousin, and Tiffany's heart broke, right there in front of these warring men. The man she loved didn't love her and never would. He was still in love with the woman his family had planned for him to marry, the woman who had married his cousin. Now the intense hatred between them made sense.

Simdan's eyes narrowed with aggression as he looked from her to Jafar, the darkness of the night unable to conceal the pure venom in them.

'What you intend to take from my wife, however, is not given willingly. My wife is not yours for the taking.' Jafar squared up to his adversary. 'Just as my kingdom is not. Go back to your wife and child, Simdan. Focus on your own kingdom.'

Guards burst out of the tunnel, grabbed Simdan, and Tiffany shrank back against the palace walls. Jafar gave instructions and, by the light of the half-moon and the stars, the foreign words, hard and unyielding, filling the night air, Tiffany almost fell to the sand. In silence she watched Simdan being taken away.

Shock at what had just happened numbed her and she barely felt Jafar's touch as he pulled her against him, but his warmth helped to soothe her panic as it gently thawed her. It did little for the pain in her heart knowing he didn't really want her in his life, that the woman he wanted was now married to his cousin.

She pulled back from Jafar, looking up at

him as the cool night breeze of the desert played with her hair. 'Your sister?'

In the darkness she could feel his relief. 'She and the baby are well.'

There was only one more thing she needed to know and she had to ask him now. 'Did you kiss Niesha?'

'I'm not proud of it, but, yes, I did.'

'Did she kiss you too?' His hard words to his cousin replayed in her mind. *What I took from Niesha was given gladly.*

Tiffany knew right there, as the stars sparkled in the night sky, that she couldn't stay with Jafar. She was a fool to think she could see their deal through to the end, salvage his reputation, but she'd be even more of a fool to stay with a man who didn't want her, much less love her. Now that she knew she was pregnant she had to leave. There was no way she wanted her child to grow up witnessing the kind of fierce rows she'd seen between parents who hadn't wanted to be together. There might well be passion between her and Jafar now, but passion never lasted, not with a man like her husband. He'd soon find another woman more desirable, then another.

'I'm leaving.' She turned with her chin held high and marched as best she could in the sand back towards the tunnel. She didn't want to go into the darkness again, but she wanted to stay out here with Jafar even less. She couldn't stand the pain of even being near him knowing there wasn't any hope of a future for her and her child with this man, despite his bold proclamations of duty and honour.

'What do you mean you are leaving?' Jafar caught her arm and pulled her round to face him.

'I'm leaving Shamsumara right now.'

'It's the middle of the night and you are not in a fit state to travel,' Jafar declared, and the lack of trying to dissuade her from leaving only made her certain it was the right thing to do.

'There is nothing wrong with me.'

'You are pregnant.'

'And we both know that was not part of our deal, not what you wanted at all.' She stood and stared at him, challenging him to say otherwise, daring him to break his terms.

'It wasn't, no.'

'Now that your sister is well and the baby too, I think it's best if I return to England.'

He looked at her without saying a word, shadows from the palace walls falling over his face rendering it as unreadable as ever. His silence, his hesitancy confirmed she was doing the right thing. He didn't want her or his baby.

'At least wait until the morning. I will arrange for my plane to be on standby and if returning to England is still what you want I will not stop you, but don't leave now. Not after what has just happened.'

Agonising pain slashed at her heart. He wasn't prepared to fight for her or even his child. Sadness percolated through her as she accepted he'd never love her. 'I won't change my mind, Jafar. I am leaving.'

CHAPTER ELEVEN

THE NEXT MORNING Tiffany woke early with a sense of foreboding, after a restless night that had seen her tossing and turning. Aaleyah had slept in one of the suite's other rooms for a second night and Tiffany couldn't decide if she was being guarded or protected. Or even worse, if it was the child she now carried that was being watched over.

With her mind still restless she sat up in the large bed she'd slept alone in. Last night, after the incident with Simdan, she'd told Jafar she was leaving and he hadn't even tried to persuade her to stay. He'd ordered Aaleyah to remain a second night in her company because he hadn't cared enough for her to do so himself.

These thoughts had whirled in her mind all night and as she'd finally given up on sleep she had come to her decision. She had to leave Jafar, leave Shamsumara and end this sham of a marriage. Not for his sake, or hers, but for the life they'd created. A baby he had admitted to never wanting.

All she could think about now was returning to England and starting a new life, where she could prepare for motherhood alone. It was ironic that she now faced this prospect when she'd come here to help Bethany do the same. Now she too was destined to be a single mother.

She ran her fingers through her hair, feeling more dishevelled than ever, but there was no way she was going to allow Jafar to see her like this. She would leave the palace full of pride with her head held high. With that thought in mind she showered and dressed in one of her own summer dresses, shunning the vast array of colourful silks Jafar had filled her closet with.

Aaleyah entered the room and stopped, the smile of greeting she always had missing from her face. 'A car is ready to transfer you to the plane.'

'Thank you, Aaleyah. There is one further thing I need you to do.' She looked at the maid, forcing hardness into her heart, trying to block out the pain of everything from saying goodbye to her beautiful dog, to walking out on the man she loved.

He will never love you.

Words that had filled her mind during the long wakeful hours of last night sounded once more. 'I need you to take care of Leah. As much as I would like to take her, I can't.'

'As you wish.' Aaleyah patted her leg and Leah trotted over to her. Neither of them seemed worried that she was leaving and it just convinced her all the more she was doing the right thing. Pregnant or not, she couldn't stay here any longer. Not when the man she loved would never love her in return.

She wanted to ask where Jafar was, wanted to know if he was going to see her before she went. He might not want her as his wife any longer, might not want to acknowledge her child as his heir, but he was still the father of her child created during a night of passion. Surely that counted for something? Pride stopped her from saying anything. His message was more than clear.

He didn't want her in his life and she wouldn't beg.

'Good, then I'm ready to leave.' Tiffany picked up the one small bag of her possessions and walked out of the suite that held such bittersweet memories for her. She bit down hard against the sadness and the tears that threatened. Crying seemed to be her default setting at the moment, but she wouldn't give in to that need. Not now. Not until she was high above the desert and well on her way back to England.

Without a backward glance she left the luxurious Royal Suite and with head held high made her way to the waiting car.

A large black SUV waited in the shade of the palace entrance, the finality of its presence taking her breath away. Jafar really did want her gone. What had she expected? That he would be here waiting to stop her, begging her not to leave, declaring undying love for her? That was the stuff of fairy tales with happy endings. That was the fantasy she knew would never happen. Jafar's absence as she walked out of his life was reality. This was the end of their deal, the end of their marriage and the start of her new life.

She'd arrived in Shamsumara a virgin and had fallen in love with the man she'd been hired to marry. She had lost her virginity to him in a night of such intense pleasure it still made heat curl deep within her to think about it and she now carried that man's child. Her life would never be the same again, but she was determined that if that child was a son she would show him so much love and affection he would never hurt a woman as Jafar had hurt her.

Her bag was taken from her by one of the palace servants, jolting her thoughts back to the painful moment of walking away. She stood proud and tall, the wind whipping the long skirt of her dress around, and waited as the back door of the SUV was opened for her. She climbed in, feeling more alone than she'd ever felt, despite the driver, dressed in white robes and a headdress, who sat patiently and wordlessly waiting. The door shut with a soft clunk, the engine started and the vehicle moved away from the palace. She wouldn't look back, didn't want to know if somewhere Jafar was watching her leave.

She didn't want to look at the desert either. Instead she rested her head back against the soft leather seats of the SUV and closed her eyes. Soon this would all be over and she allowed the motion of the vehicle to soothe her, allowed it to lull her briefly to sleep.

She woke with a start when the SUV stopped and looked out through the darkened windows. All she could see was desert, but the driver got out and she assumed Jafar had had his plane made ready at a different airfield. Maybe he didn't want her seen leaving, didn't want to make his wife's departure public knowledge yet, which would surely happen at the bustle of the one they'd landed at almost five weeks ago. So much had happened since then. Had it really only been six weeks since she'd agreed to Jafar's deal?

Her door opened and the driver, swathed in white robes and a white headdress, which he wore wrapped around his face, stood back. He averted his gaze as she stepped out into the rising heat of the morning, clutching in vain at her dress to keep her legs covered. She looked around her in alarm. This wasn't an airfield. This was the middle of the desert and all she could see were several tents. There was no sign of a plane anywhere.

'Where am I?' The man merely turned and walked towards the tents, the keys of the SUV jangling noticeably in his hand. Either he didn't understand English or refused to speak to her.

Should she follow? What if this was another attempt by Simdan? She looked at the SUV behind her but of course that was useless. Even if the driver had left the keys in it she would have no idea in which direction to drive off. She was completely at the mercy of the driver—and whoever else was here, in the middle of nowhere, waiting in the tent.

She looked across at the largest of the tents, to see the driver standing next to the opening, framed by ornately carved wood. Through the opening she could see vibrant colours and soft lighting, which contrasted completely with the plain sand-coloured exterior of the fabric that rippled gently in the wind. He didn't meet her gaze, exactly what she'd come to expect from the men who served Jafar, but should she follow him, go into the tent? As the question raced through her mind at top speed he gestured her to him, then into the tent. He obviously didn't speak any English.

Tentatively she walked towards the tent, her sandals allowing the cool sand beneath the heated surface to seep in with each step she took. Her stomach knotted in fear, but the driver now stood motionless by the intricately carved wood, which gave the plain tent a majestic look. This wasn't just an ordinary tent. She was sure of that. Fear curled inside her again. Was Simdan behind this? Was Jafar right now searching for her in his palace?

She pushed the fear-driven thoughts aside and paused as she drew level with the driver but, just as before, he gestured her inside, his eyes still downcast, his headdress making it impossible to see if she recognised him as one of Jafar's servants. With nerves racing over her, she stepped onto the carpet that covered the desert sand and into the tent. The heady scent of incense filled the air, soft seductive music weaved around her. It was the ultimate desert fantasy, the kind of place she'd imagined being with Jafar, before events had destroyed all those romantic ideas.

A noise behind her made her swing round to see the driver with his back to her, closing the tent. 'I need to get to the airport,' she blurted out as panic sluiced over her once more, but he continued his task in slow methodical movements as if he hadn't heard her, let alone understood.

'I have to go,' she tried again, not able to keep the panic from her voice any more.

This time he turned to face her and for the first time looked directly at her. There was no mistaking those eyes. 'Jafar.'

'You didn't think I was going to let you walk away so easily, did you?'

Why was it every time he needed to draw on his strength of control, Tiffany always looked so utterly vulnerable or incredibly desirable? Right now her eyes were full of doubt and vulnerability as she looked at him. They became larger as he moved towards her, but her body, today dressed in a long black dress splashed with large cream flowers, was the most desirable he'd ever seen it, reminding him of how she'd looked that Sunday morning after Damian's wedding.

Then she'd filled him with hot desire and he recalled how he'd thought that if he weren't setting out a marriage contract with her he would have taken her to his suite and made love to her. Would he have wanted the same if he'd known then she had been a virgin? Would he have put such a deal to her, knowing his ability to resist the temptation she created would be hard to achieve?

'Yes.' That one word snapped with alarming confidence from her.

'Then you are very much mistaken.' He threw the hard words into the charged atmosphere inside the tent, ratcheting up the tension to unbearable levels.

'But why here?' She spread her hands wide and looked around the desert tent he often used as his escape. This was his royal hideaway and could be assembled wherever he wanted it to be. Today it was in the middle of the desert, far away from the palace and the capital city of Shamsumara and, more importantly, far away from the airfield where his plane was on standby—awaiting his further instructions. Instructions he hoped would be to stand down, but with the fierce expression of determination on his wife's beautiful face he seriously doubted that would be the case.

'Because we can be alone.' He moved closer to her, smiling as she proudly held her ground, looking as poised as any queen could. He recalled the first time he'd thought she possessed the regal qualities fit for a queen of Shamsumara and now he was in no doubt. He also knew that he wanted her as his Queen, wanted her to be the mother of the heir to his kingdom. All he could do now was hope that it wasn't too late, that she didn't despise him for all that had happened. If he'd been the loving husband he should have been he would not only have protected her from his cousin's evil attempts to take what wasn't his, he would have protected her on their wedding night.

But then you would have no reason to make her stay.

The words chanted in his mind as he stood watching her, trying to predict her next move.

You would lose the woman you love.

'But I don't want to be alone with you,' she protested defiantly. 'I want to go home—to England.'

'And so you shall—if that is what you truly want. All I ask is to spend one last night with you.' The request was audacious, but then he was a bold and courageous man. He was also a man who would do anything to get what he wanted and right now that was Tiffany.

She gasped and this time took a step back, shaking her head slowly. 'No, Jafar.'

'Nothing will happen that you don't want to happen,' he assured her, recalling how he'd said those words to her about their wedding night, the night she had asked for more, asked him to make love to her, asked him to fulfil her fantasy. That night had been about passion, but tonight, if she allowed him to show her, would be different. Tonight would be about love—his love for her.

'We both know what happened the last time you said that.' The barb hit home, but he rebuffed it.

'You told me you were a virgin. You also told me you wanted to be mine.' His voice became hoarse with the memory of that night as guilt rushed at him again, almost unbalancing him. 'That you wanted the fantasy of a night with a desert sheikh.'

She looked down, her long lashes sweeping onto her pale skin; the freckles he'd always found so endearing were more pronounced from her recent time in the sun.

'None of this is about us any more, Jafar. It's about our child.' She looked from lowered lashes at him.

'I am well aware of that.' He moved away from her and picked up a headscarf, holding it out to her. 'Put this on. I have something I wish to show you.'

She frowned at him, but did as he asked, hiding her glorious long brown hair beneath the cream silk. 'I will show you why I come to the desert, why I have this escape route ready at all times. This way.'

He walked back out into the heat of the morning, sensing with every muscle in his body that she was following. He ducked his head and went into one of the other tents erected close to his quarters. His falcon sat patiently on its wooden perch, having been transported here ahead of them.

'My goodness,' Tiffany said from behind him as he put on the suede glove and untethered the falcon and placed her on his arm. She stretched her wings and then settled as he looked at Tiffany.

'Her name is Shae.' He ran his hand over the bird's back to calm her. 'She is excited to fly. I usually fly her much earlier in the day, but today, I wanted you here. I wanted you to see her fly.'

'What has she got to do with us? I don't understand.' She shook her head in confusion and, despite the curtness of her question, he was pleased to see she was intrigued.

'Come.' He left the tent, walking out into the openness of the desert. Then he turned to Tiffany, who was struggling to keep her dress around her legs even more than she had done at the palace. He caught a glimpse of a long slender thigh, pale and soft, and although it unleased a stab of lust he pushed it aside. 'She will now fly.'

He removed the bird's hood and she stood poised, her wings out. Then with a flurry of movement she took off, sweeping around them in the sky. He didn't take his focus off the bird. If he looked at Tiffany's body, the fabric of her dress plastered close against it by the wind, he would lose all control. This was about showing Tiffany she had her freedom, that he would set her free to fly like his falcon if that was what she wanted. He'd do it because he loved her, even though it would kill him.

'That is wonderful,' Tiffany said as she stood a little way behind him. 'To see her fly free like that.'

He smiled. That was exactly the reaction he'd hoped for. After watching the bird a while longer, he held out his arm and she returned, rewarded with the food he'd held, the protection he offered. 'And now she returns to me of her own free will.'

He looked at Tiffany. 'Tomorrow, I will do as you ask and set you free but I hope that, after tonight, you too will want to be with me and accept all I can give you.'

He wasn't yet ready to tell her that he wanted to give her his love, that he'd realised he wasn't immune to the emotion, that he'd fallen in love with her and, if he was honest with himself, it was while she was attending Damian's bride he'd done that. He'd just been too proud, too controlled and too shielded behind his defensive wall to realise it.

All he could think about was her rejection, her need to leave him, leave Shamsumara. If she loved him, then surely she wouldn't want to do that. It was her determination to leave that silenced his words, prevented him from admitting his love.

Tiffany couldn't find anything to say to Jafar's declaration. Did he really think one more night of passion would be enough to make her change her mind, to make her stay and complete the deal she'd agreed to? One more night in this man's arms, tasting his kisses, enjoying his caress was all she wanted, but she couldn't. To do that would render her incapable of doing what had to be done—walking away.

'Tomorrow I will still feel the same,' she said, annoyed he thought he only had to bring her out here, play out her ultimate desert fantasy, in order to get her to stay a little longer. He could never give her what she wanted. He could never give her his love. He'd already admitted that to her and had coldly told her he never wished to be a father.

'Then I have much to do to ensure you change your mind.' He put the hood back on the falcon and returned to the tent.

The dark coolness of the tent was a relief from the heat of the desert and the warm winds as Tiffany followed him back inside, watching as he settled the bird on her perch once more. His voice was soft and gentle as he spoke to Shae in his own language, each move he made full of tenderness, which took Tiffany's mind hurtling back to those blissful nights after their wedding. Nights that for him had been full of passion, but for her, full of love.

'Then I must change your mind.' He walked

towards her, the bird now settled, and Tiffany stood her ground despite the intent in his eyes. For several long seconds he held her gaze, challenging her, then he turned and walked out of the tent as if she hadn't spoken, as if he didn't want to listen to what she wanted. She followed him out into the hot sun and back to the luxury of the first tent, where the ambiance was far more like the fantasy she'd wanted so much but now needed to resist.

'I'm not going to stay, Jafar, no matter what you do or say.' She stood in the middle of the exotic tent, the aroma of incense mingling with the soft music and the array of colour as gold, red, purple and orange collided around her. A setting far too intoxicating when the man she loved stood in the middle of it. The desert king without a heart.

But he has my heart.

'You agreed to stay here, as my wife, for three months.' Jafar's eyes sparked with annoyance but she wouldn't allow him to talk her down. She'd made her decision. She had to leave—for her child's sake.

'Things have changed. I have a baby to consider.'

'Which is why I want you to stay, not for three months as my hired bride, but to remain here as my wife and mother of my child and heir.' He moved towards her, his expression still fierce. Those were words she'd wanted to hear but was he really offering all she'd ever wanted? Worried after the false alarm with his sister, he only wanted the heir she carried because it would keep Shamsumara from Simdan's evil clutches.

'No. I can't. My family...' She began to flounder under the intensity of his eyes, using every excuse she could, except the truth. What would he say if she told him she couldn't stay with him when she loved him, knowing he would never love her?

'In return I will ensure your sister and her child never want for anything again.' His tone was level and devoid of emotion. He was simply brokering another deal with her.

'You want to buy me?' She couldn't believe what she was hearing.

He was making another deal. Putting an offer on the table he knew she would find hard to resist. He might have bought her, but he'd never buy his child, the all-important heir. That required an altogether different currency, one he didn't trade in. Love.

'You brought me here—against my will— and then have the audacity to bribe, or blackmail me, so that I will stay and have your child?'

'It is not like that, Tiffany.' He glared at her, the white of his robes a stark contrast to the colour around them.

'Of course it is. You just want the baby.'

His eyes hardened with the anger of her accusation. 'That is so far from the truth.'

'You told me you never wanted to be a father and that was why you were prepared to even make this stupid marriage deal with me. With your sister's new baby you didn't need an heir, just a bride—a temporary bride.' The agonising hurt of saying the truth out loud almost choked her. She'd only ever been part of a deal. She'd forgotten that and fallen in love with the fantasy she'd been brought to. Worse than that, she'd fallen in love with him.

'It would be against all I believe in, all my people believe in if I allow you to leave Shamsumara knowing you carry my heir.'

'You have your heir.' She was desperate to make him see sense, to realise that forcing her to stay for the baby was even more barbaric than coldly proclaiming he didn't want to be a father.

'I did, but now I have a true heir. One of my own flesh and blood.'

'So what are you going to do? Hold me prisoner? Make me sign another contract—this time for my child?'

'No. This time there will be no contract.' He stepped closer and her heart beat in angry thuds. Or was it because he'd moved too close, because she could smell his unique scent mixed with the desert wind? As she looked into his eyes, into the depths of increasing passion, she knew without a doubt he was going to kiss her—and she wanted him to.

CHAPTER TWELVE

JAFAR SAW THE fire of desire rise in Tiffany's eyes, turning them into a tumultuous sea of emotion. However much she protested she was far from immune to him, but this wave of passion and desire wasn't what he'd intended. Neither was the kiss he was unable to resist taking. He'd intended to tell her how much he wanted her, how much he wanted their child, that he wanted to create a life with her, a family.

He needed to feel her lips against his, to taste her and crush the softness of her full lips beneath his, but the moment his lips met hers that spark of fire erupted, claiming them both.

She kissed him back, sighing into his mouth as desire drove them harder and higher, sending his plans into disarray. The wild fire of passion scorched him deeper than the desert sun ever could and he knew that whatever the outcome of bringing Tiffany here, he'd never be the same again. He wanted her. Needed her. Loved her.

'It's been too long,' he murmured against her lips as his hands held her arms. He held her close but it wasn't enough. He would never get enough of this woman.

Before she could say anything else, he pulled her against his body, holding her tightly as he kissed her harder, desperate to show what she meant to him, needing to show what he felt for her, but that explosive hot desire erupted once more.

Her tongue danced with his as her body melded against his, her curves moulding to him, fitting perfectly against his body as the haze of desire intensified, taking them to an oasis of sensual pleasure in the middle of the desert. Then it vanished, the desert becoming hostile and barren.

'No.' She pushed him away, shocking him with the force of it. 'This won't change my mind. In fact, all of this is wrong.'

She looked up at him, her breath hard and ragged. The cream headscarf she'd worn slipped back from her head, exposing the softness of her hair, reminding him how it felt, how it had looked spread out over the pale gold silk of the pillows as he'd made her truly his on their wedding night.

That last thought centred his emotions and he knew that, whatever it took, she would always remain his. 'What is so wrong with a man kissing his wife, Tiffany?'

'I'm not your wife,' she snapped at him and her eyes flashed fiery sparks through the cool darkness of the tent. 'I'm a hired bride. Nothing more.'

The conversation was going wildly off course. He should be kissing her until she wanted nothing but him, until she felt his love for her. But somehow they were still talking about the deal he'd made with her in England. A day that seemed as if it had happened a lifetime ago.

'You were more than that on our wedding night.' He was desperate to remind her of what they'd shared, the passion that had ruled so strongly they'd forgotten even the most basic things. 'That night you became my wife.'

'It's not what I want, Jafar.' A weariness entered her voice and a wave of compassion caught him off guard. 'I don't want passion and desire. I don't want nights filled with steamy sex.'

Her words sent torturous images to his mind,

but he maintained his focus, sure that those were just surface words, just as his were. She was protecting herself as much as he was, each refusing to admit what they really felt, what they really wanted. Neither wanting to say the words aloud, each still hiding in the shadows of their past.

He touched his fingers to her face, delicately tracing down the softness of her cheek with the pad of his thumb. The sigh that escaped her as she closed her eyes gave away far more than she thought. It showed the effect he had on her, the need she had for him and, most of all, that her resistance was lowering.

'What do you want, Tiffany?' He kept his tone soft and low.

'I want a man who loves me for who I am, not what I can give him.'

His heart raced as he stood facing the woman who carried his child, the woman he wanted to stay by his side, to be his Queen for ever, but the past still tormented him, still mocked the silly little boy who'd had notions of a long and happy marriage with many children. That little boy had grown up into a cold man, one who only knew how to react to desire or passion, one who'd sworn he never wanted a child to go through what he had and experience being a pawn in a big game plan. He was in line to the throne of Shamsumara and an heir would be expected, but he'd never wanted to create a new life because he had to, because the tradition he'd grown up influenced by demanded it. His sister's pregnancy had created the perfect way out of that and all he'd needed was a temporary bride.

Then he'd married Tiffany, spent an intoxicating night with her and everything had changed. Not because he'd created a child that night. It was far more powerful than that. He'd fallen in love with the woman he'd hired to be his bride.

'You can't do that, can you, Jafar?' Hurt ripped through Tiffany as Jafar stood stoically before her, the passion of his kiss just moments ago gone from his eyes. What cold and heartless plans were going through his mind now?

'You were hired to be my bride, Tiffany—'

'And that is exactly what I have been.' She cut across his words, not wanting to hear the callous truth of why she was here in his desert kingdom.

'But now it's so much more.' He looked into her eyes, a new tenderness filling his, setting light to the torch of hope within her. 'To be here like this was never what I intended.'

The light of hope flickered, threatening to snuff itself out, and she drew on her dwindling reserves of strength to protect her fragile heart. 'It isn't what I agreed to.'

He stroked her hair, then, as if realising he'd stepped over some invisible boundary, let his hand fall back at his side. 'And it isn't what I asked of you.'

'What are we going to do, Jafar?' Her reservoir of determination was sinking ever lower and an unconcealed note of hysteria in her voice was all too clear.

'We have created a new life, a child that will join us together for evermore, no matter where we are or what we do. It was not my intention at all, but it happened and we owe it to our baby to remain together.' She saw his barriers drop, watched as he lowered his guard, but his words still told her the same. He wanted her to stay because of the child she carried.

Memories of the arguments she'd tried not to hear between her parents when she was younger surfaced. Her mother and father had stayed together for Bethany's sake, even going as far as having Tiffany in an attempt to mend the marriage, but it had been a disaster. Just as it would be for her and Jafar.

What they both wanted from the marriage was completely different. She wanted his love, to be able to love him freely. He wanted his heir, to secure the kingdom he'd inherited. Staying together when they were at such polar opposites in their reasons for remaining married would be a disaster. It would be her parents all over again.

'No, Jafar. I can't do that. I can't stay here and I can't be your wife.' The pain in her voice echoed in her heart and for the briefest of seconds she thought she saw it mirrored in his eyes.

'What about your child, *my* son or daughter? They will one day rule Shamsumara.'

She moved towards him, drawn by an unknown force. A need to make him understand forced all her past to the fore, forced out words she'd never admitted out loud to anyone. 'My parents' marriage was not a happy one, Jafar. When my mother fell pregnant with Bethany, they married, as was expected of them by their families.'

'That doesn't mean ours will be unhappy. Our first week of marriage was the happiest I have ever been.'

'It doesn't wipe out the fear I knew as a child when I witnessed angry words between my parents. They didn't love one another. They were forced together when my sister came along.' His dark eyes regarded her as she struggled with ugly memories from her younger years.

'It doesn't mean our marriage will be the same.' His voice was gentle and for a moment she thought he was going to caress her cheek again. Part of her wanted that but part of her knew it would break her heart just a little more.

She continued the story of her past. 'They thought having another baby—me—would bring them closer together. It just pushed them further apart.'

'We have known much pleasure, much passion in our first week of marriage. The kind of passion which brings a man and woman closer to one another emotionally.'

His reference again to their week shut away from the world, the *honeymoon* week, crushed the hope that had started to grow within her. 'But that isn't what I want from you, Jafar.'

There was a sad resignation in her voice as she stood looking up at him. What would he do if she told him she wanted his love? What would he say if she told him she loved him?

Maybe saying those words to him was the only way to make him see that their so-called marriage could never work when they both wanted very different things.

'That week was amazing.' She blushed beneath the honesty of her soft words and averted her gaze, anything other than look into the smouldering heat of his eyes as she acknowledged the hot passion that had sparked between them so intensely. 'But it can't sustain a marriage—especially one involving children. I am all too painfully aware of that.'

He lifted her chin with his thumb and finger, forcing her to look at him once more. The heady desire in his eyes was almost too much. 'The passion was, as you say, amazing, but it is not all I want.'

'It isn't?' Her tremulous whisper must surely give away how vulnerable she felt right now. How emotionally exposed.

He shook his head gently. 'No, it isn't. I want to be loved by the woman who has captured my heart, the woman who takes it soaring across the desert as if on the wings of a falcon.'

He paused and hope flickered to life inside her again. Every barrier he'd erected around himself was stripped away. This was the man she'd fallen in love with. This was the man she'd married and given herself so completely to. A smile lifted her lips at his romantic words and the connection he was making to the bird he'd flown.

'I want to be loved by that woman as much as I love her and, if that is not possible, tomorrow I will let her fly as free as my falcon.'

'You…' Her voice wouldn't work, the words not able to form. Was he really saying he loved her?

He nodded and smiled. 'Yes, Tiffany. My wife, my love. I am madly in love with you and if you leave me my heart will search for yours for ever, miss you for ever. If freedom from me, from being my Queen, is what you desire, then out of love for you I will instruct my plane to take you home.'

Jafar watched a multitude of emotions play out over his wife's face. Did she believe him? Had he left it too late to finally bear his soul and tell her how much he loved her, how much he wanted her in his life? Even more importantly, could she ever come to love him?

'Jafar,' she said in a husky whisper, a question laced into every syllable, and he closed his eyes, not wanting to hear her rejection, not wanting to know she didn't feel the same, that he'd got it all wrong.

'Yes?' The hesitation, the hope, the raw emotion cracked so sharply in that one word he could hardly comprehend it was his voice. Tiffany looked at him, those lovely blue eyes searching his face, looking for what he didn't know. He hoped it was love, because it must surely be written boldly upon it.

He'd never been this anxious in all his life; never had one person's response mattered so much. Her silence was all too painful and he closed his eyes against the pain of the rejection that was sure to come.

The rejection didn't come. Instead soft lips brushed so lightly over his that he could be imagining it. He opened his eyes and looked right into the blue depths of Tiffany's, immediately lost.

'Your love is all I want from you,' she whispered against his lips, striking up the hum of desire in him. 'My desert fantasy. The man I love with all my heart.'

He took her face in his hands and tenderly kissed her. It was a kiss to show just how much he loved her, but now that he'd broken free of the past it wasn't enough. She'd unlocked the chains that had held his heart and now he was free. Free to love her.

'I love you, Tiffany.' He said it in English, then said it again in his own language, needing to say it aloud as many times as possible.

'I love you, Jafar.'

He smiled at her. 'So my romantic fantasy worked,' he teased her, feeling confident and surrounded by her love.

'This is just the icing on the cake,' she jested, taking his lead. 'The ultimate desert fantasy. An elaborate desert tent and a very sexy sheikh. But it is hearing you say you love me that worked.'

'And so will you stay? Will you be my wife and mother to my child?'

'Until I get a better offer.' So she still teased him, did she?

'In that case—' he swept her from her feet and carried her towards the low and wide bed, adorned with so many vibrantly coloured cushions it was almost camouflaged '—I will have to make sure you never get a better offer.'

'Is that so?' She laughed as he placed her on the softness of the bed.

'It is.' He nodded as he lay next to her, his fingers opening the tie at the front of her dress with ease, revealing her pale skin. 'And I intend to start right now.'

'There will never be a better offer.' Her voice lowered and became soft and serious as she touched her palm to his face. 'Because I love you so much, Jafar.'

He kissed her lips lightly, smoothing her hair from her face and looking into her eyes. 'I love you too, my darling wife.'

EPILOGUE

Two years later

JAFAR WATCHED HIS young son with his older cousin, as they played in the small fountain he'd had installed in the palace gardens. The squeals of delight as the toddlers splashed in the water were infectious; even Leah had abandoned her usual sedate and regal ways to chase around in the garden with the toddlers, barking excitedly as they splashed water at her.

'Our son has his father's leadership qualities,' Tiffany said as she stood beside him under the archway, her hand resting on her stomach and their second child soon to be born. 'Look at him, bossing Zaina around. Poor little girl.'

'I think he might have got that trait from his mother.' As they had done since that night in the desert tent they teased each other, but always with affection.

'I have saved that quality for our little girl.' She looked down at her tummy, at the swell of her second child.

'If she has even half the spirit her mother possesses, she will be a wonderful little girl and I can't wait to meet her.'

Tiffany reached up and touched his face. 'I love you, Jafar. Being here with you is wonderful.'

'You don't miss your old life? Your job?'

Tiffany smiled coyly at the man she was still madly in love with, her ultimate desert fantasy. Did he really question if she missed her old job?

'Bethany is doing a fantastic job running Bridesmaid Services, which means I get to relax and enjoy being an ordinary bridesmaid for Lilly.' She smiled up at him. 'I'm just thankful I will have time to get into the dress after this little one is born.'

His arms pulled her to him, as much as the baby would allow, and he kissed her tenderly. The squeals of laughter increased and they looked out again to see Aaleyah getting carried away with the fun of the water as she too joined in the fun and they laughed, pressing their foreheads together.

'We seem to have a habit of creating unplanned babies.' His sexy voice was full of the memory of the passion they'd shared since that night in the desert.

She blushed prettily and he kissed her lips softly, seductively, promising so much more once they were alone. Her heart soared high into the desert sky, swooping down to find the warm currents of air, and she knew that he had let her fly free that morning after the night of passion and love in the desert. She had been totally free to fly away but she'd chosen the man she loved—and always would.

* * * * *

If you enjoyed
HIRED TO WEAR THE SHEIKH'S RING,
why not explore these other stories
by Rachael Thomas?

VALDEZ'S BARTERED BRIDE
MARTINEZ'S PREGNANT WIFE
DI MARCELLO'S SECRET SON
A CHILD CLAIMED BY GOLD

Available now!

HOME *on the* RANCH

YES! Please send me the **Home on the Ranch Collection** in Larger Print. This collection begins with 3 FREE books and 2 FREE gifts in the first shipment. Along with my 3 free books, I'll also get the next 4 books from the Home on the Ranch Collection, in LARGER PRINT, which I may either return and owe nothing, or keep for the low price of $5.24 U.S./ $5.89 CDN each plus $2.99 for shipping and handling per shipment*. If I decide to continue, about once a month for 8 months I will get 6 or 7 more books, but will only need to pay for 4. That means 2 or 3 books in every shipment will be FREE! If I decide to keep the entire collection, I'll have paid for only 32 books because 19 books are FREE! I understand that accepting the 3 free books and gifts places me under no obligation to buy anything. I can always return a shipment and cancel at any time. My free books and gifts are mine to keep no matter what I decide.

268 HCN 3760 468 HCN 3760

Name	(PLEASE PRINT)	
Address		Apt. #
City	State/Prov.	Zip/Postal Code

Signature (if under 18, a parent or guardian must sign)

Mail to the **Reader Service:**
IN U.S.A.: P.O. Box 1867, Buffalo, NY. 14240-1867
IN CANADA: P.O. Box 609, Fort Erie, Ontario L2A 5X3

HRCBPA18